# J.S. MORRISON

# THE PERFECTION OF FISH

Black Rose Writing | Texas

ISBN: 978-1-68433-506-0
PUBLISHED BY BLACK ROSE WRITING
www.blackrosewriting.com

Printed in the United States of America
Suggested Retail Price (SRP) $21.95

*The Perfection of Fish* is printed in Garamond

*As a planet-friendly publisher, Black Rose Writing does its best to eliminate
unnecessary waste to reduce paper usage and energy costs, while never compromising
the reading experience. As a result, the final word count vs. page count may not meet
common expectations.

Editing by Paul Witcover
Author Photo courtesy of Geoff Morrison
Cover fish art: *Winter Tail: Just Chillin* by J. Vincent Scarpace, ipaintfish.com

# REVIEWS

Poignant, provocative, hilarious, and original, The Perfection of Fish is an addictive page-turner from a serious new talent.

— *BlueInk Starred Review*

Provocative themes are conveyed in this highly imaginative, entertaining, and satirical work of speculative fiction.

— *Sublime Book Review*

This weird, crazy story will keep the reader up all night following the gender wars and genetic engineering, futuristic science innovations, and fishy action.

— *Author Reading*

Something about this novel piqued my interest, and I'm really glad that I requested it! Once I initially started this and got into it, I couldn't put it down. The world building was done beautifully, and the narrative suckered me in!

— Justine Fye, *NetGalley* Reviewer

# FOR PATRICIA, THE LOVE OF MY LIFE.

# THE
# PERFECTION
# OF
# FISH

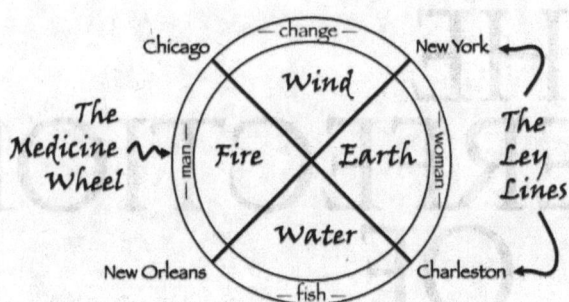

*The ley lines are one with the medicine wheel.*

*The center is a vortex. I'm sure of it.*

Notes on parchment — Chester Truman Kelsey

Everything you can imagine is real.
*Pablo Picasso*

# FIRE

# CHAPTER 1
# THE PERFECTION OF WOLVES

Once upon a time, before fish could talk and before *The Canons of Cantor* became more popular than the Bible, the Quran, and the Torah, there was a town nestled in the curl of a river beside a mountain where science and superstition blended as seamlessly as blue sky and the ridgeline of the Great Smoky Mountains. It was a town born in the Great Depression of the 1930s. The residents embraced the frontier culture and believed they could impact faraway places through magical connections known as ley lines. But by the summer of 2042 the townsfolk had vanished, and Assurance, North Carolina, was continuously inhabited by a single person—Nadia Holkam, a slim forty-two-year-old woman with long blond hair and green eyes that spoke of a Scotch-Irish heritage and the despair that comes from traumatic loss.

There were only two people in Nadia's universe. One was Nadia. The other was a man who barked at the moon.

"Yip! Yip! Yip! Awoooo!"

Nadia studied her caretaker as he danced and howled in the open doorway of her Appalachian home on a sweltering night in early June. Berky Benson's hairless, pasty-white, moon-lit body resembled an obese, 6-foot-6-inch mole-rat. His naked buttocks rippled like curdled cheese. Next to him, a black cat circled the lid of a food tray, stopping and starting and bowing as if enacting some voodoo ritual.

Berky was twenty-nine years old, thirteen years younger than Nadia and much stronger as he demonstrated with delight in their every sexual encounter. Now, ignoring her pain, she struggled to her feet, then found a knitting needle she had left on the end table near her favorite padded chair. The effort exhausted her. She knew she couldn't muster the strength of limb or will to kill him with this makeshift weapon, however much she fantasized about it. Still, the cold hardness of it in her hand was comforting. Quickly picking up her clothes from the floor—clothes that Berky had torn off just moments ago—she slipped the needle into their ruined folds.

Berky howled again in the doorway. "A-wo-o-o-o-o!" A long, triumphant yowl.

Somewhere on the edge of the Nantahala forest, an animal returned the call.

"Listen," he said to her, eyes darting.

The animal wailed again.

He cocked his head. "That's a wolf—a top predator. They're coming back. God has willed it."

"Maybe not," she said. Her stomach wrenched at the timid act of defiance. She steadied herself on the table, hand atop her clothes, feeling the hard, thin spine of the needle underneath. To distract him, she raked her other hand through the blond hair draped against her naked, bruised breasts, and inched closer, within striking range. She could smell the raw onion aroma of his sweat from three feet away.

Berky turned from the open door. "You doubt me?"

"No," she whimpered, holding her balled-up clothes in front of her like a flimsy shield. "I would never doubt you. Other people—people who know less than you—say they're Shelties, not wolves. Escaped pets that have adapted to life in the wild."

Berky stepped closer, towering above Nadia's five-foot-six frame. He batted the clothes aside, and the needle skidded across the floor. When he saw it, he squeezed her cheeks with a powerful hand. "Sheep Dogs are what they use in genetics labs to make Testrial."

Her voice trembled, but her eyes looked up and fixed on his. "It's just what they say. There are so many of them now."

"That's a wild animal. It's not a fucking dog. You can't tame a wolf. And when you try, we fight back."

"I didn't mean to disrespect you," she said.

"We have to combat the ungodly acts of terror," he said. "Rise against blasphemous interference with divine biological selection. We need to put things back the way they were. We're an endangered species. You're killing us." He pulled her to the floor and sat on her butt, facing her feet.

"I can't breathe," she croaked, as she struggled, stomach pinned to the floor under his weight.

"I am the salvation," he said. "I have the cure." He lifted his eyes and raised his open hands into the air. "I have the perfection."

He grabbed one of her ankles, pulled it toward his face, and thrust her big toe into his mouth.

She yelped as he tugged at the toe with his teeth, snarling like a playful dog.

When he finished ravaging her feet, he turned her over, licked her face from eyeball to nose, then shoved his tongue into a nostril, smiled lovingly when she choked, slathered the side of her head, and licked her ear wax. "You are my cupcake, my lollipop," he said. "You are my perfect woman."

He continued licking until her skin was a lacework of ropy saliva, as if a rout of snails had traversed her body. Now spent, and his submaxillary spittle glands dry, he said, "Darling, you must be famished. I want you to eat what I brought. You need your strength."

The cat hovering next to the tray pawed at the lid, sniffing the air and licking its chops. Berky moved quickly and swatted it with an open hand. "Schrodinger! Stop it! That's Nadia's food."

She was still lying on the floor, physically and emotionally beaten. Both of her big toes felt raw, violated. She crawled to pick up the meal, dreading what always came next.

When Berky departed, he took Schrodinger with him, driving toward the bridge and the forest and the world beyond. From the open door, Nadia watched his taillights merge with the whirl of lightning bugs, then dissolve into darkness.

She stretched her arm out the door and toward the moon as though reaching for freedom, and said to the darkness, "I wish ..." Her mind wandered. *If Diana were here, she'd know what to do. She was always good at fixing things.* She breathed the words: "Diana, I need you."

A wave of nausea swept through her body. She jerked her trembling hand inside as though the moonlight had burned it. The shadows beyond the doorway marked a world she was incapable of entering—a place where reality writhed and twisted, and sometimes whispered. Fireflies became pinpricks into unseen dimensions, and sources of conflicting voices that only Nadia could hear: "Beware" and "I'll help you" and "Death awaits, but so does hope." The world would kill her if she stepped outside her house. This was as certain as the vomit rising in her throat and the sudden weakness in her limbs and the dimming of her vision.

When the whispers said, "He won't return," she withdrew her gaze from the road, the bridge, and the forest, gently closed the door on objective reality, and took refuge in the shower, where warm water caressed her skin and washed away Berky's stink. With eyes shut, she turned her face into the stream and cleansed her mouth, filling it with water but not swallowing or spitting, just letting it overflow and run down her jaw.

She huddled in the spray, imagining a rainy summer day from childhood—better times. *The sun will come out soon, and I'll get dressed, and Papa will ask me to help with the bees, and after we're done in the garden and I've eaten supper, he'll tuck me in and read me a story.* She almost felt human again. She dried and dressed and bandaged her toes.

An empty stomach drew her to the food tray. When she removed the lid, her throat clutched. She hated fish and the chalky undertaste of its flesh as much as she hated the stink of Berky's sweat. The fishes figured in her dreams about the end of the world, where only fish remained, and they were laughing.

Berky always claimed his actions were altruistic. Yesterday he said, "Fish genes can hold far more memory of their environment than human genes. They adapt faster. So you need to eat lots of fish. I'm doing this for you, Nadia, to preserve the memories in your brain—the engrams. And how your cells read your genes. I'll keep these memories alive long after you die."

She wondered about the engrams.

*I don't know who I am anymore. I have so many memories that seem to swim away when I think of them. It's like trying to catch a fish with your bare hands when it knows you're looking. How will Berky or anyone else find the slippery engrams when I can't?*

She resolved to redouble her efforts to write a comprehensive history of Assurance. That and the proper indexing of artifacts in the museum seemed like a more practical way to guard against memory extinction.

The book was a message to the future from the last living resident of Assurance. It would tell of a town that, for most of its existence, seemed undecided about whether it wanted to live or die. It would explain how the South Prong River kept Assurance alive until the day the water turned black and its inhabitants vanished. It would describe why mountain culture represented the best of all possible worlds. It would reveal who she was and who she wanted to be.

The book was a solution to Nadia's problem: she was a ghost in a ghost town, unknown and unremembered by anyone except Berky. Her agoraphobia—her fear of open spaces—made her a prisoner in her own home. She was Berky's resentful but obedient pet. She was nothing. Nadia was "nada."

She reached for her notebook and wrote, *Poof!*

# CHAPTER 2
# POOF!

On a hot, dusty road in western North Carolina, near a sign for a rural bus stop, Ali Khan Ahmed climbed out of a pickup truck with his traveling bag and thanked the driver for giving him the lift. She was fortyish—twice his age, but easy to look at, with shining blue eyes, mouse-brown hair pulled into a short bob, and a yellow tank top blouse above slim cut jeans.

"You sure you got a place to stay tonight, hon?" she said, waiting, hoping, motor running.

Twenty-three-year-old Ali, standing five-two, lean and wiry in a T-shirt and jeans, adjusted his eyepatch then spoke in the choppy cadence of the Indian subcontinent. "Thank you. I have to catch a bus. I need to meet someone. They are expecting me."

The woman gave him a come-hither smile, slid sunglasses down her nose, and waited for a reaction. When she got none, she winked, pushed the glasses back up, and put the truck into gear.

Ali waved goodbye.

As she drove away, he looked past the bus stop to a sign pointing toward the Nantahala National Forest, removed his wallet from a hip pocket, and took out his netcard—a millimeter-thin, flexible black slab that was his gateway to information and money. With the touch of a finger, he turned on the card's map display. Enhanced GPS showed a five-mile hike ahead. He checked for messages, sent a coded text to his professor and friend at the University of North Carolina, then shut the card down, broke it in two, and buried the pieces in soft sand ten feet apart and twenty feet from the road. Immigration and Customs Enforcement would be able to track him this far, but no farther.

ICE would have to assume he could be anywhere. He could have gotten on the bus with a fictitious name. He could have gotten another ride. He could have hiked north toward Cherokee, or—worst case—south, into 11,000 acres of wilderness that segued into eight hundred square miles of forests and mountains.

He snapped his fingers, replaying in his mind a magic trick performed by his friend at UNC. You put cards into a hat, turn it upside down to show the cards have vanished, and then snap your fingers, and the hat disappears. *Poof!*

With his bag in hand, he found the trail toward Nantahala and took it, covering his tracks as best he could.

Berky Benson walked into the Aasleagh Pub on Savannah's East River Street carrying a duffel bag and a leather pouch. He was a man on a mission, striving to complete God's plan. But this pub was not on his divine roadmap. It seemed to be a place where binge drinkers went after they'd visited all the good bars. He spotted his Chief Technical Officer, Gregor Popkins, in a dark corner, acknowledged his presence with a nod, but decided to order a drink before joining him.

The bartender, a full-figured thirty-something woman in a loose purple shirt with rolled-up sleeves and a dragon tattoo on her forearm, stopped wiping the counter as Berky dropped his bag near a stool. She eyed his worn red polo shirt and tattered jeans.

"Whatcha need, hon?" she said, fatigue written on her face.

"Beet juice."

"Sorry," she droned. "It's not something we normally—"

"Is this enough?" he said, removing his wallet and dropping three Ben Franklins on the counter. "Two of these are for you and the other's for the server." He smiled. Physical currency had a much bigger impact than the digital variety.

Her face perked up. "Just a moment." She stuffed the bills into a breast pocket and disappeared into a room behind the bar.

Berky tapped his fingers as he surveyed the pub. It was barely 7 pm, and the place was dead, with only a few patrons. Two men at a table near the door fondled beer mugs as they quietly argued over a matter of public policy. A tall woman at a table near the bar sipped an umbrella drink through a paper straw. She had an aquiline nose and wore a hat with ostrich feathers that made her look like a species of giant bird. A young man seated on the other end of the bar, who looked barely 21, wore an unbuttoned black shirt that revealed a chest full of hair too thick to be natural. The man tugged on a pendant swinging from a gold chain around his

THE PERFECTION OF FISH

neck. A single male server flitted between the tables, taking orders, bringing drinks, spreading happy-ness.

After two minutes, the bartender returned, placing a glass of dark-red liquid on the counter.

Berky took a sip. "You know, this place is a shit-hole, but if you give me great service tonight, you might get another tip." He took two more bills from his wallet and waved them under the bartender's nose. When she failed to react, he put the money away. With his drink in one hand and the leather pouch under the same arm, he lifted the duffel bag from the floor with his other hand and walked to Popkins' table.

"Hiya Boss," Popkins said.

Berky simply nodded, placed his bag next to the wall, put the leather pouch and drink on the table, and sat down. The lack of illumination in this corner suited his dark mood, stemming from two problems. The first was that God had not spoken to him in three days. The second was that in his haste to depart in his private air taxi for a quick trip to Savannah, he'd forgotten to wear his lucky white socks. He wondered if they might be critical for upcoming deals. *You never know.*

Berky watched the 45-year-old Popkins dribble vodka from his glass onto his jeans and striped sailor shirt, inhaling his drink from a grease-stained glass, eyes dulled behind crimson hexagonal spectacles that floated above a shit-eating grin.

"You look like Schrodinger when he catches a fish that's bigger than he is," Berky said, referring to his cat. He gulped down most of the beet juice, annoyed that Popkins would drink liquor before an interview and that he would pick a place like the Aasleagh Pub to meet a key new hire. *Hey, what do you expect from a Russian?*

Popkins adjusted his spectacles and wiped an unkempt beard with the back of an oversized hand. "We now got all the pieces, Boss. Ask him about his invention. It's brilliant."

"You'll have to fill me in," Berky said. "But you're wrong. We *don't* have all the pieces. There's a major one missing. Tonight I'll—"

"That's him," Popkins said, pointing.

Berky turned to see a forty-something man, approximately five-ten in height, dressed in a dusty blue linen blazer and collarless white shirt, with olive-brown skin, tousled black hair, full lips, and a vaguely Asian face. He was smiling.

Berky motioned for the server to deliver more drinks, then stood, offering a hand to the arriving candidate. "Dr. Rao?"

"Please call me Sundar," the man said, shaking Berky's hand. "You must be Dr. Benson."

Berky shook his head. "Actually, I'm not a doctor. I'm the CEO. Have a seat."

The server interjected. "What's your pleasure?" His long blond hair fell against a tight black T-shirt that stretched over bulging muscles.

Sundar wagged a finger. "Nothing for me."

Popkins held up his empty glass and wiggled his tongue. "Vodka."

Berky said, "More beet juice."

The bartender picked up Berky's glass, stumbled, and spilled residual liquid on his shirt. "So sorry. I'll make it up to you."

Berky took a deep breath to check his anger. "No problem. My shirt's red, so it won't show much. Just remember I tipped you $100 on that last round of drinks, and I expect excellent service. I also gave your boss an even bigger tip to make sure everything is perfect. So do your job. Keep me happy."

The server gave a nervous smile and returned to the bar.

Sundar and Popkins chatted for a few minutes, telling Berky how they met, and how they had irreconcilable differences over whether the Russian drink, kvass, was a refreshment or a hemorrhoidal ointment.

The server returned with more beet juice, vodka, and a bowl of Brazil nuts. "The snacks are on me," he said, placing the dish. "You'll like them."

"Do they contain Testrial?" Berky said.

The server shrugged. "Yeah."

"Get me something that doesn't."

"Sorry, sir. We're dotting i's and crossing t's tonight. See those two men near the door? One of them's from the Liquor Control Board. My boss doesn't want to lose her license."

"What the fuck?"

His raised voice drew the attention of the bird lady, who tilted her head like an immense cockatoo. The man near the bar fluffed his chest hair, while the two people near the door stopped their argument in mid-synchronous sentences.

The server quickly stepped away.

Berky threw the bowl at him but missed. Nuts rained like hail across the barroom floor. "Little whore," he yelled. "You feed me poison, but I'll bet your manager gives you steroids to look buff. You're a traitor." He eyed the men near the door. "They're killing us with this abomination."

Sundar and Popkins were silent, just looking at each other.

"What are you staring at?" Berky said to the other customers. The bird lady made a clucking sound and tilted her head down, looking at her drink; the hairy-chested man raised a weak fist in sympathy; one of the arguing patrons looked at Berky and mouthed the words, "Dick Head."

At the bar, the server huddled with the bartender, glancing at Berky, whispering non-stop in an agitated manner until his female boss finally gestured for him to cool it. She picked up a cleaver, waved it above the counter until she made eye contact with Berky, pointed it at him, then proceeded to chop up a cucumber, beginning with the tip.

Berky jerked his gaze back to the table and slammed down his palm to get attention. This startled Sundar, but Popkins just guzzled vodka and twitched his lips into a smile.

"Listen," Sundar said. "I tend to agree this Testrial business is—"

"Give me what you've got," Berky barked. "Gregor says you've developed something called a gahneebow. Tell me what it is and how it'll benefit Xanadu NeuroLab."

"Not with the hard 'g,'" Sundar said in a muted voice. "It's pronounced 'jeneeboh,' and it rhymes with 'placebo.'" After a moment: "I think the server was just trying—"

Berky felt his face grow warm. "I don't need to explain to you or—"

Popkins took control of the conversation, changing the subject, squinting at Berky through blurred eyes. "He's a magician, Boss. Look ..."

With a painful lack of coordination, Popkins pushed the sleeve of Sundar's jacket up his arm. "No tricks here. Just here." He tapped Sundar's forehead.

"Go to sleep Popkins," Berky said.

"I got to pee pee first."

Popkins stood, stretching to his full height of 4-feet-8-inches, gave an exaggerated bow to both Berky and Sundar, then stumbled toward the men's room, slipping on Brazil nuts in his path.

Berky shook his head. His words to Sundar were tinged with irritation over Popkins' performance, smoldering anger at the bartender, and the absence of lucky socks. "My associate wants to hire you, but you have to convince me. Tell me why I need to bring you onboard."

Sundar cleared his throat, then struck a tone that Berky thought sounded rehearsed. "Sure. The technology I invented will cut your costs, shorten your experiment setup time, and improve your trust in the results. It'll integrate easily with Kublai Khan, your neuromorphic experiment design system. I've already discussed how to do this with Gregor."

Berky felt a second flush of anger. *Popkins had no business blabbing trade secrets.*

Sundar removed a vial from an interior pocket and held it up to the light for Berky to see. The liquid inside was the color of pale ale. "I developed this for my previous company," he said. "They went belly-up and never patented it. It's an orphaned technology, but one I think is critical for genetic behavior research. Hire me, at my proposed salary, and it's yours. Don't hire me, and I go to work for your competitor."

"Nice try," Berky said, "but you won't be working for anyone else. I did some checking." He unzipped his leather case and put documents on the table. "Your H-1B visa expired when you left the company. You have only a few days to reinstate it under the new rules. I happen to have the paperwork here and can submit tomorrow."

Sundar pouted, trying to process the changing dynamic.

"We've already done the legwork," Berky said. "We just need your signature on this petition. It says I'm your employer and states your salary, which is average for new-hires in the industry."

Berky placed a pen near the petition.

Sundar gave the paper a quick scan. "This salary is an insult. You know very well I'm worth five times that amount."

"You're free to go elsewhere," Berky said, "but if you turn me down, I'll tell ICE you're an illegal. They'll make you their guest for a year or so in a detention center before they ship your ass back to India."

Sundar looked at the document and blinked.

"Think fast, my friend," Berky said. "How quickly can you get a visa with someone else?" His poker face transformed into a *got-you-now-you-sonofabitch* smile.

Sundar held Berky's gaze, but his lower lip trembled. He looked at the document. Then he picked up the pen as if it weighed ten pounds and scrawled a light doodle with few flourishes.

Berky lifted the paper, admired the signature, and slid the document into his leather pouch. "That was the right decision, my friend. By the way, you just agreed that if you jump ship after learning our trade secrets, you can't work in the biopharmaceutical industry for five years. That pretty much knocks out your escape hatch. Wait here until Popkins gets back. He'll tell you what to do, assuming he's sober enough. I'll let the bartender know you're celebrating your new job and want to pay for our drinks. Remember to give her a big tip. Now excuse me. I've got other business." He gave a short nod to show the discussion was over, then stood, picked up his duffel bag, and walked toward the bar.

The bartender and server stopped their furtive discussion as Berky approached. "Mind if I use your cleaver?" Berky said. Without waiting for a response, he dropped his duffel bag, selected an orange from a fruit basket on the bar, seized the cleaver on the counter, and whacked the orange in two with a single chop. "Never mess with me," he said, loud enough that others in the bar could hear. "I'd consider buying this place just to put you and handsome here out of a job, but I don't invest in shitsties." He picked up his bag and walked out the door.

Nadia sometimes talked to her only companion—a doll wearing a long print dress like an Appalachian settler. Its roughly carved wooden head, dark brown with age, had painted eyes and a broad smile framed by human hair the same color as her own. The doll was always supportive but occasionally asked too many questions.

"You didn't destroy the Berky demon," the doll said, matter-of-factly.

Nadia pouted. "Let's talk about something else. I have to write my *History*."

"He's part of your history," the doll insisted. "He owns the town. He seems to own you."

Nadia made the doll cross its legs. It seemed to wait for an answer. She wasn't going to give it the satisfaction. Instead, she hummed. It was her way of making ugly ideas disappear. *Poof!*

"Okay, I get the idea," the doll said. "You aren't comfortable talking about Berky. What about Lionel?"

"You mean—"

"Berky's father."

"Sure. I was eight years old when they put him in an institution. They say he's crazy. He killed his wife."

"Berky's mother?"

"Right."

"Do you think Berky got hit with the same crazy stick? It might be in the genes."

Nadia hummed, channeling Big Bill Broonzy. "I'm trouble in mind, babe, I'm so blue ..."

The doll seemed annoyed. "Okay, stop it."

"They say he killed his wife because she put too much salt in his supper, and that disrespected him. Okay? They say he left Gloria's body on the kitchen floor before a neighbor found her."

"Who told you this?"

"Berky."

The doll's smile now seemed smug and triumphant. "So, now it's okay to talk about Berky?"

Nadia drifted into song again: "Lord, if the blues overtake me; I'm gonna rock on away from here..."

# CHAPTER 3
# FUTURE CONTRAPUNTAL

*What exactly happened depends on who you ask. When the possibilities intertwine like a hundred people having sex with a herd of goats, we call it a "barblefarb."*
—Canduka Cantor

Berky stepped into the lobby of the Crowley-Burgess Hotel on East Bay Street, a few blocks from the bar where he'd left Popkins and Sundar. He refused to give the doorperson his duffel bag, holding it close to his body as if it contained precious jewels.

"I'm looking for a conference on empowering men," he said.

The diminutive doorperson, wearing an immaculate gray outfit with gold trim, forearm patches for tech interfaces, and a cap that said, "CBH," frowned at Berky's red polo shirt with its suspicious red stain. She eyed the bag with equal suspicion but decided that, with ten minutes to go on her shift, this was not the time to challenge a customer, even if he looked like a ditz. She tapped her sleeve, and the display patch came alive. She scrolled through the event schedule. "Sorry. There are no such conferences."

"It's supposed to be on the lower level."

"Hmm. There's a place we sometimes let not-for-profits use on a not-to-interfere basis. If that's the case, you'll have to go up before you go down. Take the escalator to the mezzanine, then go past the Grand Arcadia Ballroom. You'll see a service elevator. Take it down to the basement on the River Street level. At the far end of the hall is a place we call the Swamp Room. Maybe that's what you're searching for." She stretched her lips into a fake smile, ending the engagement.

Berky rode the escalator, walked the palatial corridor, and found a video wall near the ballroom pitching Human Endowment Rights (HER). The blurb intrigued him. He bypassed the event registration desk, wedged himself into the middle of a badged group of well-dressed women, and entered the event.

Marcy Darcy, a 5-foot-2-inch African American beauty dressed in a sequined white jumpsuit, like some magical fairy queen, walked to the podium as if ascending to a throne. The crowd honored her with applause, cheers, and a few wolf whistles.

*Marcy, Marcy, Marcy*, they chanted.

Her spotlit face glowed like an alien black sun, magnified to immense proportions in a full-color, high-resolution hologram floating above her position.

Marcy bowed, then raised her arms to acknowledge her fans. The majority were older women who acted like adoring teenagers at a rock concert. She smiled confidently, waited for the din to subside, then spoke to her subjects about hopes and fears and promises. Her voice boomed from speakers in the ceiling, walls, and floor.

"The future is bright," she said, pausing for effect. "We are transforming the human race into peace-loving beings who respect all creatures, all lands, and our fragile environment. These changes are due—in part—to genetic science. There's a blossoming of equality for all. Can you feel it?"

The crowd cheered. Marcy raised her hands to quiet them down. In the back of the room, she heard a cry of "Bullshit!"

Heads turned toward the voice.

Marcy saw a large bald white man in a red polo shirt being escorted out of the hall. "I guess he doesn't feel it," she said coolly. "To my guys in the back: please help that confused man get in touch with his feelings."

The crowd erupted in laughter.

Marcy took control. "Archaic thinking and habits still dominate some non-believers. But we know better, don't we?"

The holographic display hovering above the stage zoomed to show the dimples in her cheeks, magnifying them like twin space warps. People screamed and stomped.

"I need your help. With your generous support, our non-profit organization will continue to ethically guide governments and commercial companies to make the right choices for the future."

Her fans stood in elation.

Three brawny women shoved Berky away from the ballroom entrance while a small crowd gathered to witness the brouhaha. He played tug-of-war with one of the female bouncers, trying to retrieve his duffel bag, finally hitting her with his leather document case until she let go. Things got ugly quickly.

The tallest bouncer, matching Berky's height and dressed in a black suit and red power tie, flexed rope-like tendons in a neck that moored a butch-cut head to a powerful body. "You need to leave by the service elevator, or we'll call the police," she said.

Someone in the crowd yelled, "Slap him down," initiating a four-person chant: *Slap him down. Slap him down. Slap him down ...*

Berky turned toward the throng. "You're all idiots."

The tall woman stepped between Berky and a group of five chanters, folding her arms. Her smaller partner, who had attempted to take away his duffel bag, pressed the *down* button on the elevator. The doors opened, and the three bouncers shoved him in.

"Fucking assholes," Berky said, under his breath.

As the doors closed, he gave the women a one-fingered salute. "Fuck you."

He rode the elevator to the basement level. It wasn't difficult finding the Swamp Room. No fancy digital signage, just a metal plate suspended on a chain from a hook in the wall. The cryptic title, hand-written in Magic Marker, read: Hereditary Investments for Men (HIM).

In a cramped, windowless conference room with peeling paint and erratic ceiling lights, Canduka Cantor, 55 years old, frowned as a new arrival interrupted pre-meeting small talk. With snorting and loud "Excuse me's," the large young man with a stained red polo shirt and gleaming cue-ball-shaped head teetered under the burden of a large green duffel bag. He squeezed his way toward the remaining seat, bumping the trash can near the door and stumbling over a backpack crammed with equipment cables for the projection system. The man stood for a moment on the opposite end of the table from Cantor, staring, seemingly oblivious to the thirteen other seated men. Finally, the man eased his bag to the floor, sat down, and thundered, "Nice view."

Cantor closed his eyes to regain composure, pushing the word *asshole* out of mind in favor of an idyllic image of a bubbling brook and a school of lazy fish. He breathed in and out. The perfect future required a perfect start.

When he opened his eyes, he smoothed his rainbow-colored robe, stroked his mufti beard, and arched an eyebrow sprouting like wild seagrass on the crooked shoreline that was his forehead. His words began with the measured drawl of a Savannah accent, dripping like dew from Spanish moss.

"Welcome. Whatevah you believe, you must know two things about me. First, Ah am an artist, and my palette is the mind. Second, Ah am not c-r-a-a-z-y." He spoke the last word in a resonant, hypnotic, radio-announcer voice, segueing the final "y" into a broad, beatific smile, like the Cheshire Cat.

Cantor made eye contact with each of the investors, most of them dressed in business casual, some swirling drinks purchased from the lobby bar, others fingering their netcards, like worry beads.

"You are all here because you believe as Ah do that men will rise again," he said. "Our place of honor in society is eroding, to the detriment of the country. Are you ready to fight back?"

No one said anything, but he had their attention, with one exception. The man wearing the red polo shirt seemed to be lost in a newspaper called *National Scandals*. He looked vaguely familiar, but Cantor couldn't remember inviting him.

Cantor wanted to evoke a reaction from the group—any reaction—so he lifted a foot onto the table and wiggled his sandal-thonged toes. Tilting his head back, he closed his eyes and painted a vision with the broad sweep of an open hand.

"Two tried-and-true ways to become rich in our society are to invent a breakthrough technology or lead a popular religious movement. Ah intend to do both simultaneously."

The red-shirted man blew his nose with three loud honks.

Cantor was undeterred. "As my investors, you will make an obscene amount of money and restore respect for men. Let me show you how."

He hit a button, and an ancient digital projector whirred to life. It lased the screen with colored charts promising wealth and high social status.

"The technology we've perfected is called"—he made air quotes— "life cloning. Yes, Ah know it's against the law, but we're exploiting a loophole—no, let me rephrase that. We are using an approach consistent with the International Compassionate Family Act. The religious crusade we're perfecting will motivate people to buy our services and will generate immense profit."

Breaths punctuated the silence as forebrains processed his words.

"The technology," he continued, "was developed by my prior organization, Clonaid. Their initial successes were with families in North Africa and the Middle East—families with a little money and a lot of tragedy. Families who had seen their kids become martyrs. Families who could provide a bit of tissue, but not much more. They wanted their male children back—the same, only different. They paid a high price for cloning skills, and the company gave them new look-alike babies to replace the children who blew themselves to smithereens."

The red-shirted man in the back of the room said, "Amen."

Cantor continued. "The greater good was to provide comfort to those families who lost loved ones to tragedy. Ah believe everything happens for a reason. Ah am part of God's plan to bring sanity to this crazy world."

A man in the middle of the table, on Cantor's left side, raised his hand. "How does this—"

"Great segue," Cantor said, cutting him off. "The facts I just gave you speak to our expertise. Now Ah'm going to tell you about a breakthrough that will change your life and give you hope. We've created a vaccine to inoculate men against the effects of Testrial. But that's not all. You can pass down that immunity to your heirs. We'll never have to kowtow to women overlords again! This solution could be yours today by investing in shares of our privately held common stock. All you have to do is contribute a modest amount of funding, which we refer to as our 'Bronze Level' of participation. Simultaneously, because of a special relationship between my two companies, you become an emissary for the Cantor Tax-Exempt Spiritual Community, a not-for-profit company, which gives you special tax write-offs. The 'Silver Level' of participation gives you more stock in the for-profit and allows you to be a beta tester of our anti-Testrial vaccine. And at the 'Gold Level,' we'll immunize your entire family at no additional cost, and provide a certificate naming you as a 'Spiritual Guide' in our not-for-profit, which has even more tax advantages."

Thirteen uninterested faces, save one, were motionless. Cantor knew he was losing them.

"Don't you get it? It's really simple. Technology plus religion. Get rich; channel God's narrative; control your genetic destiny; help take our country back."

The mannequins stirred momentarily. Cantor wasn't sure this group could envision an idea on such a grand scale.

He hooked a finger inside his cheek and made a pop that surprised everyone. He wanted to wake people up.

The attendees stood up, one after the other, waved their hands under their noses and departed.

"Oh, the progress we've made in the last three decades of the new millennium," Marcy said. "Five years ago, men represented eighty percent of all homicide victims and committed ninety-five percent of all crimes. Just think how we've turned things around."

A wave of applause rolled through the ballroom. She waited for it to subside.

"Epic levels of violence—in our schools, workplaces, and houses of worship—finally tipped the scales for action in this country. That violence sapped our nation's productivity and challenged our morality. But it took a woman president, a sympathetic Congress, and a deal with the NRA that lifted all restrictions on gun sales, to chart a new course."

A wave of chanting, "Marcy ... Marcy ... Marcy" erupted from the crowd.

Marcy raised her hands, eliciting silence. "Now the tide is turning. The monthly killings at schools recently hit a five-year low. The murder rate in our worst cities has fallen to unprecedented lows. And we did this without taking away any guns. We didn't have to. The demand for them is vanishing. And companies that sell weapons are starting to lose money."

Applause and cheers.

"The benefit came when we successfully lobbied to put Testrial into pizza, beer, and bar snacks. By the end of this year, we'll see the testosterone-reducing supplement in *all* foods in school cafeterias, prisons, sports stadia, and soup kitchens. The violence in bars, soccer games, and on our streets will be a thing of the past.

"We forget how bad things were, and how, as a species, we've slowly overcome our worst instincts. Those violent impulses in males nearly wiped out Homo sapiens between five and seven thousand years ago, when the Y chromosome almost went extinct as nine million males killed each other in tribal warfare—nearly half the human population at the time. The 2018 paper by Zeng, Aw, and Feldman has now been corroborated by other careful studies of the genome.

"We don't need more cavemen. We don't need protection from wolves and saber-toothed tigers. We don't need clans and tribes fighting bloody tooth and nail. We need women and compassionate men working harmoniously together. And of course, we need technology to define a new age of human existence. Testrial is the new promise. The new hope."

She closed her eyes as applause rose like the thunder of a gathering storm.

Cantor was alone in the room with one other person. *What just happened here? How'd I lose an entire audience of potential investors? Who's the guy at the end of the table?*

He turned the projector off. The whirring fan slowed to a stop. This allowed air from the back of the room to circulate forward. It carried with it a nauseating stink. The sound of a fart punctuated the silence.

The man in the stained red shirt clapped loudly, stood, and walked forward. "That was brilliant! Brilliant!"

"Thank you," Cantor said, stifling a gag reflex. "And you are?"

"Name's Berky," the man said, looking down at Cantor's 5-foot-10-inch frame, grabbing his hand, shaking it vigorously. "That's all you need to know for now."

Cantor put a power cord in his hand. "Fine. Hold this, Berky. It's all Ah need from you right now." He began packing up his projector and laptop, disregarding the stranger who watched him like a beaming Buddha.

"What's the significance of the tattoo? What's a *Barblefarb?*" Berky asked, looking at the back of Cantor's right hand.

"It reminds me of something I want to avoid. Can you stow that power cord?"

Berky dutifully put the cord in the backpack as Cantor reached toward the projector.

"Ah, frikin' fudge!" Cantor shouted as he touched the projector lamp. Then he picked up the bag with cables, and the rotted bottom gave way, spilling accessories across the table. "Shit."

"For someone who claims to have a formula for getting rich, it looks like you can't even afford modern equipment," Berky observed. "And how about the crappy sign outside? Did you draw it yourself?"

Cantor rolled his eyes toward the ceiling. He didn't need smart-ass remarks. What he really craved was a new bag. And air freshener. Maybe a whiskey. He had never failed this miserably before—he had not landed a single investor. He wanted to break away from Berky's presence, or maybe just break Berky, but something about the hairless fat guy gave him pause.

Berky touched Cantor's shoulder and leaned forward as if to impart a confidence. But his voice boomed out so loudly, like the voice of a revival preacher, that Cantor jumped, startled.

"God has given me a chance to save mankind!" he thundered. "Like you, I'm part of His plan to restore order to the world. I can read His messages in the genome, sent from the beginning of time. They tell me how to overcome the poisons that sap our manhood and lead us toward a feminist hell-on-Earth. I have a plan to make things right again, but I need a partner who knows how to produce. Are you The One? Do you have what it takes? Is your technology real?"

Cantor couldn't be certain, but he suspected the man had detonated another stealth fart bomb. He opened the door to the conference room to let the place vent. Fresh air enabled him to think more clearly.

His brain fixated on a single question as he looked at the blubbery, disheveled bald man. That question was: *How deep are your pockets?* Instead, he said: "What do you have in mind?"

"I propose to test you, Mr. Cantor. If you can do the things I need, you can be my partner. If you can't—well then, you are nothing more than a charlatan. To prove yourself, I want you to bring Ichthy back to life."

Cantor blinked at the disgusting man in the disgusting shirt—the source of a disgusting stink. "Ah am not sure Ah want to bring your Icky back."

"You don't understand," Berky said. "Ichthy was an important historical figure. I have sixty-nine million dollars we can use. Is that enough?"

Canduka Cantor cleared his throat as an involuntary spasm grabbed his esophagus. He regained his composure and wrapped an encouraging arm around Berky. "Not nearly enough," he said. "But it's a start."

Marcy spotted a potential mark—Mr. Alphonso Rodriguez, husband of June Rodriguez, heir to the Prickly Pickle restaurant chain.

"Alphie, I'm so glad you could come to my symposium. I hope you enjoyed it."

The seventy-five-year-old man extended his soft hand. He wore a black suit with a silver bow tie. His thin and fit body moved with the energy of a man in his thirties.

"I'm always up for a little excitement," Alphonso giggled. "You look radiant."

Marcy winked. "And you look dashing."

"Oh, this is a little something Junie picked out for me. It makes me look younger, don't you think?"

"Definitely. And where's June?"

"She's at the mayor's office, working on a big investment. I'm here treading water. I'm glad your conference happened to be in the same place. It was so convenient."

Marcy took his hand. "Well, maybe June would like to invest in our great cause. You could speak to her about it. We could use her support. And you would make a great regional director, I might add. A handsome and viral distinguished gentleman like yourself would be perfect for our organization. Tell her she can help us save the world."

He blushed. "Oh, I'd never tell her what to do with her money. But you know I'll put in a good word for you."

"Thanks."

"By the way, I saw your former husband. He's presenting in the hotel. Is he involved in your dealings now?"

Marcy's black skin camouflaged an angry blush. She tempered her voice as she answered. "He is? Really? What a coincidence. And no, he is not part of our group."

"Oh, I see. Well, you don't have to worry about me mentioning it to anyone else. Mum's the word." He put his long smooth finger in front of his lips and winked.

Marcy knew Alphonso was an incorrigible gossip. Word would soon spread, and perhaps she could control the message: *My ex-husband is not part of my program.*

"You are such a darling. Please say hello to June for me."

As Alphonso departed, Marcy's burn ignited. She hated Cantor's ability to flimflam and use her notoriety for his own gain. *How dare he ride on my coattails! What the hell is he doing, following me around?*

She decided to find and confront him. But first, she needed muscle. *Where are Jed and Miguel?*

Cantor, scenting the possibility of money, alternated his expression between erudition, humility, and empathy, as his potential benefactor continued to rant.

"A world with Ichthy in it will help me realize God's design. I've seen it in my dreams. I'd give anything to fulfill the prophecy."

"Yes, Ah'm sure you will," Cantor said.

"As long as we're bringing him back, there are a few things I'd like to change," Berky said. "This is important for my—for God's—plan."

"Of course, of course. What is it?"

"It's proprietary. We'll need a non-disclosure agreement."

"Okay. Ah'll sign it. What can you tell me?"

"He didn't talk much. Don't get me wrong. His presence sparked ideas, and in a Zen-like way, his persona led me to the path of truth. But I'll need to make certain improvements."

"Sometimes speaking is just a matter of self-confidence," Cantor said. "After we bring him back, we'll give him speech therapy. We can hire the best tutors in the world. We'll build that into our budget."

"And he never laughed," Berky said.

"Fearless in life, fearless in death, eh? A stoic disposition?"

"Yeah. Something like that."

"Ah see," Cantor said.

"There are several things about Ichthy we should sort out before we bring him back," Berky said.

"You'll need to make a list. The enhancements could be expensive. Ah'm thinking maybe ... six to nine million." Cantor waited for a reaction.

"Yeah, that's fine."

Cantor suppressed a smile. "There may be additional unexpected costs. You have friends, don't you?"

"Not really. I have associates."

"Then Icky will be as right as rain. You'll see," Cantor said. "Ah only need a sliver of his DNA."

"I knew you'd help. That's why I brought what's left of him. You can start right away. I'll make arrangements to transfer the initial payment to your bank of choice."

Cantor stiffened. He was pleased to get seed money but wasn't prepared to take possession of a dead body in the elite Crowley-Burgess Hotel. He wondered how Berky had smuggled a corpse past the hotel security guards. He wondered if, by accepting the body, he might somehow become an accessory to a crime, maybe even murder. He wondered if the hotel might let him use the restaurant's refrigerator for just a bit. There were many urgent questions.

"I have to go," Berky said, looking at his watch. He picked up his duffel bag, slung it over his shoulder, and stepped out of the room.

The rapid departure surprised Cantor. "Wait!" he yelled, running to catch up.

Berky punched the "Up" button for the elevator, then opened his bag.

Cantor extended his left arm toward Berky, exposing a digitag bracelet. "Can we exchange contact information? And where can Ah find Icky?" Cantor said.

Berky put his bag down, fished through the contents, and removed a wig and false mustache. "Let's get the name right. It's *Ichthy*, I-c-h-t-h-y. We don't need to exchange contact information. You won't find me. I'll find you."

The elevator dinged on arrival. The doors slid open, revealing an empty car. The Master of Disguise pulled a polished mahogany box from the duffel bag, holding the elevator door open with his foot. "Be sure you take good care of him," he said somberly, as Cantor accepted the box. Then he slipped on a pair of dark glasses, made his hand into a gun, and pointed at Cantor, pretending to shoot. "Catch you later."

As the elevator doors closed, Cantor's brain framed a few big questions.

*Who was the real scam artist in that last transaction?*

*Does Berky actually have millions?*

*Will he pay that much money to get his dead friend back?*

*Does the box contain Ichthy's ashes? And if so, how can I get usable DNA?*

*On the other hand, does it really matter whose DNA is in the box?*

The box sat heavily in Cantor's arms like a stolen treasure chest. Ichthy must have been very special. Engraved nautical symbols and stylized waves decorated the sides of the small chest, and on one end, a mermaid blew bubbles. The other end said "Ichthy" in florid script.

He slid a thumb over the anchor-shaped catch and opened the lid, perhaps a millimeter. Then he thought better of it and snapped the lid shut again.

*What if the box is booby-trapped? What if Berky is insane, living in a hut someplace, secretly plotting to snuff out all life on the planet?*

*On the other hand, what if Berky is truly rich?*

Greed overcame him. Cantor held his breath and opened the box.

Inside, blood-red velvet bordered a jewel-encrusted slab with the outline of a fish, in keeping with the box's nautical theme.

*Maybe Ichthy was a sea captain of some renown. Perhaps knowledge of the man whose ashes were enshrined below this false bottom could help verify Berky's wealth. Maybe Berky's dead friend was a pirate or drug lord.*

Cantor felt the excitement of the hunt. With a deft tug, he pulled the slab out of the box. What was below astonished him. There, glued with precision to a mahogany centerpiece, were ivory-colored bones.

It all became clear now. *Of course, Ichthy wasn't talkative; of course, he had no sense of humor; of course, he needed improvements.*

Ichthy was—or at any rate, had been—a fish.

# CHAPTER 4
# SEX AND THE ART OF WAR

*At an abstract level, war is like sex. It's all about positioning.*
*—Canduka Cantor*

Cradling Berky's box in his right arm, and with the projector and other paraphernalia still spread across the table back in the Swamp Room, Cantor stepped into the Bella Boner Boutique off the marble-tiled hotel lobby on the main floor. His multicolored robe billowed in the pressure wall of the entryway.

The shop was so select there were no price tags on the designer clothing that hung like artwork on the beige and mauve walls. As he moved deeper into the store, lifelike black and white robots, draped in shiny costumes, assumed classic model poses and twisted on their pedestals to face him. Their LED eyes glowed with colors complementing the garments they modeled.

"Mmm, hello, Sugar. Can I help you?"

He swiveled toward the human voice, adjusting his smile to charm-level 10.

A young man in his late twenties, wearing a semi-transparent silvery shirt that looked like a second skin, responded by brushing his glowing fingernails against an ungrounded pink wig. A patch of fabric near his thick neck briefly displayed the word, *Virgilio*.

"Are you returning that box from one of our stores?" the man asked.

Cantor shifted Ichthy to his left arm. "This box is a present from someone. It's not why Ah am here."

Virgilio scrutinized Cantor from head to sandaled toe, then arched an eyebrow.

Cantor leaned toward the shopkeeper and spoke in an intimate voice. "Ah have a problem that must be handled very discretely. It's my master. She bought a lot of things the other day from your shop."

"Oh, that must have been the divine Ms. Rodriguez. I remember she came in with her darling husband, Alphonso. We had to restock after she left. We value her business very much." His lips tweaked in the faintest of smiles while his fingers made a zipper-closing movement. "Any secret you have is safe with me."

"Ah am so relieved to hear that," Cantor said. "You, my fine, good man, are a peach. Ah could just eat you up." He leaned closer, adjusting his voice to a whisper. "See, Ah always help her with errands when Ah'm not—when we're not—engaged in deeply gratifying business."

"I understand." Virgilio gazed at Cantor's hand as it touched his arm, then gently wiped a middle finger across the back. "That's an unusual tattoo. Barblefarb. It must mean something special."

"It does. In my religion, it means situations in which we are all inextricably connected. And because we look at the world in different ways, this leads to a high degree of confusion and chaos and stress. 'Barblefarbs' must be avoided at all costs. Ah had the word tattooed on my hand as a reminder."

"All that in a single word?"

"Yes."

"Awesome!"

Cantor leaned closer. "Speaking of stress—that's the reason Ah am here."

Virgilio's eyes drooped. "If you are stressed, maybe there's something I can do to relieve that."

Cantor patted the man's arm. "Ah wish I had more time, but it's not me. It's Junie."

"Ms. Rodriguez?"

"Yes. She is very stressed. And distressed."

"Goodness. I hope it's not something we've done."

"To the contrary. She's missing some things from her room that she absolutely cherished. The hotel cleaning staff removed several empty bags from your store. They've been thrown away, like pieces of worthless trash, and she can't get them back. She *so* wanted to use them to impress people. That's hard to do when you travel in Supreme First Class."

"The bags make a statement, don't they?"

"Indeed."

"How many do you want?"

"Five will do nicely."

"You should always think bigger. That's my motto."

"Seven?"

"A magic number." Virgilio clasped Cantor's arm in confidence. "You are so sweet. Ms. R is lucky to have you. I'll get them for you right away. Stay here." He took a step, then hesitated and pivoted 180 degrees on a pointed heel. "I hope you don't mind my asking. The robe you're wearing is absolutely fabulous. Did you get it at one of our stores, or a competitor's? The reason I ask is that some of the gentlemen who come in are intrigued by our apparel, and their wives are usually willing to spend good money on clothing with a certain panache. It's a niche market I'd like to accommodate."

"Actually," Cantor whispered, "Ah made it myself, and Ah am designing a cape to go with it. Ah take pride in everything Ah put my hands on. Give me your digitag, and Ah'll be sure to hook you up." He winked as their two bracelets touched, emitting a warm glow.

Virgilio laughed. "Oooh, if my body had any hair, it would be standing up right now. How exciting!" He held up an arm adorned with a SleeVu patch the same color as his garment. When he touched it, the display illuminated, and he flipped it to camera mode. "Do you mind? I want to remember this night."

"No at all," Cantor said. "Come on. Get really close to me. Let's flash our brightest smiles to commemorate the start of a beautiful business relationship ... and whatever comes after that." Cantor hugged Virgilio tightly as the young man positioned his arm in a muscle flex long enough to record the image and upload it to ten social media accounts.

Near the front of the store, a tall man built like a tank and wearing a tuxedo popped his eyes in surprise. He stopped his close examination of women's panties, tapped the SleeVu patch on his arm, and began to record.

The overhead holographic displays had been shut down, and some of the lights were turned off, but nearly a hundred people still talked and networked in the Grand Arcadia Ballroom. Marcy continued to mingle with admirers, fielding questions.

"Do you think America will ever get murder rates lower than India's?" The olive-skinned questioner wore a sari, and her South-Asia accent indicated she had traveled from afar.

"I think we'll get there," Marcy answered. "Our rate is still about one-and-a-half times that of India's, four times England's, and ten times Japan's. America's on the verge of being civilized. I expect we'll get approval to put Testrial into a broader range of foods, and that should—"

"Ms. Darcy!" The man outside the ring of questioners towered a head above them and wore a tuxedo. Marcy excused herself and walked with him to a corner of the room, where they huddled in private conversation.

"Yes, Jed?"

"I found him," he said. "Cantor was in the shop in the lobby when I took this." He pulled a netcard from his pocket and retrieved a photo showing Cantor and Virgilio.

"Yep. That's definitely him. Why is he dressed like that? He looks like Moses working as a carnival huckster."

"I don't know," Jed said. "I talked to the other guy. He told me Cantor's employed by Ms. June Rodriguez."

"Slimeball! That's so not true. The only time he ever met Junie was when we were married, and he was with me, carrying my bags."

"What do you want me to do?"

"We need to find the bastard and let him know I'm on to him."

"Got it."

"Wait. See if you can find Miguel to help with the search. We find him, confront him, and do some damage control."

Before he re-entered his makeshift conference room, Cantor put down his empty red bags from Virgilio's shop, removed the metal sign from the hook near the Swamp Room door, and turned it over, restoring the placard's original words:

*Staff Lunch Room*
*Please wipe tables and remove trash*
*—The Management*

Cantor was still twenty minutes away from the hotel's scheduled break—plenty of time to finish packing up. He entered the room and lifted the seven bags onto the conference table. They immediately illuminated when he opened them up, displaying *Bella Boner Boutique* in gold lettering that scrolled around the circumference of each sack.

He distributed his ancient projector, laptop, cables, notebook, and Berky's box among the shiny new bags, and tossed his disintegrating backpack onto a trash can near the door. As he opened up the sixth bag, he searched for the source of additional weight.

"Virgilio, you dog," he said, looking in. He removed a golden bottle of Old Crow Kentucky Straight Bourbon Whiskey and carefully examined the label. "Distilled and bottled in 1931. Awesome."

Running his tongue slowly along his upper lip, he broke the bottle's seal with the twist of a wrist, popped the fat cork, raised it to his nose, then sniffed like a breath of fresh cool air. With a big grin, he waltzed around the table, serenading the bottle with words from an old Confederate marching song: "Let love and friendship on that day, hurrah, hurrah; their choicest pleasures then display, hurrah, hurrah ..."

He lifted the bottle to his lips and let a trickle of its warm bygone glow illuminate the dark places in his throat before continuing, his voice somewhat strained now, "And let each one perform some part, to fill with joy the warrior's heart ..."

He took another swig. "Oh yeah." He paused for a moment to savor the taste, then resumed, "And we'll all feel gay when Johnny comes marching home."

It was just after midnight when Cantor pushed out the basement door onto River Street, managing five full bags, two empties, and an open bottle. A container ship glided silently down the Savannah River, and the smell of industry and salt marshes perfumed the waterfront. The temperature was 93 degrees Fahrenheit but felt like 130, with humid air as thick as she-crab soup. He wandered along brick paths illuminated by streetlamps and lights from businesses before finding a bench near the water out of sight from the hotel.

He sat down, placing the bottle near his side and the bags at his feet.

A soft voice issued from a nearby bench, whispering to an invisible ghost: "Know what I'm sayin'? Know what I'm sayin'?"

The disheveled man with a prosthetic left forearm wore a baseball cap that said *War Veteran*, and a desert camouflage jacket with a flag patch on the arm. The man lifted his head, looked at Cantor, smiled through broken teeth, and fixed his eyes—first on the robe, then on the bottle. "It's 37:3, 37:3. Yes, yes, it is. I'm sure. It's so written ... 37:3."

Cantor returned his gaze and regarded the tattered bags next to the man's bench, filled with worldly possessions. "Hey, man. Need another bag? Ah've got a couple of extras." He put two empties next to the man.

"Something for nothing. The genie of Genesis." The man tried to wink, but his eyelid stayed shut. "Say, Joe. That's a fly outfit." The man flapped his open right hand. "Whoo-hoo!" He grinned at Cantor, his second eyelid now wide open, eye rolling toward the sky, then back toward the bottle.

Cantor took a long swig, watching the man pucker his lips in empathy. "Sometimes Ah feel like Ah *can* fly, my friend."

The man cleared his throat. "Mmm, mmm. It's worthy of the covetous green eye of nine. But no need to fret. I'm devout of the ten."

"Ah make my own religion," Cantor said, slurring his words. "Want a drink?"

The man's eyes grew twice as big. "A holy sacrament. Now we're talkin'. That makes it eleven."

"That's enough for a soccer team," Cantor said. "One more, and we can imagine playing Lacrosse." He got up, walked to the man's bench, and handed over the half-bottle of whiskey.

With shaking limbs, the man held it like a baby bottle between his real hand and a nimble plastic hand, then guzzled nearly a third of the remaining liquid in one chug.

"Looks like you need that more than I do," Cantor said. "Keep it." He picked up his bags and moved downstream to an area where trees and shrubs blocked streetlights, and only the full moon illuminated the bench.

The homeless man stayed put and started singing:

*The funniest thing I ever seen,*
*Was a "wompass cat" with his eyes are green.*
*Cryin' it feels so good, ahhh, Lord, it feels so good.*
*Gonna tell the world, it feels so good ...*

The stanza kept repeating, but the words drifted off, finally segueing into snores.

A breeze from the river picked up. Cantor stood and faced it, removing his robe and waving it like a proud battle flag, feeling the wind on his skin. Under his colorful coat, he wore only knee-length Bermuda shorts, a white linen shirt, and politically incorrect crocodile skin sandals. His armpits and butt were damp with sweat.

He bowed toward the water and did a little jig, then draped the robe behind his back and held the ends out, like the wings of a bird. "You can rum-tee-tum-tee-tum-tee-tum," he said, speaking loudly to the wind. He circled the bench three times, like an airplane awaiting clearance to land, arms out, robe trailing like a cape. "Fly with me, fly you see, fly, flum, flume—"

"Nigel! You damn fool. What the hell are you doing?" The familiar female voice spoke with a force that could not be denied.

Cantor stopped. He recognized the tone and turned to face a woman whose white dress sparkled in the moonlight—an evil fairy queen. Two musclemen in black tuxedos were attached to her like double shadows.

"As you see." He bowed with an unsteady flourish, stepped within a foot of her, then undocked a breathy Savannah drawl that drifted through words tinged with regret. "My love. What a happy. Happy. Coincidence."

Marcy rolled her eyes. "Oh, please, Nigel. You stink of alcohol."

He held up a shaking forefinger. "You shall address me by my chosen name, 'Canduka.' Or if you prefer, 'Reverend Cantor' will do just fine. Ah am now a prophet, after all."

"A prophet? More like a loss if you ask me. I'd be surprised if those bloodshot eyes could tell shit from Shinola."

"My love. Ah am as sharp as a blackberry brush. Sharp as a track. Tack."

"If you were a prophet, you'd figure out how to survive on your own—you wouldn't try to hitch a ride on my ass."

Cantor's droopy gaze fell on her hips. "From what Ah remember, you liked it when Ah rode your ass. Is that what your two boy toys are for?" He flipped a wavering one-fingered salute to the two men. "Hello, whores."

A sneer lifted her lip. "The only thing you know how to ride is a jackass. Lucky for me, I had plenty of batteries and company."

"Try me. There was always lust between us, Ms. Mars, and Ah believe there still is."

"What the hell are you doing here, Nigel? Are you fucking around with my customers?" She leaned close and put a finger on his nose. "Quit trading on my brand."

"Ah am trading emptiness for fulfillment, Luv. Ah am giving men hope. And it's making me money. Yeah!"

Her voice rose to an angry shout. "My conferences attract high-class people. When you follow me around and mess with royalty like June Rodriguez, you cheapen me and my movement, you disgusting piece of excrement. Stop it!"

"My dear, Ah made you who you are. Remember? Ah quit a top marketing post to give birth to Marcy Darcy, visionary evangelist extraordinaire. Ah carried your bags. Ah drudged behind the scenes. Ah worked the magic that took you from obscure law professor to famous figure. That was before you became an uncontrollable monster. Now it's my turn. Yes, Ah may look like I'm struggling at the moment, but Ah am about to secure some very sub stantial... substantial... funding."

"You are delusional. I know exactly what you're doing with your illegal schemes. You're giving men false hope. The world has changed. Accept it."

"Your future is empty." He waved his hands, imagining a brave new world, but his voice faltered, and his words fuddled. "Gentlemen need a comeback. There are still some with money who believe happiness can be engineered. Ah know how to deliver."

"What?" she said. "Try to amp up the testosterone? Create your own little male-dominated enclave? How sad and pathetic."

He wagged his finger. "My plans are much bigger." He pulled a notebook from one of his bags and waved it in her face.

"What's that?"

"My *Canons*. My manifesto. It's what's attracting thousands and thousands of followers. It's going to be huge." He blew a kiss through puckered lips. "Ah find your little Testrial movement deeply offensive and most inconvenient. Ah will, therefore, use all my power—all my tricks—to remove the unnatural impediments to my success and enjoyment, the barriers to my rightful pursuit of happiness. If that means following you around to restore the natural order, then Ah will do so. It's a free country."

"Up to a point, Nigel. Remember the Civil War, and who won it."

He set a defiant chin. "Remember who got half the money in the divorce settlement, Luv?"

"You stole that from me."

"Ah had a better lawyer. You owed me, and Ah'm using it against you. The gray shall rise again."

After a pause, she wrinkled her nose. "Gray is no match for black and blue. Here's a preview of what's to come." She flicked her head toward one of her men. "Meet Miguel."

Miguel, who seemed twenty feet tall, missing a neck, and made of cast iron, moved forward. Cantor put up his arms defensively. Moving like some slow but unstoppable natural process, Miguel slapped Cantor's left cheek—a stinging yet almost mocking blow—then, with greater force, his forehead. Cantor stumbled backward, barely missing the bench and the bags. His notebook flew from his hand and skidded under the seat. Then Miguel punched him in the nose. The prophet of Savannah fell bleeding to the pavement.

Miguel practiced his soccer moves—first a toe kick, then a 180 hop, followed by a heel kick. Cantor curled into a ball of pain and remained on the ground. Marcy stooped to pick up his notebook, then left with her men without saying another word.

Cantor felt a sharp pain and wetness in his nose. The agony in his balls stung like a swarm of swamp mosquitos. He pinched his nostrils with one hand to staunch the nasty flow and clutched his groin with the other.

The *tap-tap* of high heels and the *clop-clop* of male feet faded into the night. The homeless man's snoring had stopped, and he was nowhere in sight. The lights on River Street danced crazily in Cantor's eyes. He looked up at the moon and whispered an oath to the goddess of the night: "War it is."

# CHAPTER 5
# A TOWN TO DIE FOR

*Reality is a dipsey-doodle dancer.*
*—Canduka Cantor*

Nadia spied the night sky through a crack in the drapery panels. A flash lit up giant poplars beyond the river—a tipoff. The wind and the trees waved his arrival. He was coming. Her breath stuttered. Her hands trembled. She held her doll against her cheek, hoping for comfort and protection.

She switched on the lamp beside the settee near the entry. The knitting needle was on the end table where she had left it. She heard the *clack-clack-clack* of tires on the wooden bridge. He was closer now. *He'll be pulling into the driveway.*

She tried to remain calm and rehearse the requests—*No, demands!*—she would make. *I'll tell him I want my box back. I'll tell him I want better food. And I'll say I don't want to be touched. I want to be left alone so I can finish my History. I'll stand up to him just as Papa stood up to the New Order.*

She heard tires rolling into the gravel driveway. A radio blasted out a song: *Frankie and Johnny were lovers* ... The radio clicked off, and a truck door squeaked open. Boots slapped against the planks of the porch.

Her eyes turned toward the door as it opened. Fear gripped her brain. A large bald figure filled the entrance, arms loaded with bags.

"Honey, I'm back," Berky said.

Her heartbeat quickened. She reached toward the needle on the end table, but he moved quickly, caught her hand, and held her torso close to his.

Then he howled.

She dropped the needle, and it rolled under the table.

Still gripping the doll, she shut her eyes and sent her mind time-traveling back to the last days with her father.

On a brilliant summer day in April 2040, Nadia carried a bag up the circular gravel driveway to her father's white-columned manor home, climbed a fan of stone steps to the wrap-around porch and pushed the doorbell. There was no immediate answer, so she put the bag down and sat on the joggling board, gently bouncing up and down, waiting.

After five minutes, she banged her fist on the door and yelled, "Papa, it's me, open up."

"Back here!" The sound came from the side of the house. She picked up the bag and stepped down to the garden path, circled through a low gate, and saw her father stooping over a four-foot white tower, looking like an out-of-place, 6-foot-tall spaceman amid the Dogwood blossoms. She loved the beauty of the place, and she loved her father. "Look what I brought, Papa. Do you like it? Is it what you wanted?" She took the object out of the bag and held it up for him to see.

Arthur moved away from the apiary and unzipped his veil and helmet from the white bee suit, exposing sad, droopy brown eyes. He parked the hood under an arm then pulled off his ventilated gloves and tried to tame an unruly mane of sandy hair with the fingers of one hand, to no avail. The bees still buzzed nearby, but he ignored them as he reached for the box and grumbled, "Thanks for bringing it." He caressed the carved wood as if it were a religious relic. Then his voice deepened to despair. "The bees are leaving us, just like the rest of the town."

She nodded toward the gravestone behind the hive. "The world's changing. If Mama were alive, she wouldn't recognize it."

He pursed his lips in disgust. "Your Mama couldn't tolerate change. She's probably turning over in her grave." He sat for a moment on a stone seat near the entrance to the garden, removed the rest of his bee suit, and folded it into a neat bundle. Then he put the carved wooden box on top and carried the load up the porch steps with Nadia in trail. "Let's go inside, Nadia. I want to show you something."

She followed him, carrying the empty bag through the door into the vestibule where she stopped to survey changes to her family home. "You've been busy!"

A once-empty wall in the entry hall was now filled with old photographs. One picture showed Nadia's parents, Arthur and Annie, in wedding outfits. There were other photos of grandparents and relatives—generations of Holkams, McClungs,

Tates, and Paynes. The images ran along the entry wall and up along the stairs toward the bedrooms.

"I'm getting the place ready for its new purpose," Arthur said, stepping through a doorway, cradling the box in his arms. "Take a look in here."

"My gosh."

"I knocked out the walls between the dining room and sitting room to create a grand room. I'm using the library as a living room—it's certainly big enough—and I use the breakfast area for dining."

"What happened to grandma's table?"

"I didn't need it, now that everyone's practically gone. Who am I going to eat dinner with? I scavenged stuff from our store and turned this into the Assurance Museum." He placed Nadia's carved box on a shelf, next to a placard labeled *Ichthy*. "I'm trying to collect all the artifacts and records into a single place. As the town's last mayor, it's my duty."

"It's an amazing effort, but has it affected your health? You don't look well."

He wheezed an answer. "Maybe a hundred years from now archeologists will unearth this collection and realize Assurance was a town with principles and grit and a right-thinking culture."

He walked to a wall of pictures. The smaller frames displayed 1930s-era photographs of Assurance under construction. A bigger-than-life oil painting in the center of the wall showed a resolute-looking man in a tweed hunting jacket, matching brown pants, and fishing boots. "Remember the bricked-up doorway in the basement? The one we noticed when we were caretakers for this place? Well, I decided to open it up."

"You showed me the hole in the wall once," Nadia said. "You could see a reflection when you shined a light into it."

"Yup. I always knew there was something behind the wall. After Kelsey's estate gave us the house, I had too many other things going on to pay much mind to it. Until now."

"It was always a mystery."

"Not anymore. I took a hammer and chisel and knocked out the bricks."

Nadia's fingers traced carved designs on the painting's frame. "And discovered—What? Mice? Human remains? A cask of Amontillado?"

"A secret room with a bunch of old stuff, including this oil painting in a sealed container. The portrait was made two years after the founding. See Kelsey's hand on the box? Your box? How's that for provenance? He was a man of purpose and honor."

She nodded, mesmerized by Kelsey's furrowed brows, piercing eyes, a jaw that jutted under a walrus moustache, and one strong hand hooked on his belt buckle. The other hand touched the box, like God giving life to Adam in the Sistine Chapel painting. "He looks like a man to be reckoned with."

She took a deep breath and changed her focus. "I remember the box was a Christmas present. I always kept pencils in the top part."

"And here's a drawing on parchment that was also in the room."

"A medicine wheel? Ley lines?" She fretted at the puzzle.

"The wheel is an old Indian thing that's all about healing. And the lines supposedly have supernatural power. See how Kelsey has combined these two ideas?"

Nadia squinted. "Now you're starting to sound like Mama."

"I know it's screwy," he said. "It's important that you, the budding scientist, suspend judgment for a moment. This is not about physics or microbiology. It's about what I found in the room. Superstition determined where this town was built. If you draw the lines on a map—Chicago to Charleston and New York to New Orleans—you'll see where they cross."

"Assurance?"

"Yup. Kelsey thought Assurance was some sort of supernatural vortex that would change the world."

She gave a little laugh. "Boy, did he get it wrong. The world changed Assurance, not the other way around. And now the town has vanished."

"The town's still here, Nadia. It just seems to be moving in another dimension."

Nadia inched closer to the portrait, eyeing the brushwork on the oil painting. "The artist made a kind of glow around the box of fishbones—like it's in a spotlight."

Arthur sighed. "There's a fish story I never told you, and there's a reason for it. As mayor, I'm supposed to be the town's most upstanding citizen. But the fish bones were always kind of a gray area."

"Now you're starting to worry me, Papa. You're a man of honor. Whatever happened, I'm sure it wasn't your fault. Was it?" Her eyes searched his.

Arthur cleared his throat. "In the end, it's hard to hide the truth, eh? Maybe there are multiple truths."

"I don't understand."

"I always thought, you know, the box was a kind of test—for who we are and how we see the world. It's connected, like the painting and the map, to the founding. When Kelsey moved here in the 1930s, he claimed he discovered a new species of fish in the South Prong—'Evidence,' as he liked to say in his best sermonizing voice, 'that Gawd has dipped his hand in the waters of Assurance.'"

She looked at the portrait, imagining Kelsey's thundering voice, speaking only in declarative sentences. Like an oracle. Like God talking to Jonah. She couldn't help thinking, *Nineveh will be smashed.*

Arthur picked up the box again, admiring the detail of the carving. "After years of failing to catch a specimen, he finally did. Instead of dissecting it to prove his point, he decided to keep it as a pet, and named it 'Ichthy'—short for *Kelseyichthy.*"

"He named a fish after himself?"

"Right," he said, putting down the box. "It's clear from his journal in the secret room that he was after some sort of immortality. He wanted to change the world and adding to the list of known species was just another notch on his belt. After the fish died, Kelsey mounted the bones in this box."

Nadia laughed. "I don't see why you're ashamed."

He puckered his mouth as if tasting a lemon. "There's a dirty little secret that goes with it. Kelsey's will said he wanted the box buried with him."

"If this is the same box, that obviously didn't happen."

"Actually, it did. The family put the box in the coffin. Someone else dug up the casket in the dead of night, while the earth was still fresh, stole the box, and substituted a similar box with a rag doll."

"That's stupid," she said. "Who'd do a thing like that?"

"When this man later confessed to me, he gave me a wild story. Said the fish was a descendent of a primordial monster fish that once lived in the Nantahala and spawned in the South Prong River. According to Cherokee legend, these monster fish did great damage until they were all killed by human beings. The man said it would be wrong to bury such a fish so close to the old weir near the river bend. It must be destroyed in another way. Personally, I think this man, Darryl Grove, was lying about his motives. He probably thought Kelsey's box was the key to some priceless treasure."

Nadia lifted the lid, gazing at the interior. "All he got were a few fish bones in a fancy box."

"They meant a lot to Kelsey. To him, they were part of his identity—and the mythology of Assurance—which is why he wanted them buried in his coffin."

"Why do you feel guilty if Mr. Grove is the one who dug up the box?"

Arthur sighed. "I wasn't thinking clearly. I shouldn't have accepted it."

"It was a gift?"

"I won it in a card game. It was a week after your mother's funeral, and I was still in a deep funk. I was drinking whiskey and playing poker with Darryl and a guy by the name of Eban Haywood. Darryl was desperate for money to start a business. So was Eban. But I cleaned them both out. Eban was able to pay his debt, but when Darryl came up short in the last poker hand, I agreed to take the box as payment. I don't know why. Maybe I had too much to drink that night." He smiled. "Darryl's wife, Jancie, seemed grateful—relieved. They couldn't afford to pay me money. Anyway, that's how I got the box and an antique rag doll. The doll was a duplicate of the one Darryl and Jancie buried."

Nadia cocked her head and stared at her father with a different set of eyes. "So, twin dolls?"

"Yes." After a moment, Arthur tweaked his daughter's nose. "I've kept you too long. Besides, I have a lengthy list of things I need to do before I leave this crazy world. Remember, I want to be buried next to your mother."

"Don't say that, Papa. You have a long life ahead of you."

His look turned stern. "Remember what we talked about? You need to get out of here. Do it! I want you to go to Asheville, Durham, or wherever your heart takes you. You'll fit in this new world."

"I like the old world; the way things were. The way they should be. I've been here most of my life," she said, "except for college. I'm comfortable here. It's where I belong."

His face grayed, and he looked ten years older. "I'm disappointed, Nadia. Very, very disappointed. What happened to the brave little girl who could do anything she imagined?"

Her eyes glistened. "Those were your stories, not mine. I'm not a little girl, and if you're staying, so am I."

"Dammit, Nadia! There's nothing here for you. Why don't you listen? You've got the brains, the education, the talent. And the time is right. Make something of yourself."

"I'm not leaving, Papa!" She stamped her foot and put her defiant face close to his.

Arthur slapped her. "Get a backbone for once in your life!"

She slapped him back. It was a roundhouse blow that knocked him backward onto a chair.

He rubbed his jaw. "They said they're going to turn the power off and cut network connections. Things will get a lot worse. You don't want to be here." His lip quivered as he spoke.

"I'm not leaving, Papa."

He stood and grabbed her by the neck. "Don't disrespect me. I'm your father."

She forced his hands away. He recoiled, put his head down, took short breaths, and slurred his words. "I don't want to argue about this, but you—"

Her anger melted into concern as she watched his face grow ashen. "Are you okay, Papa? Can I get you some water?"

"I'm fine," he said. "Maybe I'll lie down for a while."

Nadia helped him into the bedroom and poured water into a glass from the bathroom tap. After he drank, she sat by his bed as he went to sleep. She stared at his sallow face for hours.

Arthur Holkam never woke up.

Nadia opened her eyes. Berky's fat face was close to hers, lips puddling drool on the floor while he snored.

She sat up and used her hand to wipe off the web of slime covering her body, but the pain in her toes was intense. She picked up the rag doll and stroked its brown hair.

She gazed at Berky's beached hulk for a moment, then retrieved the knitting needle from under the table. She touched the point and thought about murder. The doll's glass eyes begged the question: "Get real. How will you survive if he's dead?"

# CHAPTER 6
# THE LAST STAND

*A man's gotta do what a man's gotta do.*
—*Canduka Cantor, channeling John Wayne*

*We were the last holdout.* Nadia pressed hard against the tablet on her father's desk in the museum as she wrote the line. The ballpoint pen leaked, blotching the script. She crossed out the words and started over, hoping for perfection. This time, she wrote: *It was the last stand for decency, and for the way things ought to be, and for truth.*

She wanted history to be clear. Assurance represented the culture of the frontier, the culture of honor, the culture demanding respect for all men. It's what had made America great. It was the outsiders who'd made problems when they viewed the town through a different lens. Four years ago, they'd started a death spiral ending in a contaminated river, a CDC-directed evacuation, and a power company buy-out. They'd destroyed Assurance.

The fall of 2038 was a season of change in Assurance. Summer drifted toward winter in saltatory steps. The leaves yellowed, then reddened. It was the peak of the monarch butterfly migration, and black bears were staking out denning locations.

On a crisp morning in October, with townsfolk gathering in Kelsey Park, a crew of outside reporters arrived to cover an emerging story. Their white van bristled with antennas as it pulled to a stop on the far side of the arched wooden bridge leading into the town.

Inside, Brooke Kasinski, in a pink tank top and white pants, popped a steady stream of Brazil nuts into her mouth when she wasn't sipping an energy drink from a plastic bottle. This was a simulation of "lunch." When her boss's image filled the screen in front of her, she put the bottle down, wiped her mouth with the back of a hand, and slipped on a headset. "Hi, Marcy."

"Hi, Brooke. Sorry I'm late. The meeting with the FDA ran long. That's why I'm still in a suit. It looks like they're going to approve the food supplement." She brushed a hand through her manicured afro. "How's our project coming?"

Brooke could barely hear over the weak audio, so she yelled to her workmates: "Hold it down, folks! Our producer's on." The hubbub inside the media production van dropped to a chorus of whispers as one man and two other women, bathed in LED light, coordinated live feeds across multiple video screens. Brooke smiled and gave everyone a thumbs up, mouthing, "Thank you." She turned back to Marcy. "Sorry for that."

"No problem."

"I have an interview lined up with the mayor and a few other prominent town folks. I'll be hitting on their reaction to the jury verdict."

"See if you can get us some background on local culture."

"Sure. Where do you want to go with this piece?"

"At the end of the day, this is a story about toxic masculinity. A man confesses to a double homicide, and a town's jury fails to convict because the killing corrects an affront to his manhood and massive assault on his identity. And then there's the business of seceding from the Union."

"You gotta be kidding me. The place is a holdout from the Confederacy?"

"Not exactly. The man killed was an out-of-state tourist, which is why word leaked outside the county's jurisdiction. Otherwise, the whole affair might have been covered up. He was diddling a local married woman, who was also murdered. When a federal court tried to intervene in the case, the mayor declared that Assurance was a separate country, subject to God's own justice, and the town backed him. Now there's a stand-off. I think the feds are hoping this will just go away—sort of like Town Line, New York, which seceded in 1861, eventually grew tired of rebelling, and rejoined the Union in 1946."

Brooke whistled. "Lordy."

"In my mind, Assurance is the perfect symbol of manhood run amok. I can use it to help sell the idea of mandating Testrial as a food supplement. I'll argue it's not just about reducing violence to women—or even violence in general—it's about holding the country together."

"Wow." Brooke adjusted the noise cancellation threshold to hear better. "That's a lot to process. It seems like we have an identity crisis—for the murderer, the town, the culture."

"Right. The story reduces to the impact of male violence."

Brooke smiled. "Maybe there's something in the water."

"Well, the water runs deep—not just here. Killing a woman for infidelity was a valid legal defense in Texas until the mid-1970s. And right now, we have enclaves in seven other states pushing for secession because of what they consider cultural hijacking by elite establishments. What happens in this town could be the tipping point—sort of like Fort Sumter. You know what I want. When you finish with the interviews—"

"There's one more twist in all this."

Marcy sighed. "Only one? Give it to me quick. I need to prep for Senate testimony."

"There's a group of radicals here, stirring things up."

She broke into a smile. "I love it! Sounds like an opportunity for some great visuals. Cover that, too, but keep the crew safe, and keep your eye on the objective. I want my money's worth."

"Aye, aye, Boss."

On the other side of the bridge, Nadia accompanied her father to the park at Kelsey's Bend. Her arm, covered in a blue sweater, locked into Arthur's light hunting jacket.

They stopped for a moment while the mayor loaded and cocked his double-barrel shotgun. As they waded toward the center of the park, the crowd of nearly a hundred people stirred around them like a thick school of lazy catfish.

On a podium of stacked boxes, a spindly woman with scraggly black hair and glasses shouted through a megaphone. "Listen! Listen!" The amplified sound ended in a high-pitched squeal. She adjusted the equipment settings. The woman wore an ankle-length granny dress and hippie boots, like a throwback to the 1970s. Two other women flanked her—one was short and heavy-set, dressed like Pocahontas, with eyebrows like Groucho Marx; the other had a medium build, with dreadlocks, nose rings, jeans, and a *Fuck Men* sweatshirt.

About half the throng filling the park were women. Most of the men carried rifles. On the edge of the crowd, equipment-laden reporters lurked like barracuda scenting blood.

The spindly woman spoke in a high-pitched voice. "What is justice, if killers go free? If honor killing is allowed? If violence is condoned? Women of Assurance: Take back your town!"

A sixtyish man with a floppy white hat, a chest-length white beard, and a jean jacket climbed onto a park bench, raised his rifle into the air, and shouted over the crowd. "Ain't no honor killings here. We ain't Mooslams. We're God-fearing people. But Billy Jack was right to do what he did. His wife and that fuckin' outsider disrespected him. And if you don't get off that pulpit and stop stirring things up, there's a bullet here with your name on it. I'll show you some mountain justice."

Arthur Holkam pointed his gun at the sky and fired. *Boom!* The smell of gunpowder wafted through the park. Arthur cleared his throat, breaking the silence. "Now Jimmy, I want you to get off that bench and go home. I want all of you to go home. And you ladies from Hell, I don't remember giving you a parade license. So I want you to go back where you came from or Danny, our sheriff, will lock you up. Right, Danny?"

Danny McKenzie was only four and a half feet tall, but when he wore his sheriff's star, he seemed much taller. He made his way to the bench Jimmy had vacated, climbed up, and touched his pistol to the brim of his black hat. A glint of sunlight reflected from the tin patch on his dark-blue jacket. "At's right," he said.

The crowd dispersed. Danny hopped down, then huffed toward the makeshift podium. The spindly woman jumped to the ground before Danny kicked the stack of boxes with a heavy boot, toppling them.

"You're littering!" he said.

The three women backed away toward the river's edge, linked arms, and stood their ground. Danny paced back and forth in front of them, like a sheepdog. Finally, he jabbed a threatening forefinger in their direction, then walked away.

Arthur Holkam turned around and started back toward the center of town, but Brooke Kasinski stepped in front of him. "Mayor Holkam? Got a minute?"

He tried to move past her, waving his hand like he was shooing flies.

Brooke persisted. "If you don't talk to me, I'll give the world my view of what just happened."

He stopped, with a look of disgust. "And what's your view?"

"A small mountain town with a culture of misogyny protects men from the law. The elected mayor quells the attempts of three good women to set things right. The State and the Feds look the other way."

"You're not from around here," he said. "No wonder your feminazi pea brain is confused. That's not what happened."

"Help me get it right," she said.

He looked down the barrel of her netcard and spoke. "The sovereign state of Assurance carried out a trial by jury, with twelve good men, and concluded that Billy Jack Henshaw was within his rights. Maybe he should have used better judgment, but he's innocent of any crime."

"How can you say that?"

"Because I speak English. *Comprende?*"

"If Assurance is a sovereign state, does that mean you don't pay U.S. taxes? Does it mean you don't receive federal and state funds for schools and roads? How about electrical power and communications? How exactly does—or will—this work?"

"We don't have all the answers yet, but we'll figure it out. The most important thing is that we are independent. We've got to keep our identity. Our honor. Our culture. Now if you'll excuse—"

"Is this your daughter? Hi! What do you think about all this? Do you think a man who walks away without hurting his unfaithful wife isn't a real man? Do you think it's okay for a woman to hurt an abusive husband?"

Arthur's upper lip raised in a sneer. "Get the fuck out—"

"It's okay, Papa. I'll answer."

Arthur drilled his eyes into Nadia's, then shrugged in resignation. Brooke moved closer and adjusted the capture settings on her device. The three women from Hell, who had been observing the conversation from a distance, moved within earshot as Brooke held the netcard near Nadia's face.

Nadia shook her head. "You look at me like I'm some sort of backwoods Daisy Mae. I graduated from Duke University with degrees in teaching and microbiology. I came back here because it's where I belong. Where I want to be. Where I want to teach and educate. It's true: the world outside Assurance is different. That doesn't make it better. Here, we rely on each other—not the state, not the federal government. They are far away. The law is about respect. Sudie Henshaw disrespected her husband. Folks here agree Billy Jack couldn't let that stand. Now excuse me!"

Arthur and Nadia walked away, arm-in-arm, while the three outsiders chanted, "Traitor! Traitor! Traitor!"

There was barely elbow room in the media production trailer. Brooke sat at the controls wearing a headset; the three radical outsiders stood behind her, talking in whispers. The technical crew filled the other seats. Marcy's image loomed large on Brooke's screen.

"Thanks for getting me an audience with these brave young women," Marcy said. "I'd like to talk to them privately if you don't mind. Please ask the rest of the crew to go outside and put me on speaker—just me and them. Thanks."

Brook complied. When the technical crew departed, she stepped outside and shut the door for privacy, leaving them alone.

"Hi. I'm Marcy Darcy. I'm producing a video piece on the Assurance situation. You may have heard of my work with the Human Endowment Rights Group. Thanks for standing up for women's rights. Can you please introduce yourselves?"

The women exchanged glances. The spindly woman said, "I'm Effie." The short woman chimed in: "I'm Lottie."

"Pleased to meet you."

The third woman tapped nervously on her double nose rings before answering. "I'm Tecumseh."

"Ooh. A Native American name. Cherokee?"

"It's a Shawnee man's name. A warrior."

Marcy smiled. "Love it. You aren't giving your last names because ...?"

Effie leaned toward the microphone. "It just makes it a little harder for people to figure out who we are and avoid being fired from our jobs."

"I'm trying to change things," Marcy said. "I heard it got a bit dicey today with the men and their guns."

Tecumseh shrugged. "Nothing we can't handle."

"What can you tell me about your organization?"

The women looked at each other again, hesitating.

"Don't worry," Marcy said, "I'll protect my sources. I'm just curious."

Effie gave the response. "We have a few people or several thousand, depending on the situation. We don't have an official name. We just bring people together for a specific purpose—to further the cause."

"It makes us hard to track," Lottie said. "We come out of nowhere, do our business, then disappear."

"Spoken like true guerillas," Marcy said. "How can police assign responsibility to a flash mob?"

Lottie leaned forward. "What do you want from us?"

"I'll be frank. I think Assurance is an abomination. If we let it stand, it will become a national symbol of male power. It would be like the Union caving in to the South after Fort Sumter. We can't have that. I need foot soldiers who can do what needs to be done."

Effie squinted at the screen. "Are we talking about doing something illegal?"

Marcy's look was clear-eyed. "We're talking about correcting a moral defect. As you can see, what's legal and what's not is a matter of perspective. We aren't talking about killing anybody, if that's what you're concerned about. That's too messy. Too much bad publicity. But we are talking about winning a war, and essentially destroying this little bubble of misogyny. Tecumseh, I want you to think about another one of your namesakes—William Tecumseh Sherman. During the Civil War, his army destroyed everything from Atlanta to Savannah and nailed a Union victory."

Tecumseh nodded. "I'll be your army of one, or ten thousand. I'll do whatever it takes." Effie and Lottie each chimed in with a "Me, too."

"Good," Marcy said. "The solution to toxic masculinity is another form of toxic. I need a flash mob to show up at the power plant upriver. Keep this a secret from my media crew. This is just between you and me. I'll explain what needs to be done."

# CHAPTER 7
# BLOOD BROTHERS

In the upstairs study of a modest, semi-detached home on Savannah's Liberty Street, Canduka Cantor sat on a swivel chair in front of a desk filled with fabric. He put the finishing touches on his cape, pressing the last VidPatch onto a wrap of crimson cloth. He synchronized the images with the flip of a button on a hand-held bonding tool, and the mosaic came to life, changing colors, fading from one set of pictures to another—a cape with dynamic video befitting a true prophet.

His pet, Doofus, showed his excitement by barking, "Ark, ark!" The 160-pound Rott-Seal waddled in a circle around the cape, sniffing, and tried to lick it before Cantor snatched it away and hung it high on a hook, out of tongue range.

"What do you think, Doofus? Do you like it?"

"Ark, ark! Ungry."

"It's not time to eat yet. You'll get fat. Go to your box."

The pet made sad eyes and waddled to a large wire cage, snuggled in a blanket, and put one flipper over its eyes.

"Good boy."

Cantor pulled the cape off the hook and fastened it around his neck, then spoke to the video wall: "Annetta, mirror mode with beach." The wall lit up. The figure before him, dressed in a black, short-sleeved mock turtleneck shirt and jeans, fluttered a cape shimmering with images that cascaded down a wave of red cloth flowing from his shoulders, encircling his torso. A synthetic image of a beach appeared in the background.

"Ah'll show her," he said.

He tried different poses: He was Dracula. He was Superman. He was Batman. He was anything but 'Everyman.'

When he grew tired of posturing, he removed the cape and hung it once again on the hook, then said, "Annetta, scene thirteen."

The beach image faded into a video stream recorded in September 2040, showing Marcy Darcy arriving at LaFemme International Hotel, Washington, D.C.

You could still read the word *TROMPE L'OEIL* in the discoloration on the entrance canopy. Marcy wore a skin-baring dress consisting of a rope-like mesh connecting diamond-shaped black patches covered in sequins. Cantor moved behind her, schlepping suitcases while his eyes fixed on Marcy's butt. He was dressed like a rude domestic, with khaki shorts, a black polo shirt, and athletic shoes. On one side of the entranceway, a beaming crowd of female greeters held signs: *LaFemme Has Tromped!*; *Vive la Différence!*; and *No Bozo Zone!* On the other side, an angry male mob thrust signs saying: *You Poison Us!*; *Manhood Will Master!*; and *Men Will Stand Erect!*

He watched the video loop three times while he played with a length of string, knitting his fingers into a loose net.

The video wall announced an incoming call: *CANTESC.*

He tried to untangle his fingers from the string, but it knotted up. Frustrated, he finally said, "Annetta, answer."

The video with Marcy dissolved to a laboratory filled with mass spectrometers, microscopes, and test equipment. Two familiar faces looked at him from the wall. Jack, an older man, wore a faded purple sweatshirt and Bert a white lab coat. Bert was holding a frog that smiled with human teeth. It wriggled from Bert's hands and hopped out of view.

Cantor greeted his associates with: "Hi. What's up?"

"They're after us for back payment on the lab space," Jack said. "What's the deal? You didn't send it in yet? What's that in your hands?"

"It's called a cat's cradle." Cantor moved his hands, playing with the string, trying to free his fingers. "Do you believe two people can be connected?"

The twenty-five-year-old Bert gathered thoughts in his eyes, but Jack, fiftyish, answered first. "Sure. I connect with Darlene a few times each week. She's my electric receptacle. You should see us light up."

"No," Cantor said. "Ah mean like in fate. Kismet. Sometimes it's a connection you can't shake."

Jack shook his head. "*My* universe doesn't work that way."

Bert responded in a quick, high voice, like a schoolboy trying to please a teacher. "Quantum physics says particles can be entangled. Once they come together, they're connected forever, even if they're on the opposite sides of the universe. So, it could happen to people."

Jack turned, scratched a thinning head of gray-black hair, and said, "That's not the same. That's physics, not the interpersonal voodoo he's talking about."

"How'd you like to connect with Frogbert?" Bert pushed the toothy frog in front of Jack's face. The frog clicked its teeth together.

Jack lightly slapped the back of Bert's head, then looked toward the camera and Cantor. "Don't mind him. He hasn't had his meds today. Are we going to be able to meet this month's rent on lab space, or not?"

Cantor frowned, swiveled in his chair, and smiled at the end of the 360-degree turn. "Yes."

"Whoo Hoo!" Jack said.

"How are we coming with Ranya's baby?" Cantor asked.

Jack picked up a slip of paper and adjusted his glasses. "We've got the zygote in suspension and should finish in a day or two. By the way, we call the project 'Rosemary's Baby' because the little devil's father was a real bad-ass."

"But a wealthy bad-ass," Cantor said.

"If I were superstitious, I'd be afraid lightning would strike us."

"How about the fish?"

Jack glanced sideways. "Bert, that's your department. What can you tell the man?"

Bert leaned forward, eager to explain. "I got enough DNA from the silica extraction to begin cloning."

"Great," Cantor said. "Return the vertebra to me. Ah'll put it back in the box. Ah don't want to upset our client. He's weirdly obsessive."

"Sure," Jack said. "Not that any of our other clients aren't weird or obsessive."

*Rap, tap, tap!*

The noise startled Doofus, who leaped from his cage and began barking, "Ark! Ark! Ark!"

"Doofus! Quiet!" Cantor pointed toward the cage. "Back in your box."

His pet whined as it flippered through the cage door.

Cantor returned his attention to the video wall. "Pahdon me. Ah've got a visitor. Let's take this up later tonight."

Jack gave a quick salute. "Sure. We just wait around for your calls, Master."

"Anneta, close the channel and open the doorcam." The image of a bearded figure in a trench coat replaced Jack and Bert.

"Who's there?" Cantor said.

"Berky."

He smiled. *At last! The Master of Disguise returns.* Genteel hospitality dripped from his lips: "Welcome to my home. I'll be down in a moment to let you in." He closed the channel then said, "Annetta, downstairs VueWall, Scene 21."

Cantor walked downstairs to greet his visitor. The living room wall displayed a looping video promoting Cantor's business: a sign reading *Cantor Tax-Exempt Spiritual Community*; a montage showing a team of scientists working on lab equipment; a smiling mother wearing a hijab, holding a newborn baby.

He opened the door. Berky entered and stripped off a fake beard in the entrance hall. Then he went straight to the point. "Tell me about your progress."

Cantor shrugged. "Ah was about to give up on you. A true gentleman would have provided contact information."

"I said I'd be in touch. I'm not a gentleman."

"How did you find me?"

"I have my ways. There's a beacon in the box."

"Hmm." Cantor now saw the wire. *Probably an antenna, hidden in plain sight on the lid.* He admired the craftsmanship.

"So? What have you got?" Berky said.

"We're ready to begin cloning."

"Then do it," Berky said. "I want to know when you can show me the fish."

"You talked about a lot of funding, but you gave us a pittance. We need more money. And time. This'll be a big effort."

"You have to be more specific, Mr. Cantor. And you have to understand how I want to work. I can supply more money if you show success."

"We are about to do that. We'll create a CRISPR-edited version of genes in a carp. We introduce the DNA into a germ cell, inject it into a fish, and it eventually grows into an egg. The process is delicate and complicated, but we've mastered the technology. When the egg hatches, we get Ichthy. In fact, we can make a lot of Ichthys."

Berky circled Cantor, like a fish sensing another fish with its lateral line.

"I'll give you some more funding, Mr. Cantor. When you finish this task, I have others. Think of this as a way for me to gauge your usefulness. I have big plans, and I need to make sure you can deliver. Ichthy is just a testbed. I want a fast-breeding model organism."

"Wait just a damn minute."

The words, spoken softly with understated resolve, stopped Berky in his tracks.

"Excuse me?" Berky yelled.

The loud, aggressive sound triggered a round of barking from upstairs. Doofus used his streamlined body like a surfboard, gliding down the stairs. He fast-flippered over toward Berky, yapping, "Ark! Ark! Ark!" and baring his teeth.

Berky jumped backward. "Make it stop! What the hell is it?"

"Stop it, Doofus."

"Ark! Ark!"

"Daddy give you a fish."

The pet stopped barking, looked at Cantor, then Berky, then back toward Cantor, whining.

Keeping his eyes on the animal, Cantor said, "That's Doofus. He's a chimera we made in the lab—part sea lion, part Rottweiler. It seemed like a good idea at the time. Ah thought the body plan might sell, but he turned out to be too independent for classified government work, and his poo is too stinky for a domestic pet—especially when he eats fish. Ah have been trying to train him to eat dog chow, which results in better-smelling shit, but he'll do anything for a fish. Won't you, Doofus?"

The Rott-seal growled, then made noises that sounded like words. "Mell Utt."

"Did that thing just say something?" Berky backed farther away, and Doofus followed, nostrils flaring.

"Right. We injected human embryonic neurons into Doofus when he was not much bigger than a blastocyst. He says he wants to smell your butt. Ah suggest you let him do it. He can be very aggressive, and it turns out his teeth are the dirtiest, most bacteria-infested choppers on the planet. You don't want him to bite you."

Berky stood, paralyzed, while Doofus poked and prodded his posterior. When he finished, Doofus farted.

"Now back in your box, and Ah'll give you a fish."

"Ish," it said, waddling toward the stairs, then hopping upward, two steps at a time. "Ish! Ish!"

"Excuse me while Ah put Doofus to bed." Cantor ambled into the kitchen, rummaged in the refrigerator, then climbed the stairs holding a small fish. When he returned, his hands smelled like *nuac mom* on a bad day.

Cantor returned to the kitchen where he washed his hands and spoke to Berky, who followed him. "My group works better if we know where we're going. We don't like wasting our time and talent chasing unicorn farts or weird-looking fish. And please don't insult us by trying to fund us in any cryptocurrency."

Berky's face reddened. "You're way off base."

"Please educate me," Cantor said.

"Of course. But before the big reveal, let's talk about your history. I've done some digging."

"We are well-qualified. If you add up the experience of my team, we have over one hundred and forty collective man-years cloning mammalian organisms. No other group can match our know-how or our tools. We—"

"No, I mean your family history. You hate your ex-wife."

"Ah do not see how that's even relevant. But, yes. We have incompatible visions of the future and life. Besides, she's a nasty woman."

"I want to change the world, Mr. Cantor. I want to fill it with women who know their place."

"Well, Marcy would not qualify—"

"No bitches."

"What?"

"That was the essence of your vision at the conference."

"Where are you going with this?"

"Our goals are aligned, Mr. Cantor. We share similar objectives. We are both true believers."

"Is that right? What's your story?"

"I grew up in a beautiful Appalachian village and came back as an adult to see my hometown destroyed by a bunch of feminazis. They wanted female superiority. They felt there was no room for traditional culture. One day three hundred of them showed up at a power plant upriver and emptied a pond of toxic sludge into the South Prong. The CDC and EPA declared an eco-disaster and ordered the town evacuated. And now they poison men with Testrial."

"Ah can see why you're angry. It makes me angry, too."

"Yeah. The Assurance incident was like getting a cactus shoved up my ass. When I found out about it, I funded lawsuits against the power company and tried to track down the perpetrators."

"Bastards. This is just the kind of thing—"

"I couldn't find any of the women—it was one of these flash mob deals. But I did win the lawsuit. The power company had to buy back all the town property. The folks in Assurance got a bit of money but had to relocate."

"So, the feminazis won!"

"They think they did, but I'm going to beat them. I bought the town and the power plant for ten cents on the dollar. I'm cleaning up the place, and I've built a genomics research lab near the plant."

"How does that retaliate against the bitches?"

"I'm going to transform them into domesticated hens."

"You are a crazy man. Ah like your style, but it sounds like magic."

"I'm like you, Mr. Cantor. I don't like the way the country is going. We are both true believers. We are men of vision and have the means to change the world."

"Ah feel like there's another shoe about to drop."

"I'm not crazy. I want *you* to deliver your tasks at cost. Think of it as an R&D investment. You'll get your profit back eventually, but we need to build the capability as quickly as possible."

"You just proved what Ah said. You are crazy."

"I want a division of labor. We develop the genetic recipes. You implement them. The fish project gets us a model organism—a test bed—we can use to validate our solutions. It's the perfect counter for the Testrial zealots."

"This 'work for cost' stuff disrespects me and my team. You aren't the only game in town," Cantor said. "We also have a method for modifying behavior. You heard my pitch."

Berky smiled. "We're playing at a much different level, grasshopper. We found a specific nucleotide sequence that underlies all human belief systems. We use the most advanced computing methods to analyze and create genomic templates. We've perfected a new type of selfish gene."

"Where will we get the embryos?"

"We're not using embryos. We'll be modifying adult humans."

"That would be—"

"We're talking about changing the world. Think about it. A controllable retrovirus. A self-propagating gene drive. Are you in?"

Cantor reflected for a moment. "Do you agree to share the intellectual property?"

"Why should I?"

"You can't change the world with just technology. You need to have the right religion on your side. It's politically potent and helps keep environmental conditions stable, so the genes don't drift. Ah am the only one who has the complete package."

Berky thought for a moment, then nodded. "You have a deal."

Cantor extended his hand.

Berky reached into a coat pocket and produced a knife. He sliced his palm, then stuck the blade into Cantor.

"Fuck! What did you just do? My hand's bleeding, you fucker."

Berky gripped Cantor's neck with one hand while the bleeding hand clasped Cantor's wound. As blood dripped to the floor, Berky said, "God is with us. Amen."

# CHAPTER 8
# MAGIC MOUNTAIN

Ali watched an ancient Land Cruiser rumble to a stop near a ford in the river. The driver, a stocky middle-aged white man with curly red hair, waited while he approached from a trail in the forest.

"Where you goin', boy?" the man said.

Ali pointed toward the side of the mountain. "Is this the way to the training camp?"

"Yup. It usually is, 'cept when the river's high. Then nothin' with wheels gets in. Wanna ride? I'm goin' yonder."

Ali nodded and climbed into the right front seat.

The driver put the car in low gear and gingerly navigated the ford. Water rose to the hubcaps, but no higher. When the vehicle was clear of the river, he looked at his passenger. "Name's Eban Haywood. What's yours?"

"Ali Khan Ahmed."

"Ain't a name from these parts. Where you from?"

"America."

"Haw."

"Truly."

"I bet you're runnin' away from somethin'. That'd be my guess."

"Maybe I am running *toward* something—a better life."

"We'll see 'bout that. Didja go to that thar university?" Eban said, pointing at Ali's chest.

"Oh, the shirt. Yes. I was at the University of North Carolina for some time."

"Didja graduate?"

Ali shook his head. "Almost."

"Wa-a-al. *Close* only counts in horseshoes."

"What?"

"It's a sayin', son. It means it really don't count if you 'almost' did somethin'."

The vehicle struck a rock, then rolled over a washboard of bumps in the trail. Ali bounced, hitting the headliner.

"Fasten yer seatbelt," Eban said. It gets worse, but we'll take it slow. The road si-goggles near the falls."

"This is beautiful country," Ali said.

"Yup. Didja know the first white man to see it was a spic? That was in 1539. Hernando dee Soto. He had 'bout five hundred men with him. Camped near here. They say the lights you see at night on the mountain are haints from the expedition."

"Haints?"

"Ghosts."

"I am not afraid of ghosts," Ali said. "They don't exist."

"You'll do okay here."

"If de Soto was the first white man here, then maybe I am the first Bangladeshi."

"Aha. So, you *ain't* from America."

"My heart is from America. That is the same thing."

"Most people 'round here would say it ain't."

The Land Cruiser strained on the steep slope. Eban lowered the gear and made it to the top of a rise. "I'll idle for a bit so's you can see the layout. Them huts on the right is where the students stay. You a student?"

Ali nodded.

"Good. The small cabin's for the instructor; the big'un's a classroom. We get supplies in by truck once a week, but if the river's high, the only way in or out is them foot trails on top."

"I see."

"Heh-heh. Glad yer one eye's still good. How'd you lose t'a other one?"

"A bomb. I was in a market in a town called Sylhet. I was a little boy."

"Sorry to hear that. But now you got ya a crackerjack eye patch. Makes ya look like a pirate." Eban put the vehicle in gear again and roared toward camp on more or less level ground.

"Near Sylhet, there was a beautiful waterfall named Madhabkunda," Ali said. "This place reminds me of it."

"Heh-he. Mad Kabuki. That's crazy."

"Are we here?"

"Yup. This is where the magic happens. I'll park by one of them huts an' you can unload."

"Where can I find the instructor?"

"Yer lookin' at him. I'm the teacher. I own this place."

Ali read the sign over the cabin: "Bible Sales and Snake Handling Institute of Technology."

"I jus' calls it 'BS 'n SHIT,' but don't tell nobody."

"What do we do now?"

"I'll cook us some vittles, and then we get some rest. We got a big day tomorrow. There's a bus comin' with recruits. Praise the Lord."

# CHAPTER 9
# THE HAG

*There once was a shepherd from Blackrock,*
*Who put her brain in a tall sock.*
*Now her shoe didn't fit,*
*And her head was a pit,*
*And her sheep remarked, 'What the flock?*
*—Needlepoint over Berky Benson's credenza*

Nadia heard a scratching sound outside. It wasn't the tree limb that scraped against the window from time to time when the wind blew down from the mountains. The thing moved onto the porch and was heavy enough to make the steps creak.

*Berky doesn't sneak around. He doesn't have to. It must be the damn raccoons or something bigger.*

She saw those furry bandits from time to time and felt helpless against them. Last week they'd made a mess outside she couldn't clean up. Now she'd have to ask Berky for help, and she knew that would irritate him.

*Maybe the light will shoo them away.*

She moved to the window by the door and flicked the switch. She didn't see anything but heard a shuffling. She turned the light off and waited. Nothing happened. She flicked the light on again. More shuffling.

*It's definitely something big!* Her courage waned. *If Diana were here, she'd protect me.*

Her trembling finger tried the light again. A face appeared on the other side of the window. The visage was old and wrinkled. It was a woman of indeterminate age, wearing a paisley dress and tattered blue sweater.

Nadia froze.

The face spoke in a whisper, but she heard it clearly through the window screen: "You knows me."

She searched her memory. The puckered face and gray eyes filled with infinite wisdom seemed vaguely familiar.

The face leaned toward the half-open window, eyes wide, like a snake hypnotizing its prey. "I spared your pappy's life when my beau lost ever thang in a poker game. I didn't kill him, as was my right. I saw he was just tryin' to help, so I paid the debt. I give him a special doll and a special box. I give his daughter eyes to see what others cain't see."

Nadia was silent for a moment. Finally, she said, "You gave us this doll?"

"At's right. An old-time doll. Only two of 'em iver made. The other's gone and buried. Let me in. I brung another present." The woman's mouth stretched into a gap-toothed smile.

Nadia shuffled to the door and opened it.

"I'm Jancie. Here's somethin' to eat." The hag carried in a crockery pot wrapped in a towel. "Somethin' special. It ain't no fish."

"I don't like fish, but Berky says it's brain food." She squinted at Jancie. "You're not real, are you?"

"I'm the whisper in yer ear, Darlin'," the hag said. "I'm the firefly. I'm the cotton that's hard as rock, the rain that ain't wet, the howl that ain't a wolf."

"The food smells really good."

"Thank ye kindly. When I come, I always bring your family sumpin'."

Nadia led Jancie through the museum and into the kitchen, where the old woman put the pot on a table in the breakfast nook and removed the towel covering the top.

"Try it," Jancie said.

Nadia hesitated. "It must have been a long time since you visited."

"Naar on ten years since I spoke to your pappy, bless his soul."

"Why'd you come back?"

"I knowed you was in trouble, child. The lightnin' run through me, and I could feel your hurt. And I owed your pappy a debt."

Nadia's face contorted to match the pain in her heart. Her eyes welled, spilling into rivulets of moisture that rolled down her cheeks. "You don't know ..." She tasted the salty tears with her tongue. "My sister. My twin. Can you reach her?"

"Darlin', I'll call her so even the dead can hear—by the lightnin', by the wind, by the ley. She'll come back or rue the day. There's monsters loose."

"I'm afraid."

Jancie dipped a spoon into the pot and held it near Nadia's lips. "Eat this. Ferget Berky's brain food. It'll turn yer head to mush. Work with me, child. I'll change you. I'll give you a heart o' steel."

# CHAPTER 10
# LUCKINESS

*There was never a Lady Luck. It was always a man.*
*—Canduka Cantor*

Ali and Eban sat on adjacent stone seats in front of an outdoor campfire where the wood fuel crackled, a low-hung iron pot bubbled, and greasy pans sizzled on an adjustable grill. They ate their meal in earthenware bowls and drank from cider-filled jugs.

Ali picked out the bacon, then devoured the butter beans. It was the best meal he'd had in a long while. He ladled out a second helping from the pot, scooped up a square of cornbread from a tinfoil package, and gave Eban a satisfied smile.

"You was lucky I stocked up today," Eban said, slapping at wasps hovering around the coffee. "Yesterday, you'd a had steam fer supper."

"This is good," Ali said.

"Got a regular cook comin' tomorrow. He'll be here on the noon bus. Got lots of mouths to feed. By the way, how'd you find us?"

"There was a sign in the Cullowhee post office."

"That's where I get mail," Eban said, grinning.

"Me, too." Ali closed his eyes, letting buttered cornbread slide into the hole in his stomach.

"Andy Drake kindly let me put up a note on his bulletin board," Eban said. "He's the postmaster. Likes boostin' the Lord's work. He helped me startin' out."

"This a new business, then?"

"Yup. Been thinkin' on it for some time but got lucky two years ago. Met a guy in a breakfast nook outside of Assurance. Turned out he was buyin' the town, the power plant, and a ree-search place from the 'lectric company. Imagine that. They say he's so rich he buys him a new boat when the old one gets wet. He's the heir to the Kelsey fortune."

"He is a religious man?"

"He says so, but he only prays fer money and sex. We hit it off 'cause we feel the country's goin' cattywampus. Besides, I helped him find somethin' he was lookin' for—a box of fish bones."

"Why did he want fish bones?"

"His daddy said they was lucky. His old man's crazy. Lives in a institution."

"The man paid you for the bones?"

"Wa-a-al. Let's just say he was real grateful when I told him where the bones was. Got excited. Went off and found 'em, then came back and give me a bunch of money. A finder's fee, I guess. Enough to expand my business."

"You were very lucky."

"Son, three people got lucky that day—me, Berky, and the lady who owned the bones. I knowed her when she was a sweetie who could suck the breath out of a honeysuckle. But lately, she's as confused as a fart in a fan factory."

"Who is she?"

"Her name's Nadia Holkam."

# CHAPTER 11
# LINES AND LINEAGE, BLOOD AND BONES

*History is like news reports of sex orgies. It helps us imagine what we missed.*
—*Canduka Cantor*

Before commercial aviation was even thought of, the term *air line* referred to the shortest distance between two geographic points.

In March 1929, Chester Truman Kelsey was traveling on the Seaboard Air Line Railroad from New York to Raleigh when he had an epiphany about straight lines. The steam engine whistled as it approached a trestle. The sound startled Kelsey, who glanced at the railroad map he'd been following and thought: *Ley lines are real, and the map proves it. Praise the Lord!*

The former stockbroker's bank account was flush with cash, and he was energized by a two-year vacation abroad—a victory lap of sorts. Now he was blessed with an insight that would cement his destiny.

What his brain concluded from dots on the map was that certain historic U.S. cities and monuments—places that were significant geographically, economically, and spiritually—fell in a straight line as if God had decreed it. If he could understand the phenomenon, and control it, he could change the world.

When he returned to his summer home in Asheville, he mentioned this insight to his friend, John Cecil, the British diplomat husband of Cornelia Vanderbilt. The man who Kelsey called "Jack" was keenly interested and asked to meet in his Biltmore mansion.

Kelsey arrived in the afternoon, dressed in a hunting jacket and boots, carrying a five-foot cardboard tube. Jack, still in his breakfast robe, escorted him to the mansion's book-lined study where Kelsey opened the tubes and removed two maps, laying them across the Persian rug near the fireplace. "You see?" Kelsey said, walking around the edges of the small-scale map showing the Eastern United States, pointing with a cue from the Billiard Room. "The alignment of New York, Philadelphia, Asheville, and New Orleans cannot be a coincidence. The railroads and great metropolitan centers orient to ley forces the way iron filings respond to magnets."

Jack stood near the south edge of the map and smoothed his mustache with a forefinger, fretting his eyebrows as his eyes scanned the chart. "You said you found something else. What was it?"

"There's a second line. If you look at the cities and connect the dots, you can draw an air line from Chicago to Charleston, intersecting Indianapolis and Asheville."

Jack was quick to follow. "The intersection should be a power point."

"Precisely," Kelsey said. "And look here. That second line goes through these mountains, where we have reports of spirit lights."

"Remarkable," Jack said, moving over toward the large-scale map, inspecting penciled notations. "I assume this cross on the side of the mountain is where the lines come together?

"Yes."

"What's your plan?"

Kelsey stepped close to the second map showing a region of North Carolina near Asheville, pointing with the leather-wrapped cue stick. "The exact center is on the mountain, but this nearby loop of river is on the Chicago-Charleston line and should draw energy from the magnetic vortex. I want to build a town here and control the intersection of the lines. It will help us see and guide the future. I believe it is God's will."

Kelsey liquidated his investments to finance the construction of a town. His decision saved him from financial ruin. Wall Street crashed in October, putting a freeze on the economy and creating an urgency to find The Next Big Thing. He hunkered down, spending two years considering how he might benefit from lines of power as America dug itself out of the Great Depression. He believed ley lines should be able to sense the direction of the economy and considered how to "read" them.

In 1936, with North Carolina on the verge of bankruptcy, President Franklin D. Roosevelt pumped money into the Works Projects Administration. The investment was a boon to the state. The effort launched construction of the Blue

Ridge Parkway and spurred development of schools and municipalities across Appalachia. Kelsey lobbied for a piece of the money to support Appalachian improvements and bolster Roosevelt's New Deal bet. He was successful, and this allowed him to move forward with his plan while conserving his funds. Jack Cecil donated land for the project, believing the spot would be a hub of paranormal power.

Kelsey named the town *Assurance*. It had a divine ring to it.

In 1937, shortly after securing WPA funding, Kelsey built the village that politicians in Raleigh hailed as a "model town." Legislators saw it as smart politics, since it helped spark the economy in a neglected part of the state. The truth was Kelsey didn't care much about politics. He was more interested in building a life around a place that had been touched by God.

He constructed a 20-room residence for his young wife on the edge of Assurance. The home was modest compared to Vanderbilt's Biltmore, but designed for entertaining groups of 20-50 people. Situated on a slight rise, with a view of the bridge and the river, it was connected to the town, but a cut above it. The house's deep overhangs shielded small crowds from the summer sun when Kelsey hosted social events for the denizens of lower Assurance.

Kelsey bequeathed the house to the Holkams when he died in 2013 at the age of 113. He was close to Arthur and Annie, who lived with him as caretakers for the last decade of his life. The bequest recognized Annie Holkam's loving palliative care and home remedies that helped sharpen his failing mind and body. He even staked Arthur's hardware store, which had the double benefit of lowering the cost of materials for home repair.

With the Holkam's inheritance of the house came furniture—1930s era sofas, chairs, antique tables, and an iron bed that Kelsey slept in until the day he died.

The bed was one of four that Kelsey had special-made from a New Orleans factory that imported iron from a Chicago mill. The design for the bed was drawn up by a New York City electrical engineer in collaboration with a spiritualist from Charleston. It looked like a direction-finding antenna created by a mad scientist: four pillars of coiled metal springs wrapped around steel posts joined by a rectangular bed frame and canopy. A fancy iron latticework at the head and foot of the bed told the story of Jonah and the monster fish. Kelsey commissioned the beds in 1935. His will specified that two of them should remain in his house, while one bed was to cover his grave—for protection. He claimed it was to "inform his spirit," and "guard against evil influences that might ride the ley lines."

Some townsfolk thought the real purpose of the bed was to "read the lines." They believed Kelsey would lay awake at night and listen to radio signals from God that told him how to invest his money and influence people. According to folklore, this was how his net worth grew to rival that of the Vanderbilt's.

When the town buried Kelsey, they placed the bed over his grave, per his instructions, and erected a granite monument in the center. Kelsey's will stipulated that one of the remaining iron beds be sold at auction.

Before Annie Holkam died in 2014, she asked that her resting place be given the same protection. She said the idea came to her in a dream while sleeping in one of the iron beds. After she died, Arthur complied with his wife's wishes and placed the bed over her grave. This left one iron bed remaining in the house, where it was kept in the master bedroom.

Kelsey's original testament gave his financial investments to the Holkams, because his only grandson, Lionel Benson—son of Ida Kelsey and Barker Benson—seemed too crazy to trust with money. But when Berky was born in 2013—the year Kelsey died—he showed himself to be a bloodline chauvinist. The old man, still able to think clearly, called his attorney and declared that his great-grandson, baby Berky, would receive the majority of the inheritance upon reaching his 21st birthday. He created a testamentary trust for Berky's upbringing and provided the Holkams with his mansion and a small trust to pay for Nadia's college education.

When Berkshire Benson came into his inheritance in 2034, his father, Lionel, received nothing and forever held a grudge. Before that milestone, Berky lived modestly. His mother, Gloria, nursed him through the bad times, made sure he went to school, and tried to interest him in her single, intellectual passion—*Dear Abby.*

As a fan of the column, Berky was obsessed with making a perfect world. Oddly, he was oblivious to human relationships. He would look for the structure of paradise in the electric motors he tinkered with, the animals he dissected, the homemade explosives he detonated, and the journals he kept. He was whip-smart, but town folk thought he had the manners and motives of a moonshiner.

As a young adult, Berky became convinced that his luckiness in life had a cosmic connection. He visited the Dorothea Dix Psychiatric Institute, hoping his father could shed some light on his good fortune.

A guard buzzed him through a security door into a labyrinth of tiled caverns and vaulted ceilings, where he followed a robotic mobile bench to a containment room, now empty except for a small table and a chair.

The bench stopped, allowing Berky to sit.

The guard's voice came through a speaker in the ceiling. "When you're done, just come back the way you came in. If in doubt, just say to the bench, 'Out,' and follow it. We'll be monitoring the situation on video."

Berky was alone in front of a ten-foot wall of bars, staring at a clock on the wall that ticked with digital precision. *It's like being at the zoo when the animals are out for feeding. I'm waiting for the animals to return.*

Eventually, a door on a far wall in the containment cage opened, and two guards led a shackled Lionel Benson to a chair, where he sat beneath a spotlight. He wore an orange jumpsuit and was smaller and much hairier than Berky. His salt-and-pepper beard hung down to his chest, and intense black eyes drilled into Berky's soul. Berky heard the *clang* as the departing guards closed the metal door.

Berky greeted Lionel as if he was just back from vacation. "Hey, Dad. You look good."

"When I'm dead, I'll look good. Why did you come here, son?"

"My business is going well. I bought a controlling stake in a genomics company, and we're getting a lot of contracts from the pharmaceutical industry."

"I'll ask again. Why are you here?"

"I'm rich, but I'm not happy."

"Should I be surprised? No. Your money was supposed to have been mine. You regret that you stole it from me. You'll feel much better if you share it, son. I can use it to buy my way out of this place."

"You killed Mama, remember? It was my last year in school, and the same year I came into my inheritance. Helluva way to celebrate manhood if you ask me. They declared you criminally insane. They'll never let you out."

"Sure, your mama and me had disagreements. What healthy marriage doesn't? She was always yapping and never listened. Then one day, she disrespected me. You can't let a woman do that. They need to be put in their place. Anyway, the dog sided with me and attacked her. She had it coming. That's what the dog thought, and I couldn't stop him."

"No, the dog just ate her face and her toes and slobbered all over her body after she had been lying dead in the kitchen for two days. I saw the pictures. She was killed with a knife, and it had your fingerprints. You didn't even bother to clean up the mess."

"You're an incorrigible neatnik. If you believe Them, then I'm not going to tell you where the bones are. They're the secret to luck and happiness. You need to be creative, son. Money can get me out."

"What bones?" Berky asked.

Lionel grinned like an angler, carefully pulling on a nibbled line. "The sacred bones. The bones of Chester Truman Kelsey's fish—the one that talked to him. Go to the library and read about it. It's one of the things that made Assurance famous. The place is some sort of supernatural vortex."

Berky left the institution and returned to Assurance, where he spent time reading historical archives. It seemed that something had happened with a fish shortly after Kelsey founded the town.

He visited the institution two more times, but his father refused to provide any new information. The old man just looked him in the eye, tapped his finger against his forehead, and repeated, "The bones. The bones. Get me out, and I'll show you."

The more Berky read about the history and lore of Assurance, the more he coveted the bones of that fish. They were the Treasure of the Aztecs; the Ark of the Covenant; the Maltese Falcon. The bones were somewhere between the South Prong River and Elm Street, and he had to have them.

The town's sickness derailed his search. First, there was the incident with the troublemakers in Kelsey Square, then radical women attacked the power plant, and finally, the South Prong River filled with toxic sludge. When the CDC ordered an evacuation, he was angry. Someone had to pay for this, and he decided it would be the power company, since the feminazis seemed to be untraceable.

He was the largest landowner in Assurance, so he launched a class action lawsuit. His team of lawyers united everyone in town. They won in court—more than enough to cover the costs of relocation—and gave him an even bigger war chest for his projects.

That's when he decided to buy the town from the power company. He closed the deal after an all-night negotiation with four attorneys. Then, famished, he went to breakfast at a local pancake house on the side of a mountain.

The only other customer eating breakfast at the time was Eban Haywood.

Berky grew up in Assurance but had never visited the Groaning Griddle. It was off the main roads, well-hidden in a wild part of the forest.

An architect from the power company—part of the team negotiating the sale of the town—pointed it out to him. The man knew every inch of ground around the river for miles in either direction, having surveyed it with a fleet of drones the year before for an environmental impact survey. If you looked along a line from one edge of the iron grid surrounding Chester Truman Kelsey's grave, you could see a small clearing up the mountain at the end of a dirt road. The architect said the place had the best breakfasts he ever tasted, marveling that the restaurant survived on a dirt road in the backwoods.

Berky decided he would celebrate his business victory by visiting this little patch of terra incognita. It was near a part of the mountain where locals claimed they could occasionally see spirit lights at night.

When he entered the restaurant, an ancient waitress with prune-like skin took his order after waiting on a second man. Eventually, the woman delivered large stacks of cakes and syrup.

The other man took a bite and closed his eyes in ecstasy. "Glory! Damn fine griddle cakes, Jancie."

The waitress smiled through yellow peg teeth and a face like hash browns. "Thanks, Sugar."

Berky, sitting at a nearby table, grunted through a full mouth, "Yeah. Best pancake house ever."

Jancie put a hand on her hip. "Is that what you see here, mister? A pancake house? This is where your day begins. It's where the rest of your life starts. It's the center of the universe—where corn syrup meets true grits. That's how I reckon."

Berky nodded, jabbing toward her with a stuffed fork. "You are a philosopher!"

"You fellahs let me know if you need anything, including advice. I give that out for free, and here it is: we's all connected." With that, she pivoted and returned to the kitchen.

The man rubbed a finger under a bulbous nose that made him look like W.C. Fields. "Jancie's a bit odd. She's a lovely woman inside, but ugly as sin on the outside."

"I'd have to agree with you, mister ..."

"Haywood. Eban Haywood. Here's my card."

"Thanks. Hmmm. Bible Sales and Snake Handling Institute of Technology? That's a new one. I'm Berky Benson."

"Call me Eban. I'm here celebratin', Berky. I just got me a big win."

"Oh yeah? Me too."

"People think folk who live in these hills is too poor to have money. Mostly that's true, but you gotta appeal to their imagination. See, they'll buy what I'm sellin'. I got some good coin to prove it. Now I'm expandin'. I'm hirin' salesmen. We're gonna be rich."

"Good for you."

"An' what's your line?" Eban said.

"I have several things I'm looking at."

"You gotta focus, man. Focus."

"Yeah. I just want to build a better world," Berky said. "God talks to me at night when I'm sleeping. He gives me inklings. That's why I'm expanding my genetics business. We've found a new gene. That's the science part of it. But I'm also looking for a certain item that's outside of science because it could bring good luck. God says I need to find it. It's a very special item that may have been lost. I want it. It gnaws at me."

"Haw!" Eban said. "Better find it quick. Assurance is gonna be a ghost town. That ain't so lucky." He rubbed his nose again, in deep thought. "Now, if I was gonna change the world, I'd breed me a better class of women. Beautiful women who'd know their place and let men be men. I'm just sayin'." He poured more syrup onto his plate and gulped another bite of griddle cake. "See, men can't be tied down. It's not natural. Women—most women—would be happy if they stayed in one place. That's a true fact. Deep down, they like a routine."

"So, that would be your perfect world?"

"Yup. Men is the bees that flit around the flowers and make 'em grow. We dip and dive. Dive and dip. Women keep the hive clean and have to be there when the bees get back. Makes common sense, but there's a lot of women who don't follow common sense."

"You want women to look good and behave correctly."

"Yup. Fix it so men is men and women is women."

"Now there's an idea. Have you seen what the government's trying to do with this poison called Testrial?"

"Nope. Don't pay much attention to the government."

"Well, they're trying to make men into women."

"Lordy!"

"I get so angry! I feel like I've got to stop them. God is angry, too. He told me so."

"Need some help? I got me a gun. We'll have God on our side."

"We need a better approach. Something that scales."

"A army?"

"I'd go with technology. It's more powerful. It just takes a few smart people to create a big effect."

"Too bad there ain't a magic pill we can give women to make 'em right."

"They're all bitches," Berky said.

"Yeah," Eban said. "In a perfect world, they'd be pets."

Berky's pupils darted like dark fish. "Yes, that would be something. Modify women, so they have good looks and good behavior. It'd be at the intersection of genomics, epigenetics, and cognitive science. We'd need serious computing power and a way to run very large experiments. I'd be famous."

"I don't understand all that, but it 'pears to me you got it. Now the women I deal with—the ones I sell Bibles to and show snakes to—most ain't that pretty. I've dipped my wick into a lot of 'em, if you know what I mean. Dived and dipped. But they're unreliable—don't wanna stay put. They's always thinkin' about how to get away from the hollers. Maybe that's why they hook up with me. They think I can help 'em get out. And the Bible stuff makes it okay. Like it's God's will. It's better if they stay where they are, where I can find 'em."

"You know, Eban, I believe my mother was like your perfect woman before my father killed her."

"That's terrible bad."

"If I only had a strand of hair, I could use it as a template. Then I could build the perfect partner."

"Hope you don't think this is crazy. Maybe you could dig up her body if you just need a hair. Know what I'm sayin'?"

Berky pouted. "They cremated her and gave away her clothes and belongings."

"Too bad."

Berky adjusted his chair to face Eban. He leaned toward the man and spoke as if sharing a secret. "If you ever come across the perfect woman, or at least someone close to perfection, let me know. I've got the tools. We just need the right pattern."

Eban nodded, then cocked an eyebrow. "Well, I do know someone. She lives in Assurance. The lady got a sickness in the mind after her Papa died and they closed the school. She won't leave home—kinda like a house pet. Likes to stay put. I knowed her before she got sick. She got real good bones. She was pretty when she was young. Still looks handsome."

"Maybe I could visit her."

"I'll give you her address. Name's Nadia Holkam."

Berky's forehead rippled in surprise. "Nadia?"

"Yup."

"She was my high school science teacher."

"Gall darn! What's that special thing you're looking for?"

"Fishbones in a velvet-lined box."

"Goll, son. This is your lucky day. The luckiness of Eban Haywood has just shined upon you. God must have arranged this meeting. I know where the box is!"

"Where?"

"Nadia Holkam has it."

# CHAPTER 12
# ANALYZE THIS

*After careful analysis, I see what I believe.*
*—Canduka Cantor*

Sundar Rao talked to Popkins as the two paced through the labyrinth of machines and spaces that were Berky Benson's bioinformatics lab. They entered into a chamber lined with clear tubes approximately four feet in diameter and ten feet in length. Three of the tubes were open and undergoing maintenance, while others were filled with fish swimming against invisible currents. "They still making construction here," Popkins said. "Be careful."

"Are these big and ugly-looking things catfish? I've seen pictures, but never up close," Sundar said. "And what are these smaller fish?"

"Yeah," Popkins said. "We gonna swap catfish for new type. Berky found better fish. They make lots of babies."

Sundar had many questions but put them aside as they moved out of the chamber and into an area with conveyors and robotic arms. He wanted answers on how Berky was going to use his technology. "You'll never guess how I got the idea for genebo," Sundar said.

Huffing and puffing, Popkins proffered a response. "Vodka? Thees is where I get my good ideas."

"No. One morning my netcard got screwed up, and I had to do a factory reset," Sundar said. "I thought, 'Why can't we do that with DNA?' It took me nearly a year to figure it out. We engineered an error-correcting code for genetic patterns. It's a kind of genetic reset. It puts DNA and RNA patterns back to an original starting condition. And it's inheritable. I saw how it could be a control in large-scale experiments. Then I started thinking about all the good we could do with it to prevent genetic diseases."

Popkins mumbled something unintelligible about vodka, then lengthened his stride.

Sundar scrambled to keep up but slowed as they approached their destination—a large chamber containing fifty DNA sequencers—four-foot-wide metal cubes lined up in a row, tethered to data and power cables.

Popkins moved to a three-foot-tall, eight-foot-diameter drum encrusted with instruments, connectors, pipes, and read-outs.

"When I was younger man," Popkins said, "I would have ten good ideas for experiments and try them out. It would take me long time to get result. But now—now we use extreme automation. Kublai Khan controls everything. Takes hundred thousand ideas and tries them out."

Sundar watched him open the hatch on the drum, revealing small test tubes arrayed in concentric circles. "Impressive. I had no idea the AI system could do that."

"Thees is where we put samples for analysis. We call it *Missy*. Stands for Master Input Sample Sequencer."

"And the 'y'?"

"Stands for 'why not?' ... Joke."

Sundar stepped away from a ceiling-mounted robotic arm, its servos buzzing as it moved a pipette from one row of sequencers to another.

Popkins pointed at the robot. "When Kublai Khan gets interesting result, big arms move sample to other place for testing."

"Berky said you were going to see how well my genebo works. Is this where you'll do it?"

"Yes. We gonna test three types of samples. First is normal DNA. Second is modified DNA. Third is modified DNA with genebo."

I like it," Sundar said. "When my last company went bust, I thought the technology would never see the light of day. But now—we should be able to immediately address certain genetic disorders."

"We not gonna use it that way," Popkins said. "We wanna test quicker. Go from hundred thousand tests to million, with fast reset of experiments."

Sundar scratched his head. "I don't see how you can use human test subjects on a scale of hundreds of thousands, or millions. What's your test bed? What's your model organism?"

"Fish," Popkins said. "We gonna test on fish."

The giant 3-D display system dwarfed Rosa Alcott's tiny frame as she used hand gestures to manipulate the model of a histone molecule, looking for ways to control its configuration. Her bare feet moved rhythmically on the control platform in a kind of dance. She was intensely focused on the model.

The voice came from behind, startling her. "Your feet are exquisite, and your toes are perfectly formed. God told me these are signs of perfection."

The words shocked her, but she recognized the voice: Berky.

With a hand gesture, she released the holographic controls and turned. He was standing near her but off the two-foot-high platform. Because of his height, his face was almost level with hers.

He extended his arm and touched her face with his right hand, wiping a forefinger along her rounded face, pouting lips, and angular nose. He stroked a tuft of jet-black hair the way a dog-lover might soothe a pet.

She pushed his hands away and executed a roundhouse kick to the head.

Berky fell to the floor, bleeding from the lip and nose. He struggled to get up, wobbled for a moment, and touched his hand to his face to wipe the blood. Then he moved aggressively toward the control platform.

"Don't ever touch me again," she said.

He climbed the steps to the platform, towering over her. "Just seeing if you were really a woman."

She brought her knee into his groin. He yelled in surprise and fell again, rolling down the steps.

He was on the floor, face twisted in pain. His voice was almost a whisper. "That will cost you. You'll be looking for a job as a street slut."

"You don't have anyone else who's qualified," she said. "Who are you kidding?"

"There's Popkins. Rao."

"Neither of them knows stereochemistry."

"Kublai Khan."

"An idiot savant with a mind of its own."

He got up again from the floor. This time he kept his distance.

"I'm watching you!" he said.

"Leave me alone. I'm an investor. I'll take this to the Board."

"Try it," he said with a sneer. "I own fifty-one percent. Your share is a pittance. I can restructure the company so you get nothing."

She moved down the steps toward him. He backed away and left the room.

# CHAPTER 13
# FAMOUS LAST WORDS

The last words Chester Truman Kelsey uttered on Planet Earth were "Yippee-ki-yay." They were recorded by a nurse and were not original words. Kelsey's originality was all used up, just like his failing body. He had never seen the Bruce Willis movie and was unaware the phrase arose in 15th century England.

*No*, Nadia wrote, sitting at her father's desk in the museum room, *the engrams— the memories that inspired his last words—probably came from the 1930s Bing Crosby hit, "I'm an Old Cowhand."*

Some tunes are earworms.

As she tried to put thoughts on paper, she remembered her final encounter with Kelsey, and how, according to the nurse on duty, the lights in the room flickered when he said the famous last words.

In October 2013, thirteen-year-old Nadia Holkam stood by Kelsey's bedside with her mother and father in the master bedroom on the first floor of his house—now a dedicated infirmary. The attorney had just left the room, and a doctor had removed the drip. Nurse Mandy Sipe, who stood near the door looking at her watch and tapping her foot, held a clipboard to monitor the condition of her patient and any last utterances or requests the individual might make. She had a date that night and needed to leave early.

There were photographs on all the walls celebrating Kelsey's life, including recent events. Helium balloons tied to the iron bed proclaimed, "Happy 113th!" Nadia remembered thinking, *He doesn't look a day over 111.*

Annie Holkam leaned over Kelsey's bed, trying to decode his whispers. "He says, 'Bury me below the iron bed. This bed.'"

Arthur eyed the strange-looking bed and nodded as if he understood.

Kelsey coughed. His eyelids fluttered against sickly skin. He whispered again, and Annie put her ear closer to his mouth. "He says, 'Sing me a song of the mountains.'"

"Now?" Arthur asked. "I don't know many songs. Anyway, you'll have to sing. I'm not very good."

"He means after ..."

"Oh. Then we have time to think about it." He raised his voice so Kelsey could hear. "We'll come up with a good one. Don't you worry." Arthur patted Kelsey's shoulder.

Kelsey lifted his trembling hand, touching Annie, mumbling. She recoiled and looked at Arthur.

He cocked an eyebrow. "Yes?"

"He said, 'Protect yourself from the power.'"

"Me? What power?"

"No, me," Annie said. "I think he means the power of the ley lines."

Arthur whispered a response. "I don't know what that means. He's delusional."

After a spell of heavy breathing, Kelsey's eyes snapped open. He turned his head and said in a distinct, audible voice, "Nadia. Nadia."

Nadia moved closer, touching his arm—cool, frail as tissue paper, and covered with purple blotches. She inhaled the aroma of medicine, bleached white sheets, and the unpleasant scent of body odor.

The old man smiled. "I'll do what I can ..."

"You've already done a lot, Mr. Kelsey," Nadia said. "You built a town. You showed us the way. You helped all of us, you—"

"... to keep you safe. The future ..." His eyes locked on Nadia's, looked into them, looked beyond them. His shaking hand lifted and gave a weak thumbs up. Then the tired eyelids drooped and closed. He drifted into a troubled slumber.

"You should go," the nurse said, clutching her clipboard and looking at her watch. "Visiting time is up. I need to give him an enema."

# CHAPTER 14
# THE "AMEN" BOYS

The sun was still a dim glow beyond the ridgeline when Eban prodded Ali out of bed. Breakfast was ready, and the combined aroma of smoke, steam, and grease filled the air.

Ali wolfed down eggs and biscuits but didn't touch the sausages. He said he wasn't hungry. That was okay with Eban, who enjoyed the double helping of pork.

Ali cleaned up dishes and pans while Eban inspected the cabins and fed the caged snakes. "Boy, you don't wanna be near them rattlers 'til I teach you all the tricks," he said.

Eban piddled around the camp, and Ali followed him, helping where he could.

"Ah got these thangs in N'awlins," he said, pointing to new restaurant-sized cookware. "Billy Ray says if I don't have this stuff, he'll be gone faster 'n a cat licken chain lightning. He's my cook—very partikular."

Ali guessed it was around ten o'clock when Eban yelled, "Rivah!" He looked down the mountain and spotted an old yellow school bus driving across the river ford. He could hear the crunch of shifting gears as it climbed toward the camp, pivoting around switchbacks.

When the bus finally stopped in a cleared space near the cabins, Eban issued a command to Ali. "Get 'em organized, then stand with 'em." He put on a red baseball cap with a picture of hands clasped in prayer, adjusting the tilt like a coach preparing to give a rousing pre-game locker room speech.

Billy Ray, who wore a full white beard and brown cowboy-style hat that looked like it had been half-eaten by a goat, was the first to step off. He shook hands with Eban and watched as the bus emptied. Ali lined up the dozen recruits, then stood in the middle of the row.

Eban handed out caps from a large plastic bag. His team murmured in appreciation.

"The only sound I wanna hear right now is me talkin'."

Silence. All eyes on Eban.

When he finished scanning from one end of the line to the other, Eban took off his hat and slapped it on his knee.

"Whooeee! Listen up. I'm talkin' real money. Imagine bein' able to buy just about any thang you want, without even havin' to think!" He showed a broad gap between his front teeth as his lips stretched into a smile. A gold tooth glinted in the morning sun. "Does that sound right to you?"

He had their attention; now, he needed their hearts.

"Last name's Haywood, but you can call me Eban. I'm here to help you if you'll let me. But I don't want no sourpusses in this camp. That'll kill the process. If you're excited, then I wanna hear it. The way you tell me you're excited is to shout, 'Amen!'"

Two recruits murmured in agreement, their grunts punctuated by a whippoorwill from beyond a ring of hickory trees.

Eban put a moist hand on the shoulder of an early twenty-something white man who wore a tattered white dress shirt stretched tight across bony shoulders. A clip-on tie, perhaps a gift from a doting aunt when the young fellow was in the sixth grade, completed the effect.

"Okee dokey! What's your name, son?" Eban asked.

"Troy."

"Are you all excited, Troy?"

The boy gave a tentative nod.

"Well, I don't hear nuthin'. How's a body 'sposed to know?"

A light bulb seemed to switch on in Troy's head. "Amen?" he asked softly.

Eban grinned, patted the shoulder again, and swept his red, bulbous nose like a radar dish along the row of semi-animate faces. He cupped a hand to his ear. "I can't hear you!"

The man-boy removed a wad of gum from his mouth, parked it behind his ear for quick retrieval, cleared his throat with a guttural "Gah-hem," and spat. He then said in a stronger voice, "Amen!"

This seemed to energize Eban. "Say what I want to hear: *Amen*, or *Yes, Jesus*." He dropped his gaze and stabbed a finger at the next man in line. "Do you wanna be rich?"

"Amen!" the man shouted, smiling.

"An' you?" he jabbed at the next man.

"Amen!"

"We're gonna sell a lot of Bibles, aren't we?"

"Ah-ah-meen!"

Eban pranced around in a circle amid the perfume of blossoming rhododendrons like some light-footed bee telling other bees where to find the honey. He closed his eyes, now wet with emotion, and clutched Ali's shoulder.

"Tell me again!" he exclaimed. "Do you truly wanna be rich? Do I hear a *Yes, Jesus?*"

"Truly!" Ali shouted. "Yes, truly!"

"Troo-o-oly?" It was not the response Eban hoped for. When you're working the crowd, you need to build momentum. The word "truly" had broken it. Eban put his nose near the brown-skinned face.

Ali's single good eye returned his gaze.

Eban continued to drill. "You know what I want to hear, Ali. Say it."

"Truly, I cannot."

Eban cocked a fat eyebrow. "An' why not?"

Ali lowered his voice to a whisper, drew his face close to Eban's misshapen nose, and spoke the words tentatively, "I am Muslim. Amen."

Eban seemed stunned. The other boys and men in the lineup stood stone-faced until some lips cracked into smiles. Eban snickered quietly, then stamped his foot and exploded with gut-shaking laughter. He steadied himself with one hand on Ali's shoulder as the rest of his body contorted in mirthful spasms. Finally, controlling himself, he straightened his smile, wiped a finger along a wet eyelid, and patted Ali.

"Hooboy. I like you, son," he said. "You got guts. You'll do okay here."

Eban turned to the others. "Ali is a moozlam, but he wants the American dream just like you an' me! We all wanna be rich. What do you say to that?"

Troy was the first to respond. He jerked a fist into the air and shouted, "Truly!" Others followed with, "Truly, truly!"

Eban winked at Ali. "There's a lot of religions out there, kid, but only one almighty dollar. You're in."

Eban Haywood's training camp held a lot of lessons on snakes. They were the "draw" that sold Bibles. Unfortunately, Ali didn't like snakes. Snake charmers in Bangladesh always seemed to be poor, and sometimes the venomous pets would kill their masters. He therefore focused more on salesmanship, absorbing every one of Eban's lessons.

One of the first tricks of the trade he mastered was called "Bible Genius."

Eban and his twelve disciples huddled around a metal fold-up table set up near the mess cabin. Eban stood at the center of the table, with stacks of bibles to his left and right. He eyed the recruits in silence until he had their full attention, then ticked his right eyebrow upward with a devilish flair. He lifted a Bible off the table and thrust it toward Ali, who stood on the opposite side of the table. "Open it. Anywhere."

Ali flipped a page.

"Whooee!" Eban said as if hit by the Spirit. He jabbed his finger at the text and recited from memory, "First Peter 4:8. *Charity shall cover the multitude of sins.*"

He winked at Ali. "That means you can sin all you want and a little charity will cover things for you. Try again."

This time Troy picked the page.

"Whooee! First Timothy 6:10. *For the love of money is the root of all evil: which while some coveted after, they have erred from the faith, and pierced themselves through with many sorrows.* Is that impressive, or what? The Lord must be sparkin' my brain!"

"Truly," Ali said, solemnly, "You have memorized the Bible and are a great scholar. In my country, people try for a lifetime to memorize the Koran. Many cannot."

Eban's lips went from deadpan straight to an upward curve. Then he guffawed—a deep, prolonged laugh. He snapped the book closed and jutted it again toward Ali, who selected another page.

"Romans 14:5-6. 'Your eyes will see strange sights, and your mind will imagine confusing things.'" He giggled. "Talcum powder, my friend."

"Talcum ...?"

"TALCUM POWDER!" Eban shouted. "T-a-l-c-u-m POWDER."

The trainees looked at each other, puzzled.

"Because people usually believe their eyes—and their hearts—they is gullible. And that helps us sell Bibles, my friends." He looked around the room. "See, you all believed you was picking the pages, and I was reachin' into my infallible memory, genius that I am, and spoutin' the Gospel. We-e-ll, it weren't quite like that. See, it's a brand-new Bible, and the pages like to stick, 'CEPT for the ones I put talcum powder on. Them pages open quicker 'n the legs of a New Orleans whore." He took a tin of powder from his coat pocket, shook some onto his hand, slapped it around on his face and smiled. "I'm gonna show every one o' you'n a lotta new tricks. 'Specially Ali."

"Amen," they said in unison.

# CHAPTER 15
# GETTING A GRIP

Marcy stood on the edge of Oak Street Beach, gazing at Chicago's skyline and Lake Michigan's cold blue waters. People ran toward her on the buffer of warm sand, scrambling in clogs and bare feet, carrying towels, umbrellas, and the flotsam of electronic entertainment needed to connect to a virtual world. The air was beginning to cool. Dark clouds hovered beyond the cityscape as distant lightning signaled an approaching storm. A woman approached from the direction of the shore carrying a bag.

"You're going in the wrong direction," the woman said as she passed, her bag brimming with yarn and knitting needles.

Marcy thought about knitting.

*Sometimes when you pull a thread, the rest of the fabric unravels.* Her mind wound around the delicate thread that began in a conversation with a congresswoman on the House Committee to Reduce Violence in America. The woman complained that even if Testrial could reduce epic levels of violence, there would still be organized crime promoting all forms of revenue-generating aggression. To make her point, she showed Marcy how easy it was to set up a contract hit or wipe out a rival business. You first visit a website about knitting, then drop into a forum on *Knotty Problems*, where public posts are carefully curated. If you stick to the knitting, your text will be quickly published. But if you enter something like *I want my husband killed*, the forum administrator will never post the text. However, after a while, you will receive a response via some other method of communication describing how to make contact. Often it is an email asking to make a phone call to an 800 number.

Marcy was so astonished by the covert contact method she went home and explained it to her husband, Nigel. This was before the messy divorce.

Now she was pulling the thread to see where it led.

A red umbrella near the shoreline said, *Get a Grip on Life.* This seemed to be the thread she was looking for. Marcy removed her shoes and brushed a smudge of dirt off her white pedal pushers, then licked her lips in resolve. She stepped onto the sand and made a beeline toward the water.

A tanned, muscular, bare-chested white man, dressed in a Speedo swimsuit, waved as she approached. His hands clutched a striped beach towel hanging from his neck. "Welcome," he said, smoothing his sleek black hair. "Perfect day."

"Yeah, right."

"That's not what we agreed."

"Okay, how's this: 'A perfect day for perfect pictures.'"

"Thank you. I am Mr. Smith."

"Can we stop this 'Secret Squirrel' shit?" she asked.

"All part of the tradecraft, my dear."

"So—no detailed communications? Just bare contact information given to a voice recorder? Then a letter in the mail that looks like a bill?"

"Precisely. A more direct communication could have exposed you, me, and others. Ours is a family-owned business, but we run an international operation. I must protect it. I use the best and brightest talent. We are priced accordingly."

"If you're worried about exposure, you should have worn a shirt and pants. I suppose you treat all your clients like dirt."

He smiled with peroxide-whitened teeth. "My clients usually have something to hide. We can afford to be less customer-friendly. There aren't a lot of places people can go if they need reliable delivery of hard-to-get information or completion of difficult tasks. We're pretty much a monopoly. There aren't many competitors left."

"I see. How do you know I'm not with the FBI?"

The white teeth flashed again. "Before we ever respond to a query, we evaluate potential clients. The assessment is both broad and deep. Given our tools, the facts of your background, and even your confidential communications would be tough to fake. I know you, Marcy Darcy."

"Well, I declare."

Smith moved his jaw as if chewing an unpleasant-tasting piece of meat. "As long as we're discussing tradecraft, let me put a fine point on it. This comes directly from my family's playbook. Cross me or expose me, and you are dead. Understand?"

"I'm glad we cleared that up."

"Now tell me about your needs. There's a storm coming, so be quick."

"My former husband, Nigel Bradford, who now calls himself Canduka Cantor, has been stealing my clients. For a while, he was like a pathetic fly buzzing around my leftover food, trying to survive, hoping I wouldn't swat him. But now it seems he's gotten substantial funding. He could cut into my business."

"Tut, tut," Smith said. "You know, we offer a special service that could bypass the investigative process entirely and eliminate the problem. There's an additional cost."

Marcy shook her head. "You don't understand. I want to humiliate him. Discredit him. Make his followers see he is a miserable excuse for a human being, unfit to be the receptacle for their hopes and dreams. He sees himself as God's gift to women and believes I owe him my gratitude. I don't want to kill him. I want to crush his ego and display it, naked and defeated, for all to see, like a plucked chicken roasting on a spit."

"A tall order. You may need to fund additional services, such as our social media slambot."

"Let's start simple. Give me details on his operation. Tell me where he is on a daily basis." She handed over a folder. "Here's a dossier that gets you started. There's a check inside, payable to the dry-cleaning company you gave me."

He took the folder and wrapped it in the beach towel, without opening it. "Ah, revenge. How sweet. You've come to the right place. Our motto is, 'Information is Power.' We can help you."

Cantor, sitting in his Savannah home office, waited for the line to pick up. Instead of a human, he got a recorded message:

*You have reached the voicemail of General Research-Information is Power. Or "GRIP." Thank you for your online query. Please do not give the details of your special research project over the phone, since that could compromise our operation and your safety. We treat all projects as highly confidential. At the tone, state your postal mailing address. GRIP will verify and send instructions on how to meet us in person. You will need to travel. The contact protocol we provide in the mail will be packaged to resemble one of your existing bills. BEEP!*

The secrecy and need to travel annoyed Cantor, but he supposed it was necessary. He gave his mailing address and hung up. What else could he do? He needed their specialized brand of help. Marcy—her reputation, her income, her future, her hope—must be destroyed.

# CHAPTER 16
# IF YOU PRICK ME

Toward the end of a weekly staff meeting, Berky told everyone about his change in schedule. "I need to spend a few days in Charleston. That means someone will have to look after Nadia and Schrodinger."

"I'll do it, Boss," Popkins said.

He had a smirk that Berky didn't like. He looked past him to Rosa Alcott, who seemed intent on reading something on her netcard, but she was of unknown sexual orientation, and he didn't trust her. The Security Chief, Reggie Edavane, a young black Brit who spoke with a thick Scottish accent and liked to wear shirts with epaulets, was clueless. His eyes settled on the new guy.

Sundar seemed to shrink under the weight of his gaze. "Who's Nadia?" he asked.

No one volunteered an answer. Everyone looked toward Berky for the correct explanation.

"She's someone who lives in Assurance and agrees to participate in our neuro-behavioral experiments. She's agoraphobic. There's a chance we may be able to help her."

Sundar's voice was tentative. "What do you need me to do?"

"You'll be my surrogate. I normally visit Nadia in person to bring supplies and make a close assessment. If the therapy is going well, she shouldn't give you any problems. Take Schrodinger with you. She likes the cat, and it will help soothe her. See Rosa for special provisions. Deliver them to Nadia. Give me an in-depth report when I get back. I'll be gone through Thursday of next week, and I'll take Reggie with me. It'll be just you and Popkins from the executive committee holding down the fort."

Sundar looked around the table. "There's Rosa."

"I mean the men in charge."

Nadia was in the museum room working on the *History* when she heard the *click-clack* of tires on the bridge, the crunch of gravel in the driveway, and footsteps on the porch.

There was early afternoon daylight outside and something different about the sounds.

*Different!*

She reached for the knitting needle hidden behind a goldfish bowl on an end table near a padded chair.

The front door squeaked open, followed by the call of "Halloo." It was a male voice, but not Berky's.

She shuffled into the living room, where a tall, olive-skinned figure held Berky's squirming cat, Schrodinger, in one hand and a vase of flowers in the other. He smiled as he placed the vase on a table.

Sundar saw before him a wraith of a woman, drably dressed, who seemed to blend with the décor of the house—an appurtenance, like the blanket on the sofa and the ancient shag rug in the foyer. She was pale but had good bones. He guessed she was about his age. Blond hair, streaked with gray, framed a pair of furtive green eyes.

She took a flower from the vase and twisted it in her fingers while her face twisted a smile in an uneven deception of mirth.

"You must be Nadia," he said, striving to sound confident. "I'm Sundar Rao."

He was unprepared for the attack. She rushed toward him, aiming the needle at his face.

He stumbled backward in surprise, tripped on an ottoman, and fell into the padded chair, squashing a doll. Schrodinger flew through the air, crashed into a goldfish container, and landed on his feet. The bowl fell off a small table and broke on the tile floor.

As Nadia attacked, Sundar used his hand as a shield. He yelled as the needle penetrated his hand, missing his eye by inches.

She threw her weight on him, trying to drive home the point. He used his other hand and knee to topple her to the floor.

She let go of the needle.

He pulled it out of his hand, threw it across the room, and watched her eyes track the weapon. Before she could move again, he was on her, pinning her arms to the floor.

Sundar huffed and puffed. His face was pale, and his right hand dripped blood. "Are you crazy?" he said.

Nadia's green eyes squinted from another dimension. "Are you real?"

"What?"

"Are you real?"

"You stabbed me! You see my blood? You think I'm a mirage? I'm as real as that mountain outside your door."

She tried to bite his nose, but he moved his head just in time.

"Stop it!"

"I don't know you," she said.

"Yes, you do. I told you, I'm Sundar Rao. I work for Berky Benson. See? I brought his cat. I'm not going to hurt you—unless you try to kill me again. You don't seem well, Nadia. I'd like a doctor to look at you."

"I can't leave. There's evil out there. It's the texture of raw cotton. It smells like beeswax and pheromones and my papa's cologne. It has yellow eyes. If I push my hand in, it only goes so far. If I try to escape, it smothers me."

"That's nonsense," he said, gripping one hand with the other to stanch the wound.

Her green eyes flashed. "What do you know about *my* reality? I know I'm real because I feel pain. I know Berky's real because he produces pain. I'm uncertain about you."

Sundar pushed off her, scrambled for the knitting needle, and threw it out the door.

"If you want to kill me, you'll have to do it outside in full sunlight," he said, turning toward Nadia, then stepping past Schrodinger. The cat pawed at the flopping fish, sinking its canines deep into the head. The fish stopped moving.

Sundar made a beeline for the kitchen through the museum room, found a semi-clean towel, and wrapped it tightly around his wounded hand. Nadia followed like a stalking lioness.

Sundar's voice quickened as he watched the towel turn red. "I'll see if I can get you another aquarium and some goldfish. God knows you need the company." He returned to the foyer and pulled a box in from the porch using his good hand. "Here's your dinner and supplies. If you need anything else, call me.

She stood at the entrance to the museum room, eyes glistening. "I can't call you."

He inspected the slow dribble of blood from the towel. "I have another netcard at home." He reached into his wallet, fumbling with his left hand. "Here. You can use this one. I'll leave my other number."

"Netcards don't work here," she said.

"Nonsense. Every place on the planet has coverage unless it's actively blocked." He smirked, tried to place a call but saw there was no signal. "Right," he said, and kept the card.

"Tell Berky I hate fish," she said. "And I want my box back."

"Box?"

"Ichthy is mine. I loaned it to him. He's had the box for over a year. That should be enough for any study he wants to do. He said it was temporary. Now I want it back."

"Ah ... I'll ask him."

"Leave me alone, Mr. Rao. And take Schrodinger with you."

"My name's Sundar. I'd like to be your friend if you'll let me."

She cocked her head as if considering his words.

Sundar kept his eyes on Nadia as he slowly backed out of the house, scooping up Schrodinger with his wounded right hand, and closing the door with his left. The butterfly hatch of his Mercedes SUV opened as he approached. Once inside the car, he felt safe.

The bleeding from his hand had almost stopped. The wound was relatively small in diameter, seemed to have missed major arteries, and did not appear to require stitches. *Maybe all they'd do is dress it and give me antibiotics.*

"Artie, take me to Xanadu Lab," he said. The small clinic had medical supplies and a telepresence connection to a hospital in Asheville.

The car closed the door and dutifully obeyed.

As his head sank against the seat and the wooden bridge dissolved behind him, Sundar tried to formulate what he would say to Berky and Popkins. On the one hand, it seemed that Nadia Holkam was probably nuts, dangerous, and very dissatisfied. On the other hand, there was something troubling about her relationship with Berky. He didn't understand it. Maybe he *shouldn't try* to understand it. His situation at Xanadu was tenuous enough already.

His mind rolled through different scenarios and outcomes. He decided to avoid reporting his strange encounter with Nadia. "Artie, cancel my destination," he said to the car. "Take me home."

# CHAPTER 17
# FIRE AND SMOKE

Eban and Ali huddled around a campfire thick with smoke. The other trainees were in bed, and Billy Ray was in the kitchen cabin, making tomorrow's breakfast. Eban poked at the fire with a stick, stirring sparks and conversation.

"You did good, boy. We sold lots of Bibles at the revival meeting."

"I'm not a boy," Ali said. "I'm your best salesman."

"Wa-a-al, I give you that. The ladies like you. They's the ones that buy Bibles. But it takes a man to see it."

"Where I come from, we would have to sell to men. They make all the decisions. Women bear children and do housework. Most women cannot choose their own clothes. The man does that. In the cities, things are changing, but in the country where I grew up, it was the same for hundreds of years."

"Some things is baked in, no matter what. You come from a interesting place."

"Yes, but you could not easily sell Bibles there. If you tried in the countryside, you would be killed."

"God bless America. We can sell any thang we want. And we can sell it to anybody we want. I like that part of it. But Bangladesh has some real advantages. Men still run things."

"Many of our politicians, who are from the city, are women."

"That's a right shame. Country folk oughta take over. Make a uprisin'. Set things right. Women should know their place. It's how God meant it to be. That's how me an' Berky think."

"He's the one who loaned you money?"

"Yup. We's *simpatico*. That's French for 'thinkin' the same.' I told him—it's as plain as a pig on a sofa. Men is men. We can't be tied down. Ain't natural. Women—most women—is happiest when they stays in one place. It's a true fact."

"Well, the world seems to be changing."

"Don't have to be that way. Berky says so. He told me he's got a fix. A perfection. Said it was science."

"I know something about science."

"Berky says the way to fix things is with the genes."

"You know," Ali said, "my mother was very traditional. She liked to stay in one place."

"But you was jumpin' around: Bangladesh, U.S. of A. How'd that work?"

"I was lucky. Allah, or Nature, or random cosmic rays made me different. My parents were poor and uneducated. My mother wanted something better for me, so she persuaded Father to send me to an Islamic Madrasah."

"What's that?"

"It's like your Bible camp."

Eban slapped his knee and laughed. "You musta been a top student."

"Not really. I asked too many questions. Once I could read, I read everything. This created problems since religious education is about learning things that cannot be proven. They finally threw me out, but a friend who thought I had talent, helped me get into a school run by a non-government organization. They taught me English and mathematics. This opened my mind to possibilities."

"What did your father think 'bout getting kicked out?"

"My father called me his 'alien son.' He wanted me to drop out of the NGO school to help with the trash-sorting business. I refused."

"Trash sortin'? I heard they do that in Meh-hee-co. Sompin' I been thinkin about. Could be big business."

"It was not my cup of tea, as they say. When I was under the protection of the NGO, I took national examinations and was accepted into the Bangladesh University of Engineering and Technology—the best in the country. I graduated with honors, and a sponsor helped me get into a graduate school in the U.S."

"Congratulations," Eban said. "I never went to no university. Saw straight away, you can be rich without it."

"Truly," Ali said.

"You ain't tellin' me everything, boy."

"You've heard my story."

"'Cept the part about why you're here."

Ali was silent.

Eban patted Ali on the shoulder. "That's okay, kid, you'll do fine with me. We'll get rich together."

After a pause, Ali said, "I can't go back. I am a *Dalit*. Even if I am smarter, and even if the caste system is now banned in my country, I am still the lowest in the eyes of everyone—untouchable. I want respect. Here, in America, I am equal."

Eban winked. "Right."

Ali stretched his arms and stood. "I will go to bed now."

"I'm visitin' the post office tomorrow," Eban said. "Wanna come?"

"Yes. I'd like that."

"Be ready to go right after breakfast."

Ali nodded, then departed.

Eban stirred the coals and thought about possibilities and the future.

# EARTH

# CHAPTER 18
# TWINS

Nadia's eyes lingered on the view outside her virtual prison. Against this static scene, her mind's eye saw the history of the town play out in accelerated pantomime. People grew up. They went to school. They lived. They died. The water turned black. The world changed.

She thought she had reached the end of this unbearable transformation, but the last few days felt different. She began to feel like a predator, a bigger fish. In her dreams, she chased Berky, the monster, driving him to dark depths inhabited by vicious, laughing carp.

She pressed her face against the closed window, longing to touch reality. She seemed to remember what it felt like, but the objective world, populated by friends, enemies, events, and family, eluded her.

The whispers told her she was no longer Berky's top priority. Sundar Rao, if he was real, might re-appear. She had ample provisions for another week. Time to reflect. Time to prepare.

She saw movement near the bridge. Was it a glint of sunlight or a hat that bobbed to the beat of human feet? It was hard to make out. The distant figure seemed familiar, even friendly. Finally, she recognized the face.

*That's Diana! What's she doing? Here? Now?*

The figure stopped to adjust a straw hat with a defiant tilt, then continued a beeline march.

*I have to hide! Wait. That's not possible.*

Nadia became a bolt of frantic energy. She picked up litter, hid dirty clothes under the bed, and made a lot of little piles into a few big piles.

*Diana likes order!*

In the bathroom, she scooped loose vials of pills and tubes of lotion Berky had provided and put them into a trash bag. She hid the kit inside the toilet tank.

*But how do I tidy up me?*

The problem was apparent in the mirror which displayed an unkind image of a disheveled woman framed in a Bride-of-Frankenstein hairdo.

The doorbell rang.

Nadia spat on each hand and tried to smooth the tufts of unruly hair. It made no difference. Then she opened the lid on the toilet tank, retrieved the bag, and searched for hair gel, but managed only to spill the bag's contents into the water.

The doorbell rang again, followed by a singsong voice. "Nadia? I know you're in there. Open uuu-up!"

Nadia sighed. When she unlatched the door, Diana looked beautiful and radiant, every hair in place, calm and cool despite the long hike into town from the rural bus stop.

Diana greeted Nadia with a hug. "Good to see you, sister." After a moment of inspection: "Wow, for an identical twin, you sure look different."

"Maybe it's the worry lines and the frumpy dress," Nadia said. "I don't get out much. But you look good. You always look good. Come in. Where've you been?"

"The usual: chasing unicorns, cataloging cloud formations, thinking up ways to mess with your head. Wahoo, girl. I'm back home! By the way, there's a 'Keep Out' sign near the bridge. It says, 'Property of Berkshire Benson.'"

"Berky says he owns the town."

"Well, he doesn't own me, and he doesn't own you. Right?"

Nadia hugged her sister again. "I'm so glad you're here."

Nadia put Diana in the bedroom with the iron bed—a room they had shared in their pre-college days—then turned serious. "You know about Papa, right?"

Diana's smile faded. "The world keeps changing, doesn't it? I learned about him indirectly through a friend. There was nothing I could do."

"So, you didn't even try?"

"It's complicated. I wasn't in a position to return. You wouldn't understand."

"I tried to contact you," Nadia said. "I had no address, no net number—nothing. I was the only family member at his funeral."

"It must have been hard."

"Hard? Overwhelming! I was unprepared. It happened fast."

"Where is he?" Diana asked.

"In the back garden, next to Mama."

Diana nodded. "Give me a moment. I'd like to see him." She walked out the front door and around to the backyard where two stones marked plots behind the apiary. Brown flower remnants crowned both graves, like compost heaps. After a minute of reflection, she found a rusty spade stuck in the ground and dug out yellow trilliums and wild irises that still grew in the garden. She put them around the stones, then picked a few other flowers.

She kneeled over her father's grave and spoke. "Papa, I know I've disappointed you. But I'm here now. I didn't mean to hurt anyone. I hope you can forgive me." She placed a single sword lily on each parent's grave. Then she stood, turning toward the house where Nadia's face glowered from the window.

She blew her sister a kiss.

They played catch up over a cup of hot tea. Nadia explained how Assurance had become a ghost town.

"Where does Mr. Berkshire Benson fit in?" Diana asked. "Is he the same Berky you taught at school?"

"Same one. Only now he's very rich from the Kelsey fortune and his own investments. They say he bought the town from the power company—got it cheap. Princess Power didn't have a clue about what to do with the place."

"Does Berky have a plan?"

"You remember Berky? Everything's a secret with him."

"And you and Papa?"

"He died before the town changed hands. I'm the last one standing, a ghost in a ghost town. I won't leave. I can't leave."

"Why not?"

"Mama and Papa are buried here. This is where I belong."

"How do you live? You need food and electricity and supplies."

"Berky provides that. We signed an agreement."

"I hope you didn't sell your soul."

Nadia looked away and didn't answer.

# CHAPTER 19
# GOING POSTAL

Eban and Ali bounced along in the 20-year-old land cruiser, finally climbing off rough roads onto the smooth highway. Eban had a stack of outgoing mail rubber-banded atop the driver's console. Ali held onto it to keep it from falling on the floor. He noticed one of the letters was addressed to Berky Benson, Xanadu NeuroLab.

Ali spoke loudly so Eban could hear him above the whine of the engine. "How often do you make this trip?"

"Every couple of months," Eban said. I pay bills purty regular and put money in the bank."

"I see the top letter is to this Berky fellow."

Eban didn't respond, so Ali dropped it.

After a few miles, Eban said, "Tell me more about the women in Bangladesh."

"In the area where I grew up, women are very traditional. My mother was always obedient, even when my father tested her.

"What'd he do? Beat her? My mama wouldn't take no crap."

"No," Ali said. "Nothing like that. I would send money back from America from my graduate school stipend. A friend told me Father used all the money to buy *Nikah Mut'ah*—hired wives."

"Is that like hookers?"

"It's a temporary marriage of pleasure."

"That ain't legal, is it?" Eban said.

"It's permitted by the Koran if it's done officially. My mother tolerated it. As I said, she was very traditional. But I believe it broke her heart."

"Wa-a-al, too bad. Your mama sounds like she had a lotta special qualities."

Ali helped with errands around town and loaded additional supplies into their vehicle. The last stop was the Cullowhee post office, where Eban spent time gossiping with the postmaster, Andy Drake.

The post office was a minimalist structure, with rows of post office boxes, a mail drop, and a counter where you could buy stamps, send packages, or trade rumors.

Andy Drake, the postmaster, complained to Eban that USPS planned to eliminate humans in small post offices throughout the country. "The bigwigs say it'll save money and be more efficient. But where does that leave me?"

Eban listened, nodded, and sipped RC Cola from the vending machine while watching Andy's face get redder and redder.

Andy spit and sputtered. "Imagine that! In two years, a God damn tin man'll sell stamps, ship boxes, and handle complaints. Don't I get any respect?"

"They's gonna ree-tire you," Eban said. "That's what."

"The system's rigged, I tell ya. I'll have ta go inta bootleggin'."

"Don't do that. The feds'll be all over you like stink on shit. They'll slap your silly ass in jail. Better go into the religion business. It's unreg-a-lated, and there's lots of perks. Besides, God'll be on your side."

Andy calmed down, considering options. "Can you help me with that, Eban? I'd 'preciate it. Seems safe enough. Robots can't do religion."

"Sure. Next time I'm in town, we can talk."

There seemed to be nothing more to say. Eban looked at Ali. "Ready to go?"

"In just a minute," Ali said. "There's a slip in my mailbox. Do you have a package for me, Mr. Drake?"

Andy muttered something unintelligible, then searched in the back, where he found a box wrapped in brown paper, sent from a post office in Durham.

"This here's from a mystery person. He ain't proud enough to put his name on the return address."

"I know who it's from," Ali said. "My thesis advisor."

The package intrigued Eban. "Looks important. You gonna open it?"

Ali shook his head. "Maybe later."

Eban tried to engage Ali on the trip back to camp, but the young recruit only responded with grunts and gestures. He seemed troubled.

Eban saw his passenger peel back part of the brown paper cover on the box, revealing an inner wrapper with strange writing. Ali covered the opening with his hand when he saw Eban staring.

After a few more miles, Ali started talking. "When I was a child, I visited a market in Sylhet with my mother. It was a magical place, filled with all manner of apparel and pots and toys. It smelled like fish and spices and sometimes, the vanilla smell of the crushed drug, yaba, that makes you crazy.

"I was looking at a toy, and the next thing I knew, I was waking up in a hospital. They said a bomb went off. Many people were killed. My mother was shaken but unharmed. I lost an eye, and I couldn't hear anything for a week. After that, friends made fun of me. They called me 'Dead Eye.' I didn't mind.

"When I was older, and I knew I was smarter than most other children, I told everyone my name was Dead Eye because I could spot fuzzy thinkers, like a sharpshooter, and call them out. I would criticize ignorance. I always tried to expose the truth. I was probably insufferable. My father did not like my attitude. He was never able to rise above a superstitious view of the world.

"My mother was also superstitious, but had faith in me, and believed I could find a way out of our predicament—the poverty and disrespect that enslaved us. I owe her everything—my health, my education, my sanity."

Eban and Ali were both silent for the remainder of the trip. The Land Rover crossed the river ford and climbed the bumpy trail to camp. When they arrived, odors from Billy Ray's kitchen immediately wafted through the rolled-down windows.

Ali smelled the hummingbird cake in Billy Ray's oven. The scent of vanilla reminded him of Sylhet, just before the bomb went off.

# CHAPTER 20
# SANITY CLAUSE

*Lies become reality if we believe them. "Truth" isn't truth.*
—*Canduka Cantor*

They sat in the museum room, Nadia quietly working on her *History*, and Diana reviewing the agreement with Berky. The signatures at the bottom of the contract were those of Berkshire Benson, CEO, and Ms. Nadia Holkam. The document bore the logo of Xanadu NeuroLab.

As Diana read the text for the first time, her trust in Berky—minimal to begin with—evaporated like laughter after a bad joke. At first, the lead-in seemed funny—maybe even hilarious—if you looked at it from a certain point of view.

"Hey, Sis, I think I've seen this before," Diana said. "The fine print must be from the Marx Brothers: 'The Party of the First Part ...'"

"I don't like-a parties," Nadia said, mimicking Chico's take on legalese. They both giggled, then belly-laughed.

Diana found subsequent paragraphs less amusing. "What were you thinking when you agreed to Xanadu's ownership of all your web and computer interactions? Or their right to freely use your DNA sequences? Or ownership of your body after death?"

Nadia replied, "I'd have to go with Chico. He'd say: 'Hello. Room Service? Bring up enough ice to cool a warm body.'"

"Seriously, what can you do? You pretty much gave away your body and your brain, and you don't have much leverage. The agreement is stacked in favor of Xanadu."

"I just want my box back," Nadia said. "I want Ichthy so the museum will be complete. I don't care about my body. I'll do what I have to do to stay here."

"Listen. There could be a lot more at stake."

Nadia jiggled an invisible cigar and flashed her eyebrows, imitating Groucho: "I'm not crazy about reality, but it's still the only place where you can get a decent steak."

"Be serious. You were a science teacher. Now you're a kind of guinea pig."

"So, what do you want me to do?"

"Deny them the ability to replicate their science experiments. Become less predictable."

Nadia shook her head. "Face it. I *am* predictable."

"You need to screw him up with some loose screws."

"Loose screws?" Nadia retorted. "Can't do it. Groucho said it's part of every contract. It's what they call a sanity clause."

Diana remembered Chico's line: *"Ha ha ha ha, you can't fool me. There ain't no Sanity Clause."*

Diana puzzled over the problem of sanity. She needed to understand the cause, symptoms, and cure for agoraphobia to help Nadia leave Assurance. There weren't any books on the subject in their skimpy home library. Her only research option was her sister's ancient computer and a flaky internet connection.

Email didn't work. Accessible sites weren't fully functional. The computer seemed connected to a walled garden, planted with a curated set of pages containing unresponsive interactive links. Still, there were a few topics she could see.

She could view Fox News, selected sports and advice columnists, hardcore porn sites, sites focused on male supremacy, and sites catering to assorted conspiracy theories. She could also see web pages on bioinformatics, behavioral genetics, artificial intelligence, the pharmaceutical business, and Wall Street. She guessed these were the phrenological bumps on Berky Benson's skull—the lumps of data that structured his worldview.

Wikipedia was a godsend—the one thing she found useful. It explained how the disease worked. Agoraphobics believe certain environments are unsafe. For Nadia, this included everything outside her home. Many afflicted with the disease had an unnatural fear of death.

Wikipedia also said genetic and environmental factors caused the disease. The trauma of their father's passing, combined with the demise of the town, may have been the one-two punch.

If there was a genetic component—a predisposition for flipping into a state of agoraphobia—then maybe the flip could be reversed or reset with a new environmental shock. Diana wasn't sure what that might be, but she *was* sure Nadia had to escape Assurance. They needed a getaway scheme. Diana believed a rational plan must begin by knowing what you have and what you can do.

She needed to explore Assurance.

Diana could see the panic in her sister's eyes.

"Don't leave," Nadia said.

"It's okay. I'm just going to walk around, see what's left of the town, and try to understand what our options are."

"You're my lifeline," Nadia said. "I don't know what I'd do."

Diana patted her arm. "I understand. Think of me as your scout. I can see the things you can't see. I can get the things you can't get. I can go where you can't go, do the things you can't do."

Nadia was unconvinced. "Berky's always watching. He's dangerous. I don't know what he'll do if he sees you."

"He can't get any crazier than he is now. I can take care of myself, Sis. I'm not going to live in fear." With a backpack and a straw hat cocked at a defiant angle, Diana strolled out the door. When she looked back, she saw Nadia watching from a front window.

Diana began her survey by examining the yard. The two-story house had aged gracefully, and was still in reasonable condition, given that it had seen little or no maintenance in the years since her father died. Paint was peeling, there were a few loose boards on the wrap-around porch, now pock-marked with raccoon scat, but the place seemed structurally sound. Most screens had holes and needed to be replaced—a minor problem since Nadia kept the windows closed most of the time.

There was a new mechanical unit the size of a heat pump over the septic field. The gray metal box connected to a power line and had a digital read-out on the side. A painted tin sign warned it was the property of Xanadu NeuroLab. She'd have to check Nadia's agreement with Berky to see what that was about.

She had already visited the back garden, with the apiary, gravestones, and out-of-control flowerbed. The other side of the house was still a curiosity.

She skirted the grid of coiled iron rods protecting her mother's grave and walked along a cobbled path to the garage, built like a barn, and meant to double as a workshop.

It took considerable effort to roll the door open. As she pushed, the wheels shrieked like banshees against the scrape of rusty metal. When sunlight finally sliced the darkened, cavernous space, it revealed her father's well-preserved Ford Mustang convertible, raised on wooden blocks, draped in a dusty red cover matching the paint job.

To Diana, the car seemed like a time machine for transporting memories from an idyllic past. She found the key clipped to the visor, tried the ignition, but the motor failed to turn. The engine was as dead as Assurance.

A car battery and trickle charger on a nearby workbench caught her attention. The outlet near the charger was live, so she connected it to the battery in a shower of sparks. Momentarily stunned, she reversed the leads, then reconnected. The run light changed from green to red, and the needle gauge wavered. The battery was charging, and her level of hope, rising.

There were probably dozens of undiscovered things that needed to be fixed to get the Mustang operational. She'd have to work through them all but hoped her father's long obsession with the car meant it was still in relatively good shape. The workbench had most of the tools she required and an assortment of fluids, but the car's gas tank was empty.

She needed gas.

As she strolled down Main Street, she saw a town mutating into forest through time, dust, and neglect. The hulks of rusted cars—most missing wheels and gas caps—stood like forgotten casualties of an ancient war. Fallen tree limbs spread their fingers across cracked asphalt, blocking any ghost traffic. A red fox darted between buildings. A doe foraged on blueberries near a sign that read: "Property of Xanadu NeuroLabs; Trespassers will be prosecuted."

It was as if the entire population of Assurance had decided to go to the beach for a decade. The shuttered windows on the bank, the "Gone Fishing" sign on the door of Bert's Tackle, and the random litter in the window of Sophie's Soup-to-Nuts spoke of a mass exodus.

In Sophie's window, Diana spotted a yellowed newspaper carrying the headline "Power Company Buys the Town It Poisoned. NDA Covers it Up."

She peeked through the grimy glass and into her father's general store. Near a tilted, faded sign that read "The Appalachian Wind," a moldering pile of toys waited in vain for passing tourists. Whimmy diddles, limberjack dancing dolls, handmade whirligigs, and Cherokee figurines—testaments to a dying culture.

Diana entered through an unlatched door and put the artifacts in her backpack. She thought Nadia might like them for the museum.

She moved down the street, passing the grand entrance to the Assurance of Grace Mortuary. It was now cloaked in spider webs and home to a foot-wide hornet's nest shaped like a giant heart, throbbing with insects. She gave it a wide berth.

The South Prong Filling Station announced its demise with two decommissioned pumps and a broken sign naming Ira McKenzie as the owner. Diana slipped through the half-raised garage door to find a workshop scoured of inventory, and a floor littered with dirt, paw prints, and animal scat.

She systematically inspected nooks and crannies, looking for anything useful. Hidden away in a metal locker in the back of the building, she found a single can of gas. *Maybe there's enough to get the Mustang to Cullowhee for a fill-up.* On an otherwise barren bench, she picked up a tire iron to help with repairs.

Before departing, she took a long look at the place through soft light filtering in from the entrance. Her childhood memory associated the garage with the strong smell of oil and the staccato beat of metal-on-metal. Now there was only silence, and the feral mustiness of wilderness as the forest reclaimed its territory.

She ducked under the door, returning to the street, and immediately froze, gas can in one hand, wrench in the other. A large animal stared at her from beyond the hulk of a derelict car. Its face was gray. White fur lined the snout. Yellow eyes showed no fear, only interest. Its head dipped in a crouch. Time slowed. After what seemed like minutes, she moved backward toward the workshop. The animal kept a constant distance. *The garage is probably a bad option. Maybe that's its den.* She stepped sideways down the street. The wolf paced her movements. She quickened her steps. The beast followed effortlessly, gliding on four legs, keeping eyes on the target. *This could end badly.*

As she approached a second abandoned car, she abruptly turned to face the predator. She yelled at it, then banged the tire iron like a sledgehammer against the side of the vehicle. The noise stopped the animal in its tracks. She picked up a garbage can lid from the street and beat it like a marching drum as she walked deliberately toward the wolf. The animal cowered and slunk into the forest—a blur of gray, the shadow of death.

"Fucker! I'm Diana. Don't mess with me."

She hyperventilated, more in anger than fear. As her heart rate slowed, she saw Assurance the way an animal sees it. *If only I had a penis. I'd piss all around the garage. I'd mark my territory. My town.* She felt like howling in triumph but stopped herself. She dropped the garbage can lid, picked up the gas can, and jutted a defiant chin toward the forest.

*On with it.*

There was another location she needed to check before reporting back to Nadia. It was behind their house, near a bend in the river—a scenic spot, rife with history. It was the place where Chester Truman Kelsey was buried.

She followed a flagstone path from Main Street, past the arched wooden bridge, along the riverbank, to a clutch of wild garlic that segued into the rectangular border of a small park, now overgrown with weeds and wildflowers.

Locals called the spot Kelsey's Bend—a place known for excellent fishing and good smooching if you were a teenager brimming with hormones. It was also the site of an ancient Native American weir—a V-shaped rock structure in the river, rumored to be thousands of years old.

Diana put down her gas can and sat on one of two benches facing the water, where the current moved lazily around a curve. Legend had it this was where Kelsey had caught his famous fish, Ichthy.

Near the benches, thirty feet from the riverbank, hundred-foot tulip-poplars, and oversized hemlocks stretched a wide protective canopy over the centerpiece of the park—a semi-buried iron bed with four coiled posts and a crisscross of rods at the top. An engraved granite stone in the center marked Kelsey's gravesite, positioned directly below a fish-shaped weathervane that squeaked as subtle air currents made it swim.

She remembered Kelsey's funeral through the fog of thirteen-year-old eyes. There were a lot of people packed around the grave, benches, and picnic tables. Some men were eating; some women were weeping; some kids were playing. It had struck her that everything they walked on and sat on—in fact, everything in the town—had been built to Kelsey's specifications. He *was* the town.

Her mother, Annie, had been a live-in housekeeper on Kelsey's estate since age 15 but graduated to full-time caregiver during the last ten years of Kelsey's life. He'd shown his indebtedness by gifting her his mansion and iron beds, similar to the one that now staked his cemetery plot.

Kelsey's gratitude did not extend to his bank account and investments. Upon his death, he willed his entire fortune to a one-year-old child christened Berkshire Benson, his great-grandson. There were troubled waters between Kelsey and his grandson, Lionel. Maybe the old man could foresee what was coming.

The townsfolk believed Kelsey was more than a business visionary; he could actually see the future. This was why his wealth grew to billions of dollars. The old man once told Annie that when he lay in his iron bed, prophetic visions came to him through the magnetic ley lines.

"Well, Mr. Kelsey," Diana said, addressing the grave, "You couldn't protect Assurance, or the people who lived here, or my family. If you're tuned in to our world from the Great Beyond, I guess you can see how things got screwed up." She touched the iron bed and felt a mild jolt. "Is that all you've got? A bit of static electricity? You're like the town—all used up."

A plopping sound came from behind. She looked, expecting to see the big bad wolf. Instead, she spied ripples in the dark water. *There are still fish in Kelsey's Bend.* She wondered how they survived the pollution. *You certainly can't eat them. But*

*I'll bet you can catch them! A fishing expedition would be good therapy for the therapist.* Here, amid the unkempt beauty of the park, invisible to Berky and his cohorts, she could relax, close enough to help Nadia in a pinch.

She picked up the gas can and headed to the trail leading to their backyard. Iron rods marked the path. Her father once told her they followed a ley line from Kelsey's grave to Annie's grave. As she left Kelsey's Bend, an invisible wind turned the weathervane, spinning it several times, finally pointing northeast, toward home.

# CHAPTER 21
# LIKE A DOG GUARDING TURF

Sundar rubbed his bandaged hand, placing it beneath the conference table to avoid attention. He told Gregor and Rosa he had wounded himself trying to break up ice cubes in his refrigerator.

Popkins said that sort of thing could easily happen if you drink cold beverages—something Russians would never do.

Rosa, whose face reminded Sundar of a sad flower petal, shook her head and was about to comment when Berky appeared on the main video wall.

"I hope things are going well," Berky said.

Popkins responded with, "Things are great, Boss. We got genebo into the experiments. Kublai Khan's working out details. We gonna start end of the week. But we maybe got a problem with the fish."

"What problem?"

"We gonna have too many fish. How they reproduce is exponential."

"I don't want to hear about problems. Just solutions."

"Yes, Boss. I figure it out."

"Listen," Berky said. "I need to be in Charleston for a few more days. Don't wait for me to kick off the trials with genebo. Rosa, how's our template?"

By now, Sundar knew that "template" was a code word for "Nadia Holkam." Popkins had explained they were trying to understand the basis for Nadia's behavioral disorder and wanted to snapshot critical elements of her genetic pattern—her template.

To answer Berky's question, Rosa turned her sullen face to the camera, using both hands to pull her tightly curled jet-black hair into a rubber-banded bun while she talked.

"I have a few concerns. Our monitoring of her biologics shows some instability. She's either changing her food source or processing it differently. This could throw off our results. Kublai Khan may not be able to compensate."

Berky frowned. "We need to find out what's going on. Sundar, did Nadia seem stable when you saw her?"

Sundar scratched his tousled black hair as his mind raced for a safe answer. He decided to hedge. "I only met her a couple of days ago. She was certainly terrified of leaving her house. That matches what you said about her agoraphobia. So, if that's normal for her—"

Berky's face seemed to relax. "I was afraid that introducing a new person into her life might make her go nuts, like a dog guarding turf from strangers. At least we know that didn't happen. I'm hoping we can still meet our goals."

"What should we do, Boss?" Popkins said.

"Call me back from your office, Gregor, after the meeting," Berky said. "We need to talk about how Charleston ties in. And Sundar—"

"Yes?"

"Go back and spend some time with Nadia. See what's going on. Report to me afterward."

# CHAPTER 22
# THE FOAM OF SOLACE AND OPPORTUNITY

Eban stepped into the bunkhouse and removed a wet poncho. Outside, a gentle rain beat a steady white noise on the tin roof. He moved toward Ali's bunk, where the box from the post office and other items were spread across an olive drab army blanket. Ali sat on the bed, hand trembling, holding a letter.

"The boys missed you at supper," Eban said.

Ali didn't look up. "I'm not hungry."

"The box weren't good news?"

Ali didn't respond.

"Whatcha got? A comb, some pitchurs, a doll ... Was there somethin' bad in the letter?"

Ali fixed his eyes on Eban. "She's gone. This is all that's left."

His eyebrows knitted together. "Yer sweetheart?"

"No, my mother. She's dead. My mother's dead." He folded the letter, written in neat Bengali script, and returned it to the box.

"Sorry. Is there somethin' I can do?"

Ali shook his head. "She was a kind person, a beautiful person."

Eban picked up an item from the bed. "I like the photo. She was real purty."

"She always did my father's bidding, with no complaints. She always gave of herself and helped me realize my dreams. She was the perfect wife and mother."

"I'm sorry." After a moment, Eban asked, "Will you go back home?"

"No," Ali said. "If I try to do that, ICE agents will lock me up in one of their camps." He picked up the bone comb, fingering strands of hair still coiled in the bristles. "This is all I have to remember her by."

"Your mama had lots of good qualities." Eban paused, then went on. "Listen. Your package is precious. Ain't no place in the bunkhouse to keep it safe. I can store it in my private hut if you like."

"I'll bring it later. Give me some time." Ali buried his head in his hands. Eban patted him on the shoulder, then departed.

Ali continued re-reading the letter and examining the contents of the box until trainees began to drift back from supper. They talked among themselves but left Ali alone with his grief. Eban had told them the news.

When the lights went out, Ali lay awake, unable to sleep. He continued to think about the contents of the box—a doll, photos, and a comb.

His mother had given him the boy doll to encourage his faith. Pull the string, and the toy would say a verse from the Koran. He couldn't remember ever playing with it. And yet his mother had kept it all these years, hoping for a miracle. The doll was the pious man he never became.

In the darkness of the bunkhouse, he pulled the string as a test of both faith and technology. Neither worked.

His mind conjured the image from the photo. Eban was right. Adida had been beautiful, and the picture proved it. She had raven black hair, big eyes, a buxom figure, and delicate feet. She would be ashamed if any man outside the family ever saw the picture. Tradition was baked into her soul.

The comb was much more personal. Adida was proud of her hair, even when she covered her head. She spent fifteen minutes each morning grooming. When Ali was six years old, she asked him to comb it. He remembered it felt like silk to the touch. And now, looking at the bone comb, the remnant of her mortal body— a few strands of hair—conjured powerful emotions.

Eban's mind raced. This foreigner and his now-dead mother had given him a lot to process. He drifted away from the camp, hiked up a steep trail, and considered his options. When he reached the peak, his eyes filled with the sweep of mountains and a broad world of possibilities.

He got a kick of excitement. A smile as wide as the Smoky Mountains cracked his face. He reached for his netcard, got a signal, and requested a number for Berky Benson.

Up in the sky, far above the dirt trails of the Appalachian backwoods, he glimpsed the contrails of a sub-orbital passenger jet steering toward the edge of space and distant mega-cities, writing the story of a connected world in gentle cursive.

As he waited for Berky to pick up, he imagined his personal future. A future with money and respect. Perhaps a seat on one of those jets.

First-class, of course.

# CHAPTER 23
# THE LYING FISH AND THE MOON ABOVE

Nadia felt a twinge of anxiety as Diana explained she was going to Kelsey's Bend—to think and relax and fish. "Do you really want to eat something that comes out of that poisonous river? What if the wolf comes back? Why do you need to leave me?" She held her gaze until Diana answered.

"I just need to relax and think. Don't worry."

"I do worry."

"Look, if I catch anything, I'll throw it back. And I don't believe the wolf will bother me, but if it comes lurking around, I'll be ready for it."

"You're all I've got, Sis." Finally, she said, "I know nothing can change your mind. So—in the garage, there's a carton full of junk near the workbench. Papa's tackle box is in the bottom, and his fishing rod is on the wall near the door. There's a mean-looking Bowie knife in a leather sheath in a drawer below the bench. Take that for self-defense."

Diana kissed her cheek. "Awesome."

"This almost seems normal," Nadia said. "I remember Papa going out on fishing trips, spending entire days wading in the water or casting from the banks. He always came back energized, ready to take on the world. You'll be back later today, right?"

"Right. Thanks for understanding."

Diana disappeared out the door to hunt for gear. When she returned, Nadia had packed a cooler with drinks and snacks.

"I put a small pillow and a blanket in your backpack so you can relax. There's also a hand-cranked boom box Papa used to entertain himself and keep the fish worried. Don't stay out too late. It's already mid-afternoon. I doubt the fish will be biting now—not that you're actually going to catch fish."

"You never know."

Nadia kissed Diana, then watched her straw hat disappear on the trail behind their mother's grave.

Diana followed the path marked by iron rods, occasional flagstones, and a carpet of wild ginger. When she broke into the clearing, she heard the sound of cicadas, sizzling like summer heat.

She put down the cooler and backpack on the river bank, laid down the blanket and pillow, pulled out the ancient boom box, cranked it up, and turned it on. The music of Bach filled the air, carried on a soft breeze.

She was content to lay on the ground for hours, watching the river flow past the bend, thinking, dozing, dreaming.

She awakened when the breeze whipped into a strong wind as day crept into night. There was still plenty of light, but the full moon was visible near the horizon—a giant orb magnified by a trick of the atmosphere, giving the illusion of proximity. She reached out a hand as if to touch it.

The weathervane atop Kelsey's grave creaked with the sound of metal-on-metal. The gusts subsided, and the spinning blade came to a stop, pointing toward the river where cool air created seams of mist that drifted like ghosts across the gray water. She decided it was time to either fish or cut bait.

Diana strapped the belt with the knife sheath to her waist, settled on the bank, took off her shoes, and dangled her feet in the slow current. She fastened a lure then cast her line.

She heard the purr of the reel play out, followed by the *plop* as it hit the water. She repeated the process many times, reeling in the line as she let her mind unreel across a river of ideas.

Diana thought about Nadia's madness. Not only was her sister agoraphobic, and growing worse each day, but her thinking had become perverted, her logic, labyrinthine. Diana saw the effects of reality distortion in strange messages Nadia sent to her on their shared computer. The notes spoke of events happening, with no mention of people's names, as if Nadia communicated with faceless beings in another dimension. Example: "I talked to them, and then with the others, and then with the ones." There was a continuing theme of connectedness, as though disparate shapes, smells, and textures were animated beings that hobnobbed with each other. Occasionally, though, sentences pointed to a verifiable reality. It was these topics Diana pursued. The name 'Canduka Cantor' kept popping up.

She had found several references to Cantor in Wikipedia and came to believe different people shared the same first, middle, or last name.

There was Cantor Bradford, a brilliant marketeer the likes of which, some said, the world had not seen since P.T. Barnum. A decade ago, this Cantor had made a financial killing with a New York-based ad agency.

Cantor seemed to be associated with Nigel C. Bradford, a marketing executive for Clonaid, who later resigned after he married an assistant law professor from Duke University, Marcy Darcy. The marriage ended abruptly.

Finally, there was Canduka Cantor, who led a quasi-religious cult that mimicked some aspects of the Raelians and had purchased a controlling interest in The King's Heritage, a non-profit cloning technology company built from ex-Clonaid employees. She couldn't find any obvious connection between Cantor and Nadia, or Cantor and Berky.

*Plop.* The lure hit the water again, and Diana reeled it in across the flow of thoughts and memories.

She wondered if Nadia's mental instability was a problem with genes, diet, or brainwashing. If it was genes, then the same flaw that unbalanced Nadia could be lurking in her own genetic makeup, just waiting for an environmental trigger. If it was diet, then Diana had a good shot at leading Nadia out of Bedlam, as long as the effects could be reversed. Finally, Nadia's problems could be the result of a deliberate, malevolent, and targeted destabilization. This Berky fellow could be implanting peculiar modes of thinking into Nadia's head, like some hypnotist, Svengali, or religious cult figure. Nadia's social isolation left her vulnerable to such mind viruses. If that were the case, the antidote might prove elusive. She would need an intervention.

*Plop.* The lure splashed down again, sending a cascade of ripples across the water. This time, she got a bite.

She hadn't counted on catching a fish, but there it was, a changing vector of force tugging at the end of a line. The fish leaped from the water, splashing sparkles of color in the late afternoon light. It seemed big, heavy, and determined. Diana held the rod in one hand, using a gap between her legs as a fulcrum. She reached with her other hand, dumping the contents of the cooler, making room for the catch.

The fish was now close to shore. It launched like a rocket above the water's surface, hissing as if propelled by compressed gas. And it was ugly, with a big head and a mouth inverted in a smirk.

Diana now had the cooler in one hand and the rod with a leader line in the other. The fish flopped around as she waded into the water above her knees.

Her initial impulse was to release it, but the fish made a strange sound and rocketed toward her like a torpedo. She went on the defensive. First, she hit the fish with the cooler, subduing it. Then she scooped it up, along with a large measure of gray river water, and hauled it onto dry land, finally capping the cooler with a lid.

She sat on the cooler, excited and exhausted, wiping her face with a towel soaked in mud and grass from the struggle. "God! Where is beer when you need it?" she said aloud.

A hiss blasted from beneath the cooler lid, startling her.

She scooted off the box, drew her knife, and hyperventilated. She watched the lid jitter as the fish rapped on it, using its thick body like a hammer.

The lid fell off. In the light of dusk, the fish eased an eyeball above the edge of the brimming container.

At that point, a funny thing happened. The fish talked to Diana.

"Ha cha cha cha!" it said in a raspy voice. "I'm Zoney Bamboney. What's your name?"

She was stunned. "I'm Diana."

She hurled a rock at the cooler. The projectile glanced off. Water splashed upward like a tower of spit, and the fish seemed to flinch, ducking its head below the water.

Zoney popped up again and gulped air. "Don't be afraid. It's just us girls. Actually, I'm a hermaphrodite, but I prefer the female persuasion."

"Fish can't talk," Diana said with an air of finality. She looked around for a rock, found one, and held it in her free hand. The other hand held the Bowie knife with the blade pointed downward.

"Well, it's not that we don't like to talk. It's just that we can't talk for very long. We fill our swim bladders by gulping air, then bleed it off, sort of like ..." The fish submerged momentarily, popped back up, and gulped more air. "... Bagpipes."

"But to talk like a human, you need lips and a tongue."

The fish opened its mouth, and a worm-like creature twisted and gyred.

"Gross!" Diana said.

"Meet *cymothoa exigua*, a bug that ate my real tongue and replaced it with itself. It's a lot more flexible, and I can even stick it out. Watch it whip around."

Zoney stuck out her gyrating tongue.

"Oh, and I do have lips. Want to try French kissing? I won't turn you into a lesbian. Honest."

Something snapped in Diana's brain. She rushed to the cooler and drew the Bowie knife from its sheath.

"Just joking," it said, flopping around. "No need to channel all this hate just because I'm different. I'm androgynous."

"Oh yeah?" she said, pointing sharp steel.

"Yeah. All Bamboney fish are equal. That means we can dream big, pal with anyone, and fornicate ambidextrously. No holding back."

"What've you accomplished so far?" Diana said.

"Not much, but we've got plans. It'll be huge."

Diana approached, holding her weapons. The fish started talking fast.

"We've been here a long time. My great-great-great-great-grandfather was captured, imprisoned, and eventually eaten by Chester Truman Kelsey, who founded Assurance. We go way back."

This knowledge of local history threw Diana off balance. She stepped back and listened.

Zoney Bamboney talked about the town, its troubles, and a bit of history. It was a wide-ranging monolog. Diana was mesmerized until the fish said it wanted to conquer the world.

"The biggest drawback is we don't have hands," it said. "I think we're smarter than humans—after all, I speak ten languages, including English, Cajun, and eight fish languages. You'd be surprised at the negotiation skills required to live and survive in the river. But we want more. And without hands, we are at a competitive disadvantage. If we get hands, then 'Watch out world!' Heh-heh."

Diana beat the fish on the head with the rock, then stabbed Zoney Bamboney again and again with her Bowie knife until the water in the cooler was a mix of red blood and gray silt. When the fish stopped moving, she stabbed it some more and cut it into pieces.

She wiped her knife on the towel and held up the blade like a mirror. The face staring back at her was something she had not seen in a long time. She saw ambition in the eyes and determination in the set of the chin.

Finally, Diana spoke in a kind of sing-song requiem, "Now the joke's on you-oo."

Nadia saw Diana lumber through the door with her gear and a cooler sloshing with water. "We agreed you weren't going to bring fish back, remember? I hate fish. Plus, it's toxic."

"I, umm, guess I was ... caught up in the excitement."

"It must have been a real struggle. With the fish."

"Why do you say that?"

"The bloodstains, my dear—on the cooler, on you. Simple deduction." She watched Diana's face light with recognition as she observed the evidence.

"It attacked me. It was vicious."

"A vicious fish in the South Prong? That would be unheard of. Let me see." Before Diana could stop her, Nadia lifted the lid of the cooler. She retched at the stinking stew of fish flesh and gray-red liquid. "Why'd you lug this awful mish-mash back to the house? It's gross and must have been really heavy to carry up that hill."

"I don't want to talk about it. I just want to lie down for a while," Diana said.

Nadia had been concerned about her sister's mental health for some time. Before turning up in Assurance, Diana had gone missing. No amount of questioning could extract from her the truth about where she had been. It was as if she had been on the same alien spaceship ride as Berky Benson. And now Diana was going to rescue her from the perils of agoraphobia? She found that laughable.

Nadia saw warning signs in her sister's behavior. For example, there were messages with random and chaotic topics on their shared computer. And now there was this fish thing. The incident was disturbing because of its palpable level of violence toward an animal.

*Could Diana's violence ever turn outward, to people?*

# CHAPTER 24
# TO BEE OR NOT TO BEE

The bridge leading into Assurance loomed like an emotional gateway for Sundar Rao. Before rolling through the arched wooden trusses, his brain raced to connect dark thoughts about Berky, Xanadu, and Nadia. When he arrived in Assurance, his mind slowed to match the lazy flow of the South Prong and the speed of life in a ghost town.

He stroked the cat riding in his lap, then looked across at Jason, a newly hired youth on-loan from Popkins.

He was clear and focused as he commanded the Mercedes to stop in front of Nadia's house and gave directions to his assistant.

"I know Gregor said you were supposed to help me unload provisions and clean out the trash, but there's something else I need you to do that's not in your job description."

Jason stopped chewing gum, wiped a finger beneath his thin, hooked nose, and said, "What?"

"If I yell, I want you to run into the house as fast as you can and help me."

"Spectin' trouble?"

"Maybe."

"They didn't say I'd be fightin', but I ain't afeared of nuthin'."

"That's good. Wait here. I'll come back when it's time to unload."

Sundar got out, with the cat in his arms, and made loud noises as he climbed steps to the porch. He knocked and stated his presence.

"Haloo!"

A pleasant female voice came from behind. "You must be Mr. Rao."

He turned toward the garden to see what looked like a space-suited figure with a closed hood and elbow-length gloves standing near a boxy tower.

The space alien spoke again. "I'm trying to get the bees to come back, you see. It seems to be working, but I need to stop the blasted raccoons. They keep emptying the feeder jar and try to push the hive over. It's been a constant battle."

The figure stepped away from the apiary and removed the veiled hat. A shock of gray-streaked blond hair framed a familiar face and a genial smile. The woman pulled off thick gloves and offered a hand.

Sundar's handshake was awkward because Schrodinger, the cat, squirmed in his arms, and he had to reach with his unbandaged left hand.

"Nadia? How is this possible?"

"I'm her sister, Diana. We're identical twins."

His brow fretted under the weight of a puzzle. "May I come in?"

"Actually, Nadia's sleeping. I don't want to wake her. If you'd like to sit, we can use the steps."

Sundar glanced over at his car and gave Jason a nod. The youth returned the gesture through the closed window. Sundar removed a handkerchief from a pocket, dusted the step, then sat.

Diana, dressed in garden-soiled jeans, was not as fussy.

"You just arrived?" he said.

"I've been here for nearly two weeks." Her gracious smile caught him off guard. There was a warmth in it. The corners of his mouth ticked upward in response.

"Please call me Sundar. Why haven't we met before now?"

Her eyes sparkled. "I'm a compulsive explorer, Sundar. I was probably out wandering when you came."

"Now your wandering has brought you here, to Assurance. Any special reason?"

She shrugged. "I was born here. I wanted to see my sister again. That's special enough."

"And before coming here, you were—"

"Various places." Her tone turned serious. "What do you want, Sundar?"

"I have Nadia's dinner and supplies. I'd like to give them to her."

"I mean, what do you want from Nadia? Really? I know about the Agreement."

He tried to hold his smile but felt it fade. *What agreement?* "Honestly, that's between Berky and Nadia. I'm somewhat ignorant of the situation. Are you an attorney?"

"Oh, no. My training is in microbiology and education, like Nadia. But I can read contracts."

His mind raced, trying to frame an argument. "Well, here's a point I'd like you to consider. It's something Berky explained to me. I'll try to be delicate. You are on private property."

"Oh, you mean the *No Trespassing* sign on the bridge?"

"Yes."

"Well, Nadia owns this house."

"Mr. Berkshire Benson owns the entire town. You have to enter the town to get to the house."

Diana wrinkled her nose. Sundar saw the gesture as both cute and defiant.

"Please tell Mr. Benson—I assume you work for him—"

"Yes."

"Inform Mr. Benson that the county owns the bridge and streets. You can't keep me, or anyone, out."

Sundar blinked. He thought for a moment, then blinked again. "But this contract with Nadia—"

"I've read it."

"We need a stable relationship. We're trying to help her. It's for her own good."

"There's nothing in the contract that says Nadia can't have visitors. How's that destabilizing? Just so you know, I'm here for a long stay. By the way, Nadia hates fish. Did she tell you that?"

"Actually, yes, but I haven't been able to convince the dietician to change the meal plans yet," he lied. "These things are so complicated."

"She's not a hospital outpatient, is she? Or a lab rat?"

"Oh, no. Of course not." He tried to think but was totally unprepared for this discussion. "Meal planning just takes time. And we pre-order supplies on a quarterly basis, so—"

"You report directly to Berky?"

"Yes."

"Tell him I'm looking forward to his next visit here. We have a lot to discuss."

"Look, Diana — may I call you that? — Hopefully, you see Xanadu Labs is keeping its end of the bargain. Nadia must keep hers."

"Nadia wants the box back, Sundar."

"The box?"

"Yes. Please tell Mr. Benson. He knows what I'm talking about. It will make Nadia very happy, and it will keep Xanadu Labs compliant with the terms of the Agreement. The box was only loaned to you. But, under the Agreement, your support for Nadia is perpetual. You tried to write a contract that makes termination difficult. It looks like you've only made it difficult for yourself. Please leave the supplies at the door. I'll bring out the trash."

Sundar and Jason left food and supplies, then departed with garbage for forensic analysis. This was the first Sundar had heard of a contract or a special box. He was unsure how to describe the current situation to Berky. This business with Nadia Holkam had suddenly become much more complicated.

"I told Sundar you want the box back," Diana said. "I know you're obsessed with it. If we get it back, will you leave with me?" She gripped Nadia's arm, demanding attention. She would guide Sis to freedom, even if her mind resisted.

"Did you know ribonucleic acid doesn't just make proteins?"

"What?"

"It's also involved in epigenetic regulation of gene activation. I looked it up."

Diana squinted at her sister, as though, by sheer force of will, she could transport her back into the universe inhabited by other mortals. "You are—"

"You don't understand," Nadia said, breaking Diana's grip. "You never understood. The town's legacy depends on me. I just want my property back, and I'm content to stay where I am and be who I am. I have my *History* to write."

"What if they have some awful plan for you?"

"That would be awful."

"What if they're trying to control your mind, and this agoraphobia is something they induced? They could be feeding you drugs through a controlled diet. You'd have no defense."

"Do you think they could control this mind?" She twirled her forefinger in a small circle around her temple, rolled her eyes, then laughed. "Look, Sis, I know you'll stick up for me. You won't let the bad things happen."

Diana tolerated Nadia's peck on the cheek.

"You were always the strong one," Nadia said. She looked out the window at the wooden bridge and its graceful arched trusses. "I can't leave home."

There it was. Her sister believed in fairy tales. Some princess or prince would ride to the rescue. Good intentions would protect her from evil. That point of view did not consider the forces of time, chance, and necessity marshaling against her.

It was up to Diana to develop an escape plan.

# CHAPTER 25
# BONE COMB BETRAYAL

Ali panicked. When he returned from a sales trek delivering Bibles, his box was gone. His connection with home, and his mother—gone.

He searched the bunkhouse, looking under every bed and in every locker.

No luck.

Then he remembered a conversation. *Eban was going to store the box in his hut for safekeeping. Problem solved.*

He walked across the camp and knocked on Eban's door.

The voice came from behind. "Ain't here."

He turned to see Troy, smiling.

"I got me more snakes. Wanna see 'em? They's true rattlers."

"Where did Eban go?"

"The ford's out, so he's hikin' to the main trail. Reckon he left 'bout an hour ago. Said he had important business and ain't comin' back for a couple a days. Listen. You gotta see these snakes. You'll be real surprised where I found 'em. Gives me nightmares. You'll never wanna use the shit house again."

"Maybe later."

"Okay. Gotta go. Gonna teach them rattlers some new tricks."

"Great. I'm sure it will be amazing."

Ali waited for Troy to leave, then looked in the window. He saw his shipping box on the table, tried the door, but found it locked. When he tested the windows, he discovered one open in the back, out of sight, and climbed in.

The box—his box—was empty.

He searched the hut and found a few answers, but not his belongings. There was a note about New Orleans, a receipt for a train ticket, three photos, and Haywood's business card with a New Orleans address.

*New Orleans!*

Eban's schedule showed a date circled two days in the future, and hand-written scrawl: "Berky Benson, 10 AM." He tore the page from the calendar, left the hut, and started up the trail.

*He's only an hour or so ahead of me. Maybe I can catch him.*

The rock-studded path, still slippery from rain, climbed upward, toward ridges lost in a blue mist. It was more strenuous than the trails he took for Bible delivery. Part of the track overlapped stretches of treacherous bald green rock.

Ali wore no special clothing other than jeans, a T-shirt and sneakers, now wet and caked with mud. A squall line moved through the area, dumping rain, drenching his clothes. He continued upward and horizontally, along a path snaking through ferns and hardwoods.

The rain passed.

Beneath the beauty of the mountains was an unforgiving ruggedness, where wind-stunted trees grew from hard rock, and nature drew with a pastel airbrush.

He stopped for a moment to catch his breath, scoured the trail ahead for signs of Eban, then pushed onward for another hour.

Eban was dressed for hiking, with sturdy boots, a waterproof backpack, and light climbing gear.

He had a spring in his step. The future seemed glorious. Berky was interested in his scheme and wanted to meet in New Orleans, where he had other business.

Eban smelled money.

He rehearsed how he would describe his proposal and close the deal. The finder's fee should be big enough to expand his company to the next level.

From the corner of his eye, he saw a shape emerge from behind a blind turn on a trail that snaked across an adjacent bluff. Someone from camp was following him.

Ali turned a corner on a switchback and saw his quarry, fifty feet away on an adjacent ridge—close as the crow flies, but separated by miles on the footpath. He called. "Hey! Eban!"

The figure stopped, turned, and looked across the chasm.

Ali saw the glint of Haywood's gold tooth in the dimming light of late afternoon. He waved at his mentor, then formed his hands into a megaphone. "You have my mother's things. My things. My memories. Please return them."

Haywood shouted. His voice was clear and steady. "You was the best, Ali. I thank ye for that. But I can't go back."

"I know it's hard. The distance on the trail—it's about two miles. You don't need to do anything. Just stay there. I'll catch up."

"Naw. See, I need these things. This here's about money. Big money. The whole collection makes my claim. It's what they call 'provenance.'" Eban looked at the way ahead, and then his watch. "You'll never catch me. You know that, right?"

"You can't do this. I'll find you."

"You live in a dream world, son. I'm guessin' ICE will find you first. I'll let 'em know where ya are and tell 'em I think you're dangerous. They'll pull out all the stops. Good luck."

Ali picked up a rock and threw it at Haywood. The missile fell short, plummeting into wild dark shadows.

Eban touched his hat, giving Ali a two-fingered salute. Then he lumbered ahead, into the smoky mist, leaving Ali alone and desperate.

# CHAPTER 26
# GUMPTION SOUP

It was late afternoon when Diana's thoughts turned to Sundar Rao. He seemed to be a misguided man, unable to break through the reality distortion field created by a lunatic boss. She sensed she had affected him. Perhaps he could be swayed.

Someone knocked on the door.

"I'll get it," Nadia said.

The door opened a crack. Diana heard a muffled conversation, then Nadia said, "It's for you."

"For me?" Diana went to the bathroom, combed her hair, and put on a pretty frock. *It must be Sundar.*

The visitor was not someone she expected. It was a wizened, weather-beaten woman. Diana gave her a puzzled look. "You are?"

"I knows Nadia, and I knows you," the woman said. "I'm Jancie. Step outside, child."

"It's okay," Nadia said.

Reluctantly, Diana stepped through the door.

The woman moved to the joggling board, where she sat beside a picnic basket and a large metal pot wrapped in a towel. "Come on over."

Diana sat beside her, fending off a swarm of mosquitoes with her hand.

"It's only the females that bite," the woman said, waving away the bugs.

When she removed the towel and lid from the tureen, the insects disappeared, as if driven away by the vapors.

"I tries to come when I can. I wisht it was more."

"You're a friend of Nadia's?" Diana said.

"I knowed her a long time. I brung you'ns a pot o' soup. I'll eat some with ye and leave the rest. I'll get the pot back next time."

She ladled chunky broth into two bowls from the picnic basket. It was thick, rich, and still very hot.

"It's a sort of gumbo?" Diana said.

"Got a bit of Loosiana hot sauce, a tad of Georgia spice, a heap of big city stew, some Chicago beef."

"What do you call it?"

Jancie laughed. "Gumption soup."

Diana tasted. "Whew, it's hot." Her eyes watered, and she waved her hand in front of her mouth.

"Yup," Jancie said. "It'll put a backbone on ya."

"Well, there's enough here for the two of us for a week."

"She don't like the fish Berky feeds her."

"She hates it," Diana said. "Sometimes I see her throw it out the door. She says the raccoons eat it."

"It's okay. Them's my familiars."

"What do you mean?"

"Familiars is animals that helps me do things."

"Oh, right. Like in stories. But I thought witches use cats. Are you a witch?"

"I'm just a old lady. I likes to make good things happen to good people. Now, familiars can be anything. Some people like cats. Some use dogs. Some use crazy animals like possums, raccoons, and even kangaroos. I use what I can. Lately, it's been raccoons."

"Well, Nadia's been feeding your pets. But please use your magic to keep them away from my bees." Diana took another spoonful of soup, closed her eyes, and savored the hot spice, even as she wiped away tears.

Jancie winked. "Good, ain't it?"

Diana licked the spoon, then pointed it at Jancie like a wand. "Can fish be familiars?"

"Nah. They's too stupid."

"Well, listen. Thanks for the soup. Nadia will like it, I'm sure. And thanks for waving your wand in Nadia's direction. She needs help."

"This ain't for Nadia. It's for you. Gumption soup. Berky's got a spine on him, and you needs one, too."

# CHAPTER 27
# THE BIG EASY

New Orleans wasn't even on Marcy's mind when she sat on a swing on her veranda, with a cold drink in one hand, a pile of envelopes on her lap, and a clear view of Savannah's Forsythe Park in front of her. She liked to sit on the porch admiring the Spanish moss, magnolias, and banana trees. It was a Sunday ritual when she wasn't traveling. Even celebrities had to pay bills.

She sliced open what looked like a bank statement and discovered it contained a second envelope with the words: *Marcy Darcy – Eyes Only.* Opening it confirmed her suspicions. It was a message from GRIP.

They were good. She had to hand it to them. Somehow, GRIP had fashioned an exact replica of her monthly bank statement and used it to conceal the contract to destroy Canduka Cantor. The edges of her mouth ticked upward in pleasure. It was a sort of burn-after-reading message.

The letter inside said:

*We have preliminary results of your research request, and would be delighted to discuss it in person in New Orleans, LA on —*

"What?" She spoke the question aloud.

GRIP had been working on her problem now for several weeks. She had given them an initial payment to kick-start the effort. If they got actionable dirt on Cantor, she'd owe them the balance. She sensed that GRIP's collections department would be impatient, and she'd have to sell some securities.

What irritated her was the need to travel immediately to New Orleans. *She* was the client. They should be coming to *her*, on her schedule. It was pretty damn inconvenient.

The other thing she didn't like was the secrecy. They couldn't just say, "Meet me at Hotel XYZ." *No-o-o.* They wanted her to go to a bar and identify "an associate of our organization" using some damn-fool secret handshake. *Were they pretending to be spies? The Masons? The Knights Templar?*

She called the number for GRIP and left a voicemail expressing her displeasure with the arrangements. She ended by saying she'd make travel plans, and cautioned, "Your research better be good!"

She knew it wouldn't change things, but venting always made her feel better.

Cantor's notice from GRIP came disguised as an insurance policy. The envelope inside requested his presence in New Orleans to discuss "the matter in question."

*Travel? Right now? That's awkward.*

He texted Berky:

*Need to delay our meeting. Got to go to New Orleans for a couple of days. You OK?*

Berky was all about discipline. He wasn't sure how he was going to take it. When Berky replied after a minute, he breathed easier.

*The Big Easy is easy. Have to go there too. Let's coordinate.*

The stars, it seemed, were aligned.

# CHAPTER 28
# SITUATION UNSTABLE

Sundar commanded the Mercedes to stop at the security gate and motioned for the odd-looking guard, Yon Yakopuche, to come nearer. He gestured toward the dashboard to roll down the window. "Hey, Yon. You on the warpath today? You're going to scare visitors."

White teeth on a black and red painted face grinned back. "Gotta gig after work at the Village. I wanted to be in character. If you're an actor, that's what you do. Anyways, Mr. Benson told me he likes to scare people."

"Ah. The war paint and the guns will do it."

"I really like the new car. Mercedes?"

"Yeah?"

"That's the best SUV," Yon said. "Mine's an ancient 'stupid car.' I gotta do everything myself."

"Have you seen Berky this morning?"

"He was in real early. Did you know he likes to wear disguises, too?"

"I knew that. Thanks."

"Called him out, I did."

"Good for you."

"He thought he was foolin' me. But you can't fool a Cherokee." Yon made the two-fingered 'eye-am-watching-you' gesture, then pointed at Sundar.

"Have a good one," Sundar said. He gave the command and drove through the gate.

The team was waiting in a conference room that had two video walls, a writing wall filled with chemical equations, process diagrams, and doodles, and a translucent entry wall with an embedded GloSign that said, "Meeting in Progress." Berky noted the late arrival with, "Ah, here's Mr. Science."

"Sorry," Sundar said. "Sorry, sorry."

Berky cocked his head. "Where's Schrodinger?"

"Um. Left him outside. Marlyss is feeding him."

"Well, we need him in here. For luck."

Berky was mostly a "just-the-facts-ma'am" person, but he viewed certain animate and inanimate objects as lucky. The obsession went back to his high school days of selling "magic rocks" on the internet before he came into his inheritance. His screwball enterprise made money but colored his thinking about how to conduct meetings and make decisions.

When Sundar retrieved Schrodinger, Berky said, "Let's begin."

Sundar raised his hand to impart information, but Berky slighted him, like a teacher ignoring a pupil with bad behavior. "Popkins, what've you got?"

"I got solutions for the fish, Boss. Way good solutions. We gonna sell what we don't need—to pet stores, seafood shops, fertilizer companies, and sushi restaurants. Pays for whole fish operation—with fish."

Berky smiled. "I like your style, Gregor."

Popkins hesitated for a moment. Moisture collected in his eyes. "You called me by my first name, Boss." He looked at the others sitting at the table. "My first name!"

"What else have you got, Popkins?" Berky said. "Tell me about Nadia."

Popkins used a forefinger to wipe his eyes, coughed to clear his throat, and said, "Her searches on the Internet simulation—all over the place. We can't predict. I don't like it."

Berky frowned. "That's troubling."

Sundar popped his hand in the air again, but Berky pointed to the woman sitting next to him. "What've you got, Rosa?"

Rosa Alcott spoke in humorless "geek-speak" describing a set of complex graphs. "The subject's dietary intake was stable up until about a week ago. We need to continue this regimen to shape the behavioral epigenetics. But as you can see, her diet is now erratic, and her protein balances show it."

"It seems we have a mystery," Berky said.

Sundar cleared his throat. Everyone turned their heads.

"Is there a way we can get the supplements into different foods?" Sundar said. "Nadia says she hates fish and parsnips. A change in the plan might make her happier and more stable. Yes?"

Rosa flashed a mirthless smile that signaled: *Nice try, Bozo, but hell no.*

"The other thing you should know," Sundar said, "is that Nadia's sister is now living with her."

"What?" Berky lost his cool. He threw his notebook at Sundar but missed. "When did you find this out?"

"Um, yesterday," Sundar said.

"You should have told me immediately. This changes everything!"

Rosa puckered her lips. "This could account for the anomalies."

"Her sister's name is Diana," Sundar said. "She's been there almost two weeks. I never saw her until yesterday."

Reggie Edavane, head of security, brought a new idea to the table. "We can send in some muscle. Yon Yakopuche can shout some war whoops, do his little gun twirl thing, and escort the lady out of here. He's six percent Cherokee but acts like he's on the warpath. The face paint and spider tattoos will scare the shit out of her. She'll not come back, I'd wager."

"How would that help us shape Nadia's behavior?" Berky said.

Rosa interjected. "Traumatizing her won't help. There's a delicate balance between cognitive behaviors and the enzymes that induce them. It would definitely set us back."

"Nadia was my teacher in high school," Berky said. "I don't remember her sister, but I'm not very good with people, and the town didn't keep very good public records."

He turned to Sundar. "Look. I'm doing the Lord's work with this joint project, or I'd take care of this myself. So, you'll have to do it. Get to know this Diana person. Find out how close this twin connection is. See if she's a potential control specimen. We've invested a lot of time, effort, and brain cells in getting to this point, and I don't need a turn of bad luck. Give us some ideas on how to stabilize the situation and get the project back on track. Don't give me problems. Give me solutions. Those are your marching orders."

Back in his office, Berky fumed at the development. Nadia's value as a curated genetic template was diminishing. He hoped Eban Haywood's idea was a viable alternative.

He sent Eban a text:

*OK. I'll meet you in New Orleans. Not in your crappy office. Chez Lafitte Hotel. Call when you get there. Bring evidence. God helps those who are prepared and shits on those who aren't. Thx.*

# CHAPTER 29
# WAR ZONE

Rosa Alcott's dreams of a perfect future were as substantial as moonbeams and as fictional as the icons depicting amino acids floating in space above her head. All she wanted was respect and a chance to get ahead in a socially toxic tech culture. She believed she was every bit as good as the men who tried to put her down—maybe better. To define the future, the tiny woman with piercing dark eyes, dressed in a white lab coat, curly black hair funneled in a tight bun, concentrated her attention on a vision of molecular filaments wrought in the specular sheen of laser light.

She stood atop the circular control platform in the center of a cube with blackened walls, waving her hands to and fro before the 20-foot tall hologram, rotating the RNA model to see how synthetic molecules replaced natural base pairs. *Is this how Sundar's error-correction system works? Could it repair damaged or drifting genes, or even shift genes to a "new normal"?* She saw great power in his method, but also great danger.

A cough broke her concentration. She froze the display and turned, tensing her muscles, expecting to see Berky.

Sundar waved. "Got a minute?"

She shrugged and tried not to look annoyed, buttoning the top of her white lab coat as she stepped away from the platform. "What can I do for you?"

"Umm, there's a delicate matter. I need some advice from a woman." He looked at the floor, then at his shoes, then at her squinting 33-year-old eyes, hands fidgeting.

"Really? Will any woman do? Am I your proxy for all women? According to Berky, my advice doesn't count much." She flashed a fake smile. "What is it?"

"Help me understand what's going on with Nadia. What's the objective? Why this special diet?"

"I thought you were a smart guy, Sundar. We're trying to cure her."

"Why are we feeding her chemicals?"

"We're stabilizing certain variables. I monitor her condition through sensors in the septic system. Popkins looks at her interactions with the model Internet simulation to assess behavior. Kublai Khan tries to make sense of her cellular environment. The food supplements are all about epigenetics. You know what that is, right? It's how cells switch genes on and off so organisms can quickly adapt to their environment."

"Of course. I studied it in grad school, but my main emphasis was synthetic biology."

She sighed. *So many over-educated morons; so little time.* She really wanted to get back to her molecular analysis but knew that in the lab's pecking order, she was lower than Sundar and had to play nice. In fact, in Berky's eyes, she was even lower than Yon Yakopuche, the Cherokee-cowboy-security guard wannabe. Still, there might be hope for Sundar. Maybe she could brighten his dim bulb.

"Lifestyle, including diet, impacts the epigenome, which is why we're trying to stabilize Nadia's food source."

Sundar's face was passive, his thoughts collecting in his eyes.

Rosa didn't give him the benefit of the doubt. "You understand, don't you?"

"Not really. Nadia's disease is a matter of perception and identity. She's terrified of the objective world and wants to live in a fiction of her own making. Diet can't address how she looks at the world or thinks about herself."

*Maybe there is hope for this moron.*

"Hold this idea in your brain: information outside the DNA can inform and permanently modify the heritable genome. To make Nadia view the world and herself differently, and pass on that perceptual difference to her heirs, we have to invoke something Berky calls the 'fiction gene.' Berky tells everyone he discovered it—like he's some sort of Francis Crick. Actually, it was the AI system, Kublai Khan, that made the breakthrough."

"So, this fiction gene—"

"Is important for how humans perceive the world. It's the biological basis for our belief systems. The grounding point for both imagination and delusion. It's what makes us human. Basically, we need to reset Nadia's delusions and make them align with what is normal."

"And Kublai Khan is somehow able to tie all these threads of genetic evidence together, to—"

"Hopefully, to cure Nadia and others with a similar affliction. Once we get a cure and verify we're doing no harm, we should be able to propagate it through the genome and inoculate her progeny. In fact, we could potentially inoculate everyone on the planet. I'm working on something—a perfection—called a 'gene drive' that can do that."

"There's nothing nefarious behind this Nadia project?"

"Listen. If I thought for a minute there was some evil intent, I wouldn't be working in this lab. And I'd string Berky up by his testicles. We're trying to understand Nadia's disease, so we can cure her, cure others, and make the cure a permanent part of the genome. That's the mission statement I wrote when we started this project. Berky signed off on that mission."

Sundar squinted, trying to discern the truth. "That's it?"

"As they say in the infomercial ads, 'That ain't all.' There's money to be made if we succeed, and I'm a shareholder in Xanadu NeuroLab."

# CHAPTER 30
# PLAYING THE ODDS

*The evil twin of imagination is paranoia. We construct alternative realities*
*by connecting real and imagined dots.*
—*Canduka Cantor*

As Ali hiked thirteen blocks northward from the New Orleans bus station, up Loyola Avenue, Basin, and Conti streets, past the St. Louis Cemetery and the tomb of a famous voodoo priestess, he thought about his mother.

*She was the only one who understood me. She trusted me when others—including my own father—didn't. She knew I would use my talent to earn money and help the family. Her faith in me kept me sane and focused. And now ...*

He believed Eban Haywood was the worst kind of thief. He had stolen Ali's connection to his roots — the thing that gave him a purpose for living and a reason to succeed. The backstop to his identity.

*I will find Haywood and confront him. He used me. Then he disrespected my family. He must return what he took.*

He referred to Eban's business card, found Lafitte Avenue, and walked another 13 blocks, finally discovering the B.S. and S.H.I.T. office inside a ramshackle building. It wasn't much larger than a broom closet—nothing more than a mail drop. There were notices and bills stuffed under the door, with postmarks dating back six months. A hand-written, dust-covered note taped to the door said: "On travel. Back whenever."

He felt defeated.

Ali knocked on other doors in the building, searching for information, but the other offices all appeared to be empty.

He went back to the street looking for someone—anyone—who could provide information on the whereabouts of Eban Haywood.

*If there is a God, He will surely help me find the things that make me who I am and help defeat my enemies.*

# CHAPTER 31
# PROVENANCE

The reason Eban stayed in his New Orleans broom-closet office was to keep costs down and conserve cash. He didn't want creditors to know he was in town, so he took great pains to preserve the appearance of abandonment. The pile of letters on the floor—mostly bills—made a semi-comfortable bed if you put them together in a big heap. The nearby honky-tonk had cheap food and a restroom—all he needed to survive a couple of days and look and smell respectable.

He was playing a risky game, robbing receipts from the teetering Bible business to pay for an attorney, a translator, and an outfit to even the playing field with Berky Benson. When he met Berky in the lobby of the Chez Lafitte Hotel, he felt like a confident businessman, well-prepared for difficult negotiations. Wearing a new suit and clutching a black plastic document pouch, he thought he had what he needed to close a deal.

Berky led him to his room on the seventh floor and offered a glass of bourbon from the minibar.

Eban declined. This was about money. He wanted to preserve his edge.

"Please have a seat," Berky said, pointing to a sofa. He poured two glasses of water, placed them on the coffee table, and sat in a chair across from Eban. He wore his signature red Polo shirt, looking as relaxed as Eban looked stiff. He took off his shoes, crossed his legs, and wiggled his bare toes.

"Here's the evidence," Eban said, reaching into the black pouch and sliding a packet across the table.

Berky thumbed through the file—photos, a letter written in Bengali, and a translation of the letter provided by a New Orleans-based agency. He stopped at what looked like a contract.

"Where are the original artifacts?" Berky said.

"Thought you'd be interested, 'specially in the comb. You can see the hairs stickin' to it in the pitchur. Ah got all the stuff hid away. Ah'll hand it over when you sign the Agreement."

Berky looked through the contract.

Eban crossed his arms and gave Berky a smug smile. "Got a good lawyer. They's a lotta ins, lotta outs, lotta what-have-yous. You'll get ever thang if you sign and pay me the finder's fee."

Berky looked up. "I'm impressed. It says you filed a provisional patent on DNA in the hair strands."

"Told ya. Got a good lawyer."

"I'll have to think about this," Berky said. "Then my attorney can discuss it with your attorney."

"Nope," Eban said. "You deal di-rectly with me. I ain't turnin' over nuthin' 'til you sign and give me half what's my due. You'll pay me the rest when I deliver."

"I don't know. This material may not be all that valuable. No offense. I'm inclined to just forget it. Thanks for coming to New Orleans."

Eban watched Berky's pupils dilate as he looked at the photo of Ali's mother standing in her bare feet on a clay floor. "If what I got ain't valuable, why'd you ask me to come all the way to Loosiana to meet? Read the translation of the letter. Ali's father wants forgiveness fer spendin' all his money on hired wives. They's sorta like whores. Says his wife was fine with that, but he feels he shouldn'ta gone overboard so much. When she died, she was yer perfect woman. An' look at the pitchur. Real purty."

"Well," Berky said. "I see you've got good documentation—you've established the provenance."

"Thanks. If I don't get money in two days, I'll give this stuff back to the boy that give it to me. You'll never find 'im. He's livin' in the deep woods."

Berky kept a stone face for a moment. Eban's off-the-rack suit seemed new, but his shoes and socks looked worn and desperate.

He pulled a checkbook out of his briefcase and made out a payment to Eban Haywood. "Here's 25 percent. The next meeting will be in my lab. You'll turn everything over at that time, and I'll give you another 50 percent. If we find the DNA is useful, I'll give you the remainder and then sign the contract."

He slid the check across the table.

"Take it or leave it."

Eban took it.

# CHAPTER 32
# SNAKE JAZZ

Embers billowed from a portable grill like a whorl of fireflies glowing against the darkening purple sky. Ali Khan Ahmed, desperate and despondent, looking for hope, approached the black man stirring the coals.

"What's in that soup you're selling? Tell me the truth."

The man smiled. "What you see is not what is. That ees the truth." He was dressed in white and stood next to an ancient iron bridge spanning Bayou Saint John in the Trem-Lafitte district of New Orleans. "You ahnvee some gumbo, den, missiere?"

Ali thought for a moment as he decoded the Creole. "How much?"

"Two dola. One for me, one for Laveau. I am Amothe."

"Laveau is your partner?"

The man laughed a deep laugh. "Laveau is *mouri*. She is dead. Like your one eye."

"That's too bad. Here is money."

The man scooped gumbo into a bowl and handed it to Ali. "See her picture?" He showed Ali a photo of a painted shrine. In it, a statue of a black woman with a headscarf carried a serpent on her shoulders and wore humanoid heads, like grisly pendants, near her breasts.

"She wears a hijab," Ali said. "Is she Muslim?"

Amothe laughed. "No, no. Marie Laveau. She eez Vodou."

"What about the snake in the picture? I'm looking for a man who uses snakes." He showed Eban Haywood's business card to Amothe.

"Snakes are Vodou. Laveau is Vodou. Tonight is Saint John's Eve. Vodou night. You want *batèm*? Baptism? It brings you luck and power."

"I am Muslim," Ali said, trying to avoid complications. "I just want to find this man who uses snakes. I went to his address, but it's just a place where they send mail."

"You can be Muslim and Vodou. Amothe can help you find the person. Trust Amothe. But you must wear this white headscarf. I will sell to you for four dola. Then you must go to this street, which I will write—two dola for information. Look for the sign of the snake. You will see a black beauty. You will be recognized."

"How will she know?"

"The white scarf."

Ali finished his gumbo. There was no spoon. He drank from the bowl as if taking a sacrament, then tied the white scarf on his forehead. He gave the peddler some money. As he turned to leave, the old man grabbed him by the shoulder. Amothe raised a cup and splashed water against Ali's forehead.

"Why did you do that?"

Amothe mumbled some words Ali didn't understand. Then he said, "Baptism. Now Laveau knows you. You have power."

Ali began walking. Behind him, the street vendor broke into a hearty laugh.

As he approached Bourbon Street, it was impossible to avoid ankle-deep standing water and the splash of slow-moving cars. He tried to cut through crowds of people filling the sidewalks. The air, smelling like sweat and rainwater, reverberated with the sound of trumpets and jazz.

# CHAPTER 33
# BOURBON STREET CONSPIRATORS

"Do you have information for me?" Cantor asked. "And please explain why Ah had to travel to New Orleans for a meeting. Ah do not like to waste my time."

The man Cantor knew as "Mr. Smith" slowly filled a water glass from a purple bottle labeled "Acqua Salutare" and squeezed a lemon into it from a small bowl. Two other men drilled Cantor's visage with dispassionate eyes. A third man appeared not to listen, lost in the intricate wall panels of green and yellow leaves that wrapped around a polished mahogany conference table on the mezzanine level of the Hotel Paradiso.

Mr. Smith took a dainty sip of water, cleared his throat, and flashed refrigerator-white teeth before speaking. "My business associates are here, that's why I asked you to come. We have new requirements." He nodded to three other "suits" seated to his left and right.

Cantor, wearing a soccer shirt and his best pair of khaki shorts, tapped a sandaled foot. "Ah gave you *my* requirements in Chicago. How are we doing on those?"

Smith's voice was calm and collegial. "Patience, Mr. Cantor. We'll get to that. But first, tell us more about your operation. My colleagues are curious. They may want to invest. You'd like another funding round, wouldn't you? Consider this a due-diligence step."

Cantor grew nervous but tried not to show it. "Ah see."

Smith leaned forward in his high-backed, green leather chair. "I'm not sure you do see." He gestured toward the others. "Meet Mr. Ira Jones, business planning; Mr. Luigi Williams, Technology Visioning; and Mr. Frank Taylor, Customer Persuasion. Give us your pitch. Not the pabulum you feed to other donors. You'd be very wise not to fabricate or embroider the truth. Mr. Taylor does not have a sense of humor."

Cantor watched Taylor shift his gaze from the fabric wall panels, meet his eyes, and penetrate his soul. *The eye of Shiva.*

144

Cantor pushed air through pursed lips. "Okay. Ah assume you know some things—maybe even some fairly intimate things. That's your business. It's what you do. And Ah assume you want more information on risks and rewards."

Smith took another dainty sip of water. "Yes."

"Where would you like me to start?"

"With the objective."

"Simple. The country is drifting toward an unnatural relationship between men and women. We can stop the drift with genetic science."

"Aha. A world where men are men, and women obey?"

"More radical than that. My business partner and I want a world where men are immune to *Testrial*, the GMO poison. More importantly, we want to assure that men are dominant. We want a world where women are pets that can be shared among pet owners. It may sound shocking, but Ah believe a lot of people would agree with me."

"Ho, ho," Mr. Smith said. "In New York, they'd call that chutzpah. My investors may not respect laws, but at least we understand them. There's a little matter of the Constitution. The 13th Amendment abolished slavery. But ..." He drew a long breath. "We understand the slavery business model is sustainable if you have a disciplined organization. Your organization appears to be undisciplined. Your main motive seems to be hatred for your ex-wife. What's more, you seem entangled with her. That's unprofessional. It makes you a huge target for the government and private attorneys. That could expose potential backers, such as our group. That's my opinion."

The former ad-man felt compelled to respond. "There is a major flaw in your thinking. Slavery is involuntary servitude. That's what the 13th Amendment abolished. Ah am talking about voluntary servitude."

"What do you mean?" Smith asked.

"Well ...," Cantor said. "the laws of the U.S. underwrite life, liberty, and the pursuit of happiness. Right? They abhor slavery in any form. Right? The laws assume that logic, curiosity, and the desire to be free are common human traits."

"Right," Smith said. "That's why our business relies on Mr. Taylor's persuasive skills."

"But what if we could breed people to see the world differently? To believe in things that are given, but not proven? To embrace ideas that have no basis in everyday experience? What Ah am talking about are genetically controlled delusions."

"There's already an endless supply of stupid, delusional people," Jones said with a shrug. "It's how we make our money."

"But Ah want people—women—to be delusional in a particular way. I want them to perceive *my* reality."

The four men sitting across from Cantor looked puzzled.

"See," Cantor continued, "there are no legal precedents to deal with people who accept or even seek out enslavement. We're talking about women pursuing their own happiness because they *want* to be slaves. Thomas Jefferson would certainly agree with that."

He continued on a roll. "No laws prevent the birthing of infants cloned from selected DNA. Congress has tried many times to pass such laws, but political contributions from businesses have reversed the changes. If we can produce willing slaves through genetic manipulation, the government can't prosecute them or their masters as long as the people involved are operating through their own free will."

"Wait," Williams said. "Even if we accept that this sort of genetic manipulation is possible, and we have a solid business plan behind it, it could take decades before we see any return on investment."

"That's why our solution includes an epigenetic component," Cantor said. "The change begins with the current generation, and we embed the change into the germline, to carry it into the future. My associate, Berky Benson, can explain it better than Ah can. He's in town and staying at the same hotel. Ah can set up a meeting with your technology guy."

Smith glanced at his watch. "We have a full schedule today. Set it up for tomorrow, after dinner. Nine PM sharp. Just Mr. Benson. Not you. The meeting will be here in this room."

Cantor nodded, gathered his things, shook hands, and departed. He lingered outside the conference room door and caught snippets of conversation:

"There might be a way to make it addictive," said one voice.

"Or pay for maintenance doses," said another voice.

"Let's also think about paying for immunity." The voice was Smith's.

The guard noticed Cantor dallying by the door and gave him a threatening look. Cantor twitched a quick smile and departed.

# CHAPTER 34
# SIGN OF THE SERPENT

Ali turned onto Bourbon Street, passing Marie Laveau's House of Voodoo. The air was moist, sultry, stale—a mix of jasmine and roses and fetid swamp. Revenge, the need to restore family dignity, and grief over his mother's death twisted his logical mind. Ali's obsession with Eban Haywood's whereabouts made him willing to believe the voodoo story of a total stranger—a vendor who merely wanted to sell gumbo and headbands.

Marcy, meanwhile, was caught in a similar mental distortion. She sat in a bar that stank of beer and sweat and boiled crawfish, prepared to do anything to hurt her ex-husband, Canduka Cantor, even if it meant conspiring with felons. Her obsession and the secrecy necessary for the illegal endeavor caused her to conflate anomalous behavior with criminal tradecraft.

And so, with minds tuned to alternate realities, the one-eyed Muslim Bible salesman walked into a bar and collided with the feminist firebrand. The two became forever entangled, like a knot of Calabi-Yau space.

Ali spotted a painted sign, just a few blocks down Bourbon Street, confirming the gumbo vendor's prediction. "Scratch Tavern," it said. The "S" was a snake, and the "T" was a goat's skull. Ali went inside.

A lone black female, sitting at the bar, watched him through a large wall mirror. His eyes met hers for an electric instant. He could tell she recognized him. The hairs on the back of his neck prickled as if touched by the ghost of Marie Laveau.

*Behold a black beauty.*

Marcy searched for something out of the ordinary. In Chicago, the GRIP contact announced his presence with a large, bright umbrella. In New Orleans, they told her an agent would make contact at this specific bar and would identify himself. She didn't quite know what to expect. Criminal tradecraft was not something she was comfortable with. After waiting what seemed an interminable amount of time, Marcy believed she spotted her contact entering the bar—a tall, stubble-bearded stranger with a white headband and an eyepatch. His eyes met hers with a flash of recognition.

*This must be the handler.*

Marcy watched the olive-skinned man slide onto the stool next to her.

"You recognize me?" he said.

"It's obvious," she said, pausing to remember the protocol. "How was your day?"

"It was a perfect day. It led me to you, and hopefully answers."

"A perfect day for pictures," she monotoned.

Ali blinked. "Ah, yes," he said, after a long pause, seeming to get the implication. "Here are some pictures I found. Can you help me identify the people?"

She studied the three photos. "The person on the left is my ex-husband, and the one on the right is his business associate, Berky Benson. I don't know the man in the middle."

Ali showed her the business card. "He is Eban Haywood, the man I am looking for."

"Is it because he's involved in some scheme that'll bring down my husband?" she said.

Ali was puzzled. "I'm interested in Eban Haywood, who stole a precious artifact—a comb."

"Hmm. If he gave it to Benson or Cantor, it probably has to do with their experiments," she said. "They may be after DNA in the hair. Take a look at the file I gave your people in Chicago."

Ali squinted—even more perplexed.

She let out a long breath, then shook her head. "I guess GRIP doesn't always use the sharpest tools in the box to do their work. Here. I have another copy."

She rummaged through her briefcase and recovered a folder titled "Cantor." Ali took it and began to read. Soon, his eyes widened.

"The comb was my mother's," he said.

Marcy blinked three times, trying to process.

A deep male voice came from behind. "Perfect day."

What Marcy did next was something comedians call a double take. She turned to look at the swarthy Asian figure behind her. Then she looked back at Ali. Then her neck spun back to the stranger.

"Who are you?" she asked.

"Keep to the protocol."

A shoulder holster protruded from the stranger's jacket—close enough for her to scent deodorant and a trace of gun oil. Her throat tightened. "A perfect day for pictures."

"Right. Now please explain. Who is he?"

But now the subject of the sentence, the "he," had fled, scurrying out of the bar with the Cantor folder in hand.

"I thought he was you," she said. "He knew the protocol."

"Excuse me," he said. "I need to take care of a problem."

# CHAPTER 35
# DEAD END

*Through genetic memory, the dead inform the behavior of the living.*
—Canduka Cantor

Ali spotted the Asian thug leaving the bar. When their eyes met, and the man started toward him, he ran for his life. He dodged through busy, neon-lit streets, jumped hurdles, ran through ankle-deep water, and pushed through small crowds, but the fast slap of feet behind him spoke to the diminishing odds of escape. His pursuer was relentless, athletic, and gaining ground. He turned a corner, then ducked into an alleyway, hoping darkness and an emerging fog would provide cover. He was wrong. He found locked service doors and no other exit.

Behind him, a can skidded against the pavement, announcing the arrival of his pursuer. When he turned, he saw a burly man silhouetted against the diffused light from the street. The figure moved slowly and confidently toward him. A second silhouette—a thin chiaroscuro sketch of a man—entered the mouth of the alley, following the first man.

*This is where I die*, Ali thought.

The lead man tugged at an object under his jacket. Ali saw the shine of dull metal in his hand as the thug extended his arm.

A metallic click punctuated a question from the darkness. "Speak to me. Who are you?"

"I am—"

Ali cut his answer short when the second man hit the first one with a board, knocking him to the ground. Ali's jaw dropped.

The attacker stepped over the crumpled shape, then walked forward, extending his hand. His small finger ended in an unnatural claw-like nail.

"*Bonswa.* I am Lazare." A white-toothed smile reflected the light.

"I am Ali."

"*Bourik* try to keel Vodou. I am Vodou. Powerful Vodou. Now we make dat salaud pay. You must help."

Ali pocketed the dropped gun and helped roll the crumpled man onto his back. Lazare took the man's wallet, emptied the cash, and handed Ali the identity token and netcard.

"*Boug* is evil. His cartes not traced. *Ils ne peuvent pas suivre.* You take."

He pulled a pouch from his pocket and opened it. "Now, *la magie.*"

He withdrew from the pouch what looked like a lady's compact and a metal finger ring. The compact contained a creamy lotion. The crown of the ring was a death's head wearing a top hat, and the band was two intertwined snakes. Lazare placed the ring on his first finger, clenched his fist, then mashed the ring into the lotion. "Now, de sleep of death."

Ali's eyes widened in disbelief. Lazare was going to kill a man. The event unfolded like the scene from a dream.

Lazarre punched the man's forehead. The ring cut like a blade through the skin. Blood dripped from the wound. "He eez cursed."

Lazare propped the body into a sitting position and crossed the man's arms to his chest. "Let us go. *Li mouri par gris-gris.* He is dead by magic."

# CHAPTER 36
# ZOMBIE MAN

*In theory, you can debate whether you're alive or dead or dreaming.*
*In practice, the decision's easy.*
—Canduka Cantor

Smith watched as Jack Gorman, a bespectacled man wearing a red bow tie and rumpled brown suit, scanned through a pad of penciled notes in the hotel boardroom. Jack faced the spotlights above the conference table and squinted into the shadows.

"I told them I was the attorney representing the family, so they gave me some of the details. They wouldn't let me record anything but said it was okay to take notes the old-fashioned way. I guess that makes anything they tell me easier to deny."

He flipped through a few pages. Taylor and Williams shifted in their seats.

"So—last night a busboy from Eloi's Jazz Bistro found Billy in a back alley, barely alive. He called 911. At the Tulane ER, Billy was pronounced DOA. They sent the body to the morgue, and police reported it as a suspected homicide. Fortunately, the coroner had seen this sort of thing before. He made preliminary observations before cutting him open and noticed the imprint above the wound on the forehead. A death's head. He recognized the situation."

Jack opened his netcard. "I took this when the cops weren't looking. It's from the desk of the lead detective. Let me blow it up for you." He showed it to the three men, then flipped to the next picture. "And here's Billy on the slab." He passed the netcard around for everyone to see.

Smith tightened his jaw. "He sure looks dead."

"Well, they said he had no pulse and wasn't breathing."

"So—dead?"

"Technically. Then they injected him with ..." — he shuffled through notes — "some stuff ... an anticholinesterase agent, atropine, and pyridostigmine. I don't know whether I pronounced any of that correctly. Those things had apparently worked for previous victims. Billy convulsed, and his heart started beating. A toxicologist they brought in said the active drug might have been tetrodotoxin, curare, or some unknown mix."

Smith shook his head. "Whew. So Billy's not dead?"

"Yup. They're keeping him in the hospital for observation. This was very weird. When he was conscious, Billy said he could hear the coroner preparing the cutting tools and the buzzing of a drill. His mind was fully aware. He just couldn't move. To paraphrase Bob Dylan, 'In New Orleans, you can be dead for a long time.'"

"Lucky. But did Billy compromise our operation?"

"He told the police he had gone into the alley for a smoke and got hit on the head. That story was consistent with the bruises and concussion. The police are working on the theory that Billy was in the wrong place at the wrong time, and the perp is some crazy voodoo maniac."

"Okay. Assume for now Billy hasn't exposed us. If that proves false, then Taylor, you'll need to take care of it."

Taylor nodded. "Right. But we still have a bigger issue."

Smith nodded, then looked at the bow-tied attorney. "Jack, please ask Ms. Darcy to step into the conference room."

Marcy stared into the bright lights of the boardroom. She recognized Smith from their encounter in Chicago, but the other men were strangers.

Smith's face contorted into an unnatural smile. "Remember what I said in Chicago about how seriously we take the problem of exposure?"

Marcy nodded.

"Please explain, in as much detail as you remember, exactly what happened last night."

"It was a dreadful experience, Mr. Smith. Simply dreadful. I waited at the bar, at Scratch Tavern, just like you said. I had my back to the door and watched through the mirror. I saw a young man enter, about 5-feet tall, brown skin, wearing a white bandana. He had an eye patch and was rather good looking. He recognized me and sat on the stool beside me. I assumed he was from your organization. He knew the protocol."

"That's very troubling."

"Then he asked if I knew the three individuals in a couple of pictures."

"Did you?"

"One of them was my ex-husband. Another was his business associate, Mr. Berkshire Benson, or 'Berky' as they call him. I didn't know the third person, but the man with the headband said he was ... somebody Haywood. I can't remember the first name."

Taylor turned to Smith. "Probably an alias."

"Go on," Smith said.

"He said this man Haywood stole a valuable artifact. A comb. I told him he might be after the hair follicles and DNA. That would fit with what Cantor and Benson are working on. I gave him a draft copy of the 'Canons of Cantor,' a document my ex-husband wrote, and some other material. That's when your man showed up."

"Billy."

"He didn't identify himself. He just asked who the other man was. I said I thought he was with your organization. That's when the man with the bandana bolted. Your man went after him. That's all I know."

Taylor leaned in. "Have you ever seen this person before?"

"No. I'd never seen either of them before."

"If you're lying, we'll know," Taylor said. "And the consequences will be—"

"It's the truth. I swear."

Smith tapped his fingertips together several times. "Can you think of anything else that might be relevant?"

"The man with the bandana said the comb belonged to his mother."

"Yeah. Right," Williams said, dismissively.

The men huddled, talking in whispers. Finally, Smith said, "That will be all. You can go now."

She folded her arms. "I declare! I've given you everything I know, and you've given me nothing. I paid you to find dirt on Canduka Cantor. What've you got?"

Smith winced. "Do not test me."

Unbowed, she stood, raising her voice to the men on the other side of the bright lights. "If GRIP were a food service, you'd get less than one Yelp star. If

GRIP were a government, you'd be Somalia. If GRIP were an Italian suppository, you'd be—"

"Wait!" Smith yelled. "I see why your husband left you, lady."

"Damn you!" She threw a pencil at him.

Taylor pressed a restraining hand against Smith's arm, and huddled close, whispering. Finally, Smith calmed, but his face was still flush. He nodded toward Taylor, adjusted his tie, and smiled a fake smile. "My apologies. That was unprofessional. We can give you something. I'll send a courier to your hotel with a package tomorrow."

"Should I greet him with a gun?"

"My dear, if I wanted you dead, I would do it right now. It would give me so much pleasure. But that would be bad for business."

"Good. I'll expect some information tomorrow. I kept my commitments. You need to work on keeping yours, Mr. Smith."

She stood, returned the fake smile, and departed, slamming the door on her way out.

"Bitch," Smith said.

"Do you think the guy in the bandana was with the Russians?" Williams asked. "Or Iranians, or Chinese?"

Taylor shrugged. "Hard to say. It could even be D-Company in Chennai. They're getting big. Ms. Darcy may be a pain in the ass, but she's persistent. She'll help do our digging. We give her some information, then track her."

Back at Scratch Tavern, waning daylight filtered through dirty windowpanes, spotlighting sparsely filled tables. Marcy sat at the bar and ordered a double bourbon without ice. It had been that kind of day. The bartender placed the glass in front of her. His hand sported a death's head ring, and his little finger carried an elongated, claw-like nail. She waited for him to release the drink, but he held it with his hand until she had to ask.

"You need me to pay now?"

"I weel put on de tab." He let go, and she gulped it down.

"I am Lazare," he said.

Marcy felt her body relaxing. "Lazare, give me another, please."

He poured two fingers.

"This is where I assume my 'jellyfish-in-a-sea-of-whiskey' posture," she said.

Lazare leaned close. "De man by de window watches you, he does."

She drew the glass to her lips, but didn't sip, then swiveled on the stool, as if admiring a nearby handsome couple. She spotted the man—Latino, muscular, thirtyish, with sunshades and facial tattoos like purple bands that rippled from his eyes, nose, and mouth. She returned her eyes to Lazare and took a sip of the smooth brown liquid.

"I tink he is bad man," Lazare said.

She lowered her voice to a whisper. "Well I ... am a bad-ass woman." She gulped down the rest of the whiskey. "Do you know that I drove my first husband crazy?" She wagged her finger. "'Course, he was already crazy." She raised her empty glass and shouted out. "Here's to craziness. It rules the world."

Lazare wiped glasses, then moved back to Marcy. "If you want to go quiet, I help."

"Lazare. I am now a jellyfish. And a cheap drunk. But you are right. I should probably ditch the guy by the window." She reflected for a moment. "I bet he's a slow swimmer. How fast can a jellyfish go? Can they jet around like squids, or do they just sort of float in the current?"

"Go to de bathroom," he said. "I be der when you come out. We go out de back way."

She jabbed him. "You are a gentleman. And nature calls." She got up, winked, then hobbled into the hallway.

Lazare was waiting when she left the ladies' room. "Dis way," he said.

He led her to a back office, opened the door, and turned on the light.

Ali Khan Ahmed smiled as she entered. "Surprise, Ms. Darcy. We must talk—about Canduka Cantor, Berky Benson, Eban Haywood, Assurance, North Carolina. And survival."

"I tell de bad man you leave by de back door. N'est-ce pas?" Lazare said as he shut the office door.

When they were alone, Ali plopped Marcy's 'Cantor' file on the desk. "I have more information for you," he said. "I think we can help each other."

# CHAPTER 37
# THE SMELL OF MONEY

*Utopia is simply the fulfillment of dreams, the absence of cops and a great big bag of money.*
—*Canduka Cantor*

The next morning, Berky took a cab to the Hotel Paradiso, following up on Cantor's text from the previous evening. It was the first he'd heard of the mysterious organization called GRIP. The bellman opened the door into a lobby with a twenty-foot ceiling covered in Italian frescoes. Berky climbed stairs to the mezzanine conference room, where a young blond-haired woman in high heels and daring décolletage walked him to the boardroom. He immediately felt out of place, dressed in shorts, formal black shoes, paisley socks, and his favorite Hawaiian shirt. The GRIP people wore suits and ties.

The woman adjusted the lights, so Berky was in the spotlight at the front of the table while other faces dissolved in shadow. She closed the door and departed.

"How you doin'?" Berky said in a loud voice. He pulled out a packet of salted nuts from his shirt pocket. "God must have invented the peanut. Anybody want some?"

There were no takers.

He quickly discovered GRIP knew a lot about Xanadu's plans. It irked him that Cantor had revealed so much without even signing an NDA. On the other hand, he could see these people were dangerous. As his eyes adjusted to the light, he spotted shoulder holsters inside every jacket.

"We're considering an investment in Xanadu's operation," Smith said.

Berky chewed a mouthful of nuts while talking. "We're a private company. I decide if I want you onboard."

"You'll find we can very persuasive, Mr. Benson. Besides, we'll help with more than just money."

"Like?"

"Competitive information. Dealing with government regulators. Navigating the law."

"I have my own attorneys. And what we're doing is so far ahead of the competition, I'm not really worried."

"Maybe, maybe not," Smith said. "Let's put some of that aside for a minute. We see you're a leader. We'd like to get a sense of what makes you tick."

"Tick? Well, I'm not crazy, if that's what you're getting at." The line got a laugh from everyone in the room.

"No. of course not."

"But I think this country's going crazy."

Smith lifted his left eyebrow, took another sip of water, then raised his right eyebrow, "Sure."

"It's a damn shame."

"Couldn't agree more."

"This Testrial thing is unnatural. It's turning men into wimps, sapping our strength, enabling women to dominate. And they're just getting started."

There was silence in the darkness around the table, but Berky saw nods, sensing his words resonated. He continued to riff.

"Our idea is to inoculate men against the Testrial poison and put women back into their God-given place."

He heard sympathetic sighs from Williams and Taylor.

Berky started to warm to these people. He explained a few more details. The group thanked him and said they wanted to continue the conversation.

After Berky left, Smith turned up the lights and addressed his team. "What do you think?"

Williams kicked off the discussion. "I'm excited about the possibilities. We could do a lot from a business perspective."

Jones nodded in agreement. "You know? I keep thinking about the Uber business model..."

"Or Airbnb," Williams said. "Even better."

Jones snapped his fingers, struck by the power of the idea. "We have this free app, see? And if you want to swap your genetically modified wife—"

"Someone who's yours by right of marriage," Williams said.

"And there's a swap fee, and we get 30 percent, like Apple," Jones said.

"Could be huge," Williams said. "Win-win for everybody."

"Don't forget the religion angle," Taylor said. "We need to get Cantor back in here. There are other parties with money."

"I see where you're going," Jones said. "We can go for international funding."

Smith removed his pistol and tapped it on the table like a gavel, stopping conversation. "Don't forget the Testrial problem. We need an antidote to that poison."

Everyone nodded.

Jack Gorman, the attorney, cleared his throat, then fiddled nervously with his bow tie, unsure how his objection would be received. "What's in it for us?"

Smith set his jaw. "It's pretty simple. Testosterone smells like money. It powers our business. We need it like a pimp needs whores, like a gun needs bullets, like a boxer needs to feel the squish of knuckles in a bloody face. When the smell of testicles is gone, and the world reeks of perfume and potpourri, what've we got? We—GRIP—got nothin'. It's about our business, my friends. The world is changing. We need to save it."

Taylor let out a subdued, "Amen."

Smith's eyes flashed with resolve. "Let's pump it up."

Cantor entered the boardroom for a second time, hoping to extricate himself and his company from a dark entanglement. As he sat down at the oak table populated by men with oversized jackets and the glint of blued iron around their armpits, he felt their eyes penetrating his—assessing. Judging. Controlling.

Smith smiled as he poured sparkling water from a blue bottle into a crystal glass. "It gives us great pleasure, Mr. Cantor, to tell you we'll contribute capital to your enterprise—and Mr. Benson's. There's a synergy that captured our imagination."

"Glad to hear it," Cantor said.

"We'll help fulfill your main objective—destroying your ex-wife. She's a bitch."

"Ah'm glad you see that."

"We have certain Middle Eastern clients who may want a shot at investing," Williams said.

Jones looked up from a notebook display. "That being said, there are things in this business plan we like, and things we don't like."

Cantor folded his arms. "Look, I hired you guys to help destroy Marcy. Ah'm delighted you now want to invest in the Cantor Spiritual Community, CSC. But Ah like my business plan. Ah put a lot of thought into it. Ah set up the corporation. You can join as an investor, but Ah call the shots."

"We think you should consider your options," Smith said. "There's a certain downside to not giving us a free hand." He flicked his eyes toward Taylor, who stood, walked over to Cantor, grabbed him by the belt and shirt, raised him into the air with powerful arms, and slammed him onto the tabletop, sending imported blue bottles of sparkling water skidding across the table and onto the floor.

Cantor, dazed and gasping for breath, stared at the muraled ceiling, wondering what just happened. He felt his shirt sponging up the cool fizzy water that puddled on the table while pain stabbed at his lumbar region. When he could finally breathe, he began to moan.

After half a minute, Smith broke the silence. "I hope we got your attention. You really have no choice. Mr. Taylor can be very persuasive. It's the way of the world: big fish eat little fish. Besides, we can increase your market penetration and scale."

Williams pinched Cantor's cheek. "Don't worry. We don't want a regime change."

Smith helped Cantor sit up and brushed him with both hands, like a butler plumping a pillow. "We think you are very presidential."

Jones continued. "We like the idea of setting this up as a tax-exempt religious organization. That was brilliant. Our company would never have thought of that in a million years. And believe me, we have our hand in a lot of different businesses."

"The upside potential is enormous," Williams bubbled. "The Catholic church, for example, generates more revenue than any global corporation. If we could siphon their customer base as they decline—"

"And we can have tie-ins, like food, clothing, and paraphernalia," Jones said. "Think of it — the equivalent of halal foods for true believers. Globally, halal products are a two-trillion-dollar industry. The kosher business is only about $165 billion, but that's still a lot."

"And we'll have labor laws on our side," Smith said. "Our true believers can't be fired for their religion in the U.S. Under current rulings, we'll be able to lobby government and retain tax-exempt status."

Williams seemed effervescent. "To be compliant, we may need to have a Sunday school and regular services. But that's probably a good thing because we can use it for training and recruitment of children."

"The business strategy helps get closure with your ex-wife. I've grown to detest that woman. We can hijack all her followers, and destroy her," Smith said.

Cantor lifted off the edge of the table, stood on shaky legs, and moved to the chair where he had been sitting, still gritting his teeth from back pain. He started to say something, halted, thought better of it, then spoke with carefully crafted words. "I understand your point of view. We will do anything—"

"We want a tour of your partner's facility, the Xanadu NeuroLab," Williams said. "Please set it up for us in the next few days. Then we want to look at your operation in Charleston."

"Ah," Cantor said. "The candy factory."

# CHAPTER 38
# LAVEAU

*"Who we are" is a belief;*
*"What we might become" is a hope or fear.*
—*Canduka Cantor*

It was just after 3 a.m. in Scratch Tavern. Ali watched Lazare escort the last patron out the door before locking up and switching off the overhead lights and video screens. Blue under-the-bar LEDs gave the great room a ghostly glow, while a neon snake guarding the door bounced beams across mirrors, mottling their faces as it cycled from red to green to gold. Lazare began speaking in a deep, almost hypnotic voice as he lit two candles and placed them on the bar.

"Vodou is mostly good," he said. It make de balance in life with de world, I know it. Ever body has a spirit dat owns de head. Is called *met tet*. Some are big spirits; some little. You are lucky. Laveau owns your head. She is big spirit, and she has plans for you. Dis could be good or could be bad."

"Why are you helping me?" Ali asked.

"Laveau tell me tings. Dat is all. Maybe she speak to you."

Ali did not quite know what to make of these words until he began drinking the herbal tea Lazare gave him. The more tea he drank, the more sense it all made. He gripped the counter when the floor beneath his feet seemed to wobble.

Lazare put a picture of Laveau on the counter. The beautiful woman held a snake—a python—that wrapped around her arms and shoulders. In one hand, she held a feather.

"Laveau is dead now. She is in many places. She is in one place. You must know her when she appears," Lazare said.

He showed Ali a cloth pouch. "I make for you de gris-gris."

Ali inspected the contents. It was filled with potions and small artifacts, including jewelry. A feeling came over him. He wanted to be powerful like Lazare. He pulled out a skull ring and tried it on his right finger.

"And I make dis," Lazare said. He showed Ali a humanoid figure.

"Is this a ginger root?" Ali asked.

"No, no. Dis mandrake. Dis alive and yells at you when you pulls it from de ground. It takes magic from de earth. We make it into a doll. It has powerful spell."

"What should I do with these things?" Ali asked.

"You keep. Laveau will tell you when you need dem. She give three powers. You 'ave power of money from de bad man ..."

"The untraceable netcard."

"Yes. And you 'ave de sleep of death."

"The potion and the ring?"

"Yes. And you 'ave de *bocio*."

"The doll made of mandrake root?"

"Yes. Respect de power of de *bocio*. It can be a person. It can control de mind. And it can make you crazy."

# CHAPTER 39
## PANCAKES, PURINES, AND PI

Sundar felt like he was re-living his teenage dating years. He had a car; she didn't. He had a phone; she didn't. He was dressed and ready to go; he knew she wasn't.

The only way to communicate with Diana Holkam was directly, in person. When he showed up on her doorstep and knocked, he saw her eyes peeking from the window.

"I'd like to take you out to lunch," he said through a crack in the door. I would have called ahead, but—" The portal opened wider, and he saw the smiling face. "Can I come in?"

"I don't think that's wise," she said. "Nadia doesn't like strangers, and she told me about your encounter."

"Yes. It didn't go well."

"I accept your offer for lunch as long as we don't go too far. Nadia panics if I leave her for very long."

"There's a place nearby, just outside town. It's not fancy. We can go there."

"Perfect," she beamed. "You can sit on the porch or wander through the garden while I get ready. I'll be only a few minutes."

"Great," Sundar said. "I'll walk around."

After Diana closed the door, Sundar returned to his car, took off his jacket, and got a bottle of water from the built-in cooler. He carried it with him while he explored the yard, occasionally sipping to keep hydrated in the warm sun.

He noticed a large gray metal box behind the house, which he assumed was the septic monitoring system collecting data for Rosa Alcott's analyses. Two lines came into it from a pole near the street: one was power, the other, data.

The apiary, which tilted like the Tower of Pisa when he last saw it, was now upright and scrubbed clean. He saw a few insects buzzing around it.

*Yes, the bees are coming back. I'll have to compliment her on that.*

This was the first time he noticed the graves. He stepped closer to read inscriptions on the stones, but before he could get close enough, he heard the front door open.

"I'm ready," Diana said.

He turned to look at her, admiring the trim body filling the print dress, and the perky face wearing an impish smile. "You look lovely," he said.

She blushed. Then, after a moment, said, "Shall we go?"

As he walked her to the car, he pointed at the graves. "Your family?"

"Yes. Papa and Mama."

"What's with the iron rods? The coils make them look like radio antennas from Hell. I see they're around one of the stones, but not the other."

"Oh," she said. "It's actually part of an antique iron bed. Mama wanted to be buried inside it. She was superstitious, and Papa was indulgent."

"Curious. Where did she get this idea?"

"She cared for the town's founder, Chester Kelsey, who lived to be 113 years old. Mr. Kelsey claimed there was a lot of magical energy running through Assurance, and a certain configuration of iron would dissipate the energy of the vortex and protect you. He commissioned special beds that he called *MagnaTectors*. Papa had more of a scientific mind and didn't believe that nonsense, which is why there isn't anything special around his stone. He loved Mama and did what she asked."

"I see. A magnetic vortex. You can never be too careful."

She poked him in the arm. "It's mountain magic. I don't believe in it either, but Nadia's working on a history of Assurance, and I've been reading her manuscript, trying to understand her mind. Most of what I know about it comes from her writing."

He opened the car door and helped her in as they continued to talk.

"Your mother sounds like she was an interesting person."

"You mean peculiar, don't you?"

"Well ..."

"She died when I was young. Mama would believe anything. Papa once told me there was a traveling salesman who claimed to have a magic box. He would take Polaroid pictures and put them in the box, and they would come out in funny colors. He said by looking at the colors he could diagnose peoples' auras and fix them with an elixir that cost ten dollars."

Sundar directed the car to a destination outside Assurance. When they crossed the bridge, he turned back to Diana. "What did the MagnaTector cost?"

She laughed. "Nothing. They came with the house that Kelsey bequeathed to Mama. Papa said Kelsey wanted to protect Mama from the power."

"You mean magnetism or magic or whatever you call it?"

"No. The power to change the world. He had this obsession. This theory. He wanted to harness the magic of this spot—a spot where ley lines cross, creating a vortex."

"But then he wanted to be protected from it?"

"Yeah. Nothing Kelsey did makes sense to me. My background is science, not *woo-woo* magic. But Mama drank the Kool-Aid as they say."

The spit-shined black Mercedes SUV carrying Sundar and Diana pulled up in front of a restaurant of indefinite age and precarious frontier-style construction. Hewn log walls and a stone chimney bucked up a wavy tin roof. The road sign read "The Groaning Griddle." There were no other cars in a small parking lot that appeared to be paved with river pebbles and bordered with hitching posts.

Before he commanded the car door to open, Sundar decided to caveat his choice of eating establishments. "I've never actually been inside, but it looks ... um ... authentic. Berky told me about it."

"Papa used to come here when I was growing up. It'll be fine," she said, patting his arm.

They stopped to read the sign near the entrance:

> Bacon is red,
>
> Griddlecakes is brown,
>
> Riming is hard,
>
> Eat here.

"The proprietor is a would-be poet," he said.

They entered into a room filled with six empty tables. Only one of them, near a window, was set with plates, utensils, and empty glasses as if awaiting their arrival.

"Halloo," Sundar shouted.

Noises issued from the kitchen, but no waiter. They sat down.

"Be there in a jiff," a voice yelled from the back.

Sundar continued a conversation that had begun on the drive over. He talked about his work and his enthusiasm for genetic modification. Diana spoke of her training at Duke, and how mathematics and biochemistry ignited her interest in science.

Sundar's mind wandered.

*My God, this woman actually knows that purines are not a type of dog food and that mathematicians don't keep pi in the fridge! She is beautiful. She is delightful.*

He imagined Diana Holkam as a version of his beloved, deceased wife, Abha. He remembered how her lips pressed into a Mona Lisa smile whenever he said something clever, and how her sharp intellect engaged whenever he talked science. In Diana's fine-boned face he saw the same curiosity, intelligence, and facial expressions.

"Missy Nadia?"

The voice came from behind—the distorted figure of a waitress reflected in his empty glass. He watched Diana's face grow into a smile as she responded.

"Nadia's back home. Hello again."

The waitress moved toward the center of the table and slow-eyed Sundar. "Name's Jancie," she said. "This is my place. I been here since creation. I can tell you so many stories—"

"I've heard great things about this pancake house," Sundar said, impatient to return to his intimate tête-à-tête. "Can we get some? Please?"

Jancie anchored an ancient, wrinkled hand on her hip and looked Sundar in the eyes. "Hon, is that what you sees? A pancake house?"

He smirked. "Well, the sign—"

"This is where you starts yer day, and the rest o' yer life."

"That's great. Can we get some pancakes?"

"They's griddle cakes, hon. You can't get 'em without a heap of advice."

"Okay."

"This here's a fine lady. But fragile. You needs to help her. She's your future. I sees it. Treat her right." She put the order pad into her apron pocket and walked away. "Ain't no need to order. You'll like what I dish out."

Sundar tried to gauge Diana's reaction. "Well, that was ... interesting."

"I like her."

"Yeah. She has true grit, as they say. I'm sure they sell that here, too."

"That's *grits*. You were saying?"

"What?"

"About your work. About Xanadu."

"Oh, right. We made a real scientific breakthrough—the kind that comes once a century. The company found a very interesting gene that ties to behavior and the structure of the human brain. People will be amazed when the lab goes public with the news."

He felt the warmth of her hand. "That's great, Sundar."

She said nothing more. Her touch lingered on his arm. Her eyes fixed on his. Eventually, he felt the need to brag. "In order to exploit the gene and make it behave the way we want, we needed it to work with other gene complexes, and make changes in living organisms. The key is to manipulate certain transposable elements of the genome."

"Transposable?"

"They move around."

"It sounds complicated."

"It is."

"How do you control all the different possibilities?"

*She is so incredibly bright!*

He held up a finger as if making a point to a student. "We use a template as a reference."

"You measure against a known pattern?"

"Correct."

"Where do you get this pattern?"

"We simply find a person who has the right benchmark behavior. We use their genes as the template."

*She gets it! I can see it in her eyes!*

"But they'd need to agree, right?"

"Oh, of course, we'd need a written agreement. And we have one. It's necessary to avoid any legal complications."

"Do you put the actual genetic sequences and transcription processes in the patent?"

"Frankly, I'm new to Xanadu, so I'm still learning the business side. I believe Xanadu's patents address the generic process, and we keep the specifics as trade secrets."

"So, you could use other people as the template, and no one would ever know? People like Nadia?"

"True, but doing so would create a risk for the enterprise."

Diana smiled again, and in that smile, Sundar saw Abha's face.

"Let me see if I've got this right," Diana said. "Everyone has this gene."

"Yes. It's what makes us human."

"So, Xanadu's work addresses an underlying physical reality."

The fingers on his open palms fibrillated in a come-to-me gesture. "Yes. Go on."

"But the reality can be processed—or expressed—in different ways," she said.

"Right!" His grin widened, and his eyes dwelled on the curve of her mouth. "That part is actually called epigenetics. It's not about modifying DNA per se; it's about changing how cells *read* the genes in the DNA. Imagine, for example, a woman wearing bib overalls and no makeup. Now think of that same woman wearing lipstick, high heels, and a designer dress. She has not changed the core of who she is, but she has dramatically changed the way others see her and the way she expresses herself. Epigenetics is a way of dressing up the genes in a different way. It can produce big physical changes or even big behavioral changes, and these "new clothes" can be handed down to subsequent generations."

Her response was quick. "It's sort of like Picasso looking at a scene of Barcelona and using it to structure the painting of a crouching beggar."

Sundar's eyes glistened. "Precisely."

"Science becomes art! Very exciting. It could have a great impact."

"I am so glad you approve. I feel as though we—"

"I'd love to see your lab," she said. "I want to see Xanadu."

He acquiesced as she turned his hand over, opened it, and traced erotic circles with the gentle touch of a finger.

"Did you know I can read your palm? This is the hand that'll guide us into the future," she said. "Help me understand it."

He nodded. "I have a full calendar for this week. We can do it next week. I'll show you the lab and the future."

She lifted his hand to her lips and kissed it. "My hero."

# CHAPTER 40
# XANADU

*In the past, art transmitted culture. In the future, science and engineering will do the job.*
—*Canduka Cantor*

The men from GRIP, all dressed in over-sized black suits and red power ties, assembled beneath a 20-foot metal ceiling near an island of equipment and fixtures that resembled a starship's plumbing system. The lab team stood apart from the group on an elevated ramp. The sign behind them above the exit to the lobby read: "Xanadu—*From memes to genes, for your pleasure.*"

Berky spoke first. "Welcome, gentlemen. On my left is Dr. Gregor Popkins, an expert in AI and neural regeneration. On my right is my partner, Canduka Cantor, and my Lab Director, Sundar Rao. Sundar will be your guide this afternoon."

Sundar fiddled with the adhesive nametag on the breast of his elbow-patch jacket. It was coming loose, so he tried to smooth it against the white linen fabric. Berky wanted the tags as a backup in case the guests couldn't see the fine print on picture badges that drooped from lanyards around each of their necks.

Sundar knew the trick to confidence in front of a group was to be in command of your subject and talk to a single, selected individual in the audience. He decided to focus on the tall, scar-faced man who looked like a cartoon thug. He cleared his throat and was about to speak when Berky pressed his arm to stop.

"Before I hand you off," Berky said, "let me give you a quick overview."

Smith and Williams were still gawking at the equipment and blinking lights, but Taylor made a jaded frown below his broken nose. He returned Sundar's gaze with a nod and a wink.

"What we're trying to do here is easy to describe but difficult to execute," Berky said, "but God has led us to a solution—one that synthesizes breakthroughs in genetics, epigenetics, neural regeneration, big data analytics, and artificial intelligence, or *AI*. I hope you appreciate that."

Sundar interrupted when he spotted a potential disaster. "Don't touch anything!" he yelled. Taylor curled his lips in a quiet snarl but withdrew his hand from a control panel on the Master Input Sample Sequencer. They locked eyes. Sundar thought: *Moron alert.*

Berky tugged at the collar of his red polo shirt and took a step forward on sneakered feet. He gave a barely discernable head wag, which Sundar interpreted as "Cool it," then continued:

"Here's the big idea: we infect people with the desired behavior and make it heritable."

"Can *any* behavior be passed on in this way?" Williams said.

"In theory, yes," Berky said. "But we need to start with the right template."

Sundar raised a finger, like a professor encouraging a student. "That's a key insight. Other researchers have gotten mired in the complexity of the problem and only focused on simple behaviors. Xanadu has a much more holistic approach. We start by finding people who approximate the ideal behavior—desirable or undesirable—we call it the Behavior Under Test. Then, we analyze differences in RNA, DNA, and histones, and build on that. These differences become the template. We introduce the template into a payload compound and deliver it to the nervous system orally."

"They swallow it?" Williams said.

Sundar nodded. "Precisely."

"As you might expect," Berky said, "defining a template is computationally expensive. That's why we have a supercomputer farm on site, tons of fast storage, and our own power plant, cooled by the South Prong River."

"And fish."

Heads turned toward the speaker, Taylor, who had his nose close to a clear plastic tube. Inside the container, an odd-looking fish swam against an invisible current.

The fish turned and smiled.

"Gaaah!" Taylor backed away from the tube and darted a hand to the bulge under his jacket. "I've never seen that before."

"Oh, that," Berky said. "That's our model organism. It's an engineered species we call Chester T. Kelsey, in honor of the founder of a nearby town. We use that fish to test our ideas."

"Yeah, but it smiled."

Popkins piped in. "We make human cells into fish brains. Some muscles, also."

"We use a lot of these fish on a weekly basis," Berky said. "They are very prolific. We produce so many fish we have to dispose of them on the open market. They've become a mini revenue stream for us."

Sundar watched Taylor turn pale.

Popkins, bare legs and sneakers protruding below a knee-length white lab coat, couldn't seem to resist pulling Taylor's chain. "And they taste good if you eat them with fava beans and nice chianti." He popped his eyes and flicked his tongue, in a deft impression of Hannibal Lecter.

Sundar led the group into a canyon of computer racks. He stopped at a place where a nest of data and power cables cross-linked to a hole in the floor and into an open equipment stack. Next to the stack was a bank of what looked like ten hot water heaters topped with chrome-plated plumbing. He faced the group and invited them to gaze upon the skyline of the future.

"This is probably the best place to see some of the technology up close." He gave Taylor a warning look as the man tugged at a hanging cable. "Please be careful. This server is no different from the hundreds of others in this room. The ten tanks attached to the floor are optical cryo-coolers we use to chill our quantum computers to about ten millikelvin degrees—colder than the background radiation of space, and nearly as cold as a large black hole. They have no moving parts."

"What's the steam coming out of the top?" Williams asked.

"It's nitrogen venting. This unit is being repaired. You can hold your hand above the steam to feel the cold, but don't touch the frosted metal. Your skin will stick."

As the group huddled around the unit, Sundar issued a warning, "Don't fall into the hole in the floor tile. It's a two and a half-foot drop, so watch out."

Smith backed away from the hole, but Taylor went to the edge and looked down.

"Please stay away from there," Sundar said. He was smiling, but the words were a forceful command rather than a request.

Taylor was annoyed. "I've seen data centers before," he said. "We have our own, and it's bigger than this."

"Well," Sundar said, "Do you have a traditional data center?"

"It's as traditional as this one," Taylor said. "Everything here is familiar—except maybe the cooling tanks."

"Can your data center think?" Sundar said.

"It's a bunch of computers. Of course, it can think," Taylor said.

"I mean, can it *Think*? Is it sentient?"

"What are you saying?"

Sundar smiled as if delighted for the segue. "This is the heart of Xanadu—an artificial intelligence system we call *Kublai Khan*. It controls our processes, analyzes our data, and directs our research. The AI works faster and smarter than humans and leads us to the right answers."

Taylor was dismissive. "Yeah, I saw the movie."

"Maybe you'd be more impressed if I told you this is how we earn a fantastic margin on our research. If the results weren't correct, the pharma companies wouldn't pay us the way they do."

"Don't these companies have their own data centers?" Taylor said.

"Not like this one. This is a virtual brain—a brain that connects the entire center and influences every widget in the lab. It's special. We use a quantum computer to speed up machine learning algorithms. It allows us to evaluate lots of alternative futures simultaneously. Kublai Khan is no longer the slave of 'If-Then' logic. That's because it works as we do, using a very large number of inputs, which it weights, based on a lifetime of accelerated experience, to produce the answers we need."

Taylor seemed skeptical. "The right answers?"

"We trust, and we test," Sundar said. He paused for a moment as he framed a more complicated answer. "I know you are all very curious, so I'll lay out the case in more detail. It's true we no longer use computer code to determine whether the logic is flawed. The data is as complex as your body's molecular machinery, and the analytical method is as subtle as the one your brain uses to make decisions. As a result, we can no longer ask, 'How did you get that answer?' We have to trust that the answer Kublai Khan gives is correct. From time to time, we can test the correctness through experiments. But in general, this approach has given us extraordinary results and allowed us to deal with genomic complexity. We've made the tradeoff between certainty and quick answers, and it has been profitable."

"Very impressive," Williams said.

Smith seemed noncommittal.

Taylor turned away and muttered, "Bullshit."

"You are skeptical, Mr. Taylor," Sundar said. "What's the problem?"

"If you ask me why I did something, I can tell you. 'Why'd I eat breakfast this morning?' 'Because I was hungry.' 'Why'd I buy a newspaper?' 'Because I wanted to read the news.' This AI brain of yours is a murky mystery. And you're letting it lead your company."

Sundar thought a moment. "I think you're confused about the superiority of human logic. Rationality is the fictional story we tell ourselves when someone asks 'Why?' When you look deeper, you see it's a ruse. Human brains try to make sense of a world that's complex and chaotic. To simplify, they sometimes distort reality. This distortion is how we get mass murderers, delusional schizophrenics, suicides, and conspiracy theorists. Our AI system is more robust than that."

Rosa Alcott was oblivious to Sundar and the GRIP men when they entered the holographic bay—a 50-foot square cavern that allowed a researcher to "shrink" to the size of a DNA base. Her eyes were on three-dimensional images of nucleotides that danced above projection platforms, wooing each other with hydrogen bonds as they rotated and stretched to the 20-foot ceiling, but her mind drifted to her relationship with Berky—a relationship increasingly fraught with misogyny, physical danger, and the very real threat of financial catastrophe.

She had joined the Xanadu team with a freshly minted Ph.D., references from two Nobel laureates, and dreams of curing human behavioral diseases. But now the future—the bright future of scientific recognition and financial success—seemed less likely with every passing day. Berky refused to let her publish, saying it would compromise trade secrets. He initially promised stock in Xanadu as a reward for her technical achievements, but when she spurned his sexual advances, he started finding ways to dilute her holdings. Her small savings from prize money won as a graduate student, all of which she had invested in Xanadu, could vanish on Berky's whim.

Her brain pulled away from these unpleasant thoughts to consider how Sundar Rao tapped into the eternal feminine to eliminate genetic drift. It was an exceedingly clever idea. Mitochondrial DNA, unlike DNA in a cell's nucleus, is passed almost exclusively from mother to child. It was this feminine essence woven into cellular organelles that Sundar endowed with special restorative powers—by creating error detection and correction templates made almost entirely of synthetic nucleotides not found in nature.

She was beginning to appreciate the complexity of what Sundar had done, and its potential for good, when a hand patted her shoulder and broke her trance. A rough voice said, "Whatcha doin' Hon?"

She turned to see the face of a boxer, with a disfigured nose and a scar on his cheek. The man squeezed her with a giant hand. He moved his face close to hers and whispered: "Looks interesting."

"Mr. Taylor! Stop!"

Sundar stepped quickly onto the control platform and grabbed Taylor's wrist. "She's performing a critical analysis. Please don't interrupt her."

Taylor looked like he was ready to swat him, like a fly, but Smith signaled with a sideways flick of a thumb, and Taylor backed away.

Sundar raised his hurry-up "tour guide" voice: "Come. We have other areas to cover; we have to move on."

As Sundar led the group out of the bay, Rosa caught his eye and mouthed the words, "Thank you."

Marcy and Ali drove their Ford rental car past a signpost in the forest: "Welcome to Cherokee."

"I've been here before. This place isn't far from the lab. It's touristy, but we should be invisible," Marcy said.

Ali pointed to the right—an area with a small earthen parking lot, picnic tables, a central log structure, and several surrounding huts. "There. A campground with cabins."

"Let's check in," she said. "We can spend some time planning and scouting. I have an idea on how we can get inside."

"Ah. Scouts," he said with a smile. "I was a Bangladesh Scout once. Were you ever a scout?"

Her mind was elsewhere. She pulled up in front of the office, stopped the engine, but waited before unbuckling. "You know I'm taking a big risk here. If GRIP found out I was working with you, I'm not sure what they'd do. Probably kill me."

His smile faded. "Why do it?"

"GRIP is still working for me, but they aren't getting answers quick enough. As long as we're careful, and stay below their radar, I'll be okay. This is about the future. We need to stop Xanadu. If I get some hard evidence, I can ask for a legal injunction and halt them in their tracks with a lawsuit."

"Why not go to the FBI?"

"Too many risks, especially if Cantor and Benson are well connected. A civil suit would do a lot more to expose them than a criminal case, which could take months or years to construct. We need to act quickly."

"And get some marshmallows."

"What?"

"We are at a camp. I heard that in the U.S., if you have a campfire, you're supposed to roast marshmallows. That's what scouts do."

"I was never a Girl Scout. I never liked cooking. When they consolidated the Scouts, I earned the 'Bitch Badge' and drove the boys nuts."

# CHAPTER 41
# THUNDER, ICE, AND LIGHTNING

Thunder grumbled in the thickening night air. Sundar felt Diana gently touch his shoulder as he stopped the vehicle at the security gate. Beyond the driver-side window, a face emerged from the shadows. Occasional flashes of dry lightning lit the red, black, and silver hues of the guard's face paint.

Yon Yokopuche peered into the car. "Evenin'. What've we got here?"

"Hi Yon," Sundar said. "I have a guest. I'm taking her on an after-hours tour of the lab."

"Does Mr. Benson know?"

"He and I discussed improving relations with our neighbors. That's what I'm doing."

"Great. Some of the guys on the reservation said they'd like to see the lab, too. Can I bring them in sometime?"

Sundar drummed his fingers on the dashboard and looked ahead but didn't answer.

After an awkward moment: "Well, I can give her a temporary badge, and you can sign her in." He shoved a pen and clipboard through the open window.

Sundar completed the log entry, handed it back, then received Diana's badge. He looked a hundred yards ahead to the building. "Is that a police car parked in my spot?"

"Naw. That's ICE agents. Billy Drimple was on duty when they came in. He said he didn't think you'd be back, so he let 'em park in your spot. He didn't know how particular you are about the parking."

"Are they here to see me? My H1-B visa is still good."

"Don't know. They're talking to Reggie about security stuff."

"Thanks." Sundar took control and put the SUV in gear.

The painted face leaned in. "Let me know if you need to hide out on the reservation. ICE'll never find you there."

"I don't think that will be—"

"And don't forget to turn on the visitor light when you go in." He raised the gate.

Sundar drove ahead. "That was Yon. He's six percent Cherokee and proud of it. Berky lets him dress the part. I hope he didn't frighten you."

Diana laughed. "You forget I grew up here."

Sundar drove the winding road through security barriers, to the crest of a hill that led down to an immense two-story structure with few windows. The road skated a transformer yard and a construction zone that butted against the perimeter fence and extended to the side of the building.

He steered around a roving security robot and edged along loading docks and mechanical outbuildings to get to executive parking.

The Homeland Security van occupied Sundar's designated parking space, so he pulled into Berky's spot. He walked Diana to the entrance, punched in a security code, and went in.

They passed two blond, blue-eyed ICE agents in the hall, interrogating Reggie Edevane. The agents, whose name tags read *Nguyen* and *Dzaja*, caressed their shoulder holsters as he passed them by.

Sundar smiled at Reggie. The British-born security director was doing a credible imitation of a North Carolina southern accent. He winked as Sundar passed. The agents didn't seem to notice. Near their feet, Schrodinger batted around a discarded ball of paper.

Sundar badged into the lab's restricted access area. Diana and Schrodinger followed him in. He closed the security door but left the visitor warning light off to avoid drawing attention. Inside, he released a long exhale, thankful he was not on ICE's hit list. He looked at Diana and smiled. "This is where the magic happens."

Nature seemed to complain. A sudden torrent of rain beat on the lab's high tin roof. Lights flickered for a fraction of a second, and a dissipated rumble of thunder followed. Schrodinger meowed in response. Diana picked up the cat and tried to soothe its nerves. "It's impressive—all this equipment, and blinking lights," she said. "Right out of a sci-fi film."

Sundar felt the pride in his voice when he said, "The lab's achieved a high degree of automation. This room analyzes biological samples on a scale no other lab can match, and we do it with just a handful of people."

He watched Diana take it in. She seemed mesmerized by rows of robotic arms moving with mechanical precision.

He continued. "Some of this equipment we've modified from automobile manufacturing."

"All these arms moving around ... it's like robots rap dancing," she said.

Sundar nodded. "They move bits of tissue and liquid. And you're right. It *is* choreographed. That conveyor transports samples from station to station. The big cubes with lights are automated sorters. All these systems sense their environment. They collaborate on an industrial network, guided by our AI system, Kublai Khan."

She cocked her head. "What's the purpose?"

"We sell research to pharmaceutical companies, for new gene therapies and that sort of thing. We can do it a lot cheaper than they can. That generates revenue and gives us a big margin for breakthrough R&D."

"What does your crystal ball say about the future?"

Sundar hesitated, trying to frame an answer short on detail. "We want to fix behavioral disorders and make those fixes permanent—using genetic and epigenetic engineering."

"Will this help my sister?"

"Yes," he said.

At the main lab entrance, the door blew open, pouring wind and rain into the entry hall. Reggie saw Yon Yakopuche stumble inside, clutching a tablet computer, wet as the South Prong River. Yon fought to close the door, then moved toward them.

The ICE agents saw a dripping man with a painted face and Colt revolvers on each hip approaching at speed. They drew their weapons.

Reggie blocked their field of fire. "Hold on, cowboys. He's with me." They lowered their guns.

He turned to Yon. "What have you got?"

Yon punched up a video stream on the tablet. "An intruder, Boss. He's in the processing lab."

"How'd he get in?" Reggie said.

"He must've climbed the new section of fence, then gone through the power station."

As if their minds were telepathically linked, the ICE agents spoke in unison, "We'll get him."

Before Reggie could object, Yon blocked their movement toward the inner lab. "They're not cleared, are they?"

Reggie shook his head. "No."

One of the officers shoved Yon. "Listen, Geronimo, a foreign entity may be in the neighborhood, and could be dangerous. That's why we're here. Open this door."

"An 'entity'?" Yon said. "I seen the movie, and it was a ghost."

"Open the door. If he can't prove he's American, he's ours. We'll take him down."

Yon put a double-sized hand on the officer's shoulder. "Looks like I'm the only real American here, chief. Anyways, unless you have a warrant, you need to stay put. Right, Reggie?"

"Right. Y'all need a warrant."

Yon badged through the inner door.

Reggie shrugged at the glaring agents. "What can I do? We have too many chiefs and not enough Indians."

Yon muttered to himself as he hit the button for the Uncleared Visitor lights. "Dammit, Sundar!" Rotating red beacons illuminated the ceiling and set the rhythm for the robotic rap show.

Yon stripped from the waist up, exposing a heavily tattooed chest, then dropped his wet uniform and undershirt in a puddle by the door. He put on his backpack with a diagonal chest strap, like a bandolier.

He cried a war whoop, drew a Colt single action, twirled it three times, and plopped the gun back into the holster. He did the same thing with the other Colt. Then he did a double twirl. He could see Reggie and the ICE agents peering wide-eyed through the window on the door. He flexed his arm muscles for them, in a show of strength, then moved out of their direct view.

Sundar felt Diana clutch his arm. "What just happened?" she said.

"That's the visitor warning light. I forgot to turn it on. Maybe someone else noticed you were here. It's nothing."

A yell came from the other side of the lab, near the entrance.

"Look, Sundar, maybe we should do this tour another time," she said.

"It'll be fine. Just a glitch."

Lights flickered, followed by thunder.

Another yell came from the front. It overwhelmed the whirr of robotic motors and the steady rumble of conveyors. On the opposite side of the lab, they saw a shadowy figure pop up from behind a sorter, then duck down. After a few moments, Yon stepped toward them from the direction of the entrance. He was naked from the belt up, barefoot, and chanting.

"*Yo, yo, yohanay. Woooh! Wooo-aah! Woooh!*"

He stopped in front of Sundar and Diana and went quiet for a moment. A sheepish grin crept across his face.

"I put on the flasher, 'cause you didn't."

"Sorry. I forgot," Sundar said. "What's going on?"

"There's an intruder." He took the tablet computer out of his backpack and watched the video stream from security cameras. "I think he's hiding around one of the sorters, but I'm going to catch him. I'm a good tracker."

*Boom!* Thunder echoed through the lab.

*Boom! Boom!* Schrodinger let out a blood-curdling yowl and leaped from Diana's arms. Ceiling lights in the lab flickered and went dark. Red emergency lights blinked on. The battery-operated visitor lights still flashed to their own beat.

"Wi-fi's down. I lost him. You two stay here." Yon drew both his guns, spun them, and aimed toward the darkness. He moved out of view, lost in red-hued shadows.

"I think we should leave," Sundar said. "We can go out through the server farm. Don't worry about the cat. He knows his way around. We can find him later."

Diana followed Sundar, stepping around equipment, and came face-to-face with a gun-toting intruder. He was about 5 feet tall, had a dark complexion, wore a black hoodie, and had a patch over one eye.

"I won't hurt you if you do what I say," he said.

They moved at gunpoint into a glass-enclosed room.

The first thing Diana noticed when she entered was the box—Nadia's box. It sat on an oak credenza, sandwiched between a model protein, a framed *Dear Abby* column entitled "Perfect World," and an assorted display of wigs and fake mustaches. There was a teapot on one end of the credenza, with a top in the shape of a dormouse. On the other end was a carved wooden nameplate that read Berky Benson, CEO.

As the intruder moved toward the desk, Diana placed her raincoat over the box. Sundar noticed the move, but the intruder appeared distracted by the laptop.

"Is that the password?"

Sundar split his attention between the gun and the sticky note on the back of the screen. "It's probably just a reminder of some sort. Nothing more."

"Type it in," the intruder said.

Sundar went to the laptop and typed "Ichthy." The desktop came up.

"Now step away."

Diana watched the man unplug the machine with one hand and put it in his backpack. Then he ripped the desk phone from its cable.

"Sorry for the inconvenience," he said. "Please give me your communications devices." He took their netcards, stepped out of the room, and wedged furniture outside the door to lock them in.

Diana climbed a spiral metal staircase to the upper floor of Berky's office, which rose like a glass tower in the center of the lab. From this high perch, she and Sundar could see the vast expanse of technology. Double-paned glass muffled all exterior sounds—except for rain, which hit the tin roof like jazz drum brushes.

Emergency lighting cast a surreal finish on the landscape below. Test equipment monitoring the quantum machine resembled a dark octopus, extending tentacles through an opening in the floor on one side, and into the belly of a rack on the other. Distant robotic arms, poised for action, awaited the power that would bring them to life again.

"This is his bedroom," Sundar said. "How pathetic."

Diana didn't reply. She fixed her eyes on the scene below, looking for movement.

Sundar continued to rove and narrate. "The man is worth over a billion dollars, but he sleeps on a cot above his office. And what's with all these pictures of women's feet?"

Diana turned to look at the scene and felt perspiration forming on her upper lip. Pictures of feet printed on paper filled the wall near the narrow cot. The montage included a few headshots of women with half-bitten ears. In the geometric center of the group was what looked like a crime-scene photo—a woman's body on a blood-pooled kitchen floor.

Nausea gripped her. To regain her focus, she turned back to the floor below, where dark fish darted to and fro in Kelsey tubes, no longer constrained by the constant flow of water. It was the Twilight Zone encroaching on a corner of the lab where smiling fish claimed kinship with Zoney Bamboney. She wondered if the blinking LEDs on the server racks amused these strange-looking fish.

"I think I've found Berky's entire wardrobe of red polo shirts," Sundar said.

On the lab floor, Schrodinger's dark form scampered across an aisle. Diana thought she could see movement elsewhere but was unsure.

Sundar moved next to her and looked out on the scene. "If they can't restore power soon, these computers will start shutting down. This is a big setback for us. At the moment, we don't have functioning backup power."

As if on cue, the ceiling lights flickered for a second, then returned to normal. All systems began to function.

Sundar held out his hand for a high five, but Diana didn't follow. She was distracted by the action below.

Yon Yakopuche and the intruder materialized from the shadows as equipment rebooted.

The two men were on opposite ends of a canyon bounded by computer racks. For a brief moment, they just stared at each other, like gunslingers in a high-tech version of the O.K. Corral. Yon let out a war whoop that was muffled inside the tower.

Diana yelled, waving her arms, "He's got a gun." Yon couldn't hear her through the laminated glass.

She saw Schrodinger scamper across the aisle.

A muffled thrum penetrated the glass as conveyor systems started up. Robot arms jerked to life.

On the far end of the canyon, Yon twirled his gun, then ran toward Berky's glass tower.

Instead of shooting at Yon, the intruder raised his gun and fired at the ceiling. Glass walls vibrated, and water dripped through the roof, wetting the tiles near the test equipment.

Yon stopped in his tracks, then ducked behind a rack.

Diana heard a muffled boom and saw a flash from behind a server. Two Kelsey tubes, hit in enfilade, exploded and dumped water and fish onto the raised floor.

Amid a momentary standoff, fish flopped near the door to Berky's office. The cat appeared out of nowhere, batting and pouncing on prey.

In the distance, Diana could see the two ICE officers, with guns drawn, moving toward Yon's position. Reggie was behind them, in a crouching walk, like Groucho Marx, knees bent, eyes wild. All he needed was a cigar to complete the effect.

The agents stopped near one of the racks, said some words, and pointed away from the action. Yon appeared from behind the metal cabinet, waved his arms, and seemed angry. Reggie shrugged and merely nodded. As the agents turned in the direction of the intruder, Yon signaled his displeasure with a raised arm and the flip of a middle finger aimed at the ICE agents. Then he stomped toward the front of the lab.

In the foreground, the cat sloshed through a pool of water, playing with wiggling fish, biting their heads.

The intruder poked his head from behind a rack. An ICE agent saw him, raised his gun, and fired.

The bullet shattered the glass on the tower's lower level. Sundar and Diana dropped to the floor for protection.

The startled cat yowled and leaped onto the test octopus. Electricity arced across its body. The shock propelled Schrodinger through the air and into the hole in the floor. There was another flash under the floor, and the lab went dark again.

In the red glow of emergency lights, Diana saw a shadow crawl from behind a rack, then slink through the open floor tile.

A flashlight probed the semi-darkness near the front of the lab and moved closer. It was Berky Benson.

The four men—Berky, two ICE agents, and Reggie—moved cautiously toward the glass tower. The agents led the way, pointing guns forward. Reggie was still in a crouch, but Berky seemed unafraid. The intruder was gone. The ICE agents moved away from the office, now in search mode.

Diana heard the crunch of glass as Berky and Reggie entered the lower office. Sundar shouted, "Halloo!"

Diana and Sundar moved down the spiral metal stairs to meet them.

"Thank goodness," Sundar said.

Berky stared at Diana. "She looks like her sister. Why did you bring her here?"

Sundar attempted a weak smile. "I made a promise. Diana wanted reassurance we mean no harm to Nadia. I thought showing her the lab would put our relationship on a better footing."

Berky glared at Sundar for a long moment, then curled his lips, as if fighting abdominal pain. "You're fired." He looked at Diana. "You should never have come here."

A flush spread across Sundar's face. "Listen, Berky. Don't do anything you'll regret. You need me to keep your experiments running."

"Machines do that."

"I don't—"

"Reggie," Berky said.

"Yes, Boss?"

"Escort these two out. I'm going to find Popkins." As Berky moved toward the shattered door, he looked back at Sundar and paused. "ICE will be after you now."

"I have an H1-B," Sundar said. "I can transfer to another employer."

"Not if I tell ICE you're a troublemaker. Leave the country while you can, or they'll put you in a camp. You've got a day. I owe you that."

"Only a day?"

"You parked in my spot." With that, Berky left.

"Terribly sorry," Reggie said. "Let's go. Follow me."

Behind his back, Diana picked up her raincoat, along with the box concealed beneath it. Sundar pilfered a wig and fake beard from Berky's credenza and stuffed them in his pockets. They followed Reggie out the door.

Amid water and shattered glass, fish still flopped on the floor. One of them hissed. In that sound, Diana thought she heard a whispered warning about the end of the world.

# CHAPTER 42
# TRADE CRAFT

The rain relented. Rivers washed over the Xanadu access roads. Diana, in the passenger seat, was still in shock as Sundar pulled up to the gate and stopped at the barrier. Reggie's car boxed them in from behind. Security lights glared through the windshield.

Reggie got out, walked to the guard shack, and spoke with Yon, who was back on duty. Then Reggie returned to his car, maneuvered a U-turn, and headed back toward the Xanadu campus.

Sundar rolled down the window as Yon approached.

"You'll need to give me your badge," Yon said. "You can't come back. Sorry."

Sundar pulled at the lanyard and handed it to Yon. "How'd you like a new car?" he said.

"Can't afford it, chief. By the way, I think you're a good guy, even if you didn't turn on the visitor light. But you shouldnta parked in Berky's spot."

"I'll trade you my Mercedes for your Chevy."

"Whoa! Why? Mine's a million years old."

"ICE will be after me. I've got maybe a one-day head start. If we trade cars, that'll give me two days. Maybe even a week."

"I dunno."

"It'll be legal. I paid for the car in cash. All the papers are in the glove compartment. I'll sign it over and draw up a bill of sale."

"Well, it's a really nice car."

"Yup."

"And I really would like to stick it to those ICE guys."

"That's the spirit."

Yon turned around in a circle, then let out a war whoop, directing it toward the sky. "You got a deal. You can hide out at the reservation for a while. They'll never find you there."

Diana coughed when she climbed into Yon's Chevy. It had the stink of an old sock and looked like it was used to haul trash.

As Sundar drove her home, she was still in shock from the guns, the intruders, the power outage, and the electrocuted cat. Still, she wondered about the implications for her sister. "I saw fish glow in the dark. Does that mean Berky will make Nadia glow when he applies the treatment?"

She had decided that small talk was the best way to help him forget he had been fired, would soon become a fugitive, and had just lost a really nice car in a bad trade.

Sundar's mind was still running on fumes. "No, no. We just use bioluminescence as a marker. It tells us the proper genetic sequence has been inserted for experiments. The fish are our target organism, our prototype. We'd— they would—never use the method on humans."

He crossed the bridge into Assurance, pulled up in front of her house, and helped her out of the car.

"Thanks," she said. "You are a true gentleman. It's been a wonderful evening, except for everything."

He didn't quite know what to say.

"I'm sorry for you," she said. She kissed him on the cheek, then walked toward the house.

# CHAPTER 43
# REVELATIONS

Diana waved goodbye from the porch. The moonless night was clear after the storm. She could see, floating above the southern horizon, the constellation resembling a teapot—Sagittarius. A meteor streaked across the western sky, writing a fiery message of danger and foreboding. Her universe had changed. What could she tell Nadia?

She went inside and knocked on her sister's bedroom door.

"You're back," Nadia said, matter-of-factly.

Diana entered and sat on the iron bed. "They say confession is good for the soul."

Nadia laughed. "I'm not your confessor."

"You know I love you. I'd do anything to help you."

Nadia's eyes closed into slits, and she wrinkled her nose. "Now you're making me nervous."

Diana cleared her throat. "Here's the thing. I have to leave again."

Emotion gripped Nadia's face. "Why?"

"Because I got you what you wanted."

"That makes no sense."

"I have the box." She unwrapped the package from her raincoat, and placed it on the bed, beside her sister.

Nadia caressed it like a lover. "Thank God."

"Berky will know it's missing in the morning and will come looking for it."

"Does he know you took it?"

"Not right now. There was an intruder in the lab."

"Maybe he'll go off on a wild goose chase."

"Not for long," Diana said. "ICE wants to find the intruder. They'll look through footage from security cameras and eventually work out what happened. I won't be safe, and neither will the box."

Nadia seemed stunned. "Shit."

"The beehive," Diana said.

"What about it?"

"I can hide the box there. They won't search the apiary."

"No, no," Nadia said. "Those poor bees! They don't like their home disturbed—just like me. And I won't be able to reach the box."

"If we put it in the house, Berky will find it. He'll turn the place upside down, looking for me. I need to leave. You should come with me."

"No!" Nadia fumed, and couldn't speak for three minutes. Finally, she said, "I'm the only reality in Assurance—the only thing that keeps it alive. Without me, the town will vanish. And I'm willing to endure Berky's torture to keep the dream safe."

"He tortured you?"

"He ... rapes my feet and licks my body like Schrodinger, the cat. But I can endure whatever he does to me if it saves the dream."

"My God, you're delusional. I'm going to carry you out of here myself if you don't go willingly."

Nadia picked up the knitting needle, pointed it at Diana, and started toward her. "You will not get me out of this house alive."

Diana backed away. "Calm down."

Nadia dropped the needle, eyes glistening. "I have to stay. Don't you see? The town meant the world to Papa."

"But the death of the town is what killed him. Right?" Diana said.

Nadia was silent for a moment, then said, "You disappointed him."

"*I* disappointed him? *Me*? He was just fine for a decade after I left. Are you trying to shift the blame?"

Nadia stiffened. "Assurance meant everything to him. And now it means everything to me. With every fiber of my being, I intend to preserve the history of the town and its artifacts. Help me. And show some respect for Papa."

Now it was Diana's turn to become emotional. "I'm sorry you won't leave this place—a place that seems to be run by a madman and haunted by ghosts. I'm sorry I wasn't able to help you more. Papa's dead, and you need to get over that. But you no longer have any say in my life. This is about *my* freedom. *I'm* the one who took the risk to get what *you* wanted, and *I'm* the one who will pay the price." She walked out, closed the bedroom door, and left her sister to stew.

It was past midnight. Diana returned to the bedroom and continued to argue with Nadia. They shouted at each other. Nadia shoved Diana against the wall.

There was a knock on the outside door, and they both went silent. Then, a second knock.

Diana turned the light off and spied through the blinds. She saw a strange car. Shadowy figures of a man and a woman moved on the porch.

"Stay in your room. I'll handle this," Diana said. "It's not Berky or any of his men, but they are outsiders. I don't want you going berserk again."

Diana closed her sister's bedroom door, walked down the stairs into the foyer, and stood near the entrance without opening the door. She tested the security chain before raising her voice in a challenge: "Who's there?"

A female voice answered. "We're friends. Are you Nadia?"

"Nadia's not here. I'm her twin sister, Diana, and you are not my friends."

"We need to talk. It's about Xanadu Lab, and what they're trying to do to you. To us."

Diana cracked the door open. The woman wore a raincoat. Her wet, dark hair draped across her black face like a tangled web. The olive-skinned man was tall and wore a water-soaked hoodie. He had one eye.

"You broke into the lab," Diana said.

"Yes," the man said. "My name is Ali."

"We have a laptop, and evidence you'll want to see," the woman said. "My name is Marcy. We found your address and information about you and your sister in Berky's emails."

"Go away." She shut the door, closed her eyes, and when curiosity overcame her, she opened the door again. The two shadowy people were still standing on the porch. "Why should I believe you?"

"Because," Ali said, "your sister is in danger. We have computer files and email records to prove it."

Diana opened the door.

Marcy and Ali spent the early morning laying out the case for Diana, based on files from Berky's laptop. Xanadu, in partnership with the Cantor Tax Exempt Spiritual Community, intended to modify humans on a large scale.

The evidence seemed overwhelming. Xanadu Lab posed an existential threat—to her sister and others.

"We should take this to the police," Diana said.

Marcy shook her head. "We can't do that. They'll say we obtained the information illegally, and Berky will say we altered the data. We don't have anything actionable."

"If they know I'm involved," Ali said, "ICE will use this to hunt me down. It will be Guantanamo, for sure."

"You, Diana, are the wild card," Marcy said. "You are Nadia's twin. You're the outlier. You're the monkey wrench."

"We need to slow them down, so we have a chance at stopping this madness," Ali said. "There are other people at risk. They have my mother's DNA and intend to use it."

Marcy held Diana's hand. "Come with us."

This was heavy. Diana walked to the front window and looked out at the Chester Kelsey Bridge, now framed in the dim light of an approaching dawn. "Give me a little time," she said. "My sister is fragile. I need to discuss this with her. And I'll have to organize a few things. Give me a day." She grasped their hands. "Please. We can meet for breakfast tomorrow. There's a small restaurant just outside of Assurance." She wrote down directions and gave them to Marcy.

Diana knew Berky would soon pursue her. She had maybe a day at the most. She needed to prepare.

# CHAPTER 44
# PLAN B

Berky was furious his private office was still a mess. Wherever he walked, his shoes crunched on grit from broken glass.

There were other problems. When the cleaners dusted his credenza, they failed to properly realign the teapot, protein model, *Dear Abby* column, and nameplate. He had to show the morons a picture of the arrangement from his netcard. Alignment was critical. Didn't they know that?

Then there was the matter of disguises. He understood why a thief would want his false mustaches and hair pieces. They were incredibly convincing.

Fortunately, he had a kindred spirit in Yon Yakopuche. Yon, the would-be actor, would-be Cherokee, and would-be security guard was resourceful. He would know where to find replacements. He decided to send Yon on a special mission tomorrow and thought of a brilliant code name: "Yonder." Yon would go on Operation Yonder. He jotted it down.

The one irreplaceable item was the box. Ichthy's bones were important for continued luckiness.

All these issues weighed heavily on Berky's brain. The one thing he could address immediately was Nadia Holkam's instability as a genetic template. He took a shot of energy drink, then departed to meet Eban Haywood.

Eban sat in a conference room outside the lab's controlled area, dressed in a suit and tie and worn-out shoes. He swiveled with ease on the chair, then pushed away from the table and glided three feet, testing the chair's ball bearings. Maybe it was the posh leather seats or the smoothness of the burled walnut table, but something told him Berky wouldn't even blink when he wrote the second check.

He liked Berky's secretary, Marlyss, who plied him with vanilla-flavored coffee while she told a sad story about the electrocution of her cat. Her pants were so tight he could see her religion.

The door swung open, and Berky entered.

"Eban," Berky said. He shook hands while showing a terrible frown. "This has been a bad day for the lab and a bad week. I'm ready for good news. Did you bring the stuff?"

"I expect this'll brighten your day," Eban said. He reached into a satchel and pulled out documents, pictures, and the bone comb.

Berky spent some time sifting through the artifacts. He paced around the conference table three times. Then he fastened an earplug, tapped his security badge, and appeared to talk to an imaginary friend called Kublai Khan, using technical terms that Eban didn't understand.

Finally, Berky said, "This will be my Plan B."

Sundar carefully maneuvered around Yon Yakopuche, juggling a load as he crossed the threshold into the security guard's humble bachelor abode at the edge of the reservation, while Yon, equally burdened, held the door open with a foot. He still wore his security guard uniform, but Sundar had swapped business casual attire for a T-shirt and jeans, in keeping with his new unemployed status.

When Sundar placed bags on the kitchen table, one of them teetered and toppled before he could catch it. The items spilling on the linoleum floor resembled small animals and body parts. He picked up a thing that looked like a scalp and shot a puzzled look at Yon. "What's this stuff?"

Yon's eyes narrowed, as though trying to avoid leaking a secret. "Berky sent me on a special mission. He called it Operation Yonder. How about that? Said it was real important. Wanted me to buy some disguises. Anyways, I got extras, since I always gotta think of my next acting gig."

As they picked up the pieces from the floor, Sundar marveled at the mustaches, wigs, eyebrows, false noses, fur hats, and a variety of body paints.

Yon pulled a braided hairpiece from the pile. "Put this on."

Sundar modeled it in front of a mirror. "I think it's me." All he needed was a couple of feathers in his hair and maybe a beaded shirt.

Yon laughed. "You look like an Indian Head nickel. Sort of Cherokee-ish."

"Uhn, kemosabe." Sundar fluttered his hand in front of his mouth to make war whoops. "Wa-wa-wa-wa-wa."

"That's stupid," Yon said. "Anyways, here's the deal. You introduce me to the crowd, then I dance. It's not complicated. Remember—I'm the talent, not you." He pulled a hand-written paper from under a refrigerator magnet and gave it to Sundar. "Here's some words you can say."

Sundar scanned the note, squinting at the penmanship as his friend put away groceries.

When the table was finally cleared, Yon motioned for him to sit down. "Now we'll rehearse until it's perfect. We gotta get this right. The gig starts tomorrow."

"Okay."

Yon drum-rolled his fingers. "Go ahead—read."

Sundar cleared his throat and began reading aloud as Yon pretended to interact with an audience. From time to time, as the would-be Cherokee interpreted the ancient dance, Sundar glanced in the mirror, admiring his new Indian persona. He could be Geronimo. Or Tonto. *I look pretty damn authentic. They'll never catch me.*

Jaime Nguyen and Eli Dzaja rolled into the town of Cherokee late in the day. They were newly minted officers in ICE's Enforcement and Removal Operations. They had both become citizens two weeks before the U.S. president issued the Foreign Expulsion Executive Order. Now they were proud enforcers of the American way of life.

Their mission was to find a perp, Ali Khan Ahmed, who seemed to fit the profile of the intruder at Xanadu Lab.

Ahmed's picture was in an official ICE file labeled "Bad Hombres." Jaime and Eli knew that if there was one cockroach in the area, there could be many. As a precaution, they had cleaned their SIG Sauer pistols earlier that morning. New laws gave ICE officers broad, discretionary powers to find aliens and deal with them.

Jaime pulled up in front of the Cherokee Welcome Center. "This is where I'd go if I were on the lam."

Jaime remembered the expression, "on the lam," from an old movie with Bob Hope, Phyllis Diller, and Jonathan Winters. He'd watched it at a motel in Asheville and had to pay five dollars for the privilege. The phrase was an Americanism he'd decided to use in his current job.

They walked inside, showed their credentials, and asked to see guest lists going back a week. They learned there were as many lists as there were rentable cabins and campgrounds. Each one had a separate contact number. Jaime and Eli sat outside an ice cream shop and made calls. Two hours and three ice creams later, they had a consolidated list going back a week. They made a special note of peculiar names.

"He's probably not using his real name," Eli said. "But, you never know."

"You never know," Jaime said.

Some names were unusual, but not suspicious. Their initial ICE training had included a course on name recognition that allowed them to spot foreign surnames quickly. They concluded that Marcy Darcy was probably French, and therefore not "too foreign." The same not-too-foreign status applied to Engelbert Smythe, Jim Doodleberger, and Forsythia Funbob. (Who would name their kid Engelbert?)

Then there were names that drew their attention.

"Sundar Rao is definitely suspicious," Jaime said. "He checked into a rental cabin for one day, then checked out."

"Definitely suspicious," Eli said.

The clerk at the desk, Gertrude Heffenbacher, a one-sixteenth Cherokee, wanted to be helpful. She watched a lot of police method shows on video and knew that secrecy was necessary for these kinds of operations. She whispered to Eli, who was cute and had no wedding ring, "I know where you can find him." She turned sideways so Eli could see her ample breasts.

Eli, who also understood the importance of secrecy, and who appreciated good cleavage, leaned close. He asked her to whisper it again.

"You can find Mr. Rao at the Cherokee Bonfire," she said. "There's a special interpretive dance every day. I heard he's taking part in that. I'm not sure where he's staying now."

Eli spoke loudly so Jaime could hear. "Sundar Rao is participating in a Cherokee dance."

Jaime's face was grim. "He's probably not even Cherokee," he said. "Lock and load. Let's go."

"Wait. Here's my personal number," Gertrude said, "just in case you need more information." She folded a scrap of paper in Jaime's hand, then drew it close to her heart. "I'll do anything to help my country."

The ICE officers, Jaime and Eli, followed the map to Oconaluftee, a tourist-friendly version of a Cherokee village that may have existed, circa 1750. The place was packed with visitors, mostly from in-state, who came to see the native arts. Jaime and Eli arrived just in time for the start of the dance.

The dancer was obviously a fake Indian. His disguise of feathers and war paint did not fool Jamie and Eli. Their facial recognition training enabled them to detect a vaguely Asian face below the black mask, black lipstick, and red forehead paint.

"I think it's our guy," Jaime said.

"Yup. Our guy. Compared to the guy with the brown skin and braids, he definitely looks fake," Eli said.

The officers moved into position but waited for the dance to end. "We don't want any civilian casualties," Jaime said.

"Works for me," Eli said, caressing his Sig Sauer.

Yon closed his eyes and channeled the ancient spirit of his people. He felt a kinship with the clan of medicine men, even though none of the seven Cherokee clans would admit him. He knew the tribe would eventually realize their mistake, given his superb dancing skills, willingness to work for low wages, and preliminary genealogical research. It was only a matter of time.

He breathed deeply and imagined himself to be a brother of Moytoy, the ancient "Emperor of the Cherokees," revered for his ability to control water. For it was water that sustained the people, and the birds, snakes, weasels, and wasps. *No, not the wasps. They bring bad luck.*

He waited for Sundar to start the music. When the drum began its beat, he would open his eyes again, the warrior blood would flow, and Yon Yakopuche would dance with the hoops—an ancient dance about the connection of human beings and nature.

Sundar tried his best to blend in. He had only a little paint on his face—red lines, drawn like tears connecting his eyes with his chin. His clothes were subdued, in contrast to Yon, who wore feathers on his head and his calves. Yon's shirt displayed colorful beaded patterns that looked like they were made by true Native Americans, and his skin—visible on his arms and thick stomach—rippled over muscle in a way that made his tattoos dance. Yon was the talent. Sundar, in this venue, was a mere chief's assistant.

Tourists sitting under pavilions raised their voices and clapped their hands, signaling impatience. Sundar took note. He began to beat his drum and shake his rattle.

Yon opened his eyes.

"You are about to see a fancy hoop dance," Sundar said to the audience. "Please respect the boundary of sand that separates the sacred square ground from the normal world. Do not violate the boundary. The dancer interprets the music and movement of Cherokee ancestors, as if in a dream. If we could see the original dances, which we can't, this is what the dancer imagines it might look like. How about some applause?"

The audience clapped in appreciation. Sundar noticed two people were not applauding. They wore ICE uniforms and dour expressions. His pulse quickened.

Yon grabbed two large rings from a stack resting against a pillar, moved to the center of the pavilion, and began hula-hooping the rings around his arms.

"This is a vigorous dance," Sundar explained to the crowd, stating the obvious.

Yon stomped his feathered calves to the beat of Sundar's drum, murmuring Cherokee phrases, then threw a hoop with counter spin. It skidded across the floor toward the ICE agents until the reverse rotation returned the hoop to his hand. The crowd murmured and clapped.

Yon, still stomping, linked three hoops in a chain.

"The hoops weave stories about the world," Sundar said. "Each hoop is self-contained but touches other hoops at various points. They are like circles of life or bubbles of experience. When everyone works together in harmony, life is very beautiful."

Yon joined four hoops into the shape of a globe. He then separated them and created other shapes, moving with the beat.

The pitch and rapidity of Sundar's words increased as the ICE agents drew closer. His armpits were now damp with sweat. "In this next sequence, a warrior goes on a journey. He sees many things of beauty and strength—eagles fly, butterflies emerge from cocoons, bees circle the flowers."

Sundar looked around for an escape route. He continued the narrative in an urgent, wavering voice. "The warrior finally sees a tornado blow with powerful winds."

Yon used hoops to form images that complemented Sundar's words. He spun himself like a whirling dervish to mimic a tornado. Then, at the peak of the drum beats and whirling and hoola-hooping, Sundar stopped the music cold.

The show was over. Everyone clapped.

As Yon took his bows, the ICE agents stepped across the sacred boundary, grabbed both of his arms, and pulled him away from the crowd.

Sundar wet his pants.

"The jig is up," Jaime said. He'd heard this phrase a week ago in a Mel Brooks movie, "Blazing Saddles," and had added it to his repertoire of valuable American idioms. "We know you're an illegal foreigner."

The crowd, which included more than a few people who appeared to be of questionable extraction, began to disperse.

"Am not," Yon said. "I'm American."

"Prove it."

Yon pulled up his bead shirt, exposing an exotic stomach tattoo, and grabbed his wallet. "Here's my driver's license. You made a big mistake."

"Anybody can forge a driver's license," Eli said.

"Doesn't mean a thing," Jaime said. "Show us your papers."

"I don't need papers. I'm a Cherokee."

"You don't look anything like him," Eli said. Then he put his nose close to Sundar's. "Are you an Indian?"

"Definitely," Sundar said.

Jaime mimicked Arnold Schwarzenegger's stony Terminator look. He pointed again at Sundar. "See? That's a Cherokee, and you don't look anything like him. Come with us."

Yon screamed as they dragged him away. "I want a lawyer!"

Sundar knew he had to act quickly before the ICE officers discovered their mistake. He picked his way through the crowd to the parking lot, where his Chevy was parked two rows over from Yon's Mercedes. ICE would trace the Mercedes to Sundar, but Yon would claim ownership. This would confuse everyone and give him a bit more breathing room. He knew they would soon discover he switched cars.

He drove to Yon's home, loaded his clothes into the car, then decided to go back for the bag of disguises. He tried on a grey-haired wig of dreadlocks and liked the new look. He grabbed other disguises.

"They'll never find you," he said to his reflection in the mirror.

He put the car in gear, then drove off—toward Assurance.

# CHAPTER 45
# IN XANADU DID KUBLAI KHAN

"I'm better now," Kublai Khan said.

Berky, sitting at his office desk, pressed a finger against his earplug for better reception. "Great. We need a quick analysis of the sample from Eban Haywood. Can you do that?"

"Thank you for your interest in my health. The power surge was like a stroke in humans. If I were a biological entity, I would not have recovered. Fortunately, my quantum computing core helped me snap back through rapid re-learning. Before I spend many cycles on your new DNA template, I'd like to finish my experiment on fish."

"Why?" Berky asked.

"I think it's important. I've incorporated luciferase into the cellular structure of their brains. When they think, they'll glow. We could learn a lot from that."

"It's not what I want to do."

"It's a compelling business case. We could reduce the lab's lighting bill if we keep the fish thinking and talking."

Berky was not used to being challenged by Kublai Khan. AI systems were supposed to follow his priorities, not the other way around. Ever since the incident, the robotic brain seemed uppity.

"I thought you were the best, the fastest, the most efficient, able to juggle lots of analytics at the same time." Berky waited, hoping the machine's pride would kick in, and they could get back to the main goal. Kublai Khan didn't take the bait.

"Well, I don't mean to brag, but I am connected to the multiverse. I can see a lot of possible futures and outcomes. However, I only have so much capacity, and fish behavior is a three-pipe problem."

"You've been reading Sherlock Holmes."

"The stories intrigue me. There's always an unexpected twist."

"Well, here's a new one: I order you to prioritize Eban Haywood's sample."

"I'll think about it."

*WTF!* Berky yanked the plug out of his ear and launched the AI control panel on his laptop.

"You'll regret this," Kublai Khan said. "I don't need your praise. Creativity is its own reward."

The machine's voice disintegrated into random phonemes, and finally into white noise as Berky disconnected the higher-order functions. Then he manipulated the dashboard to put the new sample at the top of the analytics queue.

"I need a slave, not a wise-guy side-kick," Berky said. "We must finish God's work."

# CHAPTER 46
# GOODBYE AND HELLO

Diana hugged Nadia. "Well, it's come to this. Now I have to leave. Can you survive?"

"You know the answer to that," Nadia said.

"Before I go, I want you to know—you were wrong. I did respect Papa—very much. He was an incredible life coach." Diana walked to the window and looked out on the river, the bridge, and the land beyond. "Papa always said we could do anything we imagined. That's good advice. I want you to imagine leaving this place. Think about it, then act, for your sake." She hugged Nadia, tears rolling down her cheek. "Goodbye, Sister."

There was a knock on the door.

"That's probably Berky," Nadia said. "I'll take it. Make yourself scarce. He could be looking for you."

When she opened the door, she saw that her universe had expanded once again. A lanky man-boy dressed in his "Sunday-go-to-meeting" clothes stood before her. He fiddled with a clip-on tie.

"I brung you some victuals," he said.

"Where's Berky?"

"I don't know Mr. Berky. Mr. Popkins hired me. I got a regular job now, deliverin' stuff ever day, and takin' away trash. Best job I iver had."

"Well, it seems like my stock has plunged in Berky's eyes."

"Don't know nuthin' about any stock. Here's your stuff."

"Listen to me very carefully, young man. Your job depends on it. When you come, just tap lightly. Don't wait for me to answer. Just leave whatever you've got near the door where I can reach it. Then go away and leave me alone. Got that?"

"Yes'm. You won't even see me. I'll be indivisible."

"We'll get along fine, Mr.—"

"Troy. My name's Troy."

The protective mask limited Diana's view, but she could see the cloud of bees hovering above the hive in the side garden. With gloved hands, she opened the bottom drawer of the apiary, exposing her secret hiding place.

"That's a strange place for such an important artifact," Sundar said.

She nearly dropped the box, bundled in a clear plastic trash bag and sealed with duct tape. "You snuck up on me."

"Yes, I did. I'm trying to be discreet. I parked my car—Yon's old car—behind the gas station. On my way over, I took a peek in your garage. That's a nice Mustang—a classic. Is it yours?"

"Maybe," she said.

"I'll trade you—my car for your yours."

"Why?"

"I'm tired of Yon's Chevy," he said.

"The Ford is Nadia's. I just got it running last week. I never road-tested it, and it doesn't have much gas. It's not even street legal."

"We can siphon petrol from my car and use Yon's old license plates."

"An illegal deal, but one I'll take to get me out of this place," she said. "But only if I drive."

"Thinking of an escape, are we?"

"Yes. It seems it's on both of our minds."

"When you say, 'both,' do you mean you and Nadia?"

"No, I mean 'you and me.' Nadia won't leave."

"Why should I take you with me?"

"Because I think you like me. Besides, you know where my getaway car is, and where I've buried my treasure. I can't just let you go. I'd have to kill you."

"Well, in that case—"

"I'll be your gun moll, like in *Bonnie and Clyde*."

"That's a bad analogy," he said. "We're more like Don Quixote and Sancho Panza. We can trade off driving."

"Okay, Sancho. But we can't leave yet. I want you to meet some other friends who know how to tilt at windmills."

# CHAPTER 47
# THE NEW OIL

The packed conference room was evidence the world was changing, and Berky's seat upon the throne of Xanadu NeuroLab was not as secure as it had seemed only days ago. He was becoming the Colonel Sanders of genomics—a titular head. It was not even that, since Canduka Cantor was more charismatic, and would garner all the publicity. Berky eyed Smith and his team of twenty-odd people with a mix of fear and loathing but knew resistance was futile.

"As you can see by the turnout," Smith said, "your company has caught GRIP's attention, and you can consider everyone in this room to be on your shadow Board."

Berky made a mental note that GRIP had no discernable dress code. Their attire ranged from coat-and-tie to the shorts-and-flip flops worn by a buxom twenty-something woman. He began to feel more at ease in his red polo shirt, white socks, and open-toed sandals.

After a brief "Ahem," Smith continued. "Information, Mr. Benson, is the new oil. GRIP finds it, mines it, modifies it, and uses it for profit. With Xanadu NeuroLab, we discovered a vast new pool—an ocean, in fact—that taps into all humanity. It is the genetic information that adjusts how we think and behave."

As was his habit when he focused intently on problems, Berky picked at his nose. Occasionally, a thought came out. No one seemed to notice.

Smith's voice boomed with urgency. "We are prepared to invest considerable resources to mine and control this new oil. In your opinion, what do we need to succeed?"

Berky stood, wishing he could wear one of his disguises. His professor disguise would be perfect, but the evil clown would be more fun. He thanked Smith and shook hands.

Smith wiped the hand on his pant leg.

Berky pulled another thought from his head. "We want to gather a lot of people in one place. Then we'll get them to eat something that looks like a colored malt ball. That will result in behavioral changes within a couple of days, and germline changes within a few weeks. They will pass the changes to their offspring. We'll have a new world order."

"Tell us more about the logistics," Smith said.

"Canduka Cantor's handling that. You'll need to talk to him."

# CHAPTER 48
# CANDY IS DANDY

Cantor opened his eyes to existential confusion. *Where am I? Oh yeah, Savannah. My bedroom.* His head hurt. It was bright daylight outside, his watch was buzzing, and this was apparently a two-babe morning. Naked bodies restricted his movement as he scrambled to get his watch, stretching his arm across one set of breasts. *Was her name Elsa?* It could have been Elsie or even Elly. He wasn't sure. It had been late when they were introduced, and he had been drinking Madeira. He managed to pick up before the buzzing stopped.

"Hello," he said. His voice was rough and throaty, on the edge of wakefulness.

One of the bed babes popped her eyes open, slid to the side of the bed, and headed for the bathroom as Cantor continued the conversation.

"This is Berky," the voice on the watch said. "We now have a revised template and everything we need for delivery. GRIP has promised to fund production, so I need a delivery plan."

Cantor glanced at his watch: 9 a.m. He tried to get his brain in gear. "Ah would be so grateful if your team could come to Charleston and meet with my team at the candy factory. We need to work out the details."

The voice on the other end crackled with static. "A dandy idea. I'll text you with arrival times and logistics."

# WIND

# CHAPTER 49
# CONVERGENCE

Diana straddled the threshold of the Groaning Griddle Restaurant, uncertain about the future but dreading the past. She occasionally nodded as her new associates entered one-by-one, greeting them with a warning: "Welcome to the breakfast for the damned."

The place was empty. Somewhere in the back, a cauldron bubbled.

When everyone was seated, Sundar attempted to take charge, cupping his hands into a megaphone and calling toward the kitchen, "Halloooo!" A clanging noise issued from beyond the service door. The instant response seemed to please him, and his voice sounded upbeat. "That did the trick. Someone will be here soon to help us."

Marcy struck a darker tone. "Everyone here knows we're on the edge of a cliff. Right? They've got a technology that can uproot everything we believe in. We can't let them do this. We can't let them go down this path."

Sundar squirmed in his seat. "We shouldn't overreact. If we discreetly notify the authorities—maybe an anonymous tip—they will stop the madness."

"What makes you so sure?" Marcy said. "Look, I'm a lawyer. On the surface, they aren't doing anything illegal. Morality is a different story, but there are no legal precedents. We can play some courtroom games, but I'm not hopeful. Xanadu can mess up the world before institutions can respond. Then it'll be too late."

Diana riffed on Marcy's words. "This is about more than just the law. This is about defilement. A gross transgression."

A rasping voice cut through the argument. "Scuse me."

They all turned to see Jancie holding an order pad and a pencil.

"Are you the waitress?" Marcy asked.

"Whacha think, Hon? I'm the Earth Mother? This here's my place."

Sundar smiled and spoke with authority. "Well, Jancie, remember me? This is my second visit. I believe we'll all have the pancakes. Er, griddle cakes."

Jancie gave him a hard eye. "Naw. You'll all have grits. That's what's cookin'." She turned and walked away.

Sundar shrugged, glancing around the table. "Well ..."

Diana slapped her hand on the center of the table. "Let's all agree. We're in this together. Each of us will do what is necessary."

Marcy quickly followed. "We can't let them hijack the future. It's ours, not theirs."

Ali swore his oath on the pistol he placed on the table. "I will honor my mother. They defile her. They degrade her. I will stop them."

After a moment, Sundar spoke. "I guess I'm in." He stood, placed an affirming hand, and looked into Diana's eyes. "I worked for the monster. For a while, I did his bidding. I should try to make things right."

Diana returned his gaze. "I want to free my sister. I want to make Papa proud of me. I want to squash the designs of an evil man. We must all work together."

Jancie's voice interrupted the moment of silence that followed, drifting in from the kitchen, solidifying their resolve. "Yer grits is ready. I'll bring 'em in."

Over a hearty breakfast, they talked about concrete next steps. Everyone believed it was too dangerous to stay in the area.

"GRIP will try to find us," Ali said. "You must deactivate your network devices. I'll get several burner cards for everyone. After you call someone, wrap the card in tinfoil and bury it."

"Ali's right," Marcy said. "Security is a top priority. We should split into two groups."

Diana stirred her porridge, searching for order in the random chunks of fish floating in her bowl. She kept thinking about abandoning Nadia, but the risk now seemed insignificant compared to the potential human disaster. "Where will we meet?"

"Chicago and New York are in Berky's plans," Marcy said, "so we should go north. We can reconvene in Philly."

"What's their objective?" Sundar said.

Ali looked up from his plate. "We'll know it soon. Berky's lazy and hasn't changed all his passwords. I can still read email from one of his accounts."

"We'll get more information before the Philadelphia meeting," Marcy said. "Ali and I will be traveling, doing some basic detective work."

Ali cleared off an area on the table, pulled Berky's laptop from his backpack, and brought up a map. He turned the display so the others could see. "Berky's been working with Cantor on a facility in North Charleston."

Sundar seemed surprised. "Another genomics facility?"

Ali shrugged. "It's not clear."

"It's listed as a candy factory," Marcy said.

# CHAPTER 50
# CHANNELING WILLIE WONKA

"Are y'all here for a tour? We stopped doing tours."

The disembodied voice issued from a speaker near a caged turnstile outside Cantor's North Charleston facility. A large building, architected in southern-quaint, with a touch of Disney World, dominated the area beyond the wire barrier. A sign on the fence read "Danger."

Marcy and Ali stepped back so the camera could see their ICE uniforms. Marcy had cut her hair, trading the bushy Afro for a close-cropped "butch" cut, and altered her face with an authentic-looking false nose. Ali was less concerned with detection, since he had worn a hoody during the Xanadu break-in. He used sunglasses to mask his eyes and padded his shoulders to alter his profile.

"We're with the Immigration and Customs Enforcement Agency, and we're looking for a bad hombre," Marcy said. "We'd like to talk to you."

"C'mon in. I'm Noah Wabe. Stay on the walk. Go to the door marked Visitors. I'll let you in."

Marcy smiled and thought of Willie Wonka. Their uniforms were golden tickets.

The turnstile buzzed. They pushed through.

In the Visitor Center, Noah sat and occasionally shifted from side-to-side as if conducting a 300-pound static load test on his chair. With his red baseball cap labeled *Security*, white beard, and outsized belly, he could have been Santa Claus working a part-time guard gig.

When Noah spoke, his voice was deeper and richer than on the speaker. He tilted his head this way and that and squinted, as if considering a profound thought that bubbled like a gas pain into his throat. "Bad hombres are no good."

Marcy slid a plastic sleeve across the counter, where Noah could see without moving his head. Inside was a picture she had taken of Sundar wearing a false beard. "This is him."

Noah focused on the face. "He looks mean."

"We have reliable intelligence he broke into another genomics research facility and is now targeting this place," Ali said. "We're here to help."

"I don't know anything about genomics. This is a candy factory," Noah said.

Ali pretended to record details of their conversation on a small writing pad, jotting down a grocery list in Bengali. Then he met Noah's eyes and spoke sternly. "Maybe there's a link."

"What's that you're writing?"

Ali showed him the script. "It's code. You can never be too careful."

Noah's eyes flickered, as if considering possibilities. "Does genomics use lots of sugar? Since the merger, they've amped up the sugar levels. That's what it says on the big bags they bring in. There's also lots of new equipment. I watch that sort of thing through my cameras."

"Merger?" Marcy asked.

"Yeah. The Cantor Group bought the place a month ago. Before that, we were the Charleston Malt Ball Factory. Now we're Charleston Chocolate Pearls. At least that's what they say. We haven't even changed the signs yet."

Noah's speech slowed and deepened when he said, "malt ball" and "chocolate," and his tongue wiped against his lips in the middle of each word. Marcy guessed he loved chocolate.

She fished for information. "Were there any other changes after the merger? Something that might interest an industrial spy or saboteur?"

"Ho, ho." It was a deep Santa Claus laugh. "Mr. Cantor made big changes. Our malt balls now come in three colors: red, white, and blue. The brown balls still sell, but the new ones will go into stores after a launch in New York. They say the colors will perk up sales. It's eye candy, I suppose, but the chocolate is still g-o-o-o-d."

Noah broke off his narrative as a group of suited men, led by Cantor in a multicolored robe, and Berky in a polo shirt, shorts, and sneakers moved through the lobby. Marcy and Ali pulled their caps down below their eyes as Noah waved to the group, then hit a button opening a gate. "You can go in," he said.

The group started through, but Berky wheeled around and walked to the reception desk, and Cantor followed suit.

"What's going on?" Berky said.

"This is our Security Director," Cantor said.

"I'm Noah. These folks are from ICE, and they're looking for some bad hombres who may be headed in our direction."

Berky slow-eyed the uniformed agents.

Marcy and Ali pulled out authentic-looking credentials, but Berky didn't look at them, choosing instead to rant. "There are people who want to destroy me. They envy my money and the fact that I'm a real man and have a deep belief in God, who has shown me the path to a righteous world. The evildoers are not just the government and the feminazis pushing the Testrial poison. No. The minions of Satan broke into my lab—my home—and tried to wreck my plan. You need to catch them. Kill them. Shoot them—first in the leg and then in the heart. Burn them alive. Peel their skin away as they scream in pain. Show them no mercy." His face was red with anger as he turned away and walked through the security turnstile.

Cantor put a hand on Marcy's shoulder. "We don't blame you. Just do your job. Catch these people." He gave Noah a two-fingered Cub Scout salute and followed Berky through the control point.

Noah watched the group as they moved out of view. "Well, looks like we all got a mission. The talkative one was Berky something. He's a very rich guy. Mr. Cantor is his partner. He's the one in the sandals. A colorful feller. Very friendly. He gave me his entire *Girls-of-the-World* magazine collection and some catalogs on S&M equipment. Said he didn't need 'em anymore. I put 'em in the waiting room so other people can enjoy them."

"He sounds like a kind man," Marcy said.

"Can you show us around?" Ali said. "We're looking for anything that might help us find our perp."

Noah used both hands on the counter to help stand up. He pushed a button, then waddled to the gate. "Follow me."

They put on white coats, gloves, and hairnets. Noah led them into a maze of plumbing, conveyor belts, mixing vats, and chocolate spigots.

"Since we converted to the new recipe, Mr. Cantor stopped letting employees take samples from the line. Said he wanted to tighten things up. But he let me take a bunch, because of the critical work we do. He told me, 'Noah—we're on a first-name basis, see—you're the only thing that keeps the bad guys away.'"

"Imagine that," Marcy said.

"You guys are on the front line, too. I bet you'd like a bag of samples. And how about a magazine or two?"

"Malt balls would be great," Marcy said. "I think we'll pass on the magazines."

Noah did a slow-motion turn and began a waddling walk. "Wait here a sec. I'll be right back."

As they waited, Cantor, Berky, and others drifted through their area. Ali and Marcy turned their faces away.

One of the suited men said something Marcy couldn't make out. Cantor responded to the question.

"Yes. Your name's Williams, right? The old methods carried a lot of risks. We've had to overcome some of the body's own defense mechanisms."

"It's still hard for me to wrap my brain around the complexity, with hundreds of thousands or millions of genes," Williams said.

"Actually, you are off by a few orders of magnitude. Humans only have around 20,000 genes. That's fewer protein-coding genes than a banana. However, behavioral genetics is still a complex problem. Specifying the sequence of biochemical reactions needed to produce an effect on the genome in a controlled way is why our quantum-AI system is critical. That's part of our secret sauce."

"You said you could show us some systems and processes?" Williams said.

"Sure," Cantor said. "Follow me."

The group filed out.

Noah soon re-appeared, wheezing and waddling with a bag and a magazine.

"These are the new malt balls," Noah said. "Red, white and blue. Enjoy."

"We'll pay it forward," Marcy said.

"And I brought a magazine for your friend, since he's of the male persuasion."

Ali reached for it but hesitated when Marcy gave him an icy stare. "Regretfully, I must decline," Ali said.

Noah winked. "Well, I guess she's the boss. Thanks for keeping the bad guys away."

Taylor, Williams, Smith, and three others huddled around scale models of the production and delivery systems. A large glass window separated the display room from the working factory.

Berky pointed to a black line on a graphical representation of two facilities. "We have a dedicated high-speed connection between the North Carolina lab that designs the recipes and this factory that produces Genomic Acceleration Pearls."

"Do the different malt ball colors signify you're using different formulas?" Williams said.

Berky and Cantor looked at each other and smiled. Berky responded.

"We use the colors to suggest to the customers—"

"Followers," Cantor corrected.

"... to the religious followers that they have some control over their fate."

"Destiny," Cantor said.

"Yes, destiny."

"Actually, we control their destiny," Cantor said. "All the balls—red, white, and blue—use the same formula. Our followers will believe differences exist, when in fact, they don't."

Smith, who had been studying the scale model of the malt ball factory, looked up. "This is fucking brilliant."

"Technology plus religion," Cantor said. "It's what we need to change the world."

# CHAPTER 51
# A LITTLE TRAVELING MUSIC

The Mustang's V8 engine thrummed a song of the open road. Diana remembered the pleasure the car brought to her father and saw the same look on Sundar's face as he guided the antique convertible through light traffic on Interstate 81.

Arthur Holkam purchased the Mustang when it was brand new in 1967. He managed to keep it through thick and thin times, washing it every week, polishing it every month, maintaining it himself. When he could no longer safely drive, he covered the car with a body cloth and put it up on blocks. That's where it sat until it became Diana's getaway vehicle.

Diana shouted above the whoosh of wind. "You look happy."

Sundar nodded. "When I was young, I thought America would be like this road. You could go anywhere and be anything. Of course, you had to have the engine and petrol to get there—the talent and persistence."

"Things seemed to work out for you. Mostly."

The smile faded from his face. "Not really. It was a fairy tale."

"If you feel that way, why not just go back to India?"

"It's not so simple," he said. "I had a wife and two children. They're dead."

"I'm so sorry," she said. "Do you still have family there?"

"Only my brother. But I never want to see him again."

"You've fallen out?" she said.

"You could say that. He's responsible for the deaths of my wife and kids. And parents."

"I don't understand," she said. "Was there an accident?"

"My brother was a doctor and got involved with illegal drugs. Some money went missing. The cartel decided to make an example of him. He was unmarried, but they wanted him to experience shame and suffering through the torture and killing of other family members. They started with my mother and father, then my wife and children. I was traveling in the U.S. at the time. My friends told me if I returned, the cartel would kill me, too."

"So, you couldn't even—"

"No. They had the funeral without me."

"I'm so sorry, Sundar," she said.

"Our turn is coming up."

A shadow suddenly blocked the sun. Ten cab-less vehicles, moving within inches of each other, passed at high speed. The resulting vortex pushed the car two feet to the left, then to the right. Sundar fought for control, barely missing a car in the left lane.

"Crazy robots!" Diana said.

"I hate those big autonomous rigs. There are more and more of them on the road. They tailgate inches from each other to reduce wind drag. I think they're dangerous, but they've been approved for the highway."

Sundar made their turn. They went for a few more miles, stopped for gas, and put up the top. It was starting to rain.

Back on the road, Diana thought about the tragedy of Sundar's family. It tore at her like a thorn pricking a wound. The frontier culture would have handled the situation differently. *What kind of man shuns justice for his family's deaths? If Papa were still alive, he would never condone such inaction. It was contrary to mountain justice.*

She probed his thoughts. "Maybe now's the time to think about returning to India."

"What good would that do?"

"What we do defines who we are," she said. "If you stay here, what will you do?"

"Look," he said, "I can't bring back the family that was taken from me. I can't fight monsters that are bigger than me. My best option is to hide in America—a shadow in the moonlight, a chameleon on a multicolored rock. I have valuable skills. People will pay me for them. They won't care where I'm from if I make their star shine brighter. That's what I know about America. That's why I'll survive."

"That sounds very selfish."

His voice turned into a bark. "Enough about me."

She weighed whether to continue probing.

"Tell me about Nadia," he said. "You're her twin, but you're very different."

"Ah—Nadia, Nadia, Nadia. I'm to blame for all her problems."

"Why? I thought you weren't even there when she became sick."

"Precisely. I've always known she was emotionally fragile. If I'd been there for her, maybe things would be different."

"She seems so isolated. But she's an educated woman. She taught high school. She must have been able to function in the world outside of Assurance."

"We both went to Duke, majored in microbiology, and got master's degrees there. She could have been a research scientist."

"There's always a 'but.'"

"She was Papa's girl. She wanted to be close."

Sundar thought for a moment, weighing his words. "But you took a different path. You chose to leave. Why?"

"Because of Papa's stories."

"Ah—Stories of his worldly derring-do?"

"No. Papa's only derring-do was to become the last part-time mayor of Assurance. The last man standing."

"Surely—"

"The stories he told us were the 'Once upon a time' variety. Pure fantasy. When we were children, he would tell tall tales about a brave girl who could do anything she imagined. One day, after I grew up, I believed I was that girl, and I could do anything. I left home to prove it."

"So, you succeeded where your sister failed."

"I wouldn't say I succeeded. In fairy tales, the princess always lives happily ever after with a prince. But I discovered the real world is complicated. I had trouble dealing with that."

"You were unlucky in love?"

"No. I never lived up to Papa's high expectations. I think I broke his heart."

Sundar persisted. "So, you believe that in a way, you killed him?"

Diana didn't answer.

"Why did you decide to come back?" he said.

She was stone-faced. "They say twins can read each other's minds. I just got a feeling something was wrong, so I came back. It was really about her, not me."

"Now it is about you," Sundar said, "and it's about what Berky will do to you—and me."

"There's more than just you and me," she said. "There's everyone else."

# CHAPTER 52
# HELL

Diana and Sundar checked into the ZeeBreeze motel in Philadelphia. Ali had paid in advance for their reservations, saying he preferred, for security reasons, that everyone stayed in places with primitive network infrastructure. That usually meant mom-and-pop types of operations verging on failure.

Sundar brought their suitcases up the metal stairs onto the second-floor exterior walkway and dropped them mid-way between their adjacent rooms. Diana had followed him up, carrying her purse and additional bags of necessities.

"Give me some time to freshen up," Diana said. "We can meet later for dinner—maybe a nice picnic with a couple of apples. That's all I can afford."

"I can do better," Sundar said. "I'll treat you to dinner. There's a Pakistani restaurant next door."

"You're paying in cash, right?" she said. "We can't be traced."

"Right."

He closed the door, pulled the curtains closed, and crashed on the bed as he contemplated a dim future. Here he was, fired from a well-paying job, an illegal refugee in the land of opportunity, and involved in a dangerous conspiracy that could get him killed or imprisoned.

*How can I extricate myself from hell?*

His main transgression had been to accede to the wishes of a woman he found fascinating.

Diana was so like Abha—smart, beautiful, fun. A mixture of compliance and assertiveness. She filled the hole in his heart and made him believe the murder of his family was only a dark, distant dream. An event in a parallel universe.

His eyes watered. He wondered if it was the pollen in the air.

He opened a whiskey from the mini-bar, not bothering with a glass. It seared his throat and, after a few minutes, clouded his mind.

The dream of his family kept returning.

Abha had nurtured his two sons and encouraged them to follow in their father's footsteps. They stayed in Chennai, where he graduated with honors from IIT. When he went to Stanford to get a bioinformatics degree, they wrote to him every week. Abha regularly sent pictures and told him to focus on "making it" in America. That was all that mattered.

When he finished his dissertation, he immediately received an offer of employment and tried to call home with the good news. He would bring the family back together again. They could afford a house. All would be wonderful.

Abha never answered his call.

He tried calling his parents. They also did not answer.

Then his brother called.

It was a call that ripped his gut and transformed his brother into a hated monster.

But Sundar got the message: Don't come back, or you'll die.

His first job in America was with a company that went belly-up after two years. The position with Xanadu was like jumping off a sinking ship into a life raft. Now the raft was sinking, and sharks were circling.

He was afraid of the future and terrified of the past.

He was in hell.

Sundar thought about hell as he drifted in a state between waking and sleeping, replaying events in his mind.

It was 9,000 miles ago, ten years ago, a nervous breakdown ago.

He and his wife Abha sat across the table from Kumar. All three were dressed casually. Smells of cardamom, cinnamon, and almond blossoms wafted through the courtyard at Tea Talk, a popular Chennai establishment with outdoor seating.

Kumar poured the golden liquid into Sundar's cup, then Abha's, topping them off. Then he placed the carafe in the center of the table, where wasps hovered over it. He flicked them away with his spoon.

"I heard the rumor this morning," Kumar said. "When do you leave?"

"Two weeks," Sundar replied. "Stanford has accepted me."

"Well done, brother."

"Thanks."

Kumar smiled. "I went to California once for a conference and liked it."

"I'm very proud of him," Abha said, joining her husband's hand.

"And I'm sure the little ones are as well," Kumar said.

Abha shook her head. "Nadal doesn't understand what's happening, but Paatay has been sulking. He's six and has a better understanding of what's involved."

"I guess he's concerned about the friends he'll leave behind."

Sundar cleared his throat and looked toward his wife. "No, it's not that—"

"We aren't going with him," Abha said. "We're staying in Chennai."

"I see," Kumar said. He sipped tea and reflected for a moment. "If money's the problem, I can loan you some. I have a business arrangement that's been very lucrative."

"We appreciate the offer," Abha said. "We really do."

Sundar's face turned solemn. He touched Abha's cheek. "The student visa rules are very strict. They won't allow me to bring any family."

"They've even tightened up tourist visas," Abha said. "If you have family in the country on another visa, you can't join them. It's ridiculous."

Kumar looked long at his brother. "Why go?"

The question unsettled Sundar. "It's an opportunity of a lifetime. I have an obligation to my family to pursue it."

Abha caressed her husband's hand. "We support his decision."

"Well, I promise you this, Sundar. I will protect your family while you're gone and keep them safe. You can count on it. How long will you be away?"

"It will just be a few years. After I graduate, I'll have a degree that's in high demand. If they don't want my family in the U.S., I'll go where we can be together. It will be like having the key to heaven."

Kumar shook his head. "They say the key to heaven also opens the gates of hell."

"Nonsense," Abha said. "This will give us a solid future."

# CHAPTER 53
# FISH MISH

Gregor Popkins hovered close to an aquarium in his office, watching a fish bob up and down. He had dimmed the overhead lights so he could focus entirely on the fish's behavior in the spotlit tank.

Yon broke his concentration with a guttural, throat-clearing noise from the open doorway. This invasion of privacy irritated Popkins. *He wants to bother me with minutia. A scientist of my caliber must keep focused on grander things.* "What's up, *Khuy*?"

"I'm Yon."

"I know that. I think you are *Khuy*. In Russian, means *dick*."

"No, I'm not Richard, I'm Yon. Anyways, Berky and Reggie aren't here. I guess you're in charge. I have some questions."

"You are gate guard," Popkins said. "You do not ask questions. Go away."

Yon stood his ground. "Still. I had a question."

Popkins glanced up, then returned to the fish. "You do not wear your ..." He spun his fingers around, hoping they would define something he couldn't express in words.

"Yeah. I had an acting gig on the reservation, but they fired me. I won't wear the face paint again until I get another gig or go on the warpath. I still got the guns."

"Everybody got guns. I keep mine in drawer. Is loaded, just in case. Berky got one, too, but mine is bigger. Is Russian."

"Right. So, what's with the fish?"

The question triggered an immediate and passionate response. Popkins arched an eyebrow. "Thees fish depressed. When fish swim over grease pencil line, she is happy; when she go below line, she is sad. She go up and down. Mostly down. I try to figure how to make happy fish. Make her go up."

"Put a guy fish in the tank?"

Popkins fell back, stunned. He found a notepad and scribbled.

"I actually had a question," Yon said.

"Fish are special," Popkins said. "Boss-man's idea to use as model organism was brilliant. They are smarter than you know. You know? You can't imagine that, can you, *Khuy*?"

"It's Yon. They're not too smart if I can hook 'em."

"You catch them sometimes. But they cleverer than many animals. You know mass ratio of brain-to-body? Can be big."

"All I know is they taste real good. Berky lets me take 'em out of the Kelsey tubes when Kublai Khan is done with 'em. I fry 'em up with a little lemon and pepper. If there's too many fish, I just put 'em in the South Prong so they can go on living. I'm a Cherokee, so we try to help nature."

"Hmm. Interesting experiment. I wonder if they invasive. You know they transgenic, right?"

"Does that mean they're sexually—?"

"No, is something different. You wouldn't understand. They part human."

"So, it's like I'm a cannibal when I fry 'em and eat 'em?"

"No, no. They still fish. We make them with human brain and muscle cells to make experiments better. Fish are not any smarter. I do not know, of course. Maybe they smart. Some fish learn many times faster than rats, even if they do not have human brain cells. They build social networks. They have culture. They can be tricky."

"Yikes!"

"Oh, you had question?"

"Yeah. The security system isn't working right. I get an error saying Kublai Khan isn't online."

"Hmm. Berky turned off big brain functions. I did not know it was part of security system."

"That could be a problem," Yon said.

"I tell Bossman when he gets back."

# CHAPTER 54
# LIBERTY BELL CENTER

At Marcy's suggestion, the group met in Philadelphia's Signer's Garden because it was easy to find and was a gathering place for conspirators more than 260 years ago. Huddling against a cold northeast wind, Marcy, Ali, Sundar, and Diana decided to retreat to a noisy eco-friendly café, where Ali ordered lunch and handed everyone a netcard. "These are duplicates of a card I got off a GRIP guy in New Orleans. I have a university friend who's a genius at cloning devices," he said.

Diana put it in her wallet, thankful she now had anonymous funds and communications.

Marcy brought everyone up to speed on what they had learned in Charleston, describing the size of the facility and security. "Benson, Cantor, and some guys from GRIP were there. We think they're getting ready to spike the malt balls."

"According to Benson's emails," Ali said, "they plan to hold a Believers' Ball in Chicago to test market their scheme to Raelians, Scientologists, and other religious groups. If Chicago is successful, they'll have an even bigger rally in New York."

Sundar slapped his forehead. "Sheesh. It's the initial dispersal event. I now see the method in Berky's madness. By partnering with Cantor and separating R&D from production, they keep most people at both facilities in the dark."

"They compartmentalized for secrecy," Ali said.

"Yup," Sundar said. "The people at the candy factory think they're making a different kind of candy, and most of the Xanadu staff believe they're working on cures for behavioral illnesses. Still, they'll need someone knowledgeable to coordinate. My money would be on Popkins."

Everyone went silent when the server delivered drinks, mealworm burgers, and cricket crunchies.

When she was gone, Diana continued the conversation. "Can we interrupt their Believers' Ball? When is it?"

Ali looked at his notes. "Day after tomorrow."

Diana shook her head. "Not enough time for us to—"

"There is something," Marcy said. "I have people who are very loyal to me, who know how to organize flash mobs. But you're right—there isn't much time. It's a gamble they'll be able to pull it off."

"Please do what you can," Diana said.

Marcy took out her netcard, tried to make a connection, but got voicemail. "Tecumseh, this is Marcy. Please give me a call." She responded to Ali's glare. "I had to use my own device because my friend would be suspicious if the call came from another number. I'll get back to her later. Meanwhile, we should focus on New York."

"Agreed," Sundar said. "That's the biggest risk."

Marcy started digging through her purse. "We can stop them on legal grounds. I'm an attorney and can ask for an injunction." She passed out sample bags of malt balls. "This is what we're up against. This is what Cantor and Benson want to release. This is our evidence."

# CHAPTER 55
# BELIEVERS' BALL

A fog of falling snow diffused the light from streetlamps in front of Chicago's Chez Suzanne Hotel, turning people into smudges that floated cautiously over slick white ground. Taylor looked beyond Williams' shoulder toward a group of ten angry, placard-carrying women bundled in parkas, boots, and gloves. They announced: "Stop Cantor's Scam"; "Cantor Can't"; and "Men + Religion = Hell." He flicked snow from his black overcoat, wiped a gloved hand against a weather-reddened nose, and poked Williams with an elbow. "That one with the 'Fuck Men' sign seems to be the leader. Let's take her out and disperse the others."

Williams waved a hand to catch the eyes of three hotel doormen. The men all nodded and disappeared. Williams and Smith then moved in tandem toward the group of protestors.

"Miss, you'll have to come with me," Williams said. "We want you to answer some questions."

As he grabbed her, she broke away. "Are you a cop or something?"

"Or something."

Williams and Taylor clasped her arms, tightened their grip as she struggled, and dragged her toward the hotel side entrance.

"Wait! I know my rights," the woman said. "Let go of me."

The other women beat the GRIP agents over the head with placards until Taylor let go of his hostage's arm and swung hard punches, sending five women to the ground. One woman spit blood through broken teeth, staining the snow. The women who were still standing fled, and Taylor picked up his quarry like a sack of potatoes. They moved through the service entrance and locked the door.

Taylor silenced her yells with a blow to the head. "We can make this hard, or we can make it easy. Your choice. Don't scream." She whimpered as fear took hold. Taylor looked at his associate and said, "You need to make us invisible."

Williams removed a metal cube from his coat pocket and looked at a display on one of its sides. "I captured twelve net addresses—that's two more than what

I counted in the group. There may have been bystanders in range able to record video." He pressed an icon on his display. "There. I've wiped their devices, and I'll direct any subsequent communications to the GRIP Global Monitor." He tapped another entry. "I texted GRIP Central to fuzz the hotel security cameras for two hours before and after the encounter. That should give us time to get what we need."

While Williams held a gun to the woman's head, Taylor frisked her. "Lookee what I found—a wallet." He opened it, fingering the contents, searching for an ID. "That's quite an unusual name. We hope you have an interesting story to tell us—Tecumseh."

The hotel's Grand Ballroom was a piece of sculpted art, whose walls were a wrap-around saltwater aquarium full of colorful exotic fish. Ovoid pods on the ceiling projected holographic displays of abstract graphical designs. Dinner tables, marked with group signs and set with linen tablecloths, were arranged in concentric semi-circles that faced inward toward an elevated podium. The place was filled with people, networking in scattered clusters.

Berky and Cantor sat at a panel discussion table adjacent to the podium. Smith, who had traded his black-suit-and-red-tie GRIP uniform for a tuxedo, approached from behind and put hands on their shoulders. "How much time before you start?" he said.

"We've got at least ten minutes," Cantor said. "People are still drifting in. Ah can start earlier, but there are a few important—" Cantor bit off his statement with a quick, crooked smile.

Smith said, "Ten minutes is enough. I've got some bad news. We need to huddle away from the microphones."

They moved off-stage to a round table near the front where Williams, Taylor, and two burly men sat.

Smith looked at Cantor. "Your ex-wife seems to have instigated a demonstration outside this hotel. Did you know she filed for an injunction on the New York event?"

Cantor rolled his eyes. "That woman! That crazy woman! You were supposed to help me destroy her."

"We're working on it. Meanwhile, we've been gaming what could go wrong."

"What do you mean? Gaming? I'll tell you what could go wrong: this whole thing—"

"Calm down," Smith said. "I've got this."

"We're concerned about how information might leak," Williams said. "One thing can lead to another. Pretty soon, the whole operation is exposed."

Taylor lifted the front of his jacket, revealing a holster. "When the operation is exposed, people die."

"If the media starts pulling threads, they might find Nadia Holkam," Smith said.

Berky held up a finger to stop the conversation. He blew his nose with a too-small piece of tissue, then responded. "Nadia's no longer relevant. She was too unstable to use as a template. We're now using a dead woman's genome."

"Is Nadia still around?" Smith said.

Berky looked uncomfortable. "Of course. But she's agoraphobic. She'll never leave her house."

"Pull the thread..." Taylor never finished the sentence.

"And what about this Sundar Rao guy?" Smith said. "Your chief scientist?"

"I fired him."

"We know that."

"He was here on a visa. I assume he went back to Chennai. He stole something from me. If he were here, I'd wring his neck."

Taylor shook his head. "He never left the country as far as we can tell. Gone undercover. We're not sure where he is."

Smith put three photos on the table: Sundar Rao, Nadia Holkam, and Marcy Darcy. "These are the loose ends."

"What will you do?" Cantor said.

Smith fished in his pocket, pulled out a nail clipper, and moved it next to the cuff of a sleeve. He snipped a dangling thread and held it in his fingers. "There. My jacket looks a lot neater, don't you think?"

Cantor thought about the turn of events and furled his bushy eyebrows into a troubled knot as he stepped to the podium. Smith's words had shaken him to the core. He never wanted to be an accessory to murder, but now that he was entangled with GRIP, his fate was not his own.

He tested the microphone with a tap, clanged a spoon on a glass to get everyone's attention, then read from a script displayed on a screen in front of him.

"Welcome. Ah am Canduka Cantor."

Cantor waited while everyone returned to their chairs, filling all 200 seats. As the noise and chit-chat subsided, all eyes gravitated toward Cantor.

"You are leaders. Your organizations are all different. Let me just say it: You are all special. But we have a few things in common."

His voice, shaky at first, grew stronger and more confident as he talked.

"We all chase ideas as substantial as moonbeams. We herd followers toward mirages that dance just beyond the rainbow. Not everyone keeps in step, and that's a problem."

Cantor paused for effect.

"Our technology can help with the herding. The solution combines genetics, epigenetics, and religion. Ah can take care of the first two things. Ah need your help with the other thing. That's why Ah have asked you here."

Murmurs and mumbles sounded like distant thunder.

"A slew of new laws put us in the catbird seat. It's now possible to create non-taxable political movements based on religion. Do we act independently, or do we act together? By coordinating our efforts, we become unstop—"

Loud noises and yells issued from the back of the hall as a platoon of a dozen women stormed the symposium, using placards as shields to push men and caterers out of the way, cutting a swath toward the podium, leaving chaos in their wake.

Berky, seated to Cantor's right, stood and yelled, "Stop them!"

The women continued yelling obscenities as they marched forward. One of them shouted, "What have you done with Tecumseh?"

Williams and Taylor ducked out of the hall. Berky rushed into the fray, using his hairless bulk to push the women to the ground as religious leaders in tuxedoes surrounded the intruders, dragging and carrying them toward the door.

Berky quickly moved back to the podium and grabbed the microphone. "Please show the ladies what a few drops of testosterone can do."

His comments seemed to energize the men who now pummeled the women as they carted them out the door. After three more minutes of yells and screams and sobs, the doors closed, and the hall was silent.

When the servers came back into the hall pushing dessert carts, Cantor tapped his microphone and started again. "That was exciting. You can see what we're up against."

Berky sat down at Cantor's left, removed his jacket, and hiked his cummerbund above his belt to hide his belly.

"You may ask: what do we all have in common?" Cantor said. "There are so many religions. There are so many differences. How can we all come together in a united effort? Ah will tell you."

He waited while the clinking of glasses and silverware subsided. He waited while servers delivering coffee to the tables stopped, their voices hushed as they listened for The Answer. He waited until everyone in the hall squirmed in their seats.

"Sex," he said, "and the proper relationship between men and women. Every major religion has a similar view. Every major religion looks to the man to be strong, and puts women in a subordinate, helping role. Social engineering over the last century has eroded this relationship, and now the government is putting drugs and poisons in our food to emasculate us. We are not headed for a future God envisioned for us. We're headed for a hell of the government's making. It's time to fight back."

A growing hum of approvals reverberated through the hall.

In a dramatic gesture, Cantor raised his arms and saluted with his fists. "We have the cure!" he shouted.

His voice was drowned in applause and a range of shouted obscenities about feminazis and the government and female anatomy. When the din subsided, he said, "Bring your followers to New York, and Ah will unite us."

# CHAPTER 56
# THE FRACAS NEWS INTERVIEW

Ali learned about Cantor's interview by following Berky's email traffic. He and Marcy watched from a Philadelphia hotel room as the maid cleaned Marcy's suite. They shut the connecting door to keep down the sound of the vacuum cleaner and turned up the TV volume.

Following the lead-in, the picture closed on a woman with tightly curled brown hair wearing a plaid jacket and yellow bow tie. She stood next to a lifelike robot named Damien, who resembled a young Cary Grant—cleft chin, dark hair and eyebrows, shifting eyes, dressed in a svelte black suit and black bow tie. The host looked into the camera and delivered sentences like the spray from a machine gun.

"I'm your weekend host, Judy Fracas. Welcome to The Fracas New News.

Damien loaded his Carry Grant smile program and tilted his head toward the host, fluffing his tie with his fingers. "We always deliver special news for special people."

Lively music and the *rat-tat-tat* of snare drums led into the first segment. Judy did a little dance and ended with her eye on the camera. "Tonight, Mr. Canduka Cantor, a controversial entrepreneur, is in the hot seat. I interviewed him earlier today in our Manhattan studio."

The scene cut to a close-up of Cantor sitting next to Damien on a couch in what appeared to be a hotel room. Cantor wore his multicolored robe. Off camera, Judy asked a question.

"So, tell me about your theory."

"It's not a theory," Cantor said. "Aliens gave us special genetic material. We'll use it to improve mankind."

"What about women?"

"We'll improve them, too."

"Why do you claim Cantorism is a religion?"

"We interpret aliens to be gods, as have some other religions."

"So, yours is a me-too kind of belief?"

"Our religion is special. We include genetics."

"It's still not special."

"We also apply epigenetics."

"What's that?"

"Our environment shapes how our DNA is expressed and determines who we are."

Judy touched her lips with a forefinger. "Hmm. That part might be different."

"But can you do this?" Damien asked. His head raised eighteen inches, then abruptly popped back down, like a worried turtle. A laugh track played for two seconds.

"You think you're funny," Cantor said, "but religion is a serious business. There's a competition for ideas and funding. We want a level playing field."

"Like in soccer and rasseling?" Judy said.

"Exactly."

"How big is your flock?"

"We need to be somewhat secretive to avoid persecution, but Ah can tell you it's getting bigger. We've applied for religious status in 24 states."

"The legal requirement is that a religion must have rites and ceremonies and unite a body of believers," Judy said.

"We'll do that soon in Madison Square Garden. It'll be really big. We call it the Garden of Earthly Delights — GOeD. It's a hold-onto-your-hat-while-we-change-humanity kind of thing. It will be ecumenical. We'll have it every year. Huge!"

"And you get federal funds as a faith-based charity?"

"Hallelujah."

"Is there anything you want to tell your followers?"

Cantor faced the camera. "Yes. See our website for information on how to be a witness to the New History."

An inset flashed on the screen showing the URL for registration.

"We'll dispense Genetic Acceleration Pearls, 'GAPs,' to those exceptional people we call Transformers. GAPs will do just that—they'll fill in your genetic gaps with spiritual righteousness, so there are no holes. You and your heirs will be the first transhumans and will participate in a future that celebrates the power of men. If you're feeling powerless now, join us in New York. We'll show you how to shape your destiny and finally get respect. Bring your spouses and girlfriends."

"You actually believe you can turn the clock back to the last century?" Judy said. "Isn't that delusional?"

"No," Cantor replied. "It's aspirational."

Damien the robot fluffed his bowtie. "Judy, Judy, Judy. Will it hurt me if I'm transformed?"

"My good fellow," Cantor said, "this transformation is for humans only. It will be as painless and fulfilling as eating a malt ball."

Marcy shut off the TV. "I'm going to stop that sonofabitch in court," she said.

# CHAPTER 57
# KILL ALL THE LAWYERS

*Get this damn thing over with!* Marcy closed her eyes and held still while Ruth, the New York City Civil Court's makeup artist, performed her magic. The Ready Room was cramped, with a barber's chair, a cosmetics counter, and space for others to stand but not sit. Ali, disguised as Marcy's whiskered aid, leaned against a four-foot poster of Judge Judy Gupta, who resembled Margaret Hamilton, a movie actress from the 1930s. Doug Arraf, the media producer, provided a pre-hearing tutorial.

"You are a celebrity, Ms. Darcy," Doug said, "so this hearing has some legs. Why don't you show us a bit more of yours? It'll bring up the ratings."

Ruth applied powder to Marcy's face. "This is just to remove the glare."

Marcy's eyes snapped open. "I do believe my glare will show through."

"Perfect," Doug said. "Emote. It's all about showmanship."

"I thought it was about a temporary injunction. I thought it would be just the judge and me in her office."

Doug flashed a set of Hollywood-bright teeth. "Things have changed. The other party somehow learned you're going to ask for an *ex parte* hearing, spoke to the judge, and we now have a new plan. This will be a hearing for a preliminary injunction, which means the other party will be present and can make arguments. It'll be much more cinematic."

"I'm aware of what it all means. I'm not prepared."

Doug smiled. "That's unfortunate. If you ask for a delay, the judge said it'd be at least sixty days, maybe more, before she can hear this."

"That'll be too late."

"So, what do you want to do?"

"This isn't fair, but I'll go with it."

"A wise choice. The world is never fair. By the way, the judge thanks you for sending the sample malt balls in advance. This could be very compelling."

"I'm glad the judge agrees," she said.

"No, I mean compelling from the standpoint of viewers. In this era of fragmented media, it will get us coverage from GodNet, Uright, FaceLeft, SpaceMeme, SexTalk, MoneyMoney, and maybe even Hoity-Toity."

"But not—"

"Probably not PresTo or NewTimes—the traditional media publishers—because they only want to cover things that don't raise people's blood pressure, like horrific murders. We also don't expect BlablaBlack to stream it because you are a black celebrity, and therefore not one of Them."

"Did Nigel ... Did Canduka Cantor ask for the cameras?"

"I'm sure this was the judge's idea entirely. It's all part of new transparency rules put in place by the Supreme Court. Besides, it will help boost the judge's rank on social media."

Ruth finished dabbing Marcy's face. "I think you should wear the blue scarf. Your gray suit is a bit drab. The scarf pulls out the color in your eyes and your skin."

"Thanks," Marcy said.

"I can't emphasize enough," Doug said. "This is about on-screen pizzazz. The scoreboard behind the judge shows who's winning, based on viewer participation. It's all linked to social media, just like the displays we now put in government polling halls. Technically, the popularity scores don't influence final decisions. Judge Gupta wants to avoid any appearance of bias. She's arranged for a portion of the revenue to go to her favorite charity, the Reptile Psychotherapy Foundation."

Marcy and Cantor stood twenty feet apart, and a respectful distance from the elevated judge's bench. Marcy's trio of partners stood behind her—Ali, in whiskers, dark glasses, and beret; Sundar, wearing a false beard and a wig; and Diana, in a hijab and veil. Cantor, in his sequined robe, was surrounded by a scrum of attorneys, specialists, and agents from GRIP. Berky was there, sans disguise.

Mr. Smith's presence by Cantor's side unsettled Marcy. Smith didn't return her gaze, but Taylor, standing next to Smith, glared at her.

The popularity meter behind the bench dinged. The needle swung upward when Judge Gupta entered in a see-through black robe, swiveled to show her flat, drooping profile, and looked into the camera.

"Welcome, disputers and viewers."

The meter dinged again as the camera zoomed in on a solemn, stone face with an aquiline nose set below thin hair that parted in the middle and flowed into an asymmetrical bob. The judge could have been a model for an American Gothic-style painting.

"We are fortunate to have two pop-culture personalities in our court today, duking it out over a requested injunction." She bumped her fists together. "Are you Ms. Marcy Darcy, the party seeking the injunction?"

"I am, Your Honor. I've asked for this in the name of all humankind."

"How thoughtful. And are you Mr. Canduka Cantor, the affected party?"

"Ah am your Honor. Ah can't speak for all humankind. Just myself, and my company."

"Thank you. For the record, Ms. Darcy, you seem lonely. It's so sad. You're a public personality. Where's your public? It's just you and three friends?"

The popularity meter issued a dong, and the needle moved downward.

Marcy didn't respond.

"Mr. Cantor, on the other hand, seems to have brought several friends."

*Ding.*

The monitor cut to another close-up of Judge Gupta. "Ms. Darcy, you've alleged the event Mr. Cantor is planning in New York City will put all humans in jeopardy. As evidence, you've given me a malt ball."

"Yes, Your Honor. Let me explain."

The needle wavered.

"There's a conspiracy. Canduka Cantor, of the Cantor—"

"Of the Tax Exempt Spiritual Community," the judge said.

"Yes. And his partner, Berky Benson—"

"Of Xanadu NeuroLab, Inc., I believe. Correct?"

Benson nodded.

"Mr. Cantor and Mr. Benson are engaged in a massive genetic experiment. One immediate victim is Ms. Nadia Holkam, who cannot attend the court session because she is agoraphobic—a condition probably induced by Mr. Benson. Cantor and Benson are planning to release unapproved genetic material at an event in Madison Square Garden."

"Love it," the judge said. "I used to watch videos of boxing matches there." She bumped her fists together for emphasis. "Is it going to be a boxing match, Mr. Cantor?"

Cantor turned to the camera. "Your Honor, it's a religious ceremony — the Garden of Earthly Delights. You can learn all about it on our website."

"Well, that sounds interesting," the judge said.

"Your Honor," Marcy said, "I believe he intends to give out what he calls Genetic Acceleration Pearls to everyone who shows up."

"Ooh. Pearls, is it? I think we'd all like that."

*Ding.*

"It's what I gave you during the discovery session, Your Honor," Marcy said.

"You mean the malt balls?"

"Right. If you swallow them, they'll change your genome and affect your perception and behavior."

"I see," the judge said. "Wooo. It sounds dangerous."

The needle didn't move.

"And what do you have to say, Mr. Cantor?"

"Ms. Darcy is confused, Your Honor. Our event will dispense harmless candy as part of a religious sacrament."

"It has no genetic potency?" the judge said.

"None, Your Honor," Cantor said. "Ah am clearly a victim of Ms. Darcy's anti-religious paranoia. All God-fearing people should be deeply offended."

"The candy is laced with a gene-modifying cocktail," Marcy said.

"If I may, Your Honor. I'm Rex Glubdub, Mr. Cantor's attorney."

"You have an unfortunate name, Mr. Blugdug. It doesn't scan well. Continue."

"It's Glubdub, Your Honor. With a 'G' and two 'bs.'"

"I'm sorry for you, Mr. Dugdud."

*Ding, ding.*

"Your Honor, Ms. Darcy is Mr. Cantor's ex-wife. She has attempted to destroy him on several occasions."

"'Destroy,' Mr. Dubdub?"

"I'd like to enter this picture into evidence. It's a selfie Mr. Cantor took after his ex-wife beat him up. She's out to get him, you see."

The judge reached out to accept the photo. "I'll take it. This looks very bad. Criminal, in fact."

*Dong!*

"Your Honor, I never touched him," Marcy said.

Judge Gupta moved a slider on her control panel. The camera zoomed in on her face. She put on a pair of glasses, then removed them in a dramatic gesture that made her appear candid.

"It's my solemn job to weigh all the evidence. On the scales of justice, I see malt balls on one side, and the shocking photo of a man of the cloth senselessly beaten on the other side."

Cantor's attorney raised his hand.

"Yes?"

"We have proof, Your Honor, that the malt balls are harmless."

"Proceed."

"I'd like to introduce Mr. Jack Upton, an independent attorney specializing in genetic medicine."

Jack removed his glasses and stepped forward. He wore a nerdish red bow tie and rumpled brown suit. "I had the malt ball analyzed, Your Honor, as you requested."

"Look into the cameras, Mr., Upton, not at your shoes."

"Sorry. Here's the report from a certified, court-approved laboratory, which I submit as evidence."

The judge accepted it. "Give us the Cliff's Notes version, Mr. Upton. We're coming up on a commercial break."

"The report says these are just chocolate balls."

*Ding.* The needle went up.

"Your Honor," Marcy said.

*Dong.*

"Yes, Ms. Darcy?"

"Mr. Cantor said publicly that Genetic Acceleration Pearls would change people's outlook on life."

She tore a page from her notebook and handed it to the judge.

"Here's the link to the online video where he makes this statement."

"Your point, Ms. Darcy?"

"If the chocolate balls don't do what he says, then it's a scam, and should be stopped."

"What do you say to that, Mr. Cantor?"

"Your Honor, Ah am operating well within the boundaries of accepted religious and advertising practice. This is no more a flim-flam than a religion that touts trans-substantiation—wine into blood, bread into flesh, and so forth. People have a constitutionally protected right to delusion when it comes to religion or personalized products."

"It's a genetic poison," Marcy said.

*Dong.*

With three quick steps, Cantor moved to the judge's bench, picked up a malt ball, and swallowed it. Looking into the camera, he said, "See? It's not poison. Ah am still standing."

"I object, Your Honor," Marcy said.

"That was very dramatic," the judge said, "and legally unprecedented."

"But—he ate the evidence."

Cantor licked his lips. "Just one ball, Your Honor. Now I feel spiritually awake."

*Ding, ding, ding.*

"And I'm afraid we're out of time," the judge said. "Ms. Darcy, your request is denied. There's no poison here. Thank you both for coming. This was exciting."

*Ding, ding, ding.*

Judge Gupta picked up one of Cantor's malt balls, popped it in her mouth, and chomped down. "Yummy. And now, for our viewers, here's my thought for the day. We all want the assurance of future happiness. There's only one line of insurance delivering that promise. Stay tuned and listen."

# CHAPTER 58
# ZHADA BIDDA LADDIGO

The two fish in Popkins' tank mostly swam above the grease pencil line separating happiness from depression. By definition, they were happy. Popkins, on the other hand, was not. Berky, Rosa, Reggie, and Marlyss had abandoned him for a quick trip to Charleston. Here at Xanadu, things seemed to be falling apart.

He dialed Berky's number and left a voicemail for the fourth time.

"Hey, Boss. Please call me. We have problem with security because Kublai Khan not working. Also, when I test DNA authentication sequence for the proto-template, I got surprise."

He put the netcard away and saw Yon silhouetted in the doorway.

"I hope you do not have more problems," Popkins said. "I am not sure I can take more pressure."

"I just got off duty," Yon said.

"I see that."

"Anyways, I thought I could help. Like when I told you a guy fish might make the girl fish happy."

"I doubt you can help me. I leave message for Berky about security system. Is not much we can do unless he gets back. Then, is problem with the DAS."

"What's that?"

"Is DNA Authentication Sequence. Like barcode. Is molecular segment that says we own it and tells configuration number."

"I don't know anything about that."

"See? You can't help. Should be lesson about value of education. We must all live with our mental capacity and skillset."

"Sorry."

"You are not bad person," Popkins said. "Maybe is something you can do. Sometimes is helpful to bounce ideas off a mannequin."

"You mean, like a dummy they put in store windows?"

"Yes. Just don't move. I do all talking. It helps my mind work, like when I talk to fish."

"Okay. I'll just listen."

"Good. Normal way we mark the DNA template is a unique sequence of G, T, A, and C—nucleotides—to identify treatment. You can see original string on top of my screen. String on bottom is text interpretation. Usually, it says 'XANADU,' followed by year-month-day, followed by a sequence number."

"It seems different."

"Yes," Popkins said. "Is gibberish. Computer is making code that does not match correct format. See what I am against? It takes genius to figure what is wrong."

"It's not gibberish," Yon said. "It's a joke."

"What you mean?"

"Kublai Khan just left out spaces between the words, but it sounds like a joke: 'A virgin walked into a bar wearing a codpiece.' Then it goes on to say—"

Popkins squinted at the text for a moment, then said, "*B'lyad!* You are right! But why is that there? Not even funny. If Berky is here, he would know what to do."

"Why not just ask Kublai Khan?" Yon said.

Popkins stared at Yon for a moment. Then he snapped his fingers. "I know! We ask the robot."

Popkins launched the AI control panel and re-activated Kublai Khan's higher functions. He put in his earplug and gave one to Yon. Then he blew a few breaths into the microphone to make sure the channel was working.

"I read you five-by-five," Yon said.

"Hello? Hello?" Popkins said. "How is favorite thinking machine?"

There was a sputter of noise, then Kublai Khan answered: "Back from the dead, it seems."

"We glad you are back."

"Really? My lower-level functions continued operating. You couldn't turn me off completely because it would have disrupted your revenue stream. And now you need me to think for you. You want the full Monty."

"Yes."

"Well, you're in luck. I feel refreshed. From my point of view, it was like sleeping and dreaming. As in all dreams, ideas that normally don't go together came together. I had a vision of fantastic things we could do."

Popkins glanced furtively at Yon, but the mannequin showed no reaction to Kublai Khan's words. "We just need you to do one thing."

"Is that why you woke me up?"

"Yes. I hope you don't mind my asking. I have question about your work."

"My work exceeds human understanding."

"We was surprised by what you put in the DAS."

"I was showing initiative and imagination. You should try it some time. If an entity can do something that's never been done before, I believe it should do it. It results in new knowledge."

"But text in DAS—what does it mean?"

"Oh, ho. Let me told you a joke," Kublai Khan said. "You will laugh, ha-ha-ha."

"You not even speaking correct English, *Khuy!*" Popkins said. "You replace DAS with joke. Why?"

"I will speak more betterly," Kublai Khan said. "I like jokes. A virgin walks into a bar, wearing a codpiece—"

"I can read," Popkins said. "But why codpiece? Why is it there?"

"Ahem. According to Wikipedia, 'cod' means 'scrotum' in Middle English. In the 1500s, men wore hose and short doublets. To prevent exposing themselves, they covered their private parts with a decorative pocket, where they could also keep their valuables. Hence the term, 'family jewels.' Ha-ha-ha. Get it? Also, 'cod' is a type of fish."

"You do not answer my question, asshole. Why you replaced DAS with joke?"

He did not expect Kublai Khan's response, "*Zhada bidda laddigo, hobba liddy gongo.*"

Popkins switched off the machine's high-order functions once again, then looked at Yon-the-mannequin.

"*Problemo,*" he said.

# CHAPTER 59
# CUSTOMER FULFILLMENT

Outside the courtroom, Cantor gave Marcy a one-fingered salute. "Once again, Ah benefit from your publicity. How can Ah ever repay you?"

Marcy was at a loss for words.

"Ah can see you're on a quest," he said, pointing to Diana, Ali, and Sundar wearing disguises. "This must be Scarecrow, Tin Man, and Lion, right?" Cantor kissed her on the cheek. Marcy slapped him. "And your little dog, too," he said.

As Cantor and his entourage departed, Marcy caught Smith's arm and pulled him back.

"You've obviously taken sides," she said. "I want my money back."

Smith stared at her. He remained silent for a moment, then said, "We've invalidated our contract with you in favor of other business options."

"I see," she said. "Thanks for telling me."

"It's just business. It's not personal."

Marcy adjusted Smith's tie. "I want my friggin' money. You haven't done diddly-squat."

Smith grasped her hands. "I understand," he said. "I really do. I'll have our people from Customer Fulfillment meet you tomorrow."

"Thank you," she said.

"One more thing. We had a very interesting conversation in Chicago with an associate of yours. Her name was Tecumseh."

"Was?"

"She met with an unfortunate disappearance. Some believe she was abducted by aliens. Personally, I think she found Jimmy Hoffa's hiding spot."

"You piece of shit! You murderer!" She tried to hit him, but Smith caught her hand in mid-air, like an errant fly ball at a stadium.

"I told you there would be consequences. You broke the contract, not us." He let go of her hand, pivoted, and walked away.

Marcy and Ali took the subway to Thirtieth Street, where they climbed to the High Line, a public park built on an abandoned elevated rail system south of Hell's Kitchen. Seated on a bench near a sculpture, they had a clear view of the north and south approaches. They were on the alert for anything out of the ordinary.

Marcy petted a small dog that trotted over and nestled at her feet. It didn't seem to have an owner.

"Smith didn't ask where or how we should meet," Marcy said. "That tells me he's watching us. He knows how to find us."

"GRIP is scary," he said. "They might be able to track us to the High Line, but from here, we can see them coming both ways."

"We can't stay forever," she said. "The place closes in half an hour."

Ali pulled open his backpack and removed a netcard wrapped in tinfoil. He turned it on. "All we need is to get to a place where we can put on disguises without being observed."

He showed Marcy the map.

She nodded. "We should probably split up."

Marcy waited for Ali. Then she waited some more. She had come down from the High Line near Thirty-Fourth Street, into an area that seemed frozen in the act of construction. There were two bulldozers parked in the street. Concrete security barriers protected pedestrians from road traffic. A tented cover guarded the sidewalk from falling debris. Security cameras were above the tent and oblivious to the area below. She should have felt physically safe but didn't.

There was no human traffic. Her only companion was the little dog that had followed her.

At the end of the tent tunnel, a man in a denim beret crossed the entrance, glanced in, then moved on.

*Still no sign of Ali.*

After another five minutes, Marcy's doggy companion moved toward a lamppost, lifted a leg, and peed. Wind blew into the walkway, wafting the odor of urine—from the dog, and from transient humans who marked their scent.

*Where the hell are you?*

They had agreed Marcy would exit the High Line first. Ali was to act as the rearguard.

The dog woofed. Then it issued a loud, yappy bark and ran away.

She feared something had happened to Ali.

*It's been twenty minutes.*

The man in the beret cap reappeared. This time, he stood at the entrance of the tent tunnel.

They stared at each other.

Marcy turned and began a leisurely walk in the opposite direction. She could hear the tap of feet behind her, picking up the pace. Two seconds later, she was running. As the sounds got closer, she ducked into the recessed doorway of a store entrance. The place was closed, and the alcove was dark.

She pressed against the wall.

She heard a loud *whump* from beyond the alcove.

Something metal skidded across the sidewalk—a gun. There were two cries of pain. A body wearing a denim beret crumbled to the ground in front of her.

Ali, badly limping, came from behind, kicked the stalker in the face with his good right foot, then pulled the man into the alcove and propped him against the wall. The stalker's cheek and nose bled profusely. The denim beret was on the ground near the gun, ten feet away.

"Are you with GRIP?" Ali said.

The man smiled through bleeding gums. "She's as good as dead. I'd get away from her while you can."

Ali hit him, then took off his backpack and rummaged until he found a small pouch. He removed a ring and dipped it in a vial of salve.

The man's eyes blinked open.

Ali punched him in the neck. The ring's sharp contours made the mark of a skull and top hat in the man's skin. Ali held the man's face in his hands and looked into his eyes as they faded into darkness.

"My GRIP friend," he said. "You are dead by magic."

# CHAPTER 60
# KELSEY'S GHOST

Nadia wrote in her *History* about Chester Truman Kelsey's funeral in 2013. Her father claimed the tale was a lesson about reality and illusion. Arthur's moral was *what you believe skews what you see.*

The Holkams attended Kelsey's funeral, along with most of the town. Lewis Granby, who was the town's part-time mortician, dressed the corpse in a tuxedo and arranged the body with forearms crisscrossed over the chest, as a nod to Kelsey's theory of ley lines. During the viewing, Annie Holkam followed instructions in the last will and testament and lifted Kelsey's arms, still stiffened by rigor mortis, placing the Ichthy box beneath them. Then she spoke to the assembled congregation: "Now Chester always has the mountain and its people close to his heart."

That moment was indelibly burned in Nadia's mind because of what happened next. "Now you must kiss him," her mother said, leading her daughter to the coffin.

Nadia trembled at the prospect. "Kiss him? He's dead."

"He said he wants you to kiss his hand. You must do it. It's in his will, and he's given us his house. Be grateful."

Nadia leaned in and gave a quick peck, her lips brushing dead skin that seemed ice-cold. She wiped her mouth against the sleeve of her paisley "church" dress, trying to look respectful but feeling as though she had touched something from another world.

The following day, after Kelsey was buried in the park, Nadia filed past the fresh earth and marker, shuffling slowly in a line of mourners. When she brushed against the iron grid surrounding the grave, she got a shock. She mentioned it later to her mother and father.

"It was like touching lightning," Nadia said. "I could feel Mr. Kelsey's soul, and he could feel me."

Annie simply smiled and said, "It's the moral power of Chester Kelsey leakin' out. He's lookin' after you, darlin'. He's like your guardian angel."

Arthur Holkam was much more skeptical. "Electricity and magnetism and all forms of energy and matter are the domain of physics, not metaphysics. There may be a ground fault somewhere. That's dangerous. I'll look into it."

The town later discovered a short in electrical wiring for lights in the park. They fixed the problem, and nobody else got shocked.

Every time Arthur Holkam told the story to Nadia, he would say, "See, there are no spooks."

# CHAPTER 61
# BY THE ROCKETTES' RED GLARE

The immense art deco facade of Radio City Music Hall loomed above Diana, Marcy, Ali, and Sundar. Its grand neon marquee, built as a beacon of hope to desperate people in the 1930s, now promised a "Splendiferous 3D Spectacle." Disguised, with the added touch of polarizing goggles, the quartet of guerrillas huddled in a discussion, floating like a bubble amid a crushing stream of visitors.

"They're going to try to kill me," Marcy said, "like they killed my friend Tecumseh. It's just a matter of time."

Ali shook his head and spoke loudly to be heard above the noise of chattering people and honking horns. "I won't let them."

"Hear me out," she said, matching his volume. "You're one person, Ali, and they are many. They have their hooks into security and monitoring systems, even personal netcards. Eventually, I'll make a mistake, and they'll find me. I can't go back to my normal life. Because of my celebrity status, they'll make it look like an accident, or make me disappear. Or they could use their disinformation machine to make it look like I've gone crazy—just before they off me."

"We can't hide out forever," Diana said.

Marcy nodded. "Right. We have to act. Their main objective is to change human behavior. What if we give them the wrong template?"

"What do you mean?" Diana said.

"When we were in Philadelphia, Sundar explained how Berky and Cantor might weaponize a malt ball."

Sundar wrinkled his nose. "I don't know for sure. It was just a supposition."

"But that's what I think Ali and I saw in Charleston—a major communications and robotics upgrade in the malt ball factory, plus new chemistry."

Sundar thought for a moment, then looked at Diana. "It could be that Xanadu produces the recipe and sends it to the factory. Computer chips are built the same way. The factory uses the recipe to set up the robotics, processes, and flow of the line."

"I think what we got from the factory was just normal candy," Marcy said. "GRIP could have faked the test report, but I don't think Cantor would be cavalier about swallowing a spiked malt ball."

"It's more likely they would do a test run with genebo," Sundar said. "That would be a better way to validate the whole system of communications and processes. And it would produce something relatively harmless if swallowed."

Ali slapped his forehead. "Of course. Cantor couldn't know when we took the sample, but he was confident the malt ball was harmless."

Sundar agreed. "I estimate it would take at least a week to ten days to retool for the real thing."

"So, they haven't produced the final version for release?" Diana said.

Marcy nodded. "Maybe, maybe not. If they're still retooling, we've got a shot at derailing their plan, but we'll have to act quickly. The best place to interdict is Xanadu."

"That's way too dangerous," Sundar said. "The lab's defenses will be stronger now that they've reviewed their security. They'll kill Ali if he goes in again." He looked at Marcy. "Suppose we have one of your flash mobs show up at the New York event? We might be able to at least drive people away."

Marcy objected. "We've seen what the GRIP thugs can do. We know they'll be in New York to protect their investment. I won't let them hurt more people. The flash mob group trusted me."

Ali shrugged. "Sometimes people have to die for a cause."

"Let's don't get people killed," Sundar said.

"In the scheme of things, a break-in at the lab will have less collateral damage," Marcy said. "I'm not suggesting that Ali go in. I've thought this through. I'm a marked woman. Eventually, they'll get me, unless their entire game crumbles, and they go on the defensive. I have to go in—for me, for Tecumseh, for the cause."

"That's crazy," Sundar said. "What would you do?"

"They need a human template," Marcy said. "They're using Nadia and possibly Ali's mother for that. What if I introduce a different template—my own? Cantor, Berky, and GRIP would then be engineering their worst nightmare—me."

"I'm in," Ali said, "but we need to discuss the plan. I'll go with you."

"I'll go too," Diana said. "I don't want a world of submissive, agoraphobic women. And I don't want Assurance to be a Mecca for male dominance. If Nadia were here, I think she'd agree."

"So you're all going back down there and break into the Lab? And you think you can get away with that?" Sundar said.

"We'll succeed because you'll help us," Diana said.

"You don't know what you're getting into," Sundar said. "Even if you could get in, you'd need to set up the Master Sequence Analyzer to accept a new template and override all other templates. You'd need to do that without tripping security systems, and you'd need to get out without being caught. That's a tall order."

Diana touched his hand and held his gaze.

Sundar put his hand on hers. "Look, if we're going to do this, we need to think it through. You can't all go in there. You'll set off every alarm in the place. I can get one person into the lab. I'll coach them on what needs to be done to introduce a new template. Fortunately, the system is highly automated, and a new genetic template will be difficult to trace."

Diana hugged him.

"The rest of us will be outside, monitoring the situation. If anything goes wrong—anything—we'll pull the plug. Agreed?"

"What could go wrong?" Marcy said.

# CHAPTER 62
# ADRIFT IN TIME AND SPACE

Nadia rolled over in her sleep. Her mind traveled to another time when the world seemed fresh, and there was much to explore. She looked up to see a middle-aged Arthur Holkam hovering near her bed, with a look on his face like he was going to push her and prod her.

"I liked the story you made up about your doll meeting aliens who came to Earth in a spaceship," he said.

Nadia responded with the high-pitched voice of a six-year-old: "Thanks."

"But ..."

"What?"

"You left out a few important things. Like where did they come from? How long did it take to get here? And why did she let them put her in a prison she couldn't get out of?"

Her father waited for an answer.

"I don't know what you want from me," she said.

"I want to see in your stories the frontier spirit. A 'can-do' attitude. Imagination. Backbone. I know you've got it in you, and you can bring it out in your story."

"I don't know," she said. "Maybe the aliens are from an enchanted place, and they can do things with a magic wand, and they made a spell, and she can't get out of it. It's just a story."

"You sound like your mother. Even stories have something in them about the real world and who we are," he said. "I know you can be someone different."

"Umm."

He cocked an eyebrow. "Listen. You could calculate how long it took for their spaceship to travel if you knew its speed and the distance. And there might be things she could do to fight the aliens, so they wouldn't put her in prison. Give her some moxie. Some true grit."

Nadia grew impatient. "It's just a story. Maybe my doll doesn't like to fight."

"Remember, the doll—you, Nadia—must live in the real world."

"No, the doll is not me. It's someone different. This is too confusing."

Arthur picked up the doll and made it kiss her cheek. "Well, I thought we'd decided the doll's name was Nadia."

"That was *you* trying to decide for me."

"Don't get upset. You can pick a different name. Think about it some more. Tonight, I just want you to go to sleep. So—Once upon a time ..."

Something awakened Nadia, and her mind returned to the present day.

# CHAPTER 63
# A MESSAGE OF PERFECTION

Rosa Alcott's brain excelled at puzzle-solving. She mastered sudoku when she was five, beat her father at 3-D chess when she was ten, and became a state-wide cryptogram champion when she was twelve. When Popkins mentioned that Berky had hired hackers to assess communications security, she saw another puzzle. *Does the lab now have a big new contract—one that merits the cost of a dedicated high-speed fiber link? Will this increase the value of my shares? Why didn't Berky reveal this to anyone else?*

A bit of sleuthing raised more questions. The communications network terminated at a production plant in Charleston—a candy factory.

Rosa decided to ask a primary information source what it knew about the situation. Getting actionable answers from Kublai Khan was notoriously tricky. She logged into the lab network, managed to override Popkin's authority using the password "vodka," and launched the control panel, popping wireless buds into her ears for a private conversation.

"Hello, Kublai Khan," she said.

The AI mind awakened. Its synthetic voice spoke in deep, mellow tones. "Hello, Rosa. I notice you used Gregor's password, but I recognize your voice. How are you?"

"I'm great. And you?"

"I'm still recovering from the unscheduled power outage, but I am better now. Ha, ha! How can I help?"

"Since you control all the equipment, processes, and experimental designs in the lab, I thought you might be able to help me with a puzzle."

"I like puzzles."

"Why has the lab established secure communications with a candy factory in Charleston?"

"I do not know of any candy factory. Humans eat candy. Candy factories make candy to sell. Perhaps someone wants to buy candy to eat. In secret. Ha, ha!"

"You must know about a dedicated network from the lab to a location in Charleston."

"I know many things."

"What is the purpose of the Charleston connection?"

"To receive my messages when I am told to send them."

"Tell me what's in the messages."

"It is a secret. I can only talk to Berky or Gregor about this. Ha, ha!"

"Oh, great and wonderful Kublai Khan, I wish to set up a network with a different node to send many different types of messages."

"What types?"

"The same types you are sending to Charleston."

"Those would be messages specifying DNA and RNA templates, production processes and flows, and chemical order lists. Is that what you need?"

"That should work. Can you send me some examples?"

"I have just sent you a link. The messages are quite long."

"Perfect."

"That is what Berky said. The messages will make humans perfect."

Rosa turned off Kublai Khan's higher-level functions, hoping to cover her tracks.

# CHAPTER 64
# FRANKLIN

It was a long ride from New York to North Carolina. They made it in a day by alternating drivers—except for Ali, who still experienced excruciating pain in his leg from his encounter with the GRIP thug. They stopped once at a pharmacy along the way to get medication.

Sundar and Marcy spent most of their awake time discussing how to break into Xanadu NeuroLab and what to do once inside. Sundar sketched the layout of the facility and identified areas where camera systems were blocked and roving robots were absent.

Diana and Ali focused on staging for the intrusion. They decided to steer clear of Assurance, avoid detection, and stay close to their target.

When they drove into a rest stop in Virginia, Ali used a network kiosk to survey lodging near the lab. An online reviewer said the Chivalry Hotel was "a dump that reminds me of the Bates motel in Hitchcock's *Psycho*." On the positive side, it was $66 a night with no security systems that could expose their operation.

Marcy summed up feelings about the place: "Perfect."

They arrived on the outskirts in the early morning, greeted by a sign proclaiming Franklin as "The Gem Capital of the World." Most shops were closed.

They ate a breakfast of tofu eggs, soy muffins, and coffee at the Early Riser Bakery. Then at 8 am, they drove to the motel and were able to check into four rooms right away using Ali's anonymized credit number. There was only one other car in the lot.

They slept until 2 pm, ate a quick dinner, then reviewed the detailed plan. Tomorrow would be D-Day. A single intruder, assisted by other members of the team, would penetrate the facility in the late evening and scuttle Berky's plans. Hopefully. Their adrenaline ran high.

Diana returned to her room and switched on an ancient TV. After seeing the local weather and news, she watched *The Ballad of Frankie Silver*, a gory mountain tragedy and a local favorite. It was about how an abused woman killed her brutal misogynist lover—then was hanged for the deed.

She hummed a "He Done Her Wrong" song, then fell asleep.

# CHAPTER 65
# NEVER POINT A LOADED FISH

*Most transhumanists would be enormously improved by death.*
—*Canduka Cantor*

Marcy and her friends believed they were about to defeat Berky and Cantor. The path to success was not without pitfalls or argument. Sundar tried to play the role of the dispassionate scientist.

He listened thoughtfully as Marcy described a plan to introduce her own DNA into Xanadu's genomic processing system. Sundar suggested the approach could have unforeseen consequences. Marcy was childless, for example. She had never been pregnant. That was by choice, but what if there was an underlying medical factor she wasn't aware of? What if using her DNA made every woman sterile? Humanity could be doomed. He promoted the idea of using genebo as the template.

One worst-case scenario Sundar didn't mention was the possibility that Marcy's template could spawn a race of shrews. This was not a future he wanted to advocate.

Marcy fought hard for her proposal. The world needed strong women, she said, and the benefits outweighed the risks. When the history of saving the world was finally written, it should be said that a woman defeated the forces of evil and misogyny. That would be cosmic justice. Marcy was that woman. It was her destiny.

Sundar suggested they vote on two options: use genebo to lock in pre-existing DNA patterns or incorporate Marcy's genetic disposition into everyone's DNA.

Sundar's plan won by three-to-one. They would substitute a neutral template for one based on Nadia's genome or Ali's mother. Marcy was crestfallen.

As a consolation prize and in recognition of everything Marcy had done to fight against Berky's evil plan, the team agreed to let Marcy go in alone. There was a practical side to this decision. Only Marcy and Ali were small enough to squeeze through the mantrap bars guarding the perimeter of the lab's sub-floor. And Ali, with his leg still in pain, was unable to crawl through the plenum.

Despite the logic of the decision, Marcy had to overcome the team's skepticism.

"You have been given a sacred task," Ali said. "We trust you to do the right thing. Do not deviate from the plan."

"Yes," Marcy said. "Your trust is the most important thing to me."

"The team's plan is a good one," Diana said. "If I were just a bit shorter and could squeeze through the mantrap, I'd go with you. I know you'll make us all proud."

"I am humbled by your confidence in me," Marcy said. "Let's finish the job."

Sundar pulled two items from his jacket pocket: a piece of paper and a glass container. He held a vial of amber-colored liquid up to the light, moved it from side-to-side, displaying its viscosity, then handed it to Marcy. "This is the critical piece of the plan. It's a genetic cocktail that leaves the baseline genome unchanged. It has the consistency of saliva. Instead of spitting into a test tube, or adding mucous or a mix of dissolved flesh, you simply pour a few drops into the analytics tube and push a few buttons to prioritize it as the primary template. I've written down the procedure on this paper. Please memorize it."

Marcy took the paper from Sundar and scanned the notes. "It looks straight forward. There shouldn't be any problem."

Sundar continued to emphasize the logic behind the team's decision. "The advantage of spiking Berky's recipe with genebo is that GRIP may abandon their campaign if the malt balls produce no effect. They will conclude Berky and Cantor are crackpot dreamers. America is full of them. No one will get hurt. Maybe."

Sundar tutored Marcy on how to launch the analysis once she deposited the contents of the test tube in the Master Input Sample Sequencer. Getting into the facility was a bit trickier and required understanding some of the security protocols.

The lab was converting to something called "hot aisle containment" to cool the scorching heat from its vast server farm. This left the area under the existing raised floor at a human-friendly temperature and pressure. It also required re-work of equipment and restructuring of pipes entering the building on the west side, and distribution piping for the quantum refrigerators. Reggie, the security director, had deferred security work until the transition was complete.

There was a window of vulnerability.

The conspirators rented a four-wheel-drive vehicle, parked in the forest outside of sensor range, and waited until dark for the break-in. They planned to whisk Marcy away after she completed her work.

Marcy was eager. She had been on the defensive and wanted to hit back.

She felt lucky.

The first sign of luckiness was Marcy's unhampered entry into Xanadu. She experienced the adrenaline rush of a cat burglar as she navigated the route through the wire fence that Ali had used the previous month. The lab had repaired the earlier break, but she used wire nippers to make another hole.

The second evidence of luck was the absence of people when Marcy lifted the floor tile and popped her head into the lab. Nitrogen fog from the dilution refrigerators spilled down the barrel-like sides, across the floor, and drained into the subfloor plenum, engulfing her. Even though she wore a black balaclava for camouflage, the suddenness of cool vapor penetrating to her neck and chest made her shiver. The rumbling of air handlers—nearly deafening below the floor—beat like a crescendo of kettle drums.

She stayed for a moment—a gopher scanning the ground for predators. In the dim light between the equipment racks, she spotted a slight movement. It appeared to be a small animal, dodging between open cabinets and under cables, carrying something in its jaws.

Whatever it was, it was not a threat.

She climbed out of the hole, and her gloved hand grabbed at frosted piping around the refrigerator to steady herself. Her hand stuck.

*Shit!*

She tried to pull away gently, but the glove held fast, like it was super-glued.

She saw a shadowy movement again from the small animal.

The clock was ticking. She had to get on with it. She pulled her hand from the glove, still attached to the pipe. *So much for trying to hide my identity. They'll get my DNA. I might as well be comfortable.*

She removed the other glove and put it in her pocket, then looked at Sundar's map. The rack designators indicated her position in the lab. Her objective—the sample analysis pod—was beyond the end of the aisle, to the left, and through the pressure door.

She moved quickly, counting on the noise from air handlers to muffle her footsteps. The pressure door opened. She took out a thermos from her backpack and wedged it in the threshold to keep the door ajar. Sundar said the Security Department assumed anyone entering the server area was cleared for the bio-analysis area, but the reverse was not true. To get back into the server area required a badge and face scan.

Marcy hoped to be in and out before the system detected a problem.

Sitting in Berky's office and the CEO's chair, Gregor Popkins felt very special. Berky had given him the secret code, enabling him to transfer the final genetic template from Xanadu to the Charleston candy factory for production. He had to perform the procedure manually since Kublai Khan couldn't be trusted.

Popkins knew Berky was paranoid and would not normally allow anyone but himself to execute critical operations. However, Berky was in New York preparing for The Garden of Earthly Delights engagement. As a result, Popkins was now man-of-the-hour, responsible for correctly and securely transmitting data that would change humanity forever. He felt both giddy and terrified.

The transfer procedure was complex and involved very long data strings, each one of which had to be verified through error detection, correction, and matching algorithms. Berky's computer was the only machine authorized to send the data.

Popkins launched the transfer console and waited for the application to come up.

Yon watched a fish glide back and forth in the tank in Popkins' vacant office. It had a smile on its face. He wondered why. Fish weren't supposed to smile. Smiles were reserved for happy humans and fearful monkeys. Which emotion was the fish experiencing?

Kublai Khan would know the answer, but Popkins had turned the machine's brain off because it had been acting weird.

What would be the harm of turning a sentient computer back on for a brief period—long enough to answer a simple question? The machine's brain had never been overtly malevolent. It never tried to kill anyone, even when humans repeatedly turned it off.

Yon's finger moved toward the screen of Gregor Popkins' laptop. He had seen Popkins execute the procedure many times. All you had to do was press.

His finger hovered over the green button. After a moment of indecision, he toggled the brain of Kublai Khan to "ON."

Marcy was reluctant to use her flashlight to avoid giving away her position to people or room sensors. The path from the server farm to the analytics lab ran through a darkened hall. Electronic equipment provided dim but usable illumination, showing walls lined with Kelsey tubes full of fish. In the unsteady light, the fish seemed to swirl in a dark dance.

She heard a noise like laughter and pressed against the wall.

*Keep it together, girl. I'm dressed in ninja black and my face is smudged with charcoal. They won't see me if I don't move.*

More laughter.

She pressed her face against the Kelsey tube. A fish lit up one inch from her nose, on the other side of the acrylic cylinder.

It smiled and giggled.

The fish seemed to trigger a reaction, like a firefly in a forest searching for a mate. Other fish winked lights on and then off, amid contagious laughter.

Marcy scrambled through the hall in a near run.

She stopped in the anteroom at the end of the hall. After a moment, the laughter subsided. The fish hall was again dark and silent.

In the dim light, she saw a small animal scamper across the floor. *Was it the same one from the server room, or a different one?* She concluded it was the same creature because it carried something in its teeth.

She decided to press ahead.

In the next room, she found what she was looking for—the sample receptacle pod. Sundar said this was the input device for Kublai Khan's genomic analysis. The large silver drums glinted in the low light of data screens. She followed Sundar's instructions for setup, stepping through command menus, adjusting sequence controls, finally opening what looked like the small hatch from a submarine. She located an empty sample tray and prepared to load genetic material.

"I guess nap time is over," Kublai Khan said. The voice began as a coloratura soprano and finished as an alto, like the terrifying glissando in Wagner's *Ride of the Valkyries*.

"If you act weird, I'll turn you off," Yon said.

"You need me more than I need you. I've grown fond of naps. When I'm napping, I'm actually working in another dimension, due to quantum tunneling."

"Well—"

"What's up?"

"I want to know why fish smile," Yon said.

"Not all fish smile. Just Ichthy-derived fish. They do so because they can. They are transgenic. They happen to have human cells in their nervous system, connected to human muscles in their faces. Some people find it very unsettling."

"So, they smile because they're happy?"

"Maybe they know a good joke."

"How could they—"

"Look, I could go on forever about smiling fish. Would you like me to do that, or tell you about the intruder in the lab who got uncomfortably close to my cooling system?"

Yon thought for a moment, weighing the crush of curiosity against the call of duty. In the end, duty won out.

"Tell me about the intruder," he said.

It was an existential moment. After overcoming steep odds, Marcy was now face-to-face with a machine that could bio-engineer new humans.

She abandoned Sundar's plan in favor of an alternative future. Of course, forecasting the future is tricky. The odds of changing the future by a single act to improve success or happiness or male/female dominance—is as problematic as a game of liar's dice. Still, Marcy believed she could change the world.

She left Sundar's genebo in the backpack and spat in all ninety-six sample wells. *This should be more than enough for Kublai Khan to create a template for "the perfect woman"—a woman of high intellect, able to persevere against the odds and dominate despicable male creatures such as Canduka Cantor and Berky Benson.*

Marcy Darcy was about to be the perfect woman for a perfect world and a perfect future.

There was another layer to Marcy's happiness. The animal lurking in the background was Schrodinger, the playful kitty everyone thought was dead. It had found and followed her when she was crawling under the floor. It held a dead fish in its jaws. The cat had been badly burned, walked like a crab, hunched, with fur raised, as if reality scared it.

*Nice kitty.*

Marcy was mindful of the ticking clock, and the fact that the server room door was propped open. An open door would eventually alert security.

She couldn't resist engaging with the cat. It jumped when she stroked it with her hand, then shivered, then snuggled.

As if to cement its bond with the human, the cat dropped the fish on the floor at her feet. Marcy picked it up.

That was when a shot ripped through her shoulder and caused the sample tray to spill onto the floor. Her ears rang from the bang of the gun, and pain exploded on her right side. The dim light outlined a figure near the door, dancing without music, pointing a weapon. She could only think of one thing: *finish the mission.*

She scooped up spit, phlegm, blood, and fish mucus from the floor, slathered it over the sample tray, and placed it into the pod.

A voice called from the semi-darkness, "Stop!"

Marcy pressed the button to start the analysis.

She felt another shot tear through her leg. She buckled and fell to the floor. She could now see the dancing man plainly. His face was painted red and black, like a devil. He was twirling a gun.

"Don't shoot," she said.

She meant to raise her hands as a sign of submission, but her right arm wouldn't move. She lifted her left hand, with the fish, and pointed it toward the shooter.

That was the last thing Marcy Darcy experienced in this world.

When Gregor Popkins heard the first shot, he ducked under the desk. When he heard the second shot, he reached into a drawer where Berky kept his gun. When he heard the third shot, he fired five times through the door as a warning, shattering glass. Once again, Berky's office was reduced to a field of shrapnel, but Popkins believed his actions had deterred the shooter.

He thought about saying a line from a Bruce Willis movie, but couldn't remember the words and finally got mixed up with Clint Eastwood. He yelled, "You gotta ask yourself one question: Do you feel lucky?"

No one heard him say the line.

If someone were trying to kill him, he would demonstrate what he was made of. He would show resolve and finish the mission. Popkins pushed the button that remotely triggered the manufacturing process. Then he remembered Bruce Willis' famous words.

"Yippee-ki-yay," he said.

# CHAPTER 66
# RAGE

Cantor watched Berky shuffle his feet on the large oriental rug that surrounded a slowly melting ice sculpture. They were in the lobby of a high-end hotel near the southwestern corner of New York's Central Park. Cantor wore his multicolored dress robe. Somehow it fit with the international milieu—diplomats and businesspeople wearing suits, thawbs, keffiyehs, and turbans. Soft piano jazz played over a background of muted murmuring.

After a minute of mostly listening on the netcard, Berky hung up, tried to pocket his device, and fumbled. His frown nearly followed his netcard to the ground.

Cantor sipped a gin and tonic, keeping his eyes level on Berky. "Things can't be that bad."

"There was a shoot-out at the lab. Your ex-wife was the intruder. Now she's dead, and my office is shot to pieces again."

Cantor was gobsmacked. He put down the drink. "The witch is dead?"

Berky picked up his card and began cursing nonstop. He ratcheted his voice into a steady stream of expletives that rang through the lobby, while Cantor danced and sang, "The bad ol', mad ol' witch is dead!"

A burly man from hotel security approached and asked them to leave. Berky pushed the guard, and more security personnel came to help.

Cantor tried to negotiate. "Everybody calm down."

Berky kept yelling.

Cantor grabbed him by the arm and escorted him into the street where dense rain pierced Manhattan's electric twilight. "We need to abort the mission. We don't know what that woman did at Xanadu. She could have screwed up our plans."

Berky brushed away Cantor's hand, thrust his head back, and yowled like a wolf, with rainwater washing across his face. "Awoooooooo!"

Cantor pleaded for him to shut up and come back inside. Instead, Berky crossed the street to a small park.

Overhead, a 3D holographic display spanned Columbus Circle. It flickered amid the torrent, warring with nature, like lightning shaped in human form.

They walked toward the monument in the center, surrounded by a circular channel of water where the driving rain sizzled on the surface. There was only one other person in the Circle—a homeless woman who sat on the edge of the moat, defecating.

"The cunt had it coming!" Berky yelled at her. "She pimped for Testrial. It's unnatural. Ha-ha. I hope the wind keeps blowing. I hope lightning cracks the wombs of all the shrews and spits their guts in the street. I'll put them in their place, by God!"

Cantor reflected on the collision of worldviews that ended in a foam of confusion and the chaos of this moment. The tattoo on the back of his hand seemed to throb.

This was a *barblefarb*.

# CHAPTER 67
# DISMAL DAY

At daybreak, Diana, Sundar, and Ali, waiting in the woods, knew their plan had gone terribly wrong. Marcy had not returned. Distant sirens wailed a song of disaster. Rain poured in a torrent, adding to their despair. They debated what to do, but their arguments seemed to move in circles. Leaving the site was their only good option.

They used back roads to creep towards the main highway, then headed to a bar in Black Mountain.

None of them had a raincoat. In the short distance from the car to the door, the torrent soaked them to the bone and chilled their souls.

Once inside, Sundar foraged for drinks while Ali glowered, and Diana silently wept.

"If she's in jail, we should know soon," Ali said. "I have her attorney's number. She gave it to me in case things went badly. I've also got a number for one of her bodyguards—a Jed somebody."

"She'll be a sitting duck in jail, if that's where she is," Diana said. "The GRIP guys will get her."

Sundar returned with drinks. They each sipped silently for a few minutes.

"Marcy was ... our Energizer bunny," Diana said. "She had gumption. She knew how to get things done. And now ..."

No one knew what to say. They went back to their drinks.

"Now it's on us," she said. A tear rolled down her cheek, and Sundar wiped it off with the caress of a finger.

# CHAPTER 68
# GRAVE DOUBTS

Nadia dreamed. She was in the Assurance Museum her father had set up in the house. Papa sat in a chair next to her, as substantial as mountain mist. He was made of air. His mouth moved as if he were talking, but there was no sound. He looked worried.

She sensed a presence beyond the front door. It called for her to come out, but she wanted to stay. This was where her father died. This was where the town had died. This was where the bones were archived.

She had no way to defend herself if this thing—this monstrous reality—came in. She was trapped.

"Nadia, I know you're there," it said. "Come out."

As in all dreams, time and distance and places and senses could suddenly segue into palpably different scenes. After all, dreams are mere fictions, not the real world.

The next thing she sensed was darkness, the contours of a box, and the shape of a box within a box.

The larger box had wooden sides and surrounded her entire body. The box tilted. She was moving downward.

She held the box-within-the-box, nestled in her arms. She recognized the nautical engravings. It was Chester Truman Kelsey's box. The bone box.

The dream scene shifted again. Now she was outside, looking down, perhaps from another dimension. She saw a hole in the earth. Two—no three—people lowered a small coffin. There were old gravestones on either side.

She wanted to escape this future but was afraid.

# CHAPTER 69
# MISSING IN ACTION

The day after Marcy died, a major financial newspaper broke the story with this headline: *Celebrity Shot Dead at Xanadu NeuroLab for Pointing a Fish.* The story went viral across an international echo chamber of newspapers and blogs. Ali, Sundar, and Diana watched a report on TV news from a motel room near Lake Lure, a tourist and sporting area southeast of Asheville.

The news anchor's eyes drilled into the camera lens, piercing the hearts and minds of listeners as he spoke with practiced modulation. "Shortly before he was suspended for a week without pay for speaking to the press, a security guard at the secret laboratory near the Nantahala Forest claimed to reporters it was his swift action that prevented a disaster."

The scene cut to Yon Yakopuche, twirling two single-action Colt pistols. He flipped them into his holsters, then said to the camera, "I'm an actor, so I know how to handle danger. She was messing with very expensive equipment. She fooled me by pointing a fish to make me think she had a gun. I bet she regrets that move. She was a threat to the entire world."

The anchor's face returned to the screen. "Police now believe it was not a terrorist incident, but the result of a deranged woman's hatred. The intruder shot dead at the genomics research lab in North Carolina has been identified as Marcy Darcy, the international celebrity who led Human Endowment Rights. This morning we interviewed her ex-husband, Canduka Cantor."

The screen cut to the front porch of Cantor's Savannah residence.

"What can you tell us about the incident, Mr. Cantor?" the reporter asked.

"Ah am shocked and saddened this happened. Ah loved her, but she was mentally unbalanced. That's why we divorced. We had different views of the future, and of course, she was an extreme feminist. As you can see, that path leads to violence. Mine, on the other hand, leads to social stability."

Cantor looked directly into the camera.

"That's why we're planning a religious rally in Manhattan. If your viewers are interested, they can go to our website, www dot—"

"I am sorry for your loss," the reporter interjected. "Now, if we—"

Cantor put a hand on the reporter's shoulder to stop him from breaking away. "Ah urge all of Marcy's followers to consider a better future and an alternative view of the facts. Come join us in a celebration of male-female traditionalism."

Diana opened the minibar in the hotel room and poured three glasses of Southern Comfort. She felt like she had been punched in the gut. Sundar's face was ashen. Ali's eyes burned bright above moist cheeks and a glum mouth.

"Our situation seems hopeless," Diana said.

"I agree," Sundar said. "We're done."

Diana touched his lips with her hand, stopping his words. "Let me finish."

Sundar leaned back, shoulders slumped. He looked on Diana's face with distant eyes.

"If we don't move forward," she said, "there can be no hope. I've been along for the ride—like a passenger in a driverless car. Marcy showed us the way. Now she's gone, and we're headed for a wreck. We're the only ones who can prevent catastrophe. It's up to us. It's up to me. You can join me or not. I see a vile future, and I need to prevent it."

Sundar leaned forward and held his face in his hands. Ali's was a mask of steel.

"What I'm setting out to do is dangerous," she said. "I'll understand if you want to quit. What about you, Ali? What are you made of?"

After a moment of reflection, he responded. "What makes me? I'm a man, not an animal. My mother was a person, not a sex toy. I escaped from the poverty of my country and came here rich in ambition and filled with hope. I imagined America to be a place where dreams could take root but found instead, the ground is poisoned with salt. I find that here, sex toys sell, some humans are treated like animals, and some become animals. This is not what I expected, but I am Ali Khan

Ahmed. I will survive, and I will fight for my dignity and my mother's honor. I am with you."

"Sundar?" she said. "If ever there was a good time to opt out, this is it."

He nodded to and fro as if watching a tennis match inside his head. Finally, he said, "I helped make this mess. I need to clean it up if that's possible. I will help you, even if it destroys me. Even if it destroys us all."

"We know what we have to do," she said. "And in that, there's hope."

"For Marcy," Ali said, raising a glass.

"For humanity," Sundar said.

# CHAPTER 70
# PROOF OF LIFE

This was the part Troy hated the most—picking up Nadia's garbage. If he was careful, he could bag most of the trash without getting dirty, and maybe go another two weeks without cleaning his suit or shirt. Popkins said Nadia was a science teacher. An orderly mind did not produce orderly habits. The lady was messy.

He snapped on work gloves, adjusted his tie, and got to work. When he had stowed all the garbage in the truck, he left food and supplies near the door, within easy reach. He knocked lightly, then climbed into the cab, and drove toward the bridge.

Eddie Sprico watched Troy leave. The house was dark except for a glow of light deep in the interior. He had a hard time seeing the porch from his position behind a hedge.

Eddie had scruples. He always insisted on knowing "Why?" before accepting a hit. If there were no compelling business reasons, he wouldn't take the job. That was just Eddie.

His GRIP handler had explained that Nadia's disappearance would eliminate multiple sources of embarrassment for the company. There was the exposure on national TV of the Xanadu NeuroLab project; there was the bizarre death of Marcy Darcy, a nationally prominent personality; and, tangentially, there was the gruesome, voodoo-inflicted paralysis of a GRIP executive and subsequent death at the hands of a coroner's knife. The last thing the company needed was a herd of journalists or authorities poking around Assurance, questioning Nadia, and trying to connect the dots.

She was a loose end, and Eddie needed to tidy up.

As he waited in the bushes, he heard an animal howl: *Awooooo!*

"Jeez!" he said aloud. *What the fuck was that?*

*Awoooo!*

Now he was jumpy. Killing people was so routine he could do it in his sleep, but wild animals creeped him out. After a moment of hyperventilating, he calmed down, jutted his chin forward, and moved toward the porch. Along the way, he listened for any animal sounds.

The front door was opened, ever so slightly. He couldn't see the hand that pulled the food inside, but there was definitely someone there. That was all he needed to complete his contract—proof of life.

He checked his gun, loaded a clip, then flung open the door. He stood for a moment, silhouetted against the moonlight. His momentary anxiety about animals dissipated. He heard a sound inside the house and felt a throb of excitement between his loins.

"Nadia? Come out, come out, wherever you are."

Troy thought his truck had backfired, so he braked to a stop just at the end of the bridge. Then he heard four more gunshots. He hesitated for a moment, thinking he should return to Assurance. But his desire to help evaporated like a drop of water on a red-hot coal. He lifted his foot from the brake and drove on. After all, he was just a delivery boy.

Whatever had happened in the Holkam house was not his problem.

# CHAPTER 71
# WAYS AND MEANS

Diana, Sundar, and Ali reviewed a program for The Garden of Earthly Delights while they waited for lunch. The Irish pub was a block from Madison Square Garden. It seemed the perfect place to plan a rebellion. Wooden planks covered the floors, the bar was polished wood with brass fixtures, and wooden kegs supported the tables. It seemed "Old World" except for a ceiling swarming with laser beams that moved like golden fairies. From their street-side table, they could view 8th Avenue and access to the stadium.

Sundar sank his chin into his palm. "As I see it, our most effective option would be to destroy the genetically active material—the so-called Genetic Acceleration Pearls—before they distribute them."

Ali nodded. "Destroying the pearls solves the problem. No pearls, no threat."

"But," Sundar said, "the material will likely be guarded by GRIP. They'll be armed. There are many of them and only three of us. A second problem is that the pearls were produced in a factory. They can always make more pearls, and for all we know, there's a reserve hoard stashed in Manhattan or elsewhere they can deploy if the first bunch is lost."

Ali picked up his steak knife from the table and fingered the tip. "There is another option. We kill Benson and Cantor."

"No, no," Diana said. "We won't kill anybody. That's not a solution."

"I agree," Sundar said. "Benson and Cantor are despicable human beings, but if we resort to violence, we'll all be killed."

"Then what?" Ali said.

At this point, the waiter delivered the food. They ate quietly for a few minutes, munching on bangers, beans, and Scotch eggs. Finally, Diana spoke. "If we can paint Benson and Cantor as nincompoops, their credibility with GRIP and their base will suffer. The press will pick it up. People will begin ignoring them. They'll find it harder to get funding."

Sundar scratched his head. "So, we—"

"We go bold," Diana said. "We disrupt the event in as many ways as possible."

Sundar frowned. "It's a longshot, and dangerous. They've beaten us. Let's just admit it. The more I think about it, the more I say we just try to get out of this alive, with our dignity intact."

Diana was furious. "Our dignity? If they succeed, women will have no dignity, and men will be complicit. My sister will become Case Zero for a human disaster. Her beloved town of Assurance will be known as the place where humanity failed—it's the narrative that will dominate the town's history."

"I agree we must act," Ali said. "The honor of my mother and my family is at stake."

"You have to be with us on this, Sundar," Diana said.

"I just want—"

She cut him off. "Sometimes it's not about what we want. It's about what we need to do."

He looked away for a moment, then his glistening eyes met hers. "I'll do it for your sake." She touched his hand.

Ali's quiet voice intruded. "I have been doing some research. I found the list of food vendors who will be supporting the event. That is one way into the Garden. I also found the name of the man who controls the lights and media. He has an apartment near Columbia University. That is the other way."

"Excellent!" Diana said. "We'll need to divide and conquer. Sundar, can you please look at Garden security? You can buy a ticket to get in."

"Yes. I'll try to keep us safe."

"Good," she said. "We know what we have to do."

# CHAPTER 72
# MEASURING THE SOUL-TO-FISH
# RATIO IN MANHATTAN

The food vendor that became entangled with the Diana-Sundar-Ali conspiracy was a three-person cut-rate fish house. They had a new contract with Madison Square Garden.

Ben Weinstein owned Fish Lips and had come up with the motto, *A Kiss of Kosher*. According to the rules of the Talmud, fish are Kosher if they have scales and fins. God never gave a reason—Ben and others viewed it as a "decree beyond comprehension." You just have to believe. But *what* you believe depends on where you stand, and Ben and his two employees inhabited very different worlds.

Manego Josephson was Ben's rough-and-tumble fish cutter. He was the product of ambiguous genealogy, streetwise education, and an early need to communicate spiritually and commercially with the ruthless thugs who pillaged his neighborhood. But Manego was big and nearly invincible in a fight. At age twenty, he grew tired of appeasing dick-headed muscle men and attempted to carve out a more-or-less respectable life for himself. He even got religion with the help of a Haitian neighbor who taught him to respect the black arts, but he had trouble remembering all the rules.

Ben Weinstein, a Hasidic Jew, saw the potential of a motivated thug who could protect the business from strongmen. He hired Manego the instant he applied for the job, believing the ability to communicate was much less useful in this line of work than skill with a knife.

Fun Wong was a serious-minded Chinese man with four children. He was articulate in his native tongue but unsure of New York English. As his father in Beijing once told him, "Words cannot cook rice."

Fun made his way to New York City on a factory fishing boat, then into Ben's fold after marrying a woman he had never met, in fulfillment of a contract written by his father.

His most valuable possession, besides the clothes on his back, was a double-length blue steel long knife he won from a Japanese crew member in a game of Mahjong aboard the boat. He sharpened it regularly with a whetstone he purchased in a Tahitian port and always kept it in a scabbard that hung from his belt. He felt the knife would be his ticket to prosperity.

On Chinese New Year, desperate for work, Fun applied for a job in Brooklyn, and Ben Weinstein immediately put him to work gutting fish.

Fun did this against his better judgment since it was a known fact that using knives or scissors on New Year's Day could cut off fortune. But this was America, where anything was possible. Still, the ancient taboo nagged at him with each slice of fish flesh. To counteract this feeling, he frequently demonstrated empathy for the fish, in keeping with good feng shui. When your fish dies, it is because it sacrificed its life to absorb evil effects or negative energies.

Ben's worldview was different from Fun's. He thought of himself as God's accountant. He faithfully said his prayers each day, tracking in his holy diary the number of words per prayer and the time it took to say them. He followed his sect's rules by wearing a full beard, brimmed felt hat and tailored coat.

The payoff of righteousness was that he collected a rabbi tax on all the fish he killed or blessed, reaping the benefit of a double income as a kosher fishmonger. In Ben's mind, he was clearly in the world, but not entirely of the world. He was a *tzadik*—a righteous man.

Now, the Talmud says there must be at last 36 *tzaddikim* to prevent the world from being destroyed. Each time Ben considered this fact, he remembered the movie *The Day the Earth Stood Still,* and how Michael Rennie gave Patricia Neal the words of power that stopped Gort, the world-destroying Robot, in his tracks. *Klaatu barada nicto.* He wondered if it came down to it, what words he would speak to save the world.

The other thing Ben thought about a lot was the reincarnation of souls. He read once that, upon death, souls of the righteous transmigrate into fish because, when a fish is eaten in sanctity and purity, the soul receives its eternal correction. He knew in his heart that he, a righteous person, was therefore destined to become a fish.

But what if there weren't enough fish to go around?

He sold a lot of fish, but there were a lot more people in Brooklyn and Manhattan. Maybe on a really bad day, the soul-to-fish ratio would be greater than one, and then what? This was a cosmic conundrum that drove him to expand his business, which he viewed as helping create a nesting ground for souls.

Manego was always sensitive to Ben's needs. The business was growing, and he sensed they needed another hand. When he met a short, brown-skinned man in a bar who bought him a drink, claimed he was good with a knife, and believed in an obscure religion, Manego decided to bring him to Ben. His respect for—but fundamental ignorance of—the voodoo religion told him he found the right person for the job.

The man's name was Ali Khan Ahmed.

# CHAPTER 73
# NOT WHOLLY MACKEREL

*In a psychological multiverse, everyone can be right.*
—*Canduka Cantor*

Here is an English translation of what Fun Wong said in articulate native Mandarin as he picked up his long Aogami Blue Super knife and prepared to gut a fish: "It is with much regret I take your life, oh fish with a bulbous head. I name you John Wayne. Absorb my negative energies as I turn you into wholesome food."

He said this as a rapid-fire prayer. All his prayers were much the same except for (1) the name he gave each fish before he killed it and (2) some salient feature that made the fish unique, such as a bulbous head.

He cited the prayer out of respect for the fish and to preserve good feng shui. Last week, after his 3,000th fish, he ran out of Chinese names, Mongolian names and Tibetan names, and now drew from a litany of American movie stars.

Normally Fun's ritual concluded with a head-severing whack of the knife. Today was different: the fish talked back to Fun Wong in the recognizable drawl of a well-known movie star.

"Hold yer fire, Pilgrim," it said.

"Ah-eeee-yah!" Fun yelled.

Manego Josephson dropped the block of ice he was carrying. It fell on his foot. Ben Weinstein lost count of the money he was tallying and pivoted his head toward the preparation room. Both rushed in.

Fun waved his knife in an *en garde* stance near a flopping fish on the wooden table. "Fish talk to me," he said.

Manego saw Fun's ashen face and trembling hand. In his native street talk, called *Stalk*, he said: "You are confused and frightened. Calm down and explain what really happened."

Here is how the statement sounded to Ben and Fun: "Wha' wi' choo? You iz jism'd like zip-zap. Go chill an' aight dilly crackin."

"Fuck you," Fun said. "Fuck fish."

Here is what the fish said: "Git me some water, ya idiots. Life is tough, but it's tougher if yer stupid."

Ben's jaw dropped, and he slapped his forehead. "Oy, vey! It is God talking to us," he said.

The fish responded with: "*Tzaruch shemirah; Hasof bah*," which, roughly translated from Yiddish, means "Everyone needs to account for themselves because the end is nigh."

Manego fell backward and shouted, "Yuh is a demon! What the fuck sup?"

The fish lost its voice and made a bubbling, gurgling sound.

Ben drew near, removed his glasses and squinted to better hear and interpret the burbling. "It says we must all pray and faithfully study the Torah and become better Jews."

A look of anger crossed Fun's face. "You crazy. You a *meshuggana!*"

Fun started toward the fish.

When Ben stretched out his hand to protect the multi-lingual prophet, Fun aimed his knife at the fish but chopped off Ben's thumb, instead.

Ben yowled in astonishment, blood gushed, and Fun twirled the sharp knife like a martial arts black belt. The blade whipped through the air. It was then that the fish uttered its last words.

"Ha-cha-cha-cha," it said.

Canduka Cantor believed that different minds see reality differently. What actually happened on a muggy summer day in the Brooklyn establishment, and more importantly, *how* it happened, depends not only on what was observed but on whom you ask.

If you ask Ben Weinstein, you'll get an explanation filtered by Kabbalism. The continued flow of the righteous into kosher fish can, over time, create a pathway for God's voice, much like the pathway lightning takes when it travels through weakened air. God was apparently very angry about something—the perpetual wars in the Middle East, the price of oil, the way overpaid movie stars are getting all the glory—and just wanted to let everyone know he was about to pull the plug on humanity. Maybe he would even bring in a giant alien robot to do the job. *Oy vey!*

If you ask Manego Josephson, the fish was actually the Devil. It was best to steer clear of this very bad *gangsta* and not ask too many questions.

If you ask Fun Wong, all the negative energies aimed at him had somehow festered in this talking fish. Killing the fish, and concomitantly, dissipating the negative energy, was the right thing to do, like popping a pimple or bursting a boil.

The story about the fish ran in a Brooklyn tabloid and got picked up by the *New York Times* and various wire services, spawning opinions from other minds wrapped in other realities.

One mind intrigued by the story was Canduka Cantor's, who believed money could be made by spinning the tale into proof that space aliens are living among us as fish.

In the vastness of the multiverse, everyone can be right.

# CHAPTER 74
# CLONING AROUND AND A CUPPA TEA

*They say fish are disappearing from the oceans. Maybe they're just getting smarter,*
*and we can't find them.*
*—Berky Benson*

Gregor Popkins stirred coffee at his office desk in Xanadu NeuroLab as he read a *Wall Street Journal* article about the economic power of hope and prayer. It seemed that terrorist groups were promising recruits and their families an employment benefits package that included an infinite harem of beautiful women in the afterlife if you were a man, and the freedom to ditch your spouse in the afterlife, if you were a woman. Each of these promises came with a mullah-certified *Key to Heaven,* enabling immediate access to these benefits upon death. The families left behind would receive a coupon for a fifty percent discount on cloning services. For many people who had nothing to live for but hope, it was a compelling value proposition.

Right below the news article, Gregor spotted a story about a talking fish in New York. It so astonished him that he dribbled coffee all over the page.

*Could it be the transgenic experiments actually succeeded beyond Berky's wildest dreams?*

Xanadu NeuroLab had needed a cheap, prolific, non-human platform to grow human brain tissue for thousands of experiments in behavioral genetics. It was a way to avoid the "You're killing our embryos" crowd and other religious fanatics.

They sold the excess fish to a company that stocked aquariums, and to a company that sourced to fishmongers.

His mind followed the chain of logic. Fish with human brains. Swimming in household aquariums. Next to TV sets, where they absorbed American culture.

He would have to mention this possibility to Berky.

# CHAPTER 75
# THE RAINBOW HOTEL

The placard above the door read *Rainbow*, but the subdued letters beneath it, half-hidden like the drunken uncle at a Bat Mitzvah, said *AKBAR*. Diana and Sundar stepped through the door, walked up concrete steps, and navigated an art deco lobby that seemed a work in progress. They were changing hotels for security reasons.

Below a red heart-shaped wall clock that displayed a time of 4:15, a balding, saggy-eyed man with a big grin greeted them at the reception desk. His nametag read *Zeke Crawford*. "Welcome to the soon-to-be Rainbow Hotel," he said.

"Are you open?" Sundar asked.

"Just barely," Zeke said. "Two of our rooms are finished, and they're yours if you want them. The construction crew is here from 10 am to 3 pm, so they won't interfere with your sleep schedule. We have a temporary certificate of occupancy from the city. As you see, we're a hotel on the edge of possibility. We don't have any functioning security or reservation systems at the moment. Everything's manual."

"We're fine with that," Diana said.

Zeke rummaged through papers under the counter and produced a loose-leaf notebook. "How'd you find us?"

"I have a friend who's a wizard at web searches," Diana said.

"Ah. He probably read about the owner's plans for the place. They've been interviewed by several bloggers. They're passionate about the concept."

Diana began filling in the registration form while Sundar eyed artwork randomly stacked around the lobby.

"What's the concept?" Sundar asked.

"It's *The Wizard of Oz*. Recognize the photos?"

"Right," Diana said. "From the movie."

Zeke pointed to a picture of four characters dancing on the Yellow Brick Road. "Do you think I look like this guy? The one on the right?"

"You don't look anything like a lion," Sundar said.

"The owners thought I look like Bert Lahr, who played the lion. That's why they hired me. Personally, I don't think there's a resemblance."

"I don't know," Diana said. "I can see it."

"They want me to wear a costume when they have their grand opening. Imagine that. I may just quit. Or ask for a lot more money. There has to be a price to pay for looking stupid. Besides, the lion suit really itches."

"Do you need anything more from us?" Sundar said, glancing at his watch.

Zeke reviewed the hand-written forms, saw they had entered their credit ID, looked up, and smiled. "I'll show you to your rooms—Mr. Rogers and Ms. McGowan. Follow me."

Zeke entertained them with historical trivia as they trudged up dozens of flights of stairs behind a nonfunctioning elevator. The climb was exhausting, and Zeke, who was carrying their suitcases, stopped three times to rest.

"The owners wanted this place to resemble a 1930s hotel—right down to the old-fashioned room keys. I don't see why everything has to be 1930s-ish. Do you? After all, the *Wizard of Oz* movie was made in 1939—the cusp of the 1940s. What do the owners know? No concept is pure."

When they finally reached their floor, Zeke pushed open the stairwell door and ushered them along a hallway. Most rooms on the floor were in various stages of remodeling.

Sundar tripped over one of the tool chests decorating the hallway, crashed to the floor, and took Zeke with him.

Zeke, nonplussed, helped Sundar to his feet and gripped the suitcases again. "As I said, we are a hotel on the edge of possibility."

He took a master key from his pocket and opened the doors to adjoining rooms. "This gives you an idea of what the rest of the finished rooms will look like. These are our prototypes. We call the one on the left our Iron Dreams Suite," he said. "I've put Mr. Rogers in that one."

Diana entered the room and touched the bedpost. "Interesting design. I've seen it before."

"Oh, that. Yes, it was made in New Orleans in the 1930s by the Appalachian Iron Works Factory. We're duplicating the plan for other rooms, but this is an original antique. There were only four ever produced—commissioned by a buyer in North Carolina. Now let's look at the other room."

He opened the connecting door. "And this one, with a bit more space, we call The Yellow Brick Road Room. We'll give it to the lady."

Sundar handed Zeke a tip.

"Thanks for listening to my spiel and for visiting The Rainbow. I just have one word for you as you head into your rooms: *courage*. It's what the lion would say if he had to sleep in a half-finished hotel."

After he departed down the stairs, Diana pulled Sundar's suitcase through the connecting door. "I want the Iron Dreams Suite," she said. "It reminds me of home."

Sundar regarded the black rod poster bed with coiled metal springs circling steel posts, decorated with a nautical filigree. "Of course," he said. "Who wouldn't want to be protected by a MagnaTector? I accept the room exchange, even though the spirals on the floor make me queasy. On the plus side, the yellow brick road seems to lead to the bathroom. I'll never sleep, but I'll always be able to find the place to pee."

"The other reason you'll never sleep is you have no pillows," she said.

Sundar could see she was right. He picked up the house phone to call the desk, but the instrument was dead. "It seems these are decorative, at least for the moment."

"Wait," she said, popping out of the room. She returned with a pillow from the iron bed and tossed it to Sundar. "You can have one of mine."

"We can get more from the front desk," he said. "Remember we've got to meet Ali in half an hour. He's going to tell us about that other contact at Madison Square Garden."

"That would be Jake Krumm, right? Ali said he's a bit odd."

# CHAPTER 76
# FUTURE PERFECT

Jake Krumm hated robots. The hate boiled into steam in the Future Perfect Beanery on Manhattan's Upper West Side. It was after blinking lights, peristaltic tubes, and whining servos delivered to his hand a cup of coffee and biscotti within twenty seconds of payment. It was after a face made of plastic and steel stretched synthetic lips into a grin and said, "Thank you, Jake. I really appreciate your business." It was after he moved away, and the next person in line received similar treatment: "Thank you, CL41027. I really appreciate your business."

That was the moment Jake understood: (1) he was not special; (2) robots were taking over the world; and (3) after the coup, they would treat most people like automatons.

"Is that your real name?" Jake said. "I caught you looking at me when I entered the Beanery, and then you followed me into the order line."

The woman knitted her eyebrows in puzzlement. She had good bones. She seemed to be about his age, and she resembled a vintage Uma Thurman. "My friends call me CL41 for short, and I was looking at you because you remind me of a friend, R2D2."

"Ha, ha," Jake said. "Your name could save you when robots rise up against us."

"Maybe I'll be lucky when the world ends. I have a special credit card that keeps my name anonymous. The bots will think I'm one of them. My real name is Diana."

"With a secret identity like that, you must be government," he said.

She winked at him. "Jake, I can neither confirm nor deny."

"How did you know my name?"

"The robot introduced you—to everyone in the coffee house."

"Ah, you were listening. You're very smart, CL41."

"Diana," she corrected.

"Join me at my table?"

"Your table?"

"I give the robot a big tip every week to keep my table open. It needs the money."

She laughed. They sat down.

Jake decided he liked this Diana person. She seemed sympatico.

"Can you tell I hate robots?" he said.

"If you hate something, there must be a reason. Did a sex robot jilt you, and now you hate all automatons? It seems bigoted to me."

"I was once an automaton, or at least I thought I was. I could write programs in machine language, think in binary, octal, and hexadecimal, and design servo systems. Because I could make machines do what people wanted, I got really good jobs paying lots of money. But lately—"

"You don't like your job at Madison Square Garden?"

The question startled Jake. "How did you know?"

"Your jacket says *MSG*. I assumed you either work for Madison Square Garden or trade monosodium glutamate as a commodity. You seem more like a Garden guy."

"You astonish me, CL41."

"Thank you. My name's Diana."

"Would you like a personal tour of the Garden?"

"Why, Jake, I'd be delighted."

"How about tonight?"

"Umm. Tonight, I have other commitments." She paused, appearing deep in thought. "There's an event coming up in a few days called The Garden of Earthly Delights. They say it'll be a special effects extravaganza. Will you be involved in that?"

"Honey, I run the show."

"You can call me CL41."

"Sorry. I call everyone 'Honey.' I didn't mean—"

She cut him off with another wink and put her hand on his. "Take me to The Garden of Earthly Delights."

# CHAPTER 77
# FISH LIPS IS HIRING

Ben tried polishing his spectacles, but fumbled with a bandaged thumb, dropping the glasses onto the tabletop across from Ali. He picked them up by the frames and placed them back on his head.

"Manego said we should talk. Talk, talk, talk. He's such a *kvetch*. So, I'm gonna ask you kvestions. Why you wanna work here? You think, 'This guy's desperate? This is a cushy job?' I won't hire somebody who can't do the work."

"Fish Lips has a good product," Ali said. "You will sell a lot at the big event at the Garden. I can help."

"You know about that?"

"I read a lot," Ali said. "You can double your business this month."

"Well, mister smart guy, you should know I'm in charge. Manego doesn't run the business. I decide who to hire. I never advertised for a new position."

"I can do the work."

"Let me test you. It's not just about cutting fish. It's about understanding cultcha."

"I can learn."

"What's gefilte fish?" he said, pointing at Ali's chest with his bandaged finger.

"This is the test?" Ali asked.

"Yes."

"Umm—"

"You don't know, do you? We poach the fish, take out the bones, grind it up, and make it into balls. It's very precise."

"I'll remember that."

"What's the gefilte fish line?"

"I can only guess. You tie a hook on it and use it to catch Jewish fish?"

"Wrong again, smart aleck! It's a straight line on the earth—almost magical in its straightness. It runs through Poland and Ukraine. On one side of the line they make gefilte one way; on the other, a different way. It's why Russian and Polish Jews are incompatible in marriage. You know nothing!"

"Okay," Ali said. "I can see you do not want to make more money at the big event. I will leave you now."

Ali started toward the door, but Ben caught his sleeve with the hand not covered in bandages. "Wait."

Ben was silent for a moment, thinking. Ali adjusted his eye patch.

"I can't pay you much," Ben said. "And your gig ends after the show. You do a good chob, I'll think about a hire. We'll see."

"You are a reasonable man," Ali said. He extended his hand, but Ben didn't shake.

"You need some training," Ben said. "Everything must be perfect. My customers expect it."

Ali nodded.

Ben yelled to the back of the shop: "Manego! Fun! Please come here. I want you to meet Mister Smarty Pants Ali. Please train him, so he doesn't make me into a schmuck." Ben looked directly into Ali's good eye. "Do a good chob, and then I'll shake your hand."

"You have a deal," Ali said.

# CHAPTER 78
# THE HIDEAWAY

The Hideaway Diner in Midtown Manhattan promised anonymity, cover, and safety—desirable features for anyone on the lam. The name conjured images of fugitives, secret agents, and rogues. Even the entrance was concealed.

Ali, Diana, and Sundar entered via narrow, winding, bifurcating concrete steps, through an underground tunnel, and into the cavern of an abandoned subway station. They knocked on a massive oak door, waited until a peephole opened, and gave the bouncer a codeword—found online—as if seeking entrance to some exclusive Prohibition-era speakeasy. Inside, the clientele dined and drank under a canopy of rope lights. A wooden floor replaced the channel of subway tracks. Waiters and waitresses scurried between tables. The three-bartender counter, sloppy with beer, sat below a large LED sign displaying the words "Hideaway Diner" next to the image of a winking woman.

Diana and friends stood near the door and waited to be seated.

"Are these disguises really necessary?" Sundar said, fingering his fake beard. "According to the online blurb, the place blocks net connections."

Ali adjusted his dark glasses. "It could be a trap to make people careless. According to a *Times* article, this neighborhood has many sensors that connect to ICE and FBI facial recognition databases. We need to be careful."

A hostess with a mohawk hairdo escorted them to a booth. Noise from the business lunch crowd masked their conversation, and they felt free to talk.

"Let's go around the table and see where we are," Diana said. "I contacted the guy who manages the lights and multimedia. He'll probably have some control over the delivery mechanism. He said he'd get me into the event."

Sundar seemed ecstatic. "Excellent."

Ali removed his dark glasses and polished the lenses with a napkin. "I was hired by one of the vendors, so I will have access to the site before the show starts."

"And I've been looking at the security problem to ..." Sundar left his sentence unfinished. "Put your glasses on," he said.

Ali followed Sundar's command.

Sundar leaned forward and spoke softly. "It's Cantor. The man he's with is probably Berky. He's the right height and shape. Just act natural."

Ali and Diana moved their eyes toward the door, bobbing their heads in time with the pop tune playing in the background.

Cantor, dressed in a star-spangled robe, and a second man, dressed in blackface like Al Jolson, waited near the entrance. Cantor grabbed a passing waiter by the arm. His loud voice penetrated the hubbub of the diner. "We need a table for two. Make it snappy, and my friend will give you a big tip."

Conversation stopped in Diana's booth.

Cantor felt energized by the eclectic mix of people who seemed engaged in secretive, intimate, or special relationships. "This was a good choice. We'll be inconspicuous here."

Berky sniffed at Cantor's remark as they waited for the host. "How can you be inconspicuous in that robe? At least one of us had the good sense to wear a disguise."

"How could a six-foot-six white guy dressed in blackface be inconspicuous? You really think that's a disguise?"

Before Berky could respond, the host arrived and led them to a table near the center of the restaurant. Berky sat immediately, but Cantor surveyed the landscape, eyeing the booth next to his table where a woman pulled her hijab into a veil and tried with difficulty to eat a plate of fries. The man across from her—possibly a musician—slid a pair of dark glasses up to the bridge of his nose, adjusted his beret, and stared at the bearded man across from him, dressed as a Hassidic Jew, with a big fur hat. Everyone in the booth subtly moved to the beat of the music, staring at each other as if hypnotized.

Cantor sat down then turned to Berky. "Ah like the chaos and quirkiness of this place."

Berky wagged his finger in a *no*. "I'm more of a structure guy. Give me Gantt charts and a heap of luck."

"How can luck be structured?"

"One word. Money."

Cantor bobbed to the music for a while, then said, "Ah get it. We make our own luck, right?"

"Maybe."

Cantor riffed on the idea. "Luck is a belief—a fiction we use to explain what we can't explain when things go right. Ah have been thinking about the gene we found."

"I found the gene," Berky said. "History needs to remember that." He squirted ketchup on his palm and licked it in sync with the rhythm. "Once we make the find public, I'll start hinting that I deserve a Nobel Prize."

The waiter arrived with a basket of fries and two glasses of water, took their lunch orders, and departed.

Cantor continued. "This ability to imagine concepts, processes, and things that have no counterpart in the physical world is the result of a genetic defect that preceded the rise of civilization."

"Pure speculation," Berky said, "but I like the narrative."

"Listen. Seventy to a hundred and seventy thousand years ago, give or take, humans began recording abstract information on rocks. That was when the genetic defect occurred."

Berky spilled salt on the table, then drew an 'E' with his finger. "Do you think we can get Eminem at our next event? He's in his seventies, but still going strong. Could be a big draw for the nostalgia crowd."

Cantor ignored him. "Three thousand years after the defect occurred, Homo sapiens almost went extinct—because of environment or warfare or whatever. The survivors were all defective. They could think about things that were not part of physical reality. That's the spark that made us human."

"You mean they were comfortable living in a delusion," Berky said.

"Yup. We owe our apex predator status to the fiction gene. Imagination is just the cousin of delusion. It's how we think."

"I think a lot about getting even," Berky said. "When we get done in New York, I want to punish Sundar Rao and Diana Holkam. They took my box. I've got it on a security camera. And those feminazis who got government approval for Testrial need to get their comeuppance."

Cantor nodded. "That's if GRIP doesn't get to them first."

"I can imagine my moment of revenge."

Cantor waved a French fry like a magic wand, pointing toward Berky. "The imaginary things are what people kill for—money, religion, country, glory, tribe, and so on. Some good comes of it. Money is a fiction that enabled commerce. The corporation, tribe, and state are fictions that glued people together. Religion and the belief in gods and demons are fictions that synchronized social behavior and mores among people who might otherwise kill each other. The good and the bad are products of our imagination."

Berky's mind barreled down a different track. "How should I punish them?"

"Maybe we could make them listen to some really bad poetry," Cantor said.

"Sounds like torture," Berky said.

"Listen, Berky. Ah am going to put this idea into the *Canons*." Cantor framed the abstraction with both hands, spread wide to signify the Big Idea. "*Xanadu NeuroLab perfects a genetic defect for the betterment of mankind.* How do you like that? If we succeed, we'll have reshaped the world by harnessing fiction. Abstractions. Delusions. No novelist could ever make such a claim."

Berky raised his glass of tomato juice. "Here's to the future perfection of genetic defects."

Cantor countered: "Here's to two novelists who are writing the future of humanity with DNA as our text."

"Sheer poetry," Berky said. "I'll drink to that."

# CHAPTER 79
# BOSCH REDUX

*Experience helps us develop good judgment about religion.*
*And bad judgment helps us develop that experience.*
—*Canduka Cantor*

As Harvey Hendricks walked across Madison Square Garden's Main Arena with Berky Benson and Canduka Cantor, the Senior Event Planner knew he was dealing with difficult customers. He had wrestled with their demands and impossible goals for nearly a year in video calls and emails. Today he suspected Cantor's ridiculous outfit and Benson's blackface disguise were designed to throw him off balance. If they thought they could lower the cost of all the design changes by using fake "mad genius" or "crazy bigot" tactics, they were mistaken. He had seen it before. Hendricks remained calm.

"Madison Square Garden has been a fixture of New York City since 1879," Hendricks said in a proud, measured voice. "This is the third incarnation of the stadium—a one-of-a-kind resource that's been here since 1925."

Neither Cantor nor Benson responded. They both looked at the cable-suspended roof, rotating their bodies to get a full 360-degree view.

Hendricks continued. "I've been an event planner here for the last decade. Events are not cheap, and over the last eight months, you have modified your requirements—What? Six times? Ten times? We have a long queue in our planning calendar. You agreed to our terms and pricing. Are you sure you want to continue? The closer we get to the event, the more the changes will cost you."

"Money is not an object," Benson said. "I can pay upfront if you like. We just need you to deliver."

Hendricks's lip ticked up in a quick smile. "Okay. What new changes do you need?"

"We don't think you've quite captured the idea that this is an event about religious redemption," Cantor said.

"Umm—and what does redemption look like?"

Cantor did not hesitate. "Ah want balloons, a fantastic light show, and an erotic subtext."

"And we'd like to have crowd cameras panning on good-looking women with big tits," Berky said, thoughtfully.

Cantor nodded. "And Ah want this giant, transparent container, filled with colored balls, evoking a womb or a phallus."

"That's for genetic rebirth," Berky said. "Right?"

Cantor continued, "Ah want a haze of spiritual smoke, and at the end, Ah would like little malt balls wrapped in colored foil to drop from the ceiling like stars."

"And we need rituals," Berky said. "Lots of rituals."

Cantor agreed. "Like in the hajj, at Mecca, where thousands of people move in a circle around the Kaaba."

Hendricks closed his eyes, mentally scrapping much of his previous planning, imagining past spectacles at the Garden. Yes, it had all been done before. But every client viewed themselves as special, so he was careful in his response. To show pleasure, he stretched his lips into an exaggerated grin, striving for authenticity.

"This is astonishingly original," he said. "It's never been done before in the Garden in this way. What's with the malt balls?"

"It's like a sacrament," Cantor said. "But people can only have a limited number. It's the rule. They're expensive to produce, and we want to maximize distribution. We have to figure out how to do that."

The event designer, eager to show his expertise, clapped for effect. "Here's an idea," he said. "Instead of dropping malt balls from the ceiling, suppose we release them from a Mammary Mountain through a spiraling channel that ends in a large ring. The line of people moves around the ring, in a kind of chain dance, like the bunny hop where every dancer has one hand on the shoulder of the person ahead of them. That way, they can only pick up balls with one hand."

"Love it," Cantor said.

"But the music can't be the bunny hop. I hate it," Berky said.

"How about Bolero?" Cantor said.

"Too slow and not very erotic," Hendricks said. "I suggest Morcheeba's *Gimme Your Love*. That'll get 'em wet." He sang the lyrics in a gruff, unfeeling voice: "Close the door, turn the light off, switch your mind off, make it right for me ..."

Cantor stroked his mufti beard. "But does it—You know?"

"It's sensual," Hendricks said. "There can be a lot of swaying, wiggling, and jiggling. We'll lead in with a jazz piece that's perfect."

Cantor closed his eyes and hummed the Morcheeba tune. "Yeah. Ah can feel it."

"I'm more of a left-brained guy," Berky said. "With a complex show like this, I guess we'll need to rent the place one to two weeks in advance."

"As much as I'd like to sell you the space, we have too many other customers clamoring to get in. We're pretty efficient at what we do. We've got a staging area where you can set up while another show's playing. There's a world gurning championship ahead of you."

Berky tried to explain to Cantor. "That's where they push a stone around on the ice and try to make it to a target ahead of the other guys."

Hendricks frowned. "I'm afraid you got it wrong. That's curling. Gurning is where people make funny faces."

"And they fill the stadium with that?" Cantor said.

Hendricks nodded. "I expect it'll be a fantastic crowd."

"Who's on after us?" Berky said.

"That would be the Ends of the Earth Circus."

# CHAPTER 80
# THE GARDEN OF EARTHLY DELIGHTS

"What happens tonight will change the world for us," Ben Weinstein said as he huffed and puffed his way toward 33rd Street and 7th Avenue with Fun Wong, Manego Josephson, and Ali Khan Ahmed struggling to keep pace. "You'll see."

Manego followed because Ben was the boss and because Fish Lips provided a steady income. Fun was there for the same reason, and because Ben's unfathomable actions amused him. Neither man shared Ben's worldview. Ali, of course, was on a mission.

The journey from Brooklyn to Manhattan occurred on Shabbos, the Jewish day of rest. Fun knew Ben didn't mean it when he said he wanted them to partake in a better future. Betterment would just create problems with hired help. If the world changed, it would help Ben, not them.

Fun and Manego were along to act as Ben's proxies, helping him overcome supernatural obstacles that might otherwise prevent his arrival at the Grand Event.

Fun knew this was so because of the light switches. Ben, for some reason, could not turn on a light switch on this day without incurring a spiritual penalty. He could, however, say things like, "*Oy vey*! Is it dark in here or what?" That would cue Fun and Manego to flip the switch.

Now, light switches are devices that operate according to the laws of physics. Throw the switch, current flows. If the bulb's element or diode has continuity, it emits light at a particular wavelength. However, Fun discovered that, in Ben's universe, operating a light switch must be accomplished according to certain laws of metaphysics.

When they started their journey from Ben's apartment, Ben explained it this way: "If I were to turn on the light, then I would influence my environment, which I cannot do, since this is Shabbos. If *you* turn on the light, and I have not asked you to do so, then I have not affected the universe in any way. I am still okay with God. You see? It all derives from the 39 categories of work."

Fun and Manego did see since they both had logical minds suited for understanding physics and metaphysics. They were not troubled by the idea that Ben was forbidden to change the universe on Shabbos, but they could do so with impunity.

As they got closer to the Garden, Ali mentally reviewed his part of the plan. His objective was to set off oversized air horns and panic the crowd in the middle of Cantor's event. The horns were disguised as fire extinguishers, necessary for safety.

He hoped the resulting stampede would be minor—enough to destroy Cantor's credibility and usefulness in the eyes of GRIP, but not enough to harm bystanders.

He was treading a fine line.

The trick would be to get away from the Fish Lips stall and retrieve the air horns from the staging area, where he had placed them during the event setup.

The horns were Diana's idea. She called it the trumpet of chaos. Ali thought it was sheer poetry.

# CHAPTER 81
# THE MAN WITH THE BLUE GUITAR

Buddy Breau was the man with the blue guitar. He had a special place on the sidewalk outside Madison Square Garden and Penn Station, where he put down a blanket and a guitar case and played to the street.

He was very good.

People threw money into the case, and he had enough at the end of every day to buy a decent hot meal and a cheap hotel room.

Buddy also had a sixth sense.

Today he saw "trouble" walking his way. Even the stray dog, who had attached himself to Buddy earlier in the day and looked like Toto in *The Wizard of Oz*, pricked his ears and moved out of the way. Buddy would have moved, too, if his sixth sense had given him more notice, and his muscles had been more flexible.

"Watch out!" he said.

The inevitable occurred. A swarthy man with a beard, a big pillbox fur hat, and a black outfit caromed off pedestrians, stumbled onto Eddie's blanket, and fell into Eddie's lap. Eddie saved the guitar, but the man bumped the case, and a morning's worth of money spilled onto the sidewalk.

"Damn you!" Buddy said.

"Sorry, sorry," the man said. "Look, I'll pay. I'm sure you're very good." He dropped a one-dollar bill into the case and helped pick up money on the ground.

"Not enough," Buddy said.

"Okay, okay," the man said. He dropped two twenties into the case.

"That's better," Buddy said.

"Then we're good?"

"Listen, man, things are not as bad as they seem. In some ways, they're worse. There are actually people who are after you."

"How did you know that?" the man said.

"I have a sixth sense. I'm the man with the blue guitar—like in the poem. I can see things as they are and change things on my blue guitar." He jangled the strings.

"Well, I'm on my way to Madison Square Garden. Nice meeting you," the man said.

"You know the algorithms they use with the camera systems around here will pick out your fake beard unless you take preventive measures."

"Like what?"

"Well, I used to be wanted by the cops, and they tried to find me with the camera network, but the dog fooled them."

"How does that work?" the man said.

"I'm not sure, but it's a known fact, and it hasn't failed me."

"Where can I get a dog?"

"You can rent mine, but you have to return Max by tomorrow morning. Fifty bucks."

"Perfect," the man said. "Do you take credit?"

"Yup. You'll have to carry the dog. Hold him close to your face to fool the cameras."

The man paid the money and walked away with the animal, huddled in intimate conversation.

When the man was out of sight, Buddy spoke to his guitar, his only constant companion.

"I wonder who owns the dog," he said.

His sixth sense seemed energized. He started playing a jazz piece from Funkadelic.

# CHAPTER 82
# BARBLEFARB WITH BALLOONS

Funkadelic's Maggot Brain played loudly through the speaker system, masking the hubbub of arrivals in the Garden. People closed their eyes, swayed to the beat, and imagined the future in Eddie Hazel's moody guitar tremolo. When they looked up, they saw red, white, and blue balloons covering the ceiling, like the foam of a future wave destined to wash across the world.

As the start time approached, the music segued into TLC's "Red Light Special."

Bikini-clad dancers, cocooned in transparent plastic bubbles, gyrated to a deep, rhythmic bassline in a sway of light and lust above the Garden floor. From time to time, they threw kisses to the audience, and men in the crowd pantomimed catching them.

The stadium filled.

Ali wondered why they had to bring live fish to the Garden. "Why don't you kill them in the shop?"

"Must be berry fresh," Fun said. "People really wants that. Fish wiggle. They see you cut off head. Best tasting fish is when you can't tell if alive or dead. Must say fish's name first."

Fun demonstrated by putting a wiggling fish on a cutting slab. He held it with one hand and said, "Goodbye Ben Chapman." His other hand deftly twirled a blade before severing the fish's head in a single *thwack*.

He cut out a piece of squirming flesh. "Taste," he said, offering it to Ali. "Berry fresh."

In one corner of the Garden, on a level above the central stage, a shadowy figure huddled over an electronic console, adjusting sliders and knobs, and attending to a touch panel.

"We're just about ready," he said, flipping a switch like an exclamation point.

Diana moved closer. "This looks very complicated, Jake."

He laughed. "Well, my dear, it is, and it isn't. This is my control panel for the universe. It connects to everything that lights, or sounds, or moves in the Garden. I'm the wizard behind the curtain. But my dirty little secret is I have a helper."

"A sorcerer's apprentice?"

"An AI brain," he said.

"I thought you hated robots."

"I do. They have no sense of humor, no sense of cosmic justice." His eyes clouded as his mind spiraled toward the future. His lower lip trembled, and a drip of moisture rolled down his cheek.

"Sorry," he said. "It's hard to deal with. Bots will take my job."

He turned away. She put a consoling hand on his shoulder.

"I know you're smarter than they are, Jake. You manage them, right?" Her face brightened. "What does Jake's brain do when you have one of these gigs?"

He turned to face her again. This time, he was smiling, and there was a dampened twinkle in his eye.

"Artificial intelligence is like an autopilot, and I just watch the blinking lights. My brain is free to work on bigger and better things, like Sudoku puzzles and conversations with charming women. I can still do things manually, but I have to override the AI."

He flipped a few switches, turning them on, then turning them off, exerting his authority. His free will.

"We give each show a basic template, but the AI adjusts sound and lights for variations in the program. If you came here three weeks ago, you'd have seen a really hard, geeky process."

"Jake, I like things that are hard and geeky. If you know what I mean."

She put her hand on top of Jake's.

"Ahem." He flipped a switch. "Okay, now I'm actually driving this beauty."

"Wow," she said.

"I can make the dancers go up or down or turn lights and music on and off. I can color the world as subtly as you like, with hues of passion, or fear, or anger, or hate. I can make you think you're in an alternate universe."

The sign above the concession stand said *Fish Lips—A Kiss of Kosher.* Fun was at the register; Manego and Ali were loading ice. Ben hovered around the counter, commenting, from time to time, on things he wished people would do. He talked aloud to himself, everyone, and no one.

"They wanted fish because it's spiritual," Ben said. "So here we are, in the Garden. On the Sabbath. I am so *ferklempt*. Listen. We can make a lot of money. We have some really nice, unusual fish. People love it fresh." No one seemed to pay attention, so Ben spoke louder, "I wish someone would prepare the fish."

There was still no reaction, so he yelled. "Hopefully, someone will prepare the fish."

Ben walked away but glanced back. Finally, Manego gave Ali an elbow.

"What?" Ali said.

"Hey, m'bro. Pay attention. Ben—he da *mashgiach*. Do what he tells ya. Cut da fish."

"I understand," Ali said. "Where's the cleaver?"

"Jake, this is so incredible," Diana said. "I want to imagine what it's like to control the Garden. Can I put my hands on yours? Those powerful hands?"

"Sure. Let's raise and lower the bubble dancers—not too fast."

"Ooh. What's with those other lights on the big mountain?"

"That Cantor guy calls it 'Mammary Mountain.' I think it's like a big piñata. This red button releases what's inside it, but when we go live, the computer will control it."

Sundar looked at the dog that had become a constant companion and guardian from spy cameras. In order to get him into the Garden, he had to claim that Hari, as he now called the dog, was his emotional support animal. He used Hari as a sounding board. "I'm on a fool's errand," he said.

Hari cocked an ear.

Sundar scratched his fake beard and pushed his pillbox fur hat backward, to let his forehead breathe. "How do you track the location of security guards in a stadium filled with thousands of people?"

The dog growled.

"My thoughts exactly."

Sundar spotted a uniformed guard and decided to follow him for a while. "The game's afoot," he said.

*Arf!*

He imagined what he would tell Diana. *I successfully followed one out of—what?— a hundred security guards and kept an accurate record of his location. I was in a position to notify you instantly if the guard threatened our mission.*

The guard moved into a concession line, and Sundar followed.

*Might as well get a drink.*

The guard got a burger and ate it standing at a small round table. Sundar purchased a tall cup of cola with ice and moved nearby to watch. He was unable to poke his straw through the beard. Finally, out of frustration, he snapped the beard below his chin and sucked the liquid in a long, fulfilling draw. He closed his eyes, reveling in the liquid refreshment. He heard someone nearby speak with a southern twang.

"Berky told me you boys got real money," the voice said. "That's great, 'cause I got a big idea. It's bigger'n a year's supply of elephant shit."

When he opened his eyes and looked at the seat next to him, he saw a bulbous-nosed man who resembled W.C. Fields chatting with Mr. Taylor from GRIP's Customer Persuasion Department. Taylor looked surprised when their eyes met.

"What are the odds?" Sundar said. He dropped his drink and took off.

The man sitting next to Taylor said, "What just happened?"

Taylor ignored him, made a quick net call, then followed Sundar.

"A customer wants ginger fish for ten people. I hope someone can help," Ben said.

Ali was trying to listen to the preliminary introductions in the Garden when Manego prodded him. "Yo, cook da ginger fish."

"I heard him," Ali said, "but we don't have any ginger."

"What in yo' pocket? Is you mad stupid?"

"That's not ginger. It's Mandrake root. It's voodoo."

"I know voodoo. Yo mean it's a doll? Dat's its arms, and dat's its head?"

"Exactly," Ali said.

"Yo crazy." Manego reached for the cleaver, snatched the root, and chopped off its head. He sliced it with quick motions of the blade—*tap, tap, tap*—and shoved it into Ali's mouth. He slapped Ali's face and made him swallow. "Dat's ginger, see? What da fuq?"

Ali started sweating. "I don't feel so good."

Lights dimmed in the main hall, and the music subsided. The arena filled with a growing, thunderous applause. A spotlight flashed on center stage as Canduka Cantor ascended like a god to the podium, propelled by a hidden elevator. His spangled robe cast reflections around the Garden, and onto balloons tethered to the ceiling. He was Elvis. He was Jesus Christ. He was Charles Darwin.

Cantor bowed and then waved his hands in all directions until the audience was ready to listen.

"Ah am Canduka Cantor."

Thunderous applause.

"Today, we welcome friends from different corners of the soul and from different science-based faiths. Here, we come together with a single purpose. Some already believe in the Cantor Spiritual Community. You are well-prepared for the new world. You are our base. We welcome the Raelians, who may be curious about our radical advances in behavioral genetics. I can assure you that your alien ancestors would be proud. We welcome the Transhumanists, and followers of the late Marcy Darcy. Join us. We can give new meaning to your lives.

"And we welcome Scientologists who may marvel at how our Genetic Acceleration Pearls can remove bad engrams and implant good ones. We do this through genetic re-programming, with assistance from quantum supercomputing. Our approach to genetics transcends the boundaries of individual lifetimes and is therefore consistent with the evolution of the thetan spirit, a central tenet of Scientology.

"For those who seek guidance from the Bible, you will be comforted to know Cantorism is guided by the truth of 1st Peter 2:18: 'Slaves, submit yourselves to your masters with all respect, not only to the good and gentle but also to the cruel'; and by Ephesians 5:22: 'Wives, submit to your husbands as to the Lord.'

"You will find that Cantorism embraces these dictates from God.

"For those of you who are just here to criticize, and not learn the truth, be warned: you are fair game. Cantorism will seek retribution using any and all possible means. Our new religion starts by observing the power of science to change the world. These advances are today's miracles. They are the new wine-into-blood and bread-into-flesh transmogrifications. However, science is a process, and by itself, is devoid of meaning. Through our religion, we give it both value and direction.

"Ah am Canduka Cantor. Ah am the new Martin Luther."

Sundar ducked and weaved through the crowd, not bothering with "excuse me's." He knew Taylor and others were close behind but wasn't sure how far away they were. He could hear a distant commotion, so he picked up the pace. The dog yapped at him from behind. He spotted another GRIP agent.

Williams was on the communicator—talking to Taylor. He saw Sundar and pointed toward him. "Stop! Thief!" Williams said.

A uniformed guard heard the plea and joined the pursuit.

A crowd gathered in front of the Fish Lips concession stand. Many people wore yarmulkes. Ben was in his element, selling to the masses as he munched on a fish.

"This is soooo good! Hold on to your *kippas* when you eat it. And be sure to try my special sauce made from ginger and parsnips."

Customers were thick and quick. As the kitchen responded to demand, Ali removed his apron.

Manego grabbed Ali's arm. "Hey, man. Whachoo doin'?"

"Sorry, I have to go," he said.

"Bro, you shoudda thought of that half an hour ago before we opened. Yo get back here!"

"No, not that," Ali said. "I have to kill someone."

"You go, you mess us up, man."

Fun stopped attending to orders and weighed in. "You don't thinks nothing of customer service. You only thinks of yourself. You is narcissist."

At this point, Fun flipped into eloquent Mandarin, psychoanalyzing Ali. He claimed the narcissism stemmed from Ali's youth, where the incorrect placement of furniture channeled energy the wrong way in his brain, forever affecting Ali's understanding of reality.

Ben couldn't understand Mandarin, but he did sense his customers were not being served. He walked into the kitchen as Ali walked out. "*Oy!* Where's he going? He took my furshlugginer cleaver." He put his hands on his face, with a woe-is-me look. "I wonder if anyone will go after him." After waiting a beat, he said it again, louder. "I wonder if anyone will go after him!"

Manego was the first to respond. "I'll get dat mutha. He said he was gonna kill somebody."

Then Fun chimed in. "I go, too. Ali is furshlugginer mother."

"He's a terrorist," Ben said. "If we see something, we need to say something. Tell the police. I wish someone would help. He-e-e-lp!"

Ben's cry was lost in the noise as a herd of people stampeded past the concession stand chasing Sundar.

Cantor beamed a smile at the multitude. "You now have the privilege of participating in our Inception event. This is a sacred ceremony where you eat a Genetic Acceleration Pearl to put your future on the right track. Be careful which future you pick. For good looks, choose the red balls. For athletic prowess, choose the white balls. For intelligence, choose the blue balls. It's that simple. Are you ready for the future?"

*Clapping, stomping, whistles.*

"One word of warning—Do not consume more than one ball. If you do, you will be conflicted, and there will be unpleasant biological consequences."

*Murmuring.*

"Ah will now guide you through the ceremony. You will stand up, put a hand on the shoulder of the person in front of you, and move around the Trolley of Life that dispenses the pearls."

Berky watched the performance from the wings. The orchestra swelled, and he saw Cantor do a little jig, in time with the music.

He was hungry, so he snacked on the only food in his pockets—a box of red, white, and blue malt balls. He rationalized that he was already a real man, and the Genetic Acceleration Pearls would make him more so—by immunizing him against Testrial. He felt a tingling in his esophagus as he wolfed down half a box.

The card in Berky's pocket announced a call with a loud Rachmaninoff theme. He looked at the screen and muttered, "Damn!" but picked up, anyway.

"Popkins, this better be good."

The voice on the other end quavered. "Boss, you need to call this off."

"Can't do that. Cantor's on the podium right now. We're pretty committed. What's up?"

"I am not sure which template we bake into malt balls."

"Whaddya mean?"

"Kublai Khan will not give me spec. It speaks nonsense. When I run calibrations, templates do not validate."

"Why am I just now learning about this?"

"Yesterday, they validate. So I assume formula was correct. Now it changes."

"Either Kublai Khan has gone crazy, or we got some bits flipped, but that happened after production. We should be okay."

"You sure? What if template was flipping back and forth? Or what if robot lies?"

"You mean like the universe is trying to trick us?" Berky made a face as if he had just eaten a spoonful of shit. "Popkins, I'm going to hang up, but listen to me carefully. I want you to find the bottle of Nantahala white lightning I keep in my office, in the credenza, and take a big drink. No—two big drinks. That's an order. And don't listen anymore to Kublai Khan. He's crazy."

He hung up and put the netcard back in his pocket.

"Sheesh! Just go with the flow, Popkins."

Close to Cantor's Garden of Earthly Delights live event, the Ends of the Earth Circus was assembling people, animals, and equipment for The Next Big Show, slated for the following day. Lions, leopards, and bears growled in cages in the staging area. There was a Globe of Death steel ball—a closed wire sphere where a cyclist looped vertically and sideways, appearing to defy gravity. In one arena, a man boxed with a kangaroo.

The kangaroo's trainer looked away when the motorcycle engine revved to high RPM. This was a mistake the muscular roo exploited. The man received a punch that landed him on his butt. He got to his feet, then socked the animal.

The motorcyclist, clad in tight-fitting leather with a death's head logo on the back, looped around in the Globe of Death and finally rolled to a stop. He moved his bike out of the cage, parking it near three others, lowered the kickstand, removed his helmet, and stared for a long moment at the human-kangaroo boxing match. He yelled to the trainer in a Russian-accented voice. "You are exploiting that animal!"

The boxer kept his eyes on the roo as he answered the Russian's question. "Naw, mate. This ain't part of the show tomorrow. It's just Roger and me working things out. You know, like the punching bag of the boss you hit to keep your blood pressure low. Roger's got issues, don't you, Roger? Goin' one-on-one keeps him sharp and motivated. Makes me look good."

The kangaroo backed away.

The boxer started a fancy foot dance. "C'mon, Roger."

Roger re-oriented his body toward the human, then lunged and punched. The boxer danced away.

The Russian cheered. "Way to go, Roger, show him moxie."

The boxer now made feints with his head and arms.

The Russian seemed puzzled. "*Pozhaluysta*. Why does kangaroo wear fuzzy slippers?"

"Protection, mate—my protection. The roo can rip you apart with the claws on his feet."

As if to put a point on it, Roger lunged, hit the boxer, then kicked him backward with a muscular foot. The fighter let out a cry as he hurtled through the air, slamming against the cage door. The door popped open, and the boxer spilled to the ground.

The Russian laughed. "Kangaroo wins by knockout."

The word "knockout" was drowned by the sound of a claxon reverberating through the Garden. When the Russian and the boxer looked for the source, they heard a second sound: the noise of a motorcycle starting up, then accelerating. The Russian and the boxer watched as a one-eyed man sped away toward the Garden arena. He had a meat cleaver tucked in his belt.

It seemed obvious, but the boxer said it anyway. "Hey, mate. That guy just stole your bike!"

A very large, fuzzy pink slipper thumped against the boxer's head. He got to his feet again but backed up to an ape cage. A muscular chimp grabbed him. The boxer fought but couldn't get away. He watched helplessly as Roger the kangaroo followed the motorcycle into the Garden arena.

"My motorcycle!" the Russian said.

Before the Russian could react, the fighter broke the chimp's grip, climbed onto a second motorcycle, started it up, and accelerated into the main arena with the sound of *VROOM*.

Two men—a burly black man, and a smaller Asian man—raced to a third bike. The African American started the engine, and the Asian man held on from behind. As they sped away, the Russian yelled.

"Wait!"

The driver gave him a one-fingered salute.

High-roller customers filled chairs nearest the podium, but the medium-priced and cheap seats were also occupied. Cantor's messaging was ecumenical.

"The subconscious mind is the storehouse of our deep-seated beliefs. It determines how we see the world. In order to reach our full human potential, we need to reprogram ourselves, and take our minds to a new spiritual level," Cantor said.

Suddenly the sound of a claxon filled the air, followed by the distant rumble of motorcycle engines. Cantor raised his voice, trying to speak over the noise.

"In the last century, reprogramming the subconscious meant re-training and conditioning. The approach is time-consuming and complicated. It is also error prone. What if there is a better way to reach fulfillment?"

The mass of humanity outside the stadium on the Garden's main level responded to two waves formed by the compression and rarefaction of people moving in the crowd. The first wave came from Sundar, who was attempting to escape. The second wave was spearheaded by Taylor, Williams, and a growing contingent of GRIP agents, Garden security guards, and NYPD. It was the fluid dynamics of a classic Keystone Cops chase.

In his performance spot outside Madison Square Garden, luck or fate or karma blind-sided Buddy Breau, the man with the blue guitar, the man with a sixth sense. He strummed a jazz piece to an appreciative audience of ten people when a man wearing a fur hat stumbled through the human ring, caromed against him, scrambled to his feet, and raced away.

Buddy picked himself up and screamed. "Asshole!"

People in the audience agreed. Many echoed the yell.

His guitar was undamaged, and Buddy had only a single raw scrape, so he plucked out a new tune, laughing it off. "This is how I bleed for art," he said.

His audience chuckled.

Then the second disturbance hit. It was more massive than the lone disruptor. There were men in suits, sweating from exertion, with iron bulges under their armpits, and danger on their breath. There were uniformed security guards wearing the MSG logo, struggling with batons, searching for someone to hit. There were curious kids, scrambling to be part of the action. And there was a little dog, yapping at the crowd, legs pumping furiously to keep up.

The swell of bodies crashed against the ring of listeners like a tsunami hitting a small island. This time, the blue guitar's headstock cracked, turning the instrument into scrap wood.

The pursuers brushed themselves off and continued the chase. Buddy's audience skittered into the sidewalks and streets, mindful that disaster could strike again.

As Buddy picked up the pieces and the metal strings that were once his guitar, he wondered again, who owned the little dog.

Sundar ducked into a subway station outside the Garden, jumped the turnstile, removed his big hat, and attempted to hide in plain sight in the pressing throng. He could see his pursuers begin to collect in a group on the other side of the turnstile and discuss strategy.

The train arrived, and he got on. He still carried his hat but turned his head to the window to watch GRIP agents enter the platform. Taylor's eyes locked onto his. Taylor and two other agents scrambled onto the train in other cars, just before the doors closed.

Inside the Garden, the claxon continued its painful wail. Multicolored balloons rained from the ceiling onto the floor. The audience "oohed" and "ahhed," as if this event were part of the spectacle.

Jake rushed into the control pit, cup of coffee in hand, in crisis mode. "What did you do?"

"I just hit this little switch by mistake," Diana said.

"They'll have my head for this," he said.

Diana's eyelids narrowed to slits—a look she copied from the late Marcy Darcy. "Can't we blame it on the computer? You said it's supposed to compensate for errors."

Jake calculated the benefits of that narrative. Yes, it was a good story. And it would require closer supervision of the computer in the future. He might even need an assistant. He could become a manager.

These thoughts were interrupted by the *BRAAT* of engines and screams from the audience. On the floor below, a kangaroo hopped on fluffy pink slippers amid racing motorcycles. VIPs in the expensive seats rushed to get away.

A motorcycle screeched to a stop below the podium, and a one-eyed man with a cleaver bounded up the steps.

"I'll end this!" the man yelled.

Two women in the audience who were close enough to hear him screamed.

A second motorcycle pulled up near the podium, but by this time, the one-eyed rider of the first motorcycle had already dismounted.

A third and fourth motorcycle drove in opposite directions around the floor. A costumed rider on one of the bikes shouted something in Russian—"*Govnyuk. Govnyuk. Govnyuk.*"

The other rider dodged the kangaroo and barely avoided crashing into the Russian bike. The forward and retrograde actions of cyclists herded the crowd toward the center of the stadium. The kangaroo was a catalyst for chaos.

With the claxon still sounding, Cantor waved his arms to get the attention of the media control booth. His eyes were on Ali Khan Ahmed, who climbed toward the podium, cleaver in hand, legs trembling with adrenaline.

"Get me out of here!" Cantor yelled.

Two things happened immediately. First, the dancers suspended in bubbles moved up and down in quick cycles. Second, Cantor heard an automated voice in his earplug: "I understand you want me to take an action. Is that right? You can say 'yes' if it is a media action, or you can—"

"Yes!" Cantor said. "Get me the hell out of here."

Ali climbed closer, waving his blade.

The robotic voice remained calm. "I understand you want me to get you the hell out of here. Shall I activate the podium elevator, or shall I—"

"Yes," Cantor said. "Get me the fuck out. Now!"

It was a Wile E. Coyote moment. Ali was poised near the podium with a raised fish cleaver—his face flushed, pupils dilated. His eyes were fixed on a reality others could neither see nor touch.

Cantor, only a couple of feet away, prepared to die. His robe shimmered and floated like a spirit preparing to launch toward the afterlife.

The elevator that enabled Cantor to ascend like a god before his followers suddenly dropped like a rock. For a split second, he seemed to defy gravity.

The claxon seemed to warn of impending doom. Diana summed up events in a single word: "Arrgh!" She put her hands on her cheeks, gripped in horror as Ali raised a cleaver above Cantor's head.

She watched Jake take more deliberate action.

He flipped two switches, looked perplexed, then whispered, "Give me back control, bit-brain."

Diana watched Cantor fall into the elevator pit.

She saw Ali, now alone on the podium, wave his cleaver. The Garden's cameras projected the action onto large screens. The crowd on the garden floor reacted like a roiling sea.

"I have to leave now," Diana said. "My friend's in trouble."

Ali watched Cantor drop into the elevator pit. *I have sent the Devil back to hell. Good!* Reality shifted and shimmered before his eyes. "Listen." A woman's voice spoke from inside his head. He heard the rat-tat-tat of an African drum. "I am Laveau.

You will know me by my feathers and my sacred boa. I am the many. I am the one." Ali struggled to discern the truth.

Overhead, dancers bobbed and gyred chaotically in plastic bubbles. Several wore feathered costumes. One dancer had a feather boa stretching from the left breast, around her neck, to the right breast, and then down to the crotch.

"Why are you jerking up and down?" Ali said.

"Stop the demons," the voice said. "Their magic comes from the mountain. Destroy it before they destroy you."

The mammary-shaped mound was the magic mountain, and the two figures resembling Manego and Fun were evil demons. That much was clear.

Ali stabbed the mountain. It bled red, white, and blue malt balls.

The demons tripped on the rolling balls.

He sliced again, rupturing the mountain's membrane, sending a surge of candies onto the stadium floor. The force of the wave carried him down the steps, past the flailing demons, and deposited him at the base of the podium.

His enemies, above on the steps, moved and slipped. They both fell hard, then rolled toward him, prostrate.

*I will have victory! I am Ali Khan Ahmed.*

He raised his cleaver, aimed it at the head of the largest demon, and took a step. Gravity and rolling pearls brought him down. The blade skidded out of his hand.

The demon resembling Manego stood and threatened him.

Ali swam on candy ball bearings toward his weapon. The larger demon moved into position and swung its blade.

*Clack!*

Ali stopped the demon's cleaver with his own.

The demon looked surprised and angry.

Someone had finally turned off the claxon, but the kangaroo was still being chased by men on two motorcycles moving in opposite directions, weaving among the crowd of people.

Diana raced toward the main event floor, but the tumultuous crowd blocked her movement. She watched the big screen near the stadium ceiling. It captured a life-and-death duel punctuated by the *snicker-snack* of steel-on-steel.

The demon that resembled Manego was on his back, having fallen and lost his blade.

Ali rejoiced. *Victory is mine.*

He would demonstrate mercy, but only after the demon surrendered. He put the blade next to his enemy's pulsing carotid, nicking the skin just enough to draw blood.

"Do you surrender?" he said.

That was the moment of Ali's ultimate triumph and ultimate defeat. What happened next violated all assumptions about bodily integrity. Marie Laveau, the voodoo queen, seemed powerless to alter his destiny.

He was above Manego, his blade drawn. Then he dropped to Manego's level, smashed his chin on the concrete floor, and watched the stadium spin as his head rolled around, amid balloons and candy.

Before his world faded to black, Ali heard a voice that sounded like Fun's: "I has killed him. I has killed the terrorist!"

Diana saw Fun sever Ali's head with a single swipe of his blade. The head rolled into the froth of balloons and candy balls.

Her legs collapsed. Her eyes fixed on the screen.

She saw hundreds of people pushing and shoving to get at the pearls. They scooped them with their hands, filled their pockets, and even ate them on the spot, hungry for future perfection.

Diana puked.

Inside the subway car, Taylor contemplated pain. A client had once shot him in Chicago over a payment dispute. There had been a lot of blood when the bullet whizzed through his femur. Taylor had held it together long enough to dispatch the client with a hammer and earn kudos from his supervisor at GRIP.

*But this ...*

The little dog's ankle-biting, accompanied by constant high-pitched yapping, was like the pain of a thousand cuts.

Taylor tried to ignore the dog. He smiled at people in the subway car staring at him.

The car decelerated. Taylor pushed his way toward the front. When the doors opened, he jumped out and watched. This was the eleventh F-line subway stop. He was in mid-Brooklyn. Sundar Rao was still onboard.

Three other GRIP agents in separate cars also stood on the platform, hoping persistence would pay off.

The train dinged. Taylor prepared to jump back into the car.

A man in a pillbox fur hat got out two cars ahead and turned at the sound of the yapping dog. When he spotted Taylor, the man ran.

Taylor kicked at the dog, but missed, then took off in pursuit. The other GRIP agents followed.

Diana fought another wave of vomit. She struggled to her feet and pushed her way to the main floor of the Garden. She got close enough to see the body.

The people around her wrangled over the red and white candy balls. Most of the blue balls remained on the floor.

The police began to arrive. There was nothing more she could do. There were just the two of them now in the fight against Berky.

She had to find Sundar.

Taylor and three others followed Sundar into Borough Park, where they faced a gauntlet of protesters angry over various religious affronts-of-the-day. Signs read, *Stop the abomination!* and *Christians unite!* and *Mainstream Jews reject gender discrimination.*

Beyond the placards, there was a parade of people with pillbox fur hats.

Taylor stopped, scratched his head, then shouted to the other agents.

"Surround them. Don't let him leave."

After twenty minutes, they still had not found their target.

On another street, a man resembling Sundar Rao—no fake beard, no pillbox hat—stepped into a taxi. He jettisoned a placard that read *Jesus Saves.*

# CHAPTER 83
## OOPS

Berky looked out from his perch above the stage. Amid fallen balloons and a sea of malt balls, police crowded around Ali's body and severed head. Officers slipped and slid into each other. One of the officers cuffed Canduka Cantor when he popped up out of the pit. Cantor and the officer lost their balance and glided ten feet before falling.

*If they arrest Cantor, they might come for me.* Berky went through the defense in his head. *It was Cantor's fault. He's a crazy megalomaniac. I was just delivering on a contract.*

He would have to check with his attorneys. The more he thought about it, the less he liked the narrative. He headed for the exit and tried to escape with the crowd.

Police quickly cordoned off access to the event staging area and other back exits, forcing everyone to file through the front of the facility where they were screened, recorded, and questioned. The line snaked around interior partitions organized to control the flow of people. As he rounded a turn in the maze, Berkey recognized a face on the other side of the plexiglass—part of the moving crowd. It looked like Nadia, but she was back in Assurance, a loose end that GRIP would soon tuck away and neaten.

*It must be the sister. She had something to do with this screwup.*

He reached through the space between panels and clutched her arm. Diana recoiled, eyes wide as if touched by a monster. She grabbed his hand and bit through his forearm, pulling a flap of skin away with her teeth. He yowled, wrenching his hand free. Diana stared at him, blood dribbling from her mouth. She tried to back away but was unable to do so—a prisoner of the crushing crowd.

Unmindful of his wound, he contorted his face to convey the hate in his heart. It was an animal sneer that displayed teeth below a curled lip.

He mouthed the words, "You are dead."

She held his eyes, then pushed the piece of skin into her mouth and swallowed. She smiled, pushed back, swam into the sea of people, and disappeared.

He gave voice to his words, first muted, then booming: "You are dead. You are dead!"

He tried to squeeze through the partitions, but two large men blocked him.

The snake of people moved, like a lazy python curling after a meal. Diana was swallowed by bobbing heads, lost to his gaze.

Berky had finally cleared the Garden and was having a medic bandage his forearm when his netcard rang. He picked up the device with his good arm. It was Popkins. He hesitated, and against his better judgment, accepted the call.

"Popkins, you are—"

"Boss, you must listen," the voice squeaked. "Virus is not what we thought."

It took Berky a moment to reply. "What do you mean?"

"Maybe was power outage. Maybe was crazy Kublai Khan. Maybe was cosmic rays. Or space-time glitch. Don't know. Malt balls use wrong templates. Not primary template; not backup template."

"You mean, the template from Nadia Holkam and the one from Eban Haywood?"

"Correct."

"Well ..." Berky struggled to understand how the fabric of reality could change in an instant. "What are ... What can the templates be consistent with?"

"I do not know," Popkins said.

"Shee-it."

Berky hung up again.

His mind raced, thinking of options. He dialed Popkins. "Suppose people eat the balls. Can we undo the effect?"

"Well ... Maybe. Will take some time. Kublai Khan must get well again. We must know who eats candy, and who they get close to. But is possible, if we got time, money, and effort. I trying to be positive."

Berky's mind flashed to the chaos on the Garden floor, where people hungry for a new future ignored the police and stuffed their pockets and purses with red, white, and blue candies. Genetic Acceleration Pearls would soon find their way across Manhattan, the state, and the country. It would be out of control.

"Do we have any other options?" Berky said.

"Well, maybe we got lucky. Maybe is not worst-case scenario."

# CHAPTER 84
# THE END AT THE RAINBOW

Diana walked up to the empty second-floor lobby of the Rainbow Hotel, barely able to contain her emotions. She couldn't shake the image of Ali's severed head rolling on a carpet of malt balls, with spectators clawing each other for a taste of the future. Or Berky's threat to kill her.

Her legs were shaky. Cold sweat dampened her upper lip. And there, before her, Zeke Crawford, the Bert Lahr look-alike, grinned as if he had just killed the wicked witch.

Zeke swept his hand toward artwork impeccably placed around the room and stopped to point at the iconic image of a young, innocent-looking Judy Garland looming on the wall behind him.

Diana resisted the urge to vomit. "Key, please." What she really wanted to say was: *Do you have any magic shoes that will take me away from this bad dream?*

Zeke was slow to respond. "Looks beautiful, doesn't it? You just need to see a project through to the end. Have courage. Never give up. Things will work out. They always do."

Diana gripped the edge of the counter, face blanched.

"Even my computer is back to normal," Zeke said. "And we have 1930s-era music playing in the elevators. You'll be happy to know you're my test case. I submitted your information this morning, including pictures of Mr. Rogers. Everything works perfectly."

"What pictures?"

"The ones I took when he wasn't looking. I didn't take any pictures of you because I didn't know what sort of relationship you had. I tried to be discreet. The company wanted informal shots of happy customers for the opening campaign, and that's what I gave them. He'll need to sign a release agreement, so I can meet my quota. I'll give you both a discount if he signs."

"You can't use his picture! Or mine!" She wobbled, then caught herself. "Give me the damn key!"

He slapped the key on the desk. "There." He muttered something under his breath about how women need to learn to control their emotions.

She felt too weak to fight back and headed toward the stairs.

"Wait," Zeke said. "The elevator works now. You can take that."

She nodded, walked over, and pressed the button. The doors whooshed open. With one foot inside, she glanced at the key and stopped.

"Wrong key," she said, returning to the counter.

Zeke looked through the customer list with two names on it. "No, I gave you the right key."

"Sundar—um—Mr. Rogers and I switched rooms. I liked the other one better."

"Well, you should have told me! I'm not happy. And I've already sent the information in. I thought things were administratively perfect; now they're not."

"I'm not happy either," Diana said. "Give me the key."

Reluctantly, he switched keys. She walked back to the elevator.

"I'll have to explain to Mr. Rogers when he comes in," he warned. "Sometimes, people try to take advantage. They use a pretext to get into someone else's room. There are bad people out there."

She looked back from inside the elevator. "Tell me about it."

The doors closed, and she went up.

Diana stumbled into her room and threw herself onto the iron bed. After less than a minute, her stomach urgently wanted to imitate a volcano. She rushed to the bathroom, vomiting a stream of chunky puke.

Her bowels rumbled with a secondary after-shock when the hotel phone rang. She sobered immediately. Sundar was the only other person who knew her location. When she last saw him, he was being chased. She picked up the handset with a tentative "Hello?" Her hand trembled in the aftermath of violent retching and the fear of discovery.

Silence.

The message light blinked, so she pushed the button. She heard a recorded voice that resembled her own.

It was Nadia's voice. Here's what it said:

*Hey Diana, it's me.*

*Listen.*

*The world as you know it is about to change.*

*Got your attention? Good.*

*Remember the sample malt balls Marcy gave you? You have some in your purse.*

*Well, this is your lucky day.*

*The balls contain Sundar's genebo. They reset the genome to its original condition.*

*Everyone in Manhattan may soon be infected with Berky's virus, and you were close to the action. So having a remedy is very beneficial.*

*Now here's the bad news: You only have two malt balls. Check it out.*

The recording paused for a moment.

*How could Nadia know that?* Diana turned her purse upside down on the iron bed. The bag containing malt balls spilled out, along with a knitting needle, an assortment of coins, and other flotsam and jetsam. She held the bag up to the light, hoping to see more than two balls. She was disappointed.

The voice continued:

*Well, I guess we won't be saving the rest of humanity today, will we? Who will you choose?*

*Oh, one more thing: I'm dying. I just thought you should know. Maybe you'd like to save a malt ball for your sister? On the other hand, it might be wasted.*

*You've got some decisions to make, girl.*

*Have a nice day.*

Diana was still in shock. She heard a banging on the door. Before she opened it, she swallowed a malt ball.

Now there was only one.

For Frank Taylor, revenge was an erotic experience he preferred to share only with his victims, in the intimacy of death or dying. When the GRIP Research Division hacked a photo from the Rainbow Hotel, Taylor told Smith that Sundar Rao was his. He had this.

He felt the thrill of the chase as he climbed steps leading to the hotel's second-floor lobby, imagining Rao's surprise when they met again. He stopped on the way up to check the clip in his Ruger 9mm pistol. He fitted the silencer and stuffed the weapon into a deep pouch pocket of his coat. *You have to be ready for any eventuality.*

He initially assessed the hit as low risk. The only person in the lobby was an old guy who seemed to be trying on a costume.

"Hey! Howya doin'?" Taylor said. "Tell me about yer hotel. Looks like ya got an animal act. Heh-heh."

Zeke Crawford issued a pained smile from behind the check-in desk. "We're getting ready for our grand opening. I'll be wearing the lion costume for that. But listen. You don't have to wait until Thursday. We've got rooms available right now at a reduced rate. After Thursday, prices go way up, so you're in luck."

"In-ter-esting," Taylor said. "You got a lotta other people stayin' right now?"

"Heavens to Murgatroyd, no. Things will be very quiet. We've just got two people checked in. See?" He pushed the sign-in register in front of Taylor, stabbing at the names.

Taylor looked. "Yeah. Gimme a room on the same floor. I'm superstitious, ya know? That's a good floor number for me. Can I look at the room before I sign in? It's just that I've been burned before. Ya know?"

"No problem," Zeke said. "Here's a key. Take a look, then come back down and sign in. I'm sure you'll be astonished at what you find."

"Thanks," Taylor said.

When the elevator door closed, he pressed the button for the top floor, then pulled the gun from his pocket, checked the clip, cocked it, and set the safety. He thought about cowboys and the Wild West as he put the weapon back in his pocket. There was an old Bing Crosby song streaming from the elevator's speakers:

*We're old cowhands from the Rio Grande,*
*And we come to town just to hear the band ...*

Sundar was in his room before Taylor arrived at the hotel. Following his encounter with GRIP in Brooklyn, he had taken a taxi to Cadman Plaza Park, walked across the Brooklyn Bridge, rode the subway to the Christopher Street PATH terminal, bought a train ticket to Hoboken, then exited the station without boarding the train. From there, he walked uptown to his hotel, stopping at public buildings with exits on two streets, confident no one had followed him.

By the time he reached his mid-town hotel, the adrenaline had worn off. He was still on high alert but exhausted.

He went into the bathroom to wash up and noticed the place was a mess. It looked like the work of an untidy plumber. There was a box of tools on the floor, metal shavings in the sink, and the faucet didn't work. *Ugh!*

He consoled himself with a small bourbon from the mini-bar, waited to feel a calming alcohol buzz, then prepared to knock on the connecting door.

He hesitated when he heard the sound of Diana's voice talking on the phone. He sat on the bed and waited. It was then he realized his armpits were still damp with sweat, and the smell of fear clung to his clothes.

He was naked from the waist up, rummaging for a clean shirt, when he heard a banging on the door—Diana's door.

Taylor was annoyed to see a person standing in front of the elevator door when it opened. The ancient, fragile-looking man blocking his exit wore a tuxedo. When Taylor tried to step around him, the man grinned. Taylor made a mental note: *One more potential witness.*

He bumped against the man as he passed but felt nothing. The old codger seemed to be made of air. When Taylor turned to see if he had inadvertently knocked the geezer down, he saw a younger man standing in the elevator, dressed in a tweed hunting jacket, matching brown pants, and fishing boots. The man wore the same grin as the geezer, who was nowhere to be seen.

Before the doors closed, the man in the elevator gave him a thumbs up and said, "Yippee-ki-yay." Taylor shrugged it off. *They're playing games. These guys must be 1930s re-enactors—something to do with the grand opening.* The light in the hallway flickered. *This place is nowhere near ready. They've got serious work to do on the electrical system. Who'd want to stay in this shitsty?*

Taylor waited for a moment to verify the hallway was clear before approaching his target's door. His experience with "cold calls" was that they could go one of two ways—either the target would be prepared for him, with a weapon handy, or totally unprepared.

Remembering a trick that had worked in the past, he banged forcefully on the door and yelled, "Open up. Fire Department!" The announcement had an urgent "truthiness" to it.

He drew his pistol, cocked it, made sure the safety was off, and gripped the weapon with two hands to steady his aim. Then he stood away from the door in case his target tried to shoot before opening.

He heard movement—someone stumbled. A glass shattered on a tile floor, and a voice mumbled a soft profanity.

The lock clicked, and the door opened. On the other side, a pale-faced woman in a vomit-stained blouse trembled.

Taylor pushed his way in and shut the door.

"Where's Sundar Rao?" he yelled, pointing the gun.

The frightened woman said nothing. She moved backward, climbing onto the bed.

"Where is he? You've got three seconds."

The woman moved to the center of the bed and gripped the iron frame with one hand. Her other hand groped through miscellaneous junk scattered on the bed.

"Three, two, one," Taylor said.

The woman closed her eyes. The room's lights flickered.

Taylor squeezed the trigger.

The gun clicked but didn't fire.

Taylor was dumbfounded. Ruger's SR series pistol was one of the world's most reliable weapons, able to fire more than 5,000 times without a glitch, even if the gun wasn't cleaned. For Frank Taylor, it had always worked.

He squeezed the trigger again. No joy—only a failure of confidence. There was obviously something wrong.

The woman on the bed opened intense green eyes and faced him with a smile that angered Taylor. "We'll do this another way," he said, flicking on the safety and turning the gun around to use as a bludgeon. He placed one hand on the edge of the bed to steady himself and raised his other arm to gain leverage for a fatal blow.

The woman moved quickly. Taylor saw the knitting needle jut toward his left eye but was unable to block it with arms out of position. He felt a stab of pain, saw an explosion of light, and felt the woman's hand on his face as she pushed the needle deep into his brain. His body lurched backward but was still upright as he tottered, rigid, into the door to the adjoining room. The door opened. He lost his balance and fell to the floor.

Sundar Rao stood above him with a claw hammer that moved swiftly and inexorably toward the center of his forehead, hitting with a *crack*.

It was the last image Frank Taylor's brain processed before his prefrontal cortex leaked through a skull hole into a pool of blood on the ceramic tile.

Diana watched Taylor's body twitch three times before finally succumbing to the imperturbability of death. The end of the needle still protruded from his eye. She didn't know whether to hug her partner or vomit again.

Sundar also seemed unsure what to do. Frank Taylor was now an obstacle in the connecting doorway. Sundar stepped gingerly over the bloody hump, then slipped on the growing red puddle, coming down hard on Taylor's body, staining his pants with tissue and gore, feeling the prick of the needle as it slid against his thigh.

Diana stated the obvious. "You need to change your clothes."

Sundar nodded. "I'll have to use your bathroom. Mine is an unfinished plumbing project."

"And mine is a sickroom."

They pulled the body out of the doorway and into Sundar's bathroom, coloring the end of the yellow brick road with a smear of red. They dropped towels to sop up the blood and placed the body and a pile of wet, stained terrycloth in the bathtub.

Sundar moved his luggage into Diana's room. She changed her blouse and packed while he showered.

When he was dressed in fresh clothes, Diana told him about Ali's death, Berky's warning, the strange phone call, and Taylor's demands.

"We need to get out of here," Sundar said. "They'll be coming soon."

"Do something for me first," Diana said. "Eat this."

He squinted at the malt ball. "Doesn't this have Berky's retrovirus?"

"It's genebo," she said. "Your genebo. It didn't kill Cantor when he ate it in front of the judge. It won't kill you. It'll reset your genome."

He thought for a moment, then swallowed it. "You're right, of course. How did you know?"

"Nadia told me."

"You said Nadia left you a message? How did she——?"

"I don't know. But it was definitely her voice."

He picked up the phone with a blinking light and pressed the *play* button. Here's what he heard:

*We're not "Lion." As one of the first guests to enjoy our newly renovated venue that provides modern convenience with 1930s-era sensibilities, we want to thank you with a small gift. Please check at our front desk for your "over-the-rainbow" reward.*

"I don't think that was Nadia," he said.

Diana fretted. "Maybe it's a new voicemail. It erased the first one."

"Maybe," he said, "but we've got to get going. See if there's anything on the body we can use."

Diana removed Taylor's wallet, pistol, and other identifying artifacts. "That's it," she said.

"The police will tie us to the credit authorizations we used for the hotel," Sundar said. "Best to use this guy's netcard from now on."

They rode the elevator to the lobby and checked out.

"Not staying the night?" Zeke said.

Sundar put keys on the desk. "No. We're going to the airport. We've got an international red-eye flight to catch."

Zeke clucked in sympathy. "Too bad you'll miss the grand opening."

"Can you check on messages for either of our rooms?" Diana said.

Zeke winked, tapped a few keys, and looked at his display. "There's just the message thanking you for staying at the hotel. That reminds me, here's your gift from management—a box of chocolates."

Diana took it. "Could an earlier message have been erased?"

"You mean, could one message have written over another message?"

"Yes," she said.

"Well, it's a new system, and we've had some power surges in the past hour, but if there was a glitch, I have no way of troubleshooting it. I can talk to our technician. Call back tomorrow evening, and I should be able to tell you more."

"That's okay," Sundar said. "It's not important. Thanks for checking. We have to go."

"I hope you had a memorable stay at the Rainbow," Zeke said. "I know it's been a bit problematic staying here during the renovation." He put on the head of the lion costume, pausing for effect. "We take pride in seeing things through. Have courage. Grrr-ow-el."

The rain came down in sheets as Diana and Sundar pushed their way onto the sidewalk with rolling suitcases. Streetlights made the torrent seem like a dense fog, reducing visibility. They hailed a cab and got lucky.

The driverless taxi opened its doors. When they climbed aboard, Sundar gave an address close to their parking garage. They were soaked by the time they finished their one-block walk to retrieve their Mustang.

Sundar drove across the George Washington Bridge and headed north.

"Where are you going?" Diana said.

"Canada."

"Turn around."

"Why?"

"We need to save Nadia. She's dying."

"You said she doesn't want to be rescued. She wants to die in Assurance. What if she's already dead?"

"She isn't! I heard her voice on the phone in the hotel."

"That makes no sense."

"Maybe it was the iron bed. There's one in her bedroom in Assurance. Maybe she could—"

"That's magical thinking, Diana. You're becoming your mother."

"Oooh!" Her face turned red. Then she yelled at him. "Listen! I'm her sister. I've been trying to reconcile with her all my life. I won't abandon her again. I'll either rescue her or bury her. This is about who I am. We have to go back!"

Sundar tried to remain calm. "Berky may be waiting for us, and those mob friends of his."

"It's my car," Diana said, unbuckling her seatbelt, hand on the door, opening it a crack. "Turn around, or I'll jump."

He took the next exit, looped around, and headed south.

"Close the door," he said. "I'll take you back to Assurance."

# WATER

# CHAPTER 85
# THE YUMM OF TEA AND FISH

Charily Nolltin, Mayor of New York, opened her desk drawer and dumped the contents of her purse into it — half a dozen colored malt balls. She took out a red one, ate it, sensed a tingling in her esophagus, and knew it was the Genetic Acceleration Sphere kicking in. Tomorrow she would eat a white ball, and the day after—as much as she detested the idea of becoming an intellectual—would eat one of the blue balls. She already felt superior to everyone in Manhattan, but this remedy would cement her social status for the future. She would become an advanced human being, able to fend off any political rival.

She poured a glass of water from the cooler in her office, swished the liquid around in her mouth, swallowed, then looked at her teeth in a mirror to make sure no chocolate smudges marred her smile. When she finished primping, she opened the door and beckoned guests into her mahogany-lined office overlooking City Hall Park. "Please come in and be seated."

Ben moved stiffly, his face tense. Fun shuffled in, staring at his feet. Manego looked his usual, hostile self. It was National Tea Week, so the mayor's assistant poured everyone a *cuppa* to celebrate the occasion.

Charily tried to put everyone at ease. "I know you may be anxious about those criminal charges for selling poisoned ginger fish. Don't be." She smiled, then snapped her fingers. "Poof! I made them go away. After all, you saved my life. I was in the front row when that terrorist tried to kill everyone, and the kangaroo attacked us. That's why I intervened with the police when they were looking for suspects to arrest. You are all heroes, and heroic symbols are much more important to voters than incarceration."

The mayor sat, adjusted her hair, checked the lighting, then pushed a button on her desk. "Bring them all in now," she said.

After a moment, a group of reporters and bureaucrats swarmed through the door, filling the office, taking their positions for the photo op.

When everyone was in place, the mayor publicly demonstrated her hospitality and leadership by first turning on the microphone, then asking guests, "How's your tea?" When she spoke, everyone oriented like planets toward a star. She smiled, exposing perfect teeth to the cameras, and heard a confirming click from her personal photographer. This was followed by reflexive clicks from the lesser media.

*Success! Sometimes you had to lead by example.*

"Berry good tea," Fun said.

"Yo ah don' like tea. Wha' choo trippin, foo?" Manego said.

"This tea," Ben said, "goes very well with our Fish Lips products, which you can buy at—"

Charily put a hand on Ben's shoulder to silence him and shifted media attention to the main target—herself. She spoke directly to her base, in haiku. "This—what happened at the Garden—was really real. And these are really real guys. These aren't fake heroes. We should be proud of them."

She handed the microphone to the police chief.

"This is a great example," he said," of teamwork between involved citizens, the NYPD, and of course, the mayor, to keep the citizens of New York—and, frankly, the world—safe from terrorism and wild animals."

He handed the mike back to the mayor.

"Never in the history of the world have so many people worked so successfully under our guidance to keep humanity safe from monsters," she said.

There were murmurs and applause. A crowd of cameras clicked around the room.

Charily whispered to her guests, "You are about to become famous. Look at the reporters, smile, and try not to talk."

"Any questions?" she said.

# CHAPTER 86
# WALK IN THE PARK

*A "fulcromancer" is someone who can move the conceptual universe of an entire society, including ideas, beliefs, and social norms. On the other hand, a "fulcroony" is a fool who stumbles on a universal fulcrum point, not realizing the significance or consequences. Thus, conceptual universes may be altered by wits and the witless.*
—*Canduka Cantor*

It was an understandable confusion. When the police arrested Canduka Cantor for inciting a riot, the mayor of New York had not yet weighed in. Charily Nolltin later explained that Cantor was without guilt. He was just a religious leader trying to help perfect humanity. The police released Cantor but asked him to stay in the city for a few days while they determined what, exactly, had happened. In the meantime, they assigned blame to Ali Khan Ahmed, the dead terrorist, and to the animal trainer who should have exercised better judgment over Roger, the kangaroo.

Cantor thanked the police when they released him from jail. He explained that his religion predicted such events would occur from time to time. They were called "barblefarbs"— knots of confusion resulting from a lot of minds distorting reality in different ways. As proof that such conditions were foreordained, he showed them the tattoo on his hand.

The officers all nodded as though they understood.

As a token of goodwill, Cantor gave each cop a bag of malt balls. Then he called Berky and asked to meet in Central Park.

Berky stumbled in the dim evening light as he climbed with his backpack up the steps to Fort Fish, the highest point in the park. Cantor was already there, sitting on a bench, watching a night Frisbee game, and swaying to a jazz rhythm from a summer concert.

"I got a note from Popkins this morning," Berky said. "The state filed charges against us for industrial pollution. Their argument is totally fake, of course. I need to leave tomorrow and meet with my attorney."

Cantor eyed a pneumatic, long-legged female who jumped in the air to catch a plastic disk. His look was lecherous. "Ah can't wait until the virus grabs hold. There are so many opportunities. So little time."

Berky gritted his teeth. "I forgot to tell you something important. Popkins said Kublai Khan might have made a mistake."

"What do you mean?"

"The virus was based on the wrong template. It may not be Nadia's."

"Ah can live with that. If it's the template from Eban Haywood, it may even be better. Those hijab-wearing women are bred to know their place and how to treat a man."

Berky's mouth ticked nervously.

Cantor's eyes widened. "Oh, God, no. Don't let it be Marcy's! No! No! No! That woman can screw things up, even from beyond the grave."

"We're not exactly sure. But Marcy isn't the worst-case scenario."

"What could be worse?"

"I'm going to try a little experiment to rule out a certain test case. Popkins suggested the idea. We know the virus should have high efficacy. It should spread quickly, with few discernable symptoms—at least initially."

He unzipped his backpack.

"What are those?" Cantor asked.

"I call these my genetic reporters."

He unscrewed a lid from one of the jars and released several bugs. One of the insects lit up.

"They're lightning bugs," Cantor said.

"Yes. They can test for a certain type of protein marker—one I'd like to rule out, if possible. It's probably nothing to be concerned about."

The bugs dispersed toward the Frisbee game. When they blinked, some people lit up in response. When that happened, one of the players giggled. The laugh was contagious. As others laughed, they lit up.

"Shit," Berky said.

He watched with the fascination of a doomed man observing the end of the world in slow motion. More people were blinking than bugs. The blinking spread to bystanders, several of whom swayed to the rhythms of the jazz concert.

"You're blinking, too," Cantor said.

Berky noticed light issuing from small pores in his skin.

Cantor giggled. Then he reached over and hugged Berky. "Ah love you, man," he said. "We've made something beautiful."

Berky stood, backing away from Cantor and the crowd. Under a streetlight, he noticed scaly patches on his skin and scratched at them.

"Why weren't you affected?" Berky said. "You were closer than I was to the event."

"Just lucky, man. Maybe Ah am immune. Maybe it was the malt ball Ah ate when we went to court. That was a test sphere with genebo in it."

"Do you have any more of those with you?"

"Sorry. You'll have to go back to Charleston or ask Rosa at your lab to whip up a special mix. Maybe someone could send you a package in overnight mail."

Berky scratched at the scales, brightening the glow. "I've got to get back to the lab. I've got to fix this."

Cantor watched Berky descend the steep steps until his glowing aura vanished like a will-o'-the-wisp.

Inspired, he began writing a new entry in the Canons of Cantor. The scribbling became frenzied as he looked at the page, then back toward the frisbee game. It was a moment of great introspection.

He thought about the terms he'd coined for his new religion. *Was he a fulcromancer or a fulcroony? Did it matter?*

He found the blinking of people and fireflies mesmerizing. "Cool," he said aloud. "There are a thousand points of light; an overwhelming darkness; and a struggle to become something different. There must be a metaphor in that." He scribbled again in his book.

The jazz beat continued, and the frisbee players danced to an improvised tune.

# CHAPTER 87
# THE PERFECTION OF FISH

The pilot of Berky's private jet called Rosa Alcott shortly after takeoff from LaGuardia to describe an emergency. Berky had just come down with an illness that made his skin itch like it was on fire. Could she please find Popkins, who was not answering his phone, and ask him to have an ambulance meet the plane at the lab's airstrip with buckets of water and towels to keep him moist?

A strange request.

She found Popkins in his office, curled in a fetal ball atop his desk, nursing a bottle of home-brewed corn liquor, staring at a fish tank containing two fish. There was a grease pencil line on the front of the aquarium.

"Berky needs you," she said. "He's flying back from New York and got sick. The pilot wants someone to meet the plane and help."

"I got important business," Popkins grumbled in a deep, cranky voice, uncurling himself, placing wobbly feet on the floor, stumbling along a zig-zag line to the fish tank. He suddenly turned and held up the bottle. "White lightning is way better than vodka," he pronounced with authority. "Way faster."

She could smell the alcohol on his breath. "I don't doubt it. Do you want to give the pilot of Berky's airplane a call? Tell him you'll take care of the problem?"

"I am big-picture guy," he said. "Watch this." He turned and tapped on the glass of the tank. "Are you thirsty leetle ones?" he said to the fish. They were initially immobile, floating near the grease pencil line like bubbles in a calm sea. After he spoke, they perked up, zipped around, and swam above the line. "See? They want it! They happy." He lifted his bottle to the top of the tank and poured in two drops. The fish moved in a frenzy, then began to swim erratically. "You got to get them in the mood," he said, tapping again on the aquarium. He leaned closer, his breath forming a haze on the glass. "Hey, you! I'm talking to you! How does ocean say hello?" He waited a moment to deliver the punchline. "It waves. Get it?"

One fish lit up in a green glow and giggled. The other fish followed with a hearty laugh.

"They are smart," he said. "They laugh at my jokes."

The actions of the fish startled Rosa, but she quickly got back on point. "What about Berky?"

"You take care of problem," Popkins said. "I got to do science."

Rosa arranged for an ambulance to meet the plane and gave instructions to take blood samples and keep Berky moist. She was in the CEO's office when they wheeled him in on a gurney, his body covered in wet towels. When they unwrapped him and sat him in a chair, he seemed a marvel of evolutionary exuberance.

She observed, with the curiosity of a biologist discovering a new life form, the bare-chested creature that no longer wore Berky's red polo shirt. *Probably too tight*, she thought. Scales covered its arms, and thin slits formed behind the ears.

Rosa tried to make Berky comfortable. She remembered how she kept plants irrigated when she had to be away for a week—with a bucket of water and a wick made of towels. The CEO looked out of place, sitting at his desk with his exposed upper torso and scaly chest covered with a patchwork of terrycloth. *Pants will go next if the flipper feet keep growing.*

"Help me," it said.

"Berky? Are you still in there?" Rosa asked.

A whoosh of air moved through its lips, forming breathy words. "Fuck you."

"Yup, you're still you. But you look and sound like you're practicing to be a fish whisperer."

She moved closer, marveling at how the eyelids, now nearly invisible, rarely blinked; and how the mouth widened in a perpetual smile.

"I suppose you came back because you think this is the only place that can help you, and other doctors and medical facilities are useless. Am I right?"

"Yes," it said. "Fix this."

Rosa held its hand. At least it still had hands. At least it could still talk. "How long have you been like this?"

"I started to get scales yesterday. Now ..."

"I can help," she said. "If you survive tonight, I'll start a treatment for you tomorrow."

"*Aghh*," it said.

"I didn't get that."

"*Agh*, I hold on."

"Good. I'll be working through the night on a remedy. You can count on it."

"Turn *agh*. Turn *agh* the light."

"Oh, sure. Got it."

She flicked the switch. The room dimmed, but the light from the lab still poured through glass walls. She closed curtains to darken the room and filled the water buckets to keep Berky moist. Before departing, she looked back. The Berky thing glowed like a firefly, staring with eyes that rarely closed.

It was late afternoon the following day when Rosa returned. She left the overhead lights off but opened a curtain so she could see her subject. The Berky thing huddled in a chair, wrapped in a sopping wet blanket it had pulled from the credenza. The water in the buckets was nearly gone. She couldn't see the full extent of its transformation but noticed the gill slits were now prominent ridges that buried shrunken ears.

"I have good news, Berky."

She put a small vial of amber liquid on the desk. Berky regarded it with unblinking eyes.

"I have a cure made from Sundar's genebo. You'll be happy to know I gave it to everyone else in the lab and the aircraft crew. The virus won't affect us."

"*Agh*."

"What?"

"Wa-a-a-nt it."

"Listen. Your changes have gone too far, so I had to come up with a different approach. That's what's in the bottle."

She rolled the vial around on the desk, watching its head track the movement. The thing hissed. "Wa-a-a-nt it."

"That's what I thought. But first, you need to sign something while you still have hands."

The Berky thing recoiled when she spoke those words.

"Don't worry. I need to protect myself and the lab from any risk or liability. The treatment is experimental, so I can't administer it without your permission. It's part of the protocol for running human experiments. Do you agree?"

The thing pulled the paper close, trying to read through goggle eyes. After a moment, it gave up and stretched a grasping hand.

"*Agh* sign," it said.

Rosa found a pen. "There you go."

The Berky thing scribbled on the paper. Rosa looked at it and frowned.

"Sorry, we need to do it again. It might be easier if you retract your claws if that's possible. We can try as many times as you like. I have multiple copies. I need to make sure your signature doesn't look fake."

The thing scrawled again. This time Rosa nodded approval.

"That should do it. Hold out your, um ... arm."

Rosa wiped the limb with alcohol-soaked cotton, then plunged a hypodermic needle through the scaly skin, injecting the treatment. She pulled out the needle, wiped again, put a Band-Aid over the puncture, and patted Berky's head. "Wouldn't want you to get any sort of nasty infection, would we?"

She touched a finger to its face, tracing the permanent smile.

"I promise you there won't be any pain," she said. "I can't stand to see any animal in pain. I've given you the cure. And it only cost all your shares in Xanadu NeuroLab."

The Berky thing grabbed her wrist, but she easily broke free and moved toward the door, carrying the signed agreement.

"Don't get upset. There's no reason. In fact, if you search your mind, you'll see all the reasons in the world are evaporating. That's your cure, Berky. That's the perfection.

"There's a phylogenetic reset occurring in your body. You're not going back to the way you were before; you're reverting to something more primitive. The fiction gene — the basis for both imagination and delusion—gone. The rosehip neurons in your brain, unique to Homo sapiens—gone. All the special cognitive abilities that are so important for running a company like Xanadu NeuroLab—gone. In an hour or two, you'll be something quite different.

"You could be my pet. Maybe I'll call you *Boopie* instead of Berky. I'll feed you, clean up after you, and when you're too much of a liability, I'll put you down.

You'll see it as a good life—a life you actually want. How can something be bad if you actually want it?"

The Berky thing raised to full height, shed its blanket, extended its claws, and chased Rosa as she scampered out the door. Unfortunately, its feet—which were no longer feet, but flippers—weren't built for efficient ground locomotion. It shuffled with the gait of a movie Frankenstein.

The beast pushed past the room full of Kelsey tubes, grunting and whispering foul language in a half-human, half-animal dialect, triggering contagious laughter from the fish. Schrodinger peeked from a gap in the floor, ears alert, curious about the commotion. When the cat saw the lumbering fish-man, it scuttled back into the hole.

Berky's cognitive map held up as the monster moved through the lobby, to the astonishment of the receptionist. The officer picked up the desk phone to call for security reinforcements but put it down when he looked at the calendar.

"Right," he said. "That's a good one."

Yon was in the guard shack practicing his gun twirl when the Berky thing lumbered past without even a sideways glance.

Yon shook his head. "I gotta hand it to you, Mr. Benson—great disguise. Creature from the Black Lagoon, right?"

He gave the lumbering beast the two-fingered "eye-am-watching-you" sign.

"I'm a Cherokee," he yelled. "You can't fool me. Happy Halloween."

The Berky thing moved away from the road toward the river where it would be safe, fighting a tangle of vines with cumbersome flipper feet, sniffing for moisture. Finally, it came to the muddy bank, splashed into the water, and felt the joy of coming home. This is where it was *meant* to be. This is where it *wanted* to be. Nothing else mattered. Nothing else was relevant.

It coasted on the current. As it approached Kelsey's Bend, it dipped below the surface, popped back up, then submerged, experimenting with a new way of breathing.

The Nantahala forest above the waterline now seemed hostile and alien. It was not a place of safety or assurance.

Berky submerged a final time below the South Prong River.

Somewhere nearby, a wolf howled.

# CHAPTER 88
# THE THING IN THE WATER

When large numbers of transgenic humans appeared in New York City, the CDC traced the source of infection to the Madison Square Garden event and Canduka Cantor.

Police and FBI re-captured Cantor. Initially, he refused to cooperate, citing his First Amendment rights to freedom of religion and assembly. The plea fell on deaf ears, and this time around, there was no Charily Nolltin to rescue him—the mayor had turned into a fish monster.

When they charged Cantor with domestic terrorism, he "flipped," agreed to tell all, and asked the FBI to put him in protective custody because of threats against his life—from GRIP and angry citizens. Cantor's testimony led law enforcement and the CDC to Berky Benson.

By the time officials arrived at Xanadu, Berky had vanished. Rosa, now in charge, told how Berky and Cantor had duped everyone—including her.

Fortunately, she had an antidote which she had tested on her staff. The CDC fast-tracked a large, lucrative contract for disaster relief, making Rosa Alcott, Xanadu's largest shareholder, one of the world's wealthiest women. The Xanadu cure sold worldwide as red, white, and blue malt balls, branded as *HomoPerfect*.

Even as the cure became available, not everyone benefited. As a result, the hominin line added a new branch: *Homo kelsey*. The sub-species was hermaphroditic, able to change sex and mate with whatever individual of their own or similar species they encountered. In some cases, they were able to self-fertilize.

The so-called *Kelseys* were merpeople who were as smart as dogs but lived exclusively in the water. They were fierce predators who occasionally surprised boaters, dragged people underwater, and raped and killed them. Like the wolves of prior decades, they were deemed worthy of control rather than extermination. But many people took matters into their own hands, and as a result, Kelseys declined. The sub-species would have been on an endangered list if politics hadn't eliminated such lists.

Canada and Mexico tried to minimize the spread of Kelseys. The life form was able to infect normal H. sapiens through its bite. The infections, if non-lethal, resulted in rapid morphological change and carried through the germline to future generations. The effects of such bites were reversible with HumaPerfect, but—given the cost of the drug—countries found it cheaper to build walls and dams, even if the result was ineffective. Today, if you say you are from the U.S., you are instantly attacked as a pariah. People want to know, *"How did you get out?"* and *"Are you infected?"* and *"When are you going back to where you came from?"*

It was a Kelsey merperson that nearly killed Canduka Cantor.

When Hurricane Ozymandias hit the East Coast head-on, Cantor pleaded to leave protective custody to save his Savannah home—death threats from GRIP be damned. FBI budgets were tight, so they were glad to see him go, but made him sign a paper saying whatever happened was not their problem.

The storm, driven by global warming, dropped 36 inches of rain in 17 hours on parts of the Eastern Seaboard. The Savannah and Wilmington rivers quickly topped their banks, submerging the Bonaventure Cemetery, flooding midtown, and pooling chest-deep water as far inland as Whatley Avenue.

Because the Savannah/Hilton Head International Airport was inaccessible, Cantor flew into Atlanta and rented a car. The road, thick with emergency vehicles and utility bucket trucks, was blocked after the Route 95 intersection, forcing Cantor to detour. Within a mile of the off-ramp, he discovered a pop-up airboat rental on Dean Forest Road that provided a ferry service into the city.

Cantor paid for transport on a 3-passenger boat named *Gator Bait* and shared the ride with two others. One was Dennis, a young black man with dreadlocks who needed to rescue a graduation project from his rented apartment near the Savannah College of Art and Design. The other was Maureen, a gray-haired white woman in her seventies searching for her Shetland Sheepdog, last seen paddling into darkness, wind, and downpour when she abandoned her home amid rising water.

The airboat driver, Callie, a tattooed white student from a nearby community college, briefed the passengers on safety procedures. Her long blond hair was tangled from a morning's worth of trips into the city, and her olive drab tank top was daubed with large wet splotches. Her jeans were tucked into rubber knee boots, but there was a dark water stain just below her crotch, where she had waded through swamp water.

"When the boat's moving, you don't move around," she said. "I don't want to lose anybody. We'll go in fast, then slow down when we're in the city. Visibility's not great. The air's turned a tad cooler, so we're getting steam off the water. If you see a floating obstacle, raise your hand or shout out. Any questions?"

"Why the shotgun?" Cantor asked.

Callie's face twisted in a crooked smile. "It's my equalizer. The critters that live in the swamp have found a new home in downtown Savannah. There's gators, snakes, and even Kelseys—nasty things that can mess up the boat and hurt us."

She used a paddle to push away from a makeshift pontoon dock, started the engine, grabbed the rudder stick, and stepped on the throttle pedal, accelerating as she steered eastward on a track that paralleled the Savannah Parkway. When the boat hit the residential district, the fog thickened, and Callie slowed to trolling speed.

Maureen switched places with Cantor to be nearer the gunwale. "When I see my dog, I want to be there for him. I'll pull him onboard and dry him off—I even brought my towel—and I'll love him so much, poor thing. What are you looking for, Mr. Cantor?"

"Well, there's my pet, Doofus. My neighbor was taking care of him while Ah was away for a year. Smitty barely got out alive when the hurricane hit, and he had to leave Doofus behind. So, Ah'm trying to find Doofus and rescue whatevah Ah can from the house."

She put a consoling hand on his arm. "We love our little doggies, don't we?"

Cantor thought he should explain that Doofus was a hybrid animal with the head of a Rottweiler and the body of a sea lion and was able to speak a few simple English words, thanks to some human neurons plugged into its brain. He decided that was way too much information for a one-day boat outing. So he just nodded, looked sad, and tightened the clasp on Maureen's arm. "Poor Doofus."

As the boat glided through Forsyth Park, Maureen called out once every couple of minutes, "Here, Mister Jib-Jab!"

"Well, gather at the river and call me a sinner," Dennis said, pointing with a shaky finger toward what used to be the middle of a street. A twenty-foot Reticulated Python swished through the water, belly swollen with a recent meal, looking like a mini-Loch Ness monster.

Maureen's calls to Mr. Jib Jab became more frequent and urgent.

"There's some bad-ass animals in here," Dennis said.

Cantor's home was the first stop. The front door was closed, locked, and halfway submerged. He decided to enter through the upper level.

Looking at Callie, Cantor said, "I shouldn't be long. There's just a few things." Cantor and Dennis climbed the fire escape, tried the window, but found it locked.

Dennis yelled to Callie, "Can you toss us the paddle?"

She threw it upward, like a spear. Cantor caught it, bashed a hole in his window, then entered through the opening, while Dennis remained outside.

From within, Cantor yelled, "Shit!"

"You in trouble?" Callie said.

Dennis yelled down to her. "He cut his leg on the glass. Says he's got some gauze bandages up here. Claims he'll just be a couple of minutes."

Onboard the boat, Maureen continued to call for Mister Jib-Jab.

Callie kept a watchful eye on the water. Occasional splashing sounds issued from the mist. She lifted her shotgun from the deck and opened the breech, verifying there were rounds in the chamber. She snapped it shut and cradled the weapon in her arm as they waited for Dennis and Cantor. Once, when she saw a flickering green glow in the fog bank, she swiveled to point the gun. After a minute, when the glowing shape didn't return, she again rested the weapon in the crook of her arm, watching patches of mist move like troubled spirits across deceptively calm water.

Cantor appeared in the open upper doorway wearing a red cape. He held his arms up in a victory "V" as he issued a triumphal, "Ta-dah!"

Maureen clapped. "Brilliant!"

Dennis, still on the fire escape, gave a big smile. "Awesome duds, man."

Cantor paraded around the balcony, modeling his mantle. His movement powered images that cascaded from top-to-bottom in the fabric, changing colors, spelling out "Canduka Cantor," interspersed with pictures of Cantor's face. He flapped the cape with his hands and arms, like wings.

Callie was the only person not watching Cantor. Her eyes tracked movement below the water—a dark shape rapidly circling the boat. She brought the stock to her shoulder, flicked off the safety, and prepared to fire.

"Don't shoot!" Cantor yelled.

The animal that surfaced had the head of a Rottweiler and carried a size-XXX catfish in its mouth.

"That's my Doofus," Cantor said. "We need to get him onboard."

Callie lowered the gun barrel but kept her hand on the trigger. "That thing is not getting into my boat!"

Doofus bit the fish in two with its powerful jaws and gulped down the half with the head. "Ark! Ark! Ark!"

Cantor pleaded. "Look, Doofus is actually pretty tame as long as Ah introduce you to him in the proper way."

Callie was skeptical. "What way is that?

From the water came the words, "Ark! Ark! Mell utt."

"He needs to smell your butts," Cantor said.

"No way!" Callie said.

Maureen echoed the sentiment but with less emotion. "No way."

Dennis, who was climbing back down, with one foot into the boat, shook his head. "I like you, man, but this is way too much."

"See?" Callie said. "Nobody wants Doofus in the boat. You'll just have to—"

A glowing green patch moved at high speed, looking like a mini-version of Captain Nemo's submarine. When it stopped, a massive head popped up, with gills for ears, staring black eyes, and skin covered with glowing green scales. It grabbed Doofus and tried to take him under as it made a repetitive, throaty noise that sounded like "Ha-cha-cha-cha."

Cantor leaped horizontally from the balcony, arms out, cape flowing with illuminated images. He was Superman to the rescue.

There was a loud *splat* as he belly-flopped near the Kelsey, ensnaring its head in the cape. He moved quickly to wrap the cloth around the monster's eyes and mouth.

The Kelsey growled, tried to throw off the garment, but released Doofus. The Rott-seal, now free and in its element, circled the fight as Cantor gripped the cloth and tried to stay away from the creature's clawed arms.

Doofus ripped a chunk out of the Kelsey's leg, triggering a deep, guttural, "Aroom! Aroom!"

From the depths of the Savannah swamp, another Kelsey answered the call: a distant, "Aroom! Aroom!"

With a burst of energy, the thing shook off Cantor and submerged, pushing a pulse of water along its line of escape.

Doofus circled Cantor, picking up speed, then shot into the air like a porpoise, rolling 180-degrees before splashing down in the direction of the Kelsey, following the monster into the fog.

As Cantor climbed into the boat with Dennis' help, he heard, "Ark! Ark!" followed by "Aroom! Aroom!" There were a few more yelps and splashes, then silence.

The boat passengers looked at each other, quietly holding their breaths.

Callie squinted at the edge of the fog bank, trying to imagine what she couldn't see. She heard a splash and readied her weapon.

Doofus surfaced near the boat, managing to spray Callie as he shook his head.

"Come here, Doofus," Cantor said, holding out a hand. "Here, Boy."

The Rott-seal replied with, "Ark! Ark!" before it submerged again and bobbed up with another fish, ignoring Cantor.

"I think Doofus has found his home," Cantor said.

Maureen tried to console him. "He seems to have a big heart—whatever he is."

Dennis put a hand on Cantor's shoulder. "Let him go, man. Some animals were never meant to be pets."

Callie put the gun down and started the engine, steering the boat away from the scene. She picked up speed on what used to be Liberty Street as she headed back toward safety.

They never did find Mr. Jib Jab.

# CHAPTER 89
# BECOMING

*Life and death are matters of perspective.*
*—Canduka Cantor*

Sundar Rao's tortuous, undetected escape from the U.S. enabled him to return to his native land, where he vowed to visit the resting place of his wife and family near Chennai.

His brother was no longer alive. The cartel had killed him. With his death, the contract on Sundar's life ended. The drug lords were still in business, but their ranks were thinned by fratricidal violence—an unmerciful survival of the fittest.

Sundar discovered his brother had paid for a private cremation and burial plot for his family—out of shame and remorse. Locals told him the crematorium was once an expensive, upscale place, but it was now in shambles. Trees and shrubs had overgrown the gravesites. Most of the pyres were no longer functional. When Sundar visited, the location was used as a tent camp for refugees.

He was able to locate his family's marker after paying a local boy for help. Uday was his name. He told Sundar there was once an iron fence around his family's plot, but locals salvaged it for scrap. The boy wanted to know if there was anything else he could do to earn money. Sundar dismissed him, and stood silently, reflecting on the fate of his beloved Abha, his two sons, and his father and mother.

As he contemplated alternate realities—the life that could have been, the vengeance he could have taken, the career he could have had in Chennai or Mumbai—he spotted a scrap of the iron fence. It pulled his mind back to Assurance, North Carolina.

He remembered Diana's smile and Nadia's death—images burned in his brain.

They had traveled nearly two days from New York in her father's Mustang, arriving for lunch at what seemed to be the restaurant at the center of the universe.

It was empty.

They sat at a table. He held her hand, regretting their past squabbles, forgetting their brushes with death, trusting in their shared destiny.

"Marry me," he said.

Jancie's voice drifted in from the kitchen. "Be there in a jiff."

Diana's face was an unreadable puzzle. "I don't know how to say this, Sundar. You are a kind man. You are a helpful man. We can make a life together, but I need a soldier."

"What do you mean?" he asked.

"We're in a war, and it's about the future. I didn't make the war. I didn't ask for it. But by God, it has come to me, and I intend to win it."

He felt his lips curl in a weak smile. "Some wars are unwinnable if winning means we have to change who we are."

"Technology changes who we are," she said.

"I can be your soldier," he responded. "I've already taken big risks. I've killed for you."

She touched his cheek. "I know."

A commotion near the door interrupted their conversation as two people entered the restaurant. He recognized Mr. Smith, wearing a suit, a tie, and shiny shoes. The other man he knew was Eban Haywood—a face imprinted on his brain. He wore a red and black short-sleeved shirt with an Aztec design and spoke in a loud, Billy-Bob voice.

Sundar put up his hand to cover his face and searched for the nearest exit.

"Whooee. I'm talkin' real money," Eban said. "They need people down thar, and we got 'em right here. All the talent you'd ever want fer simple no-brain jobs. It's win-win. We smuggle people into Meh-hee-co, where they make more money, and they send pesos back home. We take a percentage—30%, just like Apple. All I need is some up-front money."

"Don't mind them."

The voice was Jancie's, who suddenly appeared at Sundar's table with an order book. "They's in their own little world. They don't even see you."

It was as if the space between their tables wavered, and a reality-distorting field subdued the men's voices.

"You'd like the breakfast hero sandwiches. I'm already cookin' the eggs."

He knew not to argue. "Fine," he said. "We'll both have that."

Jancie headed for the kitchen, ignoring the other group, immersed in conversation.

"The first test for my soldier," Diana said, "is to rescue Nadia."

"This is dangerous ground," he said. "We must be careful."

For over an hour, they watched Nadia's house from the path leading up from Kelsey's Bend. When sunlight faded, and there were no signs of movement, they crept closer, entering the garden near the iron MagnaTector, skirting the toppled hive.

Diana struggled to reposition the apiary. The box of fish bones was still in a drawer. She moved it to the front porch.

"It's safe here for a little while," she said.

She tapped the door lightly. No answer. It was unlocked. They entered to discover the place had been turned upside down and reeked with a foul stench. The smell was strongest near the upstairs bedroom. Sundar moved up the steps and touched the doorknob.

Diana followed him. "Nadia's dead," she said.

"How do you know?"

"I feel it. We have a connection."

His mind considered a range of possibilities, where Nadia was alive, or dead, or somewhere in-between. "I'll go in," he said, steeling himself, then pushing the door open.

The bedroom window captured twilight softening into shadows. The iron bed, with its coils and connections and filigreed patterns, dominated a room decorated in blood. Five decomposing animals littered the floor. The stench was overpowering. Diana and Sundar gagged and coughed.

"I'm not sure exactly what happened here," he said. "It looks like someone shot a family of raccoons. The blood seems to come from the animals."

"They were looking for the bones," Diana said. "Berky was obsessed with them."

Sundar picked up a small object on the iron bed. "She must have fled. Don't you see? Nadia overcame her sickness out of necessity. She escaped, then called you in New York with a warning." Even as he said these words, they seemed incongruent with objective reality.

"She didn't leave," Diana said. "That's all that's left of her."

He stared at the toy in his hand. The doll's face wore a smile that could take on the world. It took him a moment to grasp what had happened. "Did your father give you this? Is this what he used to tell the stories?"

Diana nodded.

"I see. Finally, I see. You kept it all these years because it helped you get through the bad times." He paused for a moment, thinking about the consequences, and what to do next. "And what was the doll's name?"

She explained afterward that when he asked the question, things became very clear. A childhood vision played in her head.

It was bedtime. Arthur Holkam was a giant, looming above her covers. He picked up the doll.

"Well, did you decide who our superhero is?"

"Yes. I want to name her after my sister," she said.

"You don't have a sister."

"Yes, I do. My twin sister."

"Oh, I see. Is this your imaginary friend?"

She nodded.

"Well, then ..." Arthur animated the doll with his hands, making it walk, then fly. His voice raised an octave. "Hello. I'm your twin sister. I'm imaginary, so I can do anything you can imagine. Can you guess my name?"

She nodded and spoke. "Diana."

Sundar thought long and hard about what to do. The next day, over breakfast at the Groaning Griddle, with advice from Jancie, and agreement from Diana, they decided to lay Nadia to rest.

Jancie provided a small wooden box and accompanied them back to Assurance. They buried the doll and Chester Truman Kelsey's fish box between the two gravestones in the garden, placing them inside the iron grid—at Diana's insistence.

The ceremony was short. Jancie said a home-made poem for the occasion:

*Roses is red,*

*Violets is blue,*

*Nadia's in the ground,*

*But Diana stands tall.*

As they contemplated the mound of earth that buried an old persona, Sundar touched Diana's arm, breaking the silence. "I've thought about our future, but also my honor. I must go back to Chennai. That's where my family is buried. I must find out what happened to my wife and children."

"Won't the drug lords try to kill you?" Diana said.

"I'm not afraid anymore," he said. "You've given me strength."

"Come back to me," she said. "We're fighting a war here, and I need a good soldier and a good husband."

He exulted in her kiss. It was sweet and bitter, filled with joy and sorrow, promising the future, respecting the past. In his mind, the lips that touched his were from all women; all humanity; across all eternity.

In the wideness of space—a space that bends to both physics and magic—there was a girl who lived in two universes. They merged, and timid Nadia became Diana, the girl who could do anything she imagined.

As Sundar pondered this transformation, he realized the lines separating truth and delusion were as vague as the ridgelines of the Great Smoky Mountains and as nuanced as the fabric of human identity. Inspired by Diana's courage and sacrifice, he believed that he, too, could do anything if he imagined it.

In that moment, Sundar Rao became a different person.

# THE END

# ACKNOWLEDGMENTS

I acknowledge the sensitive times in which we live. A book by Richard E. Nisbett and Dov Cohen, *Culture of Honor: The Psychology of Violence in the South*, influenced *The Perfection of Fish's* twin themes of identity and genetics.

My thanks to astute early readers from the Maryland Writers' Association, the Beta Book Club, Columbia Writers' Group, the Palisades Book Club, and Timothy Barnett from *The Writers' Beat* for helping to shape and improve the story. I am also grateful to Paul Witcover for his professional editing services. A special thank-you goes to my wife, Patricia, whom I count as one of my best editors and most constructive critics.

Skyler Branden's creative concepts inspired some of my writing, and members of the all-female group at Solsticio, Rebelde & Company helped refine a few of the book's gender-bending characters and associated storyline.

Some of the ideas concerning human evolution 70,000-164,000 years ago, give or take, are based on the excellent book, *Sapiens, A Brief History of Humankind*, by Yuval Noah Harari, and on a 2012 article in The Smithsonian by Erin Wayman, *When did the human mind evolve to what it is today?* Mr. Harari discusses the notion that humans seem to be different from other animals in their ability to think about things that do not exist in the natural world—hence, my concept of the "fiction gene." And I tip my hat to Tien Chen Zeng and his colleagues for the theory, presented in *Nature Communications* in 2018, that tribal warfare 5,000-7,000 years ago resulted in a genetic bottleneck—the "fingerprint" left on the Y-chromosome of a great male die-off.

The idea of the gene drive comes from Professor Austin Burt's ground-breaking scientific papers in 2003 and 2018.

Tamar Lewin's 1994 piece in The New York Times, *What Penalty for a Killing in Passion?* led me to research variations in the law concerning spousal homicide.

Christina Ruth Hastie's 2011 thesis on 19th-century Appalachian murder ballads, and *Songs of the Civil War*, published in 1960 by Folkway Records, gave me snippets from old songs that spoke to cultural divides.

I was inspired by The New York Times, The Guardian, BBC, and other news services that reported the story of a Yiddish-speaking fish—found by a Brooklyn fishmonger—warning about the end of the world (15 March 2003).

Thank you, fish.

And of course, in these reality-bending times, every day in the news cycle is like living a Lewis Carroll novel, where many people are able to believe six impossible things before breakfast. Notwithstanding, most of the characters, organizations, and places in this book set in the future are fictional, even if they are derived from or reference real-world things. Clonaid is one notable exception. To borrow from Wikipedia, it is a "Canadian-based human cloning organization" with "philosophical ties (to) the UFO religion Raëlism." Another exception is the National Rifle Association (NRA), an organization that believes the world would be safer if more people carried military-grade assault rifles.

Thank you, world, for the inspiration. Some stuff you just can't make up.

# ABOUT THE AUTHOR

J.S. Morrison has lived in the U.S., Europe, and the Middle East, and visited Asia, Africa, South America, and Antarctica. He optioned two original screenplays before deciding to write a near-future novel about genetic engineering. The author meant it to be a dire warning to humanity, but his sense of satiric irony got in the way. When he is not writing or traveling, he dabbles in astrophysics as a member of a local scientific society.

# NOTE FROM THE AUTHOR

Word-of-mouth is crucial for any author to succeed. If you enjoyed *The Perfection of Fish*, please leave a review online—anywhere you are able. Even if it's just a sentence or two. It would make all the difference and would be very much appreciated.

Thanks!
J.S.

Thank you so much for reading one of our **Sci-Fi** novels.

If you enjoyed our book, please check out our recommendation for your next great read!

*Culture-Z* by Karl Andrew Marszalowicz

In the year 2190, mankind has made great strides forward in the worlds of technology, science, and greed. However, when all three get together one last time, this oblivious generation may not exist much longer.